THE HIDDEN BONES

By Nicola Ford

The Hidden Bones

a&b

THE HIDDEN BONES

Nicola Ford

Allison & Busby Limited
12 Fitzroy Mews
London W1T 6DW
allisonandbusby.com

First published in Great Britain by Allison & Busby in 2018.

A CIP catalogue record for this book is available from the British Library.

First Edition

HB ISBN 978-0-7490-2362-1
TPB ISBN 978-0-7490-2367-6

Typeset in 11/16 pt Adobe Garamond Pro by Allison & Busby Ltd.

The paper used for this Allison & Busby publication has been produced from trees that have been legally sourced from well-managed and credibly certified forests.

Printed and bound by
CPI Group (UK) Ltd, Croydon, CR0 4YY

For Manda

PROLOGUE

[illegible]

[illegible] reach out and touch the people who'd built them [illegible] mounds that dominated the skyline in these parts.

[illegible]

PROLOGUE

1972

It was a single glint of sunlight piercing the hanging mists of the October morning that caught his attention. The incessant rain of recent weeks had stopped, but the sodden chalky soil clung to his boots, making every step along the freshly cut furrows more difficult than the last.

He'd expected flint. It seemed to grow better than wheat up here. The Downs were littered with the shattered white fragments of ancient tools. When he held them he felt he might almost reach out and touch the people who'd built the turf-covered burial mounds that dominated the skyline in these parts.

He bent down to retrieve his find. Spitting on his fingers, he rubbed away the soil that smeared its surface. He stood motionless – it wasn't flint. In his hand he cradled the most beautiful thing he'd ever seen. Not much bigger than a ten pence piece, an orange-red disc lay at its centre. The ruddy amber disc was encased within a circle of gold decorated with four delicately incised concentric grooves that ran right around its rim.

Running his fingertips over the still-glittering metal, he felt a pang of regret as they encountered a small tear where something sharp had ripped it. Four thousand years had passed since the disc had been laid to rest. And if it hadn't been for the unforgiving efficiency of the plough, there it might have stayed for another four millennia.

He'd searched these fields a hundred times. Every new discovery collected and exchanged for the telling of a tale. But this one was different. This one was meant for him. He slipped his prize into the soft flannel of his shirt pocket and he turned for home.

As he neared the bottom of the field, he cast a sideways glance at the dark pool seeping from the belly of the chalk, its swelling waters seeking out their path towards the village in the valley bottom far below. The locals called it the Hungerbourne. But he knew it by an older name – the Woe Waters.

CHAPTER ONE

2013

There was a flutter of excitement in the pit of Clare Hills' stomach when she stepped out of her coupé onto the gravel drive of Hungerbourne Manor. It had taken two deaths and nearly fifteen years, but she was finally going to get what she wanted. The day was shaping up to be everything she'd hoped for. The journey through the rolling chalk hills of the Marlborough Downs reminded her how much she loved this landscape. The pale blue sky was streaked with gauze-thin clouds and despite the gusting March wind she'd driven the thirty miles from Salisbury with the top down.

Until his death last year, the manor had belonged to archaeologist Gerald Hart. It had started life as an elegantly understated Palladian villa, but the addition of an unbecoming low-slung porch and bay windows by its Victorian owners set it at odds with the gentle folds of the upland valley it inhabited. Clare was only too aware that the house was somewhat less of an intruder than she was. David had avoided using the word 'widow', but she knew his invitation to help him salvage what he could from Gerald's records was born out of pity rather than any genuine need for her assistance. The fact of Stephen, and now his death, hung between them like a freezing fog. But whatever David's motives, she was glad to be here. For the first time in months she was looking forward to something.

There was no sign of his Land Rover. He'd never been known for his timekeeping and she was acutely aware that she'd never actually met the new owner of Hungerbourne Manor – Gerald's nephew, Peter. She hoped this wasn't going to prove awkward.

As it turned out, she needn't have worried. David's familiar baritone boomed out of an open sash window at the front of the house. 'Front door is open. Let yourself in!'

The paint-flaked door juddered open to reveal a dark but lofty hallway. The air smelt stale and musty, and in places the fading wallpaper had peeled from the walls, revealing grey-blue patches of mildew. She found David kneeling on an old Turkish rug amid piles of papers and open filing cabinets in the oak-panelled study. He was wearing a pair of baggy brown cords and a dark blue rugby shirt with a small hole in one elbow. His six-feet frame now erred on the comfortable side of well-built, and the close-cropped sandy hair and neatly trimmed sideburns were tinged with grey. But he still looked reassuringly like the eager young doctoral student she'd known in her undergrad days.

David Barbrook wiped his palms down the front of his cords and knelt down. What the hell had he been thinking of? When Clare had contacted the university's archaeology department, it had seemed the most natural thing in the world to ask her down here. She needed a distraction from Stephen's death and he needed another pair of hands. But, as the day drew closer, he'd become increasingly uncertain about the wisdom of the invitation.

When the hinges of the front door creaked their un-oiled warning, he grabbed a random sheaf of papers from the rug. The echo of footsteps on the tiled hall floor stopped and he looked up. The figure in the doorway was a million miles from the Oxfam-clad student he remembered: designer jeans, cashmere polo-neck, chestnut-brown hair cut short to frame her face. And so thin.

He threw his arms wide in a redundant gesture, indicating the sprawling array of books and papers that covered the floor. 'Can you believe this? How can a man who hadn't published a word in four decades have this much paperwork?'

A hint of amusement sparked in her hazel eyes. 'Didn't you say that was why Peter asked you here in the first place?'

He bent forward, pretending to examine a pile of papers. 'Would've been a bloody sight easier if the cantankerous old sod had answered my letters.'

Clare gestured at him to lower his voice.

'It's alright, Peter's not here. He had an appointment with a client.'

Without waiting for an invitation, she joined him on the rug and began tidying the documents that littered the floor into neat stacks. 'What letters?'

'I wrote to Gerald to ask if I could help him publish the Hungerbourne excavations.'

She looked at him from behind a stack of journals. 'Write the report for him, you mean.'

He leant back on his heels and nodded. 'If that's what it took.

British Heritage was going to fund it. Part of their Backlog Project. I just needed access.'

'And Gerald wouldn't play ball.'

He shook his head. 'Peter did his best to persuade him. But the mardy old sod wouldn't have it. And now it's too late.' He sighed, then blasted Clare square-on with what he hoped was one of his more disarming smiles. 'This doesn't need two of us. You OK with ladders?'

She nodded but said nothing. Was he imagining it or was there a hint of reluctance? 'Good. Peter said the rest of Gerald's papers are in the loft. Why don't you take a look up there and I'll crack on with this lot.'

.

Whatever she'd envisaged today would be like, this wasn't it. Two flights of increasingly narrow stairs had led her up past the old servants' quarters. And now she found herself clutching the sides of a rickety loft ladder and bracing herself for the short climb through the hatch set into the ceiling of the upper landing.

At the top, she felt for the light pull and tugged. A fluorescent strip light flickered on, revealing a room lined with wooden shelving that was crammed from floor to ceiling with boxes of every shape and size. Reassured by the sight of stout wooden floorboards, she clambered through the opening. She ran her hand over the lid of the nearest box, disturbing a thick layer of dust she knew her mother would consider unacceptable. But the intimation of age and the musty smell only served to induce a tingle of anticipation. There were no external clues to the contents of any of the boxes. She would just have to work her way through them one by one.

They were mostly crammed with offprints from academic journals and photocopies of old articles, randomly interspersed with the sort of old lampshades and discarded china that could be found in every attic in the country. After an hour searching she had nothing to show for her efforts except an aching neck. David definitely had the better end of the deal, sorting through Gerald's study.

Straightening her spine, she brushed her hands down the front of her polo-neck in an effort to dislodge the dust that clung to the soft wool. Black hadn't been the most practical choice. She adjusted the waistband of her jeans. She'd lost weight since Stephen's death; maybe it was time to treat herself to some new clothes.

As she turned back towards the loft hatch, she caught sight of four large wooden packing crates wedged into the bottom run of shelves by the far wall. They weren't at all like the collection of decaying cardboard boxes she'd been rummaging through. Dangling from the side of the nearest crate was a small length of twine, at the end of which hung a mildewed luggage label. In the shadows of the corner of the room, she screwed up her eyes, trying to make out what was written on it. Kneeling down beside the crate, she fumbled for the penlight on the key ring in her pocket. She peered at the small circle of light illuminating the faded ink, but it was too indistinct to read. She turned the label over. Clearly marked in capital letters were the words *HUNGERBOURNE BARROWS*.

She knelt, motionless, unable to believe what she saw. She could feel the pulse in the ends of her fingers and realised she'd been holding her breath. Hungerbourne had been Gerald's most famous site; the most spectacular Bronze Age cemetery dug in modern times. But in September 1973, after just one season's digging, he'd announced the dig was over.

She'd seen the beautifully crafted goldwork in the British Museum. But the rest of the archive had remained closed to public view. During the dig, Gerald had published a painfully brief magazine article with photographs of some of the more spectacular finds. And the archaeological world had held its breath waiting for the final report – the great man's pronouncements on what he'd unearthed. But none came. And gradually the Hungerbourne excavation had been forgotten. Until last year, when, a few months before Gerald's death, the nationals ran a story on the destruction of the finds and all of the records in a fire in the manor's coach house.

So how could they be sitting here in front of her? Far from being reduced to a pile of ashes, they appeared to be untouched in their original crates. She knew she should tell David. But no one had seen this stuff for forty years. It wouldn't hurt to keep it to herself for a few minutes more. Besides, David would think she was a complete pillock if she told him and it turned out to be nothing more than some reused packaging.

She stood up and leant over the first crate, scanning its contents with the small beam of light. It was full to the brim with crumpled newspaper. Rummaging through the crinkled pages, her hand came to rest on a rusty metal box. Its lid lifted easily, revealing an assortment of hardback notebooks, out of one of which poked the corner of a photo. She opened the book and withdrew the photograph, stepping back into the glare of the fluorescent light for a better view.

The black-and-white image showed a small group of people in front of a dilapidated wooden shed. Above the door, a hand-painted sign read 'The Brew Crew'. The figures were arranged in two rows, the men standing at the back with the women sitting on wooden boxes at the front. They were all clutching tin mugs raised aloft in a gesture of salute. In the middle of the back row, a slim, dark-haired man of middle years grinned into the camera lens. He wore an open-necked shirt with its sleeves rolled up above the elbows and stood two or three inches taller than his colleagues: Gerald Hart. This must have been his dig team. They looked a happy bunch. But why wouldn't they be? Fabulous finds, burials, gold – the Hungerbourne Barrows were every archaeologist's dream.

Clare stood on the back doorstep of the manor, trying without success to remove the last vestiges of dust from her jumper. She'd left David in the study, trying to reach Peter on his mobile. Across the courtyard, the mouth of the coach house gaped open, the fire-blackened hinges where its double doors had once stood jutting out like the decaying pegs of some hideous hag.

Picking her way across the moss-covered sets, she stepped inside. At the centre of the smoke-scarred room rested the burnt and twisted wreck of an old Volvo, its once sturdy and dependable hulk reduced to a mass of blackened metal and contorted plastic.

She caught a sudden whiff of petrol. The sharp acrid smell, the warped metal struts – she stood transfixed, gripped by the sudden realisation that this was how the end had been for Stephen.

'I don't know what the fuck you're playing at, but if you're not out of there in ten seconds I'm calling the police.' It was a male voice and its owner was clearly mad as hell.

She stood stock-still, unsure of what to do. As the stranger's footsteps approached, she swung round to find herself standing on the foot of a tall, slim man, in his mid-fifties. Dressed in an open-necked blue-checked shirt and neatly pressed jeans, his distinguished angular features morphed from anger to bafflement in a split second.

'What the . . . ?'

'I'm so sorry, I didn't mean to . . . What I mean is . . .' She could hear the words spilling from her lips like a guilty child, but appeared to be unable to control them. Eventually, she managed to pull herself together enough to say, 'I'm here with David.'

He looked around at the innards of the gutted building. 'Best we don't hang around in here. I don't know how safe it is.'

She nodded. Out in the courtyard, standing in front of a new BMW four-by-four that looked as if it had never ventured further off-road than its current location, she drank in a long draught of fresh Wiltshire air.

He bent his head towards her. 'Sorry if I startled you.' He made as if to extend his hand, but then seemed to think better of it, letting it drop by his side. 'Peter Hart.'

In the daylight, she could see his eyes were a cool, deep blue, their colour accentuated by his well-cut coal-black hair. She couldn't take her eyes off him. It was remarkable. The man standing in front of her was the living embodiment of the figure in the Brew Crew photograph.

She shook her head and pieced together a smile. 'Clare Hills. And I'm the one who should be apologising. I just came out for a breath of air.' She wasn't sure how to explain what had drawn her into the burnt-out structure. 'They said in the papers that's where he kept it.'

He nodded. 'I wanted him to pack it off to a museum, but he wouldn't have it.' He shrugged. 'Uncle was something of a traditionalist when it came to security. One damned great padlock to which he held the only key. Add a couple of old jerry cans full of petrol and . . .' He mimicked the rising flames with a gesture from his upturned hands.

She shivered and closed her eyes, concentrating hard on her

breathing. When she opened them again, he was looking back towards the gutted building.

'If Gerald hadn't seen the flames he'd have lost more than a few old pots.'

He doesn't know. David can't have spoken to him yet.

He said, 'The police thought it was someone local.'

'It was started deliberately?' She couldn't disguise her shock.

He nodded. 'When I heard someone poking about in there just now I thought they'd come back.' He paused, before adding as if by way of explanation, 'There was a lot of trouble over the visitor centre proposal. Some of the locals got the idea they could make a few quid by opening up the barrow cemetery as a tourist attraction. The village was split right down the middle. Half of them could see the pound signs lighting up in their eyes and the other half didn't want anything that would spoil their rural idyll. But after the fire destroyed the archive there was nothing to put on show, so it all fizzled out.'

Clare couldn't conceal her shock at the idea that a bunch of NIMBYs might have done this. 'Someone could've been killed.'

'I think they were.'

He beckoned her back towards the doorway of the coach house, pointing to the back wall. In the dim light, she hadn't noticed it before; but, barely discernible beneath the soot-streaked filth, someone had scrawled in red spray paint, BEWARE THE WOE WATERS: BRINGERS OF DEATH.

For a moment, she struggled to make sense of it all. Then, with a horrifying clarity, she realised what he was trying to tell her. 'You think whoever did this killed Gerald.'

'As good as. This was only the tip of the iceberg. He had so many silent phone calls that he would unplug the phone when he was here on his own. It was a nightmare trying to get hold of him.'

'Couldn't the police do anything?'

'They tried tracing the calls, but they were all from pay-as-you-go mobiles. Uncle worried himself sick about it. He never really recovered. In the end, his heart just gave out.'

CHAPTER TWO

'Take a look!' Muir stabbed his finger at the sheet of A4.

David glanced down at the paper lying on his head of department's desk without speaking.

'Well!'

'Well what?' To everyone except Muir himself and the vice-chancellor, the bald-headed Glaswegian was known as the Runt. He was renowned for both his complete disregard for anyone or anything other than his own future prospects and his apparent obliviousness to the universal detestation with which he was regarded by other members of the department. The VC had parachuted him into the chair of archaeology over the tops of the heads of several better qualified candidates – David included. But it wasn't personal jealousy that was fuelling the Runt's ire this morning. Today's topic of conversation was David himself.

'Don't play games with me, Barbrook. You won't like the consequences.'

'Is that supposed to be a threat?'

'I don't need to make threats.' He gesticulated at the sheet of paper that lay between them. 'The figures speak for themselves.'

Muir seemed to have acquired his management style from old Jimmy Cagney films. It was all David could do to stifle his urge to laugh. Normally he wouldn't even try, but something in the Runt's demeanour this morning told him he'd be wise to suppress his natural inclinations. He picked up the paper and made a show of examining it. In reality, he was only too well aware of the contents of the departmental email. It demonstrated beyond a shadow of a doubt that he had brought in significantly less research funding than any of his colleagues in the department.

'Well! Don't you have anything to say? You might be determined to spend your entire academic career in the gutter, but I'm damned if I'm going to let you drag the rest of us into it with you. I won't have it.'

David replaced the email on the desk and settled himself into the sleek leather chair that Muir reserved for favoured guests. He could see that his choice of seat hadn't improved the Scotsman's humour. 'Look, can we drop the amateur dramatics?'

'How dare you—'

Before he could finish his sentence, David raised his hand. Starting from his chin and working its way upwards across his balding pate, Muir's face flushed a vibrant shade of pink. For a moment, David thought the Scot was going to have some sort of seizure. 'I could sit here and listen to you outlining my manifold failings, but frankly I'm tired of playing that scene. So why don't I save us both the pain of enduring unnecessary time in one another's presence. There is absolutely nothing wrong with my academic credentials; my submissions for the last research assessment exercise scored higher than anyone else in the department. I'm not some simple-minded dullard. I know the game has changed. Research scores are only a means to an end. We both know that the bottom line is cash.'

Muir made no effort to contain his sarcasm. 'Well, glory be – he's seen the light. Now what exactly do you propose to do about it?'

David was well aware that from the moment Muir had set foot in the department he'd viewed him as nothing more than an irritating tick whom he had every intention of crushing underfoot. But thus far he'd failed to do so. And David had every intention of ensuring he remained firmly embedded under the Runt's skin.

His adversary leant back in his chair, arms folded, drumming the fingers of his left hand against his right forearm, anticipating victory. It was clear from the Scot's face that he had absolutely no idea what was coming.

'I have British Heritage project funding to the tune of half a million pounds.'

'Pull the other one, Barbrook. You haven't managed to pull together a viable funding application in the whole of the three years I've been here.'

'Well, I have now.'

'And exactly what is this fictional funding for?'

'To analyse and publish the Hungerbourne archive.'

Muir's mouth broke into a self-congratulatory smile. His target was within range. 'You're a fantasist, Barbrook. The Hungerbourne archive went up in smoke – in much the same way that I intend to see that your academic career does, unless you can provide me with some genuine evidence that you're pulling your weight in my department.'

David reached into the bag that he had placed by his chair. He extracted its contents and slapped them down on Muir's desk. Before the Runt had a chance to respond, David turned the hardback notebook through one hundred and eighty degrees so that the Scot could read the fading black ink on its tattered cover.

Muir glanced down. There was no mistaking the words on its label, but they clearly weren't what he was expecting. *Hungerbourne Barrow Cemetery Excavation Diary 1973. G. Hart.*

Muir opened the book and began leafing through it. He looked up, his eyes boring into David's. 'Where did you get this?'

'Hungerbourne Manor – along with . . .'

'Why didn't I know about this?'

Muir knew full well what the answer was. David didn't dignify it with a response. If he'd told the Runt that he'd found the Hungerbourne archive, he would have insisted he head up the project himself.

David picked up the notebook and, placing it carefully back in his bag, turned to leave.

As he opened the door, Muir said, 'Make no mistake, Barbrook. One more fuck-up, just one, and it will be the last thing you do in this department.'

David closed the door behind him without a backward glance.

CHAPTER THREE

'God, that's good.' Clare watched David take a second large bite from his eclair and wash it down with a gulp of Darjeeling.

By the end of a week incarcerated in the archaeology department's laying-out room, she'd had her fill of listing, counting and weighing artefacts from the Hungerbourne archive. So she'd been only too happy to accept David's invitation to join him at the tea rooms next to St Thomas' church.

She finished dividing her poppy-seed cake into bite-sized squares. 'You always had a knack for knowing how to cheer me up.'

He licked the chocolate from the ends of his fingers and flushed. 'There aren't many situations that can't be improved by a cuppa or a decent pint.'

She laid her knife down on the edge of her plate. 'I do appreciate you letting me work on the Hungerbourne stuff, you know. It's given me something to get my teeth into. There was so much to sort out right after the accident. But later . . .'

He stared down at the pristine white tablecloth, rubbing his fingertips distractedly over some imaginary speck on the linen. 'You don't need to explain.'

But she wanted him to understand. The first few weeks after her husband's car crash had been hell, but she'd held it together. Stephen had been a successful solicitor and he'd ensured everything was taken care of even when it came to his own death, appointing a colleague from his practice as his executor. But that had seemed to make things worse. She'd spent all of her time consumed with worrying about the funeral arrangements, writing thank-you letters for the sympathy cards and then finally sorting through his possessions. It all seemed so pointless; everything done for show. She wasn't allowed to do anything of substance that might make a difference.

Her words were spoken softly, but her tone was determined. 'When I phoned the department, I had no idea you were working in Salisbury. I just needed to be somewhere familiar – to have something to focus on.' He shifted uncomfortably in his seat. 'I suppose I hoped to be allowed to do a bit of pot washing or some finds drawing. I didn't expect to be indulged like this.'

He snapped his head upwards. 'I wouldn't have asked you if you weren't up to it. You're a bloody good archaeologist.' His broad face eased into a smile. 'When I used to take you for seminars, you knew as much as I did half the time.'

'That was a long time ago.'

'Doesn't seem it.' He swirled the dregs round in the bottom of his cup before repositioning it on its saucer. 'So, are you going to tell me what's in that archive or not?'

Clare brightened, grateful to be dragged back to the

present. 'Gerald seems to have run a pretty tight ship. His notebooks are in good shape, which should make it easier when you come to write up. You know the goldwork is in the British Museum.' He nodded. 'There's a complete small finds catalogue cross-referenced to the site plans. So we'll be able to work out where everything came from.' She paused. 'But what I'm really looking forward to is excavating the cremation in the Collared Urn.'

'What?'

She'd known what it was as soon as she'd seen the pot's heavy brown rim protruding out of the scrunched-up balls of time-cracked newspaper. What she hadn't anticipated was what she'd find inside. 'It's still got the ashes in situ. I presume you'll want to analyse it yourself.'

'Not a chance. We need to get someone in – a specialist.' He was staring out of the window towards the church.

'Why do you think he left it like that? Do you suppose he wanted to leave something for posterity? . . . David!'

He was looking straight at her now. But he didn't seem to have registered a word she'd said. 'A human bone specialist. Someone with experience in prehistoric cremations. Lloyd or Granski, maybe.'

'Fine.' She couldn't disguise her impatience. 'But what do you think?'

'About what?'

She'd forgotten he could be like this, entirely absorbed by the past. Sometimes he seemed to inhabit another world, a world that excluded everyone and everything around him. The world of the long dead.

She sighed. 'Why do you think Gerald stopped?'

'No idea.'

'And why let everyone think it had all gone up in smoke like that?'

He shrugged.

'His site diaries are so methodical. Everything recorded down to the last flint flake. But they just stop. No summary. No conclusions. It's like he just gave up.'

David remained silent. She could see she wasn't making any headway.

'Then there's this.' She handed him a folded sheet of faded blue writing paper.

Painstakingly cut out from newsprint, the first two words were individually glued to the paper while the last two had been cut out in a block. The words BEWARE THE WOE WATERS obscured the Basildon Bond watermark.

'Where did you find this?'

'Stuffed into the back of one of Gerald's site journals.' She withdrew a small spiral-bound notepad from her bag. 'He talks about it. "Arrived on-site to find a note addressed to me pushed under the door of the finds hut: more of the usual rubbish about the Woe Waters. Another amateurish effort by one of my more unstable fellow residents to make the Harts feel at home in Hungerbourne. I had hoped they might have come to terms with our presence by now." Don't you think it's a bit of a coincidence?'

He passed the letter back to her. 'Gerald was right. Best off ignoring rubbish like that. If I'd stopped work every time some nutter had spouted mumbo-jumbo about my sites, I'd never have dug anything.'

'But it's the same as the warning in the coach house.'

'Probably some local with a grudge against the bloke in the big house. People have long memories in villages like Hungerbourne.'

'Maybe.' She wasn't convinced, but she knew him well enough to know there was no point arguing. And he was obviously determined to change the subject.

'I'll put a funding bid in to British Heritage to get radio-carbon dates from the intact cremation. It'd look piss poor if they don't stump up the cash on something as big as this.' For a few seconds he sat motionless, before pushing his cup and saucer away from him. 'What would you say if I asked you to work on the project?'

'Isn't that what I'm doing?'

'Not voluntarily. I mean professionally – a paid post as project manager.'

'What?'

'I'd be the director, but I don't have time to deal with the day-to-day stuff. The pay wouldn't be great and it would depend on the BH funding being confirmed.'

She hadn't expected this. She replenished her pot of Earl Grey with hot water, aware he was scrutinising her face intently.

'Well?'

'I'm not bothered about the money.'

'I sense a "but" coming.'

'I need to be sure you're not doing this because you feel sorry for me.'

He placed his right hand over his heart and grinned. 'Promise.'

'I mean it, David.'

He leant forward. 'Look, I couldn't get anyone half as good as you for the money I'll be paying. And' – he hesitated – 'we understand how one another work.'

'OK, but if I'm working on this I need some background information.'

'Like?'

'What was Gerald really like?'

'How the hell would I know?'

'You're mates with Peter.'

'Belonging to the same rugby club doesn't make us bosom buddies.'

'Doesn't he ever talk about his uncle?'

He rested his elbows on the table. 'From what I can make out, he was very fond of him. A bit of a father figure after Peter's old man did a bunk. But I gather he was pretty much a recluse in his later years.'

'It's difficult to picture him shutting himself away in that draughty old house. His site diaries are so full of life. His ideas and plans for the site. According to the early entries, when he started he intended to dig the whole barrow cemetery.'

David laughed. 'You've got to admire his ambition.'

'So why stop? He had so much talent.'

David made no reply, yet his expression articulated an accusation she understood but was determined to ignore.

'Judging from the papers we found in the house, he didn't lose interest in the subject.'

'Some people choose to do other things with their life. You of all people should know that.'

She said nothing, her gaze fixed intently on the teapot in front of her.

It was David who spoke first. 'Look, it's the barrow cemetery we're trying to piece together, not Gerald Hart's life story.'

'Oh, come on. Aren't you even a tiny bit curious?'

'Archaeologists normally wait until people have been dead for a few hundred years before they start poking round in their lives.'

They both laughed.

David leant back in his chair. 'Now you're signed up for the long haul, do you fancy a day out on expenses?'

She narrowed her eyes in mock suspicion. 'Where to?'

'The Big Smoke.'

She wrinkled her nose. She'd come here to try to get away from London and the memories it held.

'Pity . . .'

'Why? What did you have in mind?' Licking her index finger, she dabbed it distractedly at the last few poppy seeds on her plate.

'A visit to see Daniel Phelps.'

She stopped dabbing. 'Who?'

'Keeper of Prehistoric Antiquities at the British Museum. I've arranged to go through the finds they hold from the dig. And Daniel is expecting two of us.'

'You're very sure of yourself, Dr Barbrook.'

'Well, do you fancy getting your hands on the Hungerbourne gold or not?'

David returned from his foray to the buffet car of the Salisbury to Waterloo service bearing two paper cups, an assortment of sachets and small plastic containers, and a bulging paper bag. All balanced precariously on an ill-designed cardboard tray. He handed Clare a cup.

She looked up from her newspaper. 'Thanks. I didn't have time for breakfast.'

'God help us, woman, it's nearly midday.'

She brushed his concern aside. 'I had more important things on my mind.'

He emptied two of the sachets of sugar into his coffee, stirred, took a slurp of the hot tarmac-coloured liquid and grimaced. 'Such as?'

She patted the laptop lying on the seat beside her. 'Creating a database from Gerald's finds records.'

She'd only seen a couple of pieces of the Hungerbourne

goldwork before and then they'd been trapped inside a glass case. Now that she was actually going to get to handle it, she had every intention of making the most of her opportunity.

He raised an eyebrow. 'Always one step ahead of the class.' He ripped open the paper bag in front of him, revealing a BLT sandwich. 'You should still eat.' He tore the sandwich in two and thrust half in her direction.

She shook her head. 'I'll stick to caffeine.'

He gestured at her copy of *The Independent* with an unopened sachet of sugar. 'I can barely bring myself to read one of those things these days. Too much doom and gloom.'

'I was reading Gerald's obit. Written by a Margaret Bockford.'

He nodded. 'Professor Margaret Bockford to mere mortals like you and I.'

'Well, whoever she is, Peter's not going to enjoy reading it.'

'Why?'

She passed him the newspaper. As he rifled through his jacket pockets for his reading glasses, she turned her attention to her coffee, burning her lips in an attempt to take on-board caffeine as rapidly as possible. Before she'd managed to sip her way down more than an inch of the scalding liquid, David looked up at her.

'She hasn't held back, has she? ". . . an unforgivable lapse in academic standards from a man who should have known better . . . Generous, supportive and brilliant in his early years, the discovery of Hungerbourne should have been Hart's finest hour. Instead it became the scene of his spectacular demise. From a starring role in academia, Hart rapidly and obstinately receded into the shadows of obscurity, taking the knowledge of the Hungerbourne excavation with him."'

'I don't understand. If Gerald was such a model professional before Hungerbourne, why did he pack it all in without writing up the site?'

'Maybe he enjoyed digging more than publishing. He wouldn't be the first to be guilty of that.'

She didn't reply. She didn't like being flannelled.

He said, 'By the look of some of the newspaper pieces I found in his filing cabinets, he became quite a celebrity when he started unearthing goldwork during the dig. One of the tabloids called him the Howard Carter of Wessex. Maybe . . .' He leant across the table, hands raised in front of his face, snapping away with an imaginary camera. '. . . the media intrusion pushed him over the edge.'

A portly gentleman in a Savile Row suit sitting on the opposite side of the aisle raised a disdainful eyebrow and rustled his *Telegraph*.

Clare bent forward until she was almost nose to nose with David, barely able to contain her laughter. 'Behave! You're meant to be a respectable academic.'

'Know where you're going?' The attendant in the British Museum held open one of two enormous double doors.

David nodded. They found themselves in a long tiled passageway that ran like an artery into the heart of the great building. Down either side of the corridor stretched a series of offices trapped behind plate-glass windows set into solid oak frames. Clare could almost taste the centuries of learning.

It took a sharp dig in the ribs from David to break her reverie. 'It's the door at the far end.'

Reaching the spot he'd pointed to, she paused to remove her overcoat, tugging at the elegantly cut black jacket beneath to ensure no wrinkles were present.

'Ready?'

She nodded. David turned the worn brass knob, and the solid oak door swung open to reveal a slim man in his early sixties, with thinning grey hair and spectacles, sitting behind a desk on the far side of the room. The exact dimensions of the room were difficult to gauge. It was crammed with desks covered with dishevelled piles of journals and paperwork, its walls lined from floor to ceiling with books.

He rose to greet them, sticking out a hand, which David shook warmly. 'Clare Hills. Dr Daniel Phelps.'

'Pleased to meet you, Mrs Hills.'

Mrs Hills. The name crashed around in her brain. She found herself overwhelmed by a sudden feeling of emptiness. She was vaguely aware of Daniel gesturing at the seat opposite his own and sat down gratefully. She'd been so caught up in her rediscovery of the world of archaeology she'd almost managed to suppress the memory of Stephen. How could she allow herself to forget him? And so soon. She fought back a wave of nausea. Digging her fingernails hard into the palms of her hands, she forced herself to concentrate on what David was saying.

'Thanks for seeing us at such short notice.'

There was the hint of an Ulster accent in Daniel's reply. 'Not at all. In museum terms, I'm a sort of descendant of your man Hart. He was Keeper of British and Medieval Antiquities. So it's always been a particular source of frustration holding the Hungerbourne gold, but having so little information about his excavation.'

'Well, I hope we can change that for you.' David smiled. 'We're intending to publish Hart's work at Hungerbourne and to carry out an excavation of our own.'

She glanced sideways, not quite believing what she was hearing. Since when had he been planning a dig? He was smiling at her, his expression betraying his satisfaction at her reaction.

The study room was large, bright and entirely free from the books and clutter of Daniel's office. Clare and David had both donned thin blue plastic gloves to protect the precious treasures that lay in a large foam-lined wooden drawer on the desk in front of them. Four small holes had been cut into the foam, in each of which rested an artefact. First David and then Clare examined each in turn.

The largest of the objects was a cone-shaped button measuring little more than four centimetres across. Fashioned from shale, it was entirely covered in gold that had been beaten to the thinness of tinfoil and decorated with four pairs of delicately incised lines. Alongside the button lay what looked like a miniature gold bangle with its out-turned terminals resembling a cow's horns. Slightly smaller than a matchbox, a rectangular pendant sat next to the bangle, a criss-cross of narrow lines forming a chequerboard pattern incised into its gleaming golden surface. According to David, the whisper-thin metal enveloped a piece of human skull; the Bronze Age equivalent of a mourning brooch.

Her eyes were drawn to the smallest piece – a tiny imitation of a halberd. She knew full-sized halberds were capable of inflicting vicious wounds, with their dagger-like blade jutting out at right angles from one end of a long wooden pole. But this exquisite wonder was no bigger than a thimble, its handle crafted from lustrous red amber and wrapped around with four narrow bands of ribbed gold. Out of the thicker end projected the broken remnant of a tiny copper blade.

She opened her laptop and turned her attention to checking

each item against the finds database she'd missed breakfast to create. All four pieces matched Gerald's meticulous descriptions, but he'd also listed another that wasn't present: a gold and amber artefact he referred to as a 'sun disc'. She pointed out the omission to David.

'Maybe it's on display. You carry on here and I'll have a word with Daniel.'

Clare set about measuring the dimensions of each object with a pair of grey plastic dial callipers, the soft clicking of keys signalling the entry of the information onto her computer.

David returned accompanied by Daniel, who placed a small opaque plastic box on the desk in front of her that looked as if it should contain his sandwiches. 'I think this is what you're after. It was under a different accession number because it was deposited separately from the rest of the Hungerbourne material.'

'Isn't that unusual, depositing two parts of the same archive separately?' Clare asked.

'Strictly speaking, it's not part of the same archive. It came from the Hungerbourne barrow cemetery but it was found before the dig started,' Daniel explained.

She couldn't believe what she was hearing. 'Are you sure? In his site diaries Gerald describes it being found during the dig.'

'Take a look.' Daniel lifted the lid of the box to reveal a circular disc about three centimetres across, lying on a bed of acid-free tissue paper. At its centre was an orange-red amber disc encircled by thinly beaten gold, decorated in turn with four concentric circles traced into the glittering metal.

She lifted the disc gently out of its container, turning it round in her hand. Except for some pitting of the amber, the disc was perfect in every way. Taking the callipers, she measured its width and depth, and returned it to its box before beginning to click through the database on her laptop.

She frowned and looked up at the two men waiting expectantly beside her. 'It can't have been found before the dig started. It matches the description of the one found by Gerald during the excavation exactly.'

David leant over Clare's shoulder, peering at the laptop screen, then turned to face her. 'You're certain there can't have been an error transferring Gerald's records to the computer?'

'Positive. The gold was listed separately to everything else in the catalogue and the details in the database match everything else here.'

David turned to Daniel. 'Can we be absolutely sure the accessions record for this piece is accurate? It definitely wasn't part of the excavation archive?'

'Mistakes do happen, especially with older items, but I'm certain about this one. We've still got the letter of gift that accompanied it when it was given to the museum.'

'Could we take a look?'

'I'll dig it out for you.'

Sitting in the corner of the coffee bar opposite the gates of the British Museum, two sheets of paper lay on the table between Clare and David. The first, a photocopy of a handwritten letter dated 20th June 1973, detailed the gift to the museum of what its author, a Richard Jevons, called 'the Jevons sun disc'. Jevons had apparently owned the field in Hungerbourne where the disc had been found in the autumn of 1972. He had decided, the letter went on, that the most suitable place to house the piece was in the nation's most prestigious museum, 'so that all might benefit from the gift of such a magnificent example of ancient craftsmanship'.

David skimmed the chocolate from the top of his cappuccino with his spoon. 'Sounds a bit of a pompous old git.'

'Generous, though.' Clare sipped her coffee. But even the double shot of espresso failed to make her feel any better.

'Anyone can make a mistake.'

She placed her cup forcefully but not quite accurately down on its saucer, causing a little of the hot liquid to spill onto the table. 'I didn't make a mistake. Gerald not only lists that sun disc in his finds catalogue, he describes it being found during the dig by some woman called Joyce Clifford.'

David picked up the second sheet, a copy of a typed inventory bearing Gerald's signature. In the bottom right-hand corner, a British Museum date-stamp read 25th October 1973. It comprised a list of all the goldwork found during his excavations and subsequently handed over to the museum. David read through its contents for a third time before placing it purposefully back on the veneered tabletop that divided them.

He looked up at her. 'Well, that's not what it says here.'

She held his gaze, struggling to control the rising pitch of her voice. 'I know.'

'We'll just have to check through the original catalogue again when we get back.' He leant across the table, looking into her eyes, his tone softer now. 'No one would blame you for making the odd error after what you've been through.'

Later, replaying the scene in her head, she would picture herself depositing the dregs of her hot coffee into his lap. But what she actually did was to ram her left arm into the right sleeve of her overcoat; then, abandoning the attempt, thrust her chair backwards, clattering it into an unsuspecting Italian student sitting at the table behind her.

David stood up. 'Clare, I'm sorry.'

For several seconds, they stood looking at one another. Then he reached down to where her bag sat on the floor and handed it to her.

'Thanks for the support!'

It wasn't until she was picking her way alone through the deepening puddles in Great Russell Street that she finally lost the struggle against her tears.

CHAPTER FOUR

David edged his head round the door of the laying-out room. 'Can I come in?'

Clare was sitting behind a Formica-topped desk, a hardback notebook open in front of her. Her expression wasn't encouraging. He should have left it longer.

'Only if you promise not to try the sympathy thing again.'

Her chastisement was an improvement on the studied silence of the last few days. He tilted his head towards her deferentially. 'I promise to remain entirely unsympathetic in future.'

Her face softened into a smile as she beckoned him towards her.

He pointed in the direction of the notebook. 'Any luck?'

'If you mean have I found my mistake . . .' He opened his mouth to speak, but seeing her raise her hand towards him immediately shut it again. '. . . the answer is no. My transcription from Gerald's finds catalogue was spot on.'

He pulled up a chair alongside her. 'So why don't you look as smug as hell?'

She fixed him with a warning glare. 'Don't think I'm not tempted.'

He felt a sudden urge to laugh, but managed to suppress it.

Clare said, 'If we can't trust Gerald's records, how can we make sense of the excavation?'

'We don't know all his records are unreliable.'

'Don't you see? Now we don't know how much of his record-keeping we can trust. If he faked his excavation records, it would explain why he kept the archive under lock and key for so long.'

He sat with one arm folded across his chest, the other stroking his chin, considering the proposition. 'Why go to the bother of faking them if he never intended them to become public knowledge?' He leant back in his chair. 'It doesn't make sense.'

They sat in silence. For the first time since Clare's return to Wiltshire, he felt despondency creeping over him. Over the past few years he'd experienced a growing hopelessness every time he'd opened his inbox and tried to wade his way through the endless bureaucracy that the twenty-first century academic was forced to endure. They didn't tell you about that on the Discovery Channel!

Finding the Hungerbourne archive had given him the kick up the backside he'd needed. He had the chance to get out and do some real archaeology – something that actually mattered. And having Clare back alongside him was more than he could have hoped for. A once-in-a-lifetime opportunity had fallen right into his lap and he wasn't going to let anyone screw it up – not even Gerald bloody Hart and his sodding record-keeping.

'Got it!' Clare slammed the flats of her hands down on the

desk. Picking up one of Gerald's notebooks, she waved it in front of David's face. 'Other than these and Gerald's magazine article, what have we got?'

'Bugger all.'

She replaced the volume on top of the pile on the corner of the desk. 'Not true. We've got Richard Jevons' letter.'

'How does that help?'

'The letter says Jevons owned the field the sun disc was found in – and the disc came from the Hungerbourne barrow cemetery.'

David pulled himself upright in his seat. 'So he owned the field where the dig took place.'

She nodded enthusiastically. 'If we can track him down, we might just get to the bottom of this.'

'If he's still alive.'

The golden flecks in her hazel eyes sparkled with the same glimmer he remembered when he'd first seen her put trowel to soil as an undergrad. 'Are you teaching this afternoon?'

'No, thank God.'

'Right.' She grabbed her fleece from the peg on the back of the door and ushered him into the corridor.

'Where are we going?'

'I'm going to buy you a pub lunch in Hungerbourne. Let's see if we can run Mr Jevons to ground.'

'I don't give much for our chances, but I always think better on a full stomach.'

Clare glanced down at his waistline. 'That, Dr Barbrook, explains why you've done so well in academia.'

David luxuriated in the warmth of the spring sunshine as he sank into the leather passenger seat of Clare's smart new coupé, an altogether welcome improvement on bumping along in his ancient Land Rover. As Clare manoeuvred the Mazda precisely round the sweeping bends, his gaze drifted to the River Avon meandering its way through the valley floor below. What wouldn't he give to have seen the huge grey sarsen stones being transported along this river from the Marlborough Downs towards their final resting place at Stonehenge. Being an archaeologist, he reflected, was akin to having a mental illness, his head populated with long-dead voices and images.

Despite their avowed intent to track down Richard Jevons, neither of them was able to resist the draw of the small green footpath sign that pointed them towards the barrow cemetery as they entered the village of Hungerbourne. And now as they stood on top of the hill overlooking the burial ground, David imagined he could feel the presence of the people who'd inhabited the ancient landscape. Immediately below where they stood were the round barrows. Overlooking the modern village, all that remained to be seen above ground was one large round mound lying between two slightly less well-defined grassy hummocks, spaced at about fifty-metre intervals, tumbling down the side of the hill.

Clare was standing beside him, hands jammed into the pockets of her chunky fleece, which was zipped right up to her neck. It looked decidedly warmer than his old army jacket, though he would never have admitted as much.

She glanced sideways at him. 'You're very quiet.'

'I was thinking.'

'About Gerald's excavation?'

He turned to give Clare his full attention. He shook his head. 'About rivers. Watercourses were treated as special places in prehistory. Around here, a bourne is a name for a stream or small river.'

Clare looked puzzled. 'But I've looked at the maps. There isn't a watercourse anywhere near here.'

He rubbed his hands together gleefully. 'That's where you're wrong. Every few years a spring appears just over there.' He pointed at a spot just upslope from the topmost barrow. 'It flows right past our barrow cemetery and on through the bottom of the valley.' He swept his arm downwards in a series of sinuous arcs, emulating the gentle folds of the hillside in front of them and finally coming to rest not far from the car park of the pub they were aiming for in the modern village. 'It's where the village gets its name.'

'But why Hungerbourne?'

'The waters only run in really wet years. So they were associated with bad harvests and famine.'

Clare shivered. 'The Woe Waters.'

'Cold?'

She shook her head. On the leeward side of the uppermost barrow, a recently born lamb was tenaciously trying to headbutt its sibling away from their mother to ensure its own supply of life-giving nourishment. 'People must have had to make some harsh choices up here at the end of winter when the food ran out.'

David followed Clare's gaze towards the grassy mounds.

Without moving, she asked, 'Do you think the association with the rising of the waters and death is why they chose this as a burial site?'

'Let's say I think it's a bit more than a coincidence.'

Hungerbourne was a typical downland village. Perched on a small plateau on the southern slope of an upland valley, to the casual observer its thatched cottages and rose-filled gardens gave it a timeless quality. It looked a long way from the bleak grit-stone uplands of his Derbyshire childhood, but David knew appearances were deceptive.

Until a few decades ago it had been a tiny isolated settlement, its inhabitants struggling to eke out an existence. But one glance at the Mercs, Volvos and Audis that peppered the high street told David that today's residents had a decidedly easier time of it. An impression reinforced by the low-slung beams and tastefully decorated interior of the Lamb and Flag, inside which he and Clare now found themselves.

Handing Clare her orange juice, he settled himself into a seat next to the open fire and took a long appreciative slurp of his pint. It took him less than half an hour to demolish an out-sized portion of steak and ale pie, followed by an unfeasibly large apple crumble and custard. As he cast his spoon into the bowl and wiped his mouth on a paper napkin, a short thick-set man in his late fifties with a smile that matched his gleaming pate approached their table.

David whispered, 'Natives seem friendly.'

Clare leant across the table towards him. 'Good. That'll make it easier when you ask him about Jevons.'

'Me?'

'Everything OK for you?' The harshness of the Estuary accent was mellowed by both the hint of a Wiltshire burr and the affable intonation of its owner.

'Great.' David patted his stomach appreciatively before proffering his empty glass towards the man. 'Could I have another pint?' He cast an enquiring glance at Clare, but she shook her head, giving him a look obviously intended to encourage him to further his conversation with the man waiting patiently beside their table.

'Had this place long?' he asked.

'Me and the wife bought it about ten years ago.'

'You've made a good job of it.'

'Wasn't easy. A couple of townies rolling up in the sticks.' He lowered his voice, bending his head towards them. 'But old man Clifford, who had the place before us, wasn't the most congenial host. The only reason anyone came here when he had it was cos it's the only pub for miles. Things picked up once they had a taste of Shirl's cooking and found out what it was like to have a landlord who could keep a civil tongue in his head.' He smiled contentedly.

'You must know most of the locals round here, then,' David said.

He nodded.

Clare widened her eyes at David and he felt a sharp kick to his shin.

He acquiesced. 'Would you happen to know a Richard Jevons?'

'Out of luck there, mate. Died a few years back.' A concerned expression crossed his face. 'Are you two coppers?'

David laughed. 'God, no! Archaeologists.'

The anxiety in the landlord's expression vanished as David introduced himself and Clare.

Their landlord, now known to them as Tony, asked, 'What brings you looking for Jevons?'

'We're trying to find out about an excavation on his land in the seventies.'

'The dig up on Old Barrows Field?'

'You've heard of it.'

'Can't avoid it. There was a hell of a to-do about the site a while back.' Tony leant across the table and in a stage whisper said, 'See the bloke at the bar talking to Shirl?'

A well-built man in his mid-fifties, wearing a crisply pressed NFU-issue white and green checked shirt and sober tie beneath a tweed jacket, was drinking a gin and tonic, and conversing easily with the landlady.

'That's Richard Jevons' son, Ed. A couple of years back, the agro company that owns Old Barrows Field wanted to go into some sort of agreement with British Heritage. Open the place up for tourists. Some of the real old locals were quite keen on it. Bring in a bit of money to the village. There's not much work round here for the youngsters.'

David said, 'I take it not everyone was quite so keen.'

Tony nodded. 'Ed got up a petition. Said it wasn't "appropriate to the spirit of the place". Kept banging on about the barrows being the inheritance of the people of Hungerbourne and how he didn't want it destroyed by a bunch of "yobs and day-trippers".'

David said, 'Bet that went down a storm.'

'The commuters loved it. Didn't want anything wrecking their peaceful Sunday strolls. But some of the old-timers weren't so happy. To tell you the truth, I was quite keen on the idea. But I steered clear of making my views too well known. Doesn't pay to take sides. Ed's one of my best customers and this place wouldn't stay open without the weekenders.'

'So the Jevons family don't own Old Barrows Field now?' David asked.

'Not any more. Ed spent years trying to persuade his old man to hand the land over to him so he wouldn't get stiffed with inheritance tax. But Richard was a cantankerous old sod. When he died, Ed had to sell all the family land to stay afloat. He did some sort of deal to lease most of it back as a tenant. But the way he acted you'd think he still owned it.' Tony glanced up at the bar and then back to David and Clare. 'He took a pot shot at a couple of blokes with metal detectors and spades up on the barrows a couple of years back.'

David suppressed a grin. He could see the shock on Clare's face. 'Was anyone hurt?' she asked.

Tony shook his head. 'Ed's a pretty good shot. If he'd meant to hit 'em he would've. Caused a splash in the local rag, but it never came to court.'

'Do you think he'd be willing to talk to us about the excavations?' Clare asked.

Tony chortled. 'Once he finds out who you are you'll have trouble stopping him. Would you like me to have a word with him?'

Clare nodded, and Tony scurried away towards the bar.

David sat back and drained the dregs of his pint. Clare delved into her shoulder bag and withdrew a copy of the Brew Crew photograph and placed it on the table in front of him. 'Look! Second row, far end.'

David followed Clare's finger to the image of a sturdy-looking young man, the image a foreshadow of the stocky, middle-aged man now engaged in conversation with Tony.

David looked Ed up and down as he made his way towards them. His dark curly hair was well cut, with tinges of grey just beginning to show through in his sideburns. Not tall, but when David saw the smile Clare gave Ed he felt aware that, despite the slight crook in his patrician nose, some women – Clare included – might definitely consider him handsome. David's eyes alighted on the conker-brown sheen of Ed's Oxford brogues. Beneath the table, he rubbed the muddied and scuffed insteps of his walking boots on the back of his cords. Clare flashed him a warning look and he settled instead for tucking his feet beneath his chair to remove them from view.

'I hear you're after some information about the Old Barrows Field dig.' Ed's accent, like the shoes, said minor public school.

David gestured for him to pull up a chair. 'We're from the

University of Salisbury. We're working on the Hungerbourne excavation archive.'

David thought he saw the expression on the older man's face tighten for a moment, but Ed responded without hesitation.

'Wasn't that destroyed in the fire?'

'That's what we thought. But after Gerald Hart passed away we found the archive in the attic of the manor when we were helping his nephew sort through his effects.'

'I'm surprised Peter didn't mention it.'

'I had to ask him to keep it quiet. British Heritage put a media embargo on the story. We're intending to re-excavate the site and, given what they found the first time, they don't want to compromise security.'

Ed seemed distracted. Clare filled the silence. 'Are you a friend of Peter's?'

'We grew up together.' Ed turned towards her, as he did so catching sight of the photograph on the table in front of her. 'Good Lord. Is that a photo of the dig team?' She nodded. 'May I?'

Clare pushed the picture across the table towards him. Ed picked up the image and studied it, lost in his own thoughts.

'Do you remember any of the other diggers?' Clare asked.

Ed raised an eyebrow and looked up at her. 'I see my secret's out. You spotted me.'

She said, 'You haven't changed much.'

Ed smiled. 'Most of them were locals. You'll recognise Gerald, of course. The one standing next to him is his younger brother, Jim – Peter's father. And in front of him is Jim's wife, Estelle. The woman on the end there is Joyce Clifford.' Ed pointed at a curvaceous young woman, blonde hair piled high, standing hands on hips at the end of the row.

'Was she related to the chap that used to own this pub?' Clare asked.

'The grass doesn't grow under your feet, does it, young lady?' David noticed Clare prickled, but Ed seemed unaware. 'Joyce was married to George Clifford, the old landlord here.'

'Was?' Clare asked.

'She left him years ago.'

'Does he still live round here?'

Ed nodded. 'Bought himself a little ex-council place in Hackpen Close when he sold this.'

'Do you think he'd be willing to have a chat about the excavations?'

'You can try.' Ed had a twinkle in his eye.

'You don't think he'll be much help?' David asked.

'He wanted nothing to do with the dig. But Joyce was keen on getting involved right from the off. A bit too keen for George's liking. She was always up for a bit of fun.'

The knowing look Ed gave him made David feel distinctly uncomfortable. He pointed to the photograph again, this time indicating a petite young brunette in a floral print blouse and slacks. 'Who's that standing in front of you?'

Ed still seemed amused by David's reaction, but returned his attention to the photograph. 'Peggy Grafton. You'd think butter wouldn't melt, wouldn't you?' His tone was one of undisguised resentment. 'Local girl made good. You know the type. Got a scholarship to an Oxford college, then hooked herself a biochemist by the name of Bockford. She always knew which way her bread was buttered.'

Picking up the photograph, David mumbled, 'Margaret Bockford.'

He'd thought the face was familiar, but the Margaret Bockford he knew was a studious, well-respected professor of archaeology approaching retirement, not a pretty young girl in her early twenties.

'That would be it. She only took to calling herself Margaret once she was amidst the dreaming spires. Plain old Peggy had always been good enough for us simple Wiltshire folk.'

David exchanged a glance with Clare. This was progress. Maybe the scathing obituary of Gerald that Margaret Bockford had written was less impersonal than they'd thought.

'Would you be willing to provide us with a list of everyone in the photo?' Clare asked.

Ed inclined his head in Clare's direction and smiled. 'I'd be delighted. Some of them are dead now. But if it helps . . .'

David stood up. 'Can I get you a drink by way of recompense?'

'Very decent of you. A G and T would hit the spot nicely.'

David made his way to the bar, leaving Ed to dictate the details of the rest of the dig team to Clare. When he returned, she was listening to Ed with rapt attention.

'So you didn't have access to any of the records during the excavation?' she asked.

'I'm not much help to you there, I'm afraid. I was just a teenager helping out in the holidays. Gerald only let me take part to humour my father. All of the important stuff was done by Gerald, Estelle and Jim. Oh, and Peggy, of course; Gerald's star pupil. The rest of us were pretty much cannon fodder.'

Clare asked, 'Do you remember any of the goldwork being found?'

Ed looked thoughtfully into the bottom of his gin and tonic before replying. 'I remember the sun disc being discovered. That was what sparked Gerald's interest in digging the cemetery in the first place. Of course, he knew the barrows were there, but he'd never shown any inclination to excavate them until the disc turned up.'

Clare leant forward. 'You mean the disc found before the excavations?'

'That's right. It was turned up by the tractor in the autumn ploughing. As soon as word got out everyone wanted a piece of the Hungerbourne treasure. We owned the land the barrows were on. Manor Farm had been in my mother's family for generations.'

'I thought the Harts owned the manor,' Clare said.

'They do. My grandfather sold the house to Gerald's father. Gerald's old man made an absolute packet, in soap of all things. Then set about buying the accoutrements of a gentleman.' He laughed, evidently enjoying a private joke. 'Whiter than white, the Harts.'

'What happened when the sun disc was found?' Clare asked.

'There was an inquest.'

'I thought inquests happened when someone died.'

'Keep up, Clare! A solicitor's wife should know better than that.' As soon as the words were out of David's mouth, he regretted them. He couldn't bring himself to look her in the eye. Stephen was dead, for God's sake. Surely now he should be able to overcome the jealousy and resentment he'd felt towards the man. He took a slug of his bitter.

When he finally looked up and started to mumble an embarrassed apology, she waved his words aside, her expression more one of disappointment than of hurt. 'It's alright. Really.'

Ed looked quizzically between the two of them.

David cleared his throat as if to speak. But it was Ed who offered the explanation. 'It was a treasure trove inquest to decide who owned the sun disc. They held it at the village hall. Local press, the nationals – they were all here. Father loved every minute of it.'

Clare said, 'And he very generously gave the find to the British Museum.'

'"Donating it for the greater good", he said.' Ed's face reddened. 'He never gave a damn about the greater good.'

The first half of the drive back from Hungerbourne passed in total silence. David was unsure whether to try again to apologise for his gaffe in the pub. But despite the silence, Clare looked unperturbed. And he had no desire to make things any worse than they already were. Better to let sleeping dogs lie.

He turned his thoughts to what they'd learnt. Ed had been a bit of a dead end as far as information about the finds from the excavation had been concerned. But at least he'd been able to tell them the names of the other members of the dig team.

He turned to Clare. 'Bit of a turn-up for the books, Margaret Bockford being on the dig.'

'She might be able to shed some light on the confusion over the sun disc.'

'Ed seemed pretty sure the disc was found before the dig started. It all tallies with the BM's records.'

'If what he says about the dig is right, there are only three people who can help us get to the bottom of when that disc was found: Margaret Bockford, and Jim and Estelle Hart. Didn't you say Jim left Peter and his mother when Peter was still a kid?'

David nodded.

'Do you think Peter might have any idea where he is now?'

He shook his head. 'Hasn't seen him in years.'

'What about Estelle?'

'Peter's been beside himself with worry about her.'

'Why?'

'She had a bit of a health scare a while back. When she got out of hospital she just couldn't cope on her own. Needed round the clock care, apparently, but he had the devil of a job persuading her she needed to go into a nursing home.'

'And did he?'

'Eventually, but given her condition I don't want to bother her if we can avoid it.'

'Well, that just leaves us with Professor Bockford. Think you can blag us an appointment for a chat with Peggy?'

He laughed. 'Only if you promise not to call her that to her face.'

CHAPTER FIVE

David had met Margaret Bockford at numerous academic conferences over the years. She was forthright to the point of being blunt, and possessed an unerring instinct for sniffing out bullshit and bringing academic poseurs to book. It was widely acknowledged that if you valued your career you stayed on your intellectual toes in Professor Bockford's company. And that was why, despite the fact that she unnerved him, David rather admired her.

Her office was a bit more than twice the size of his. Encased as it was with heavy wooden panelling that betrayed the fact that Oxford's colleges had been built with more masculine inhabitants in mind, it might have possessed a tomb-like quality. But a small vase of purple freesias softened the otherwise imposing character of the dark rosewood desk that dominated the room. The sweet heavy scent of the flowers wafting towards them on the breeze from the open window reminded him of the pretty young woman in the floral print blouse in the Brew Crew photo.

Now that he was in the presence of the original, he could see there was still something of Peggy Grafton about Professor Margaret Bockford. More than a hint of the girl in the photograph was visible beneath the grey hair and businesslike rectangular spectacles of the small, neat woman who faced them across the desk. The room was west-facing and, as she rose to greet them, her still-trim figure silhouetted against the window created the illusion of a much larger presence. The backlighting forced both Clare and David to lower their gaze momentarily as she indicated they should sit; a neat trick. He had no doubt that, like everything else about Margaret, the positioning of her chair and desk had been carefully considered to achieve the desired outcome.

'What can I do for you, David?'

'As I said on the phone, we're working on a project to publish the Hungerbourne excavation archives.'

'It's nice to see some of the younger generation have a sense of academic responsibility. It's a trait sadly lacking in some of your predecessors. That site should have been written up years ago. It's a miracle the archive survived.'

'I understand you participated in the original excavations.'

Margaret peered deliberately over the top of her spectacles at him. 'The use of the word "original" makes me sound like some sort of artefact.'

He shifted uneasily in his seat.

The desired response achieved, Margaret smiled. 'I was born and brought up in Hungerbourne. It was the vicar, Reverend Hemmings, who got me and one or two of the other local children interested in archaeology. He used us as his legs and eyes. When he got too old to do it he sent us out to walk the fields around the barrows looking for finds – stone tools in the main. For most of the villagers, the barrows were just a backdrop for everyday life; they took them for granted. But when the sun disc was found, Gerald persuaded the British Museum they should be investigated. Once the newspapers got hold of the story, the locals began to sit up and take notice.'

'Was Hemmings involved in the excavations?' David asked.

Margaret shook her head. 'He died not long before I went up to Oxford.'

'Gerald's site journals suggest he originally intended to excavate all of the barrows in the cemetery,' Clare said.

Margaret turned towards Clare, looked her up and down, and, seemingly satisfied with the assessment, smiled. 'That's right. These days we tend to try to conserve something for future generations, but the approach to excavation then was somewhat more robust. Gerald and his brother both inherited the Hart gene for persuasion. Because of all of the publicity surrounding the discovery of the goldwork, Gerald secured enough funding from the BM to carry out a sustained campaign of excavations on all of the barrows in the group.'

'But his records show he only actually excavated one of them.'

Margaret nodded. 'That's right.'

'Why did he stop?' Clare asked.

The older woman's face darkened. 'That's a question only Gerald could answer.' Margaret sat back in her chair. She opened up her hands, which had been loosely clasped together on her desk, scrutinising her palms as if they might provide the answer to Clare's question. Finally, she looked up at her. 'The dig had gone better than we could possibly have hoped. We struck lucky. Picked a round barrow that hadn't been ransacked by nineteenth-century antiquaries. There was some plough damage to the mound, but most of the funerary deposits were intact. Gerald had planned an open day for the public on the bank holiday Monday. We'd been preparing for weeks. But when we got to site on the Monday morning, he called the dig team together and announced we were going to start backfilling.'

The long-case clock in the corner of the office struck the half hour. Margaret raised her hand to pre-empt further questions and hit the hands-free button on her phone. 'Emma, be a dear and bring us through three coffees and the usual, would you?' She returned her attention to Clare. 'We'd all worked so hard. And Gerald was so passionate about his work; it took a while before we realised he meant it. Gerald and Reverend Hemmings were the only people who took me seriously when I said I wanted to be an archaeologist. So with Hemmings dead, when Gerald told us . . .'

Margaret faltered. She looked pale and all at once seemed every one of her sixty-odd years. David had never seen her like this before. 'You see, it wasn't the sort of job a working-class girl from a Wiltshire village was meant to have. My mother and father thought I should aspire to something a little more reliable – like working in a bank. But Gerald used to say archaeology gets in your blood. Once it's running through your veins, you can't escape. And I was young enough and naive enough to believe he meant it.' Her expression of disdain was unmistakable.

Clare spoke softly. 'Hungerbourne was his last excavation.'

'He cut himself off from archaeology completely.'

'Did you ever ask him why?'

Margaret nodded. 'Once I got over the shock. But he wouldn't discuss it. Just kept saying he had no choice.'

'What do you think he meant?' Clare asked.

'I've always supposed it was something to do with internal

politics at the BM. He left the British Museum within weeks of the end of the dig. I've heard rumours since that his boss didn't like his public grandstanding with the media and withdrew funding.'

David began to feel some sympathy for the man. He knew what it was like to work for a boss who threw obstacles in your path because he resented your success. 'So it wasn't entirely Gerald's fault. Professional jealousy was at the root of it.'

Margaret wasn't having any of it. 'It was a complete dereliction of his duty as an archaeologist not to have published that site. You should know as well as anyone, David, that the most unforgivable sin in archaeology is to excavate a site without making the record of it publicly available. It's tantamount to looting.'

He knew she was right, but still couldn't help feeling shocked by the vitriol of her response. She rose from her desk and turned to look out of the window behind her. 'It's weak-willed to give in to bullying from one's superiors just to keep one's job. Gerald was a man of independent means. He didn't need the job at the BM. He wanted the prestige.' She turned to face Clare and David. 'That is not the way in which an archaeologist should behave.' No one could be in any doubt of the force of Margaret's convictions.

The door of the office swung open, and a besuited and bespectacled woman in her mid-fifties entered carrying a tray bearing the requested coffee together with a bottle of Irish whiskey. She deposited it on the desk and, after receiving a smile of thanks from Margaret, departed wordlessly.

Margaret dispensed the coffee, pouring a generous tot of Jameson's into her own mug. 'I find one's metabolism needs a little stimulation at this time of day. Care to join me?'

Clare declined, but David smiled encouragingly and Margaret poured a splash of whiskey into his coffee. His admiration for this woman was coming on in leaps and bounds.

Margaret took an appreciative swig of her coffee before setting it down on the desk and looking directly at David. 'You didn't come here to listen to a lecture on archaeological ethics. Why are you really here?'

He cleared his throat. 'You said Gerald was passionate about his work. Would you have said his record-keeping could be relied upon?'

'The majority of the day-to-day recording was done by me, Gerald's brother, Jim, and Jim's wife, Estelle. We did the initial recording and Gerald wrote everything up in his site diary at the end of each day. It was obvious from the start that Jim was there under sufferance, so after the first couple of weeks all of the recording was left to Estelle and me.'

'Was there any possibility of a mistake being made with any of the major finds?' Clare asked.

David held his breath. He'd seen too many of his colleagues' academic reputations destroyed by Margaret's politely worded rapier thrusts not to be aware of her destructive potential.

'I like to think I maintained a high standard even in my younger days, and Estelle was assiduous in her work. You obviously have something specific in mind. What exactly is this about?'

Clare looked towards David, and he nodded. 'The British Museum holds the Jevons sun disc. Richard Jevons donated it to them in June 1973, just before the dig began.'

Margaret nodded. 'That's right. In fact, somewhere in my files I have a copy of a newspaper article with a photograph of Richard handing over the disc after the inquest. I'll ask Emma to hunt it out and send you a copy.'

Clare said, 'But the excavation records describe the sun disc being found during the course of the excavations. In his site diaries, Gerald says it was found in the same pit that contained the largest cremation urn.'

Margaret smiled. 'That's right. Joyce Clifford found it. I have to admit to being somewhat envious of her at the time. To discover the second of a matching pair was unbelievably good fortune.'

'There were two sun discs?' Clare looked as horrified as David felt.

He felt a distinctly queasy feeling in the pit of his stomach. British Heritage weren't going to like this.

'I was away at university when the first one was found, but I saw them both. We needed to be able to compare the entire goldwork assemblage so Gerald kept them together at the manor.'

David raised an eyebrow.

'It was quite secure. He kept the whole assemblage in his safe.' For a moment, the irony of Margaret's assertion seemed to escape her. Then a shadow of dismay fell across her face. 'Am I to infer that one of the sun discs is missing?'

Clare nodded. Margaret raised a hand to her mouth and, for a few seconds, appeared to be lost for words. This was obviously a day for firsts.

Then she muttered, 'Of all the things I imagined, I never thought . . .'

'Was Gerald ever in monetary difficulties?'

'Clare!' David snapped his head round to face her.

Margaret turned to face him. 'It's a perfectly reasonable question. Gerald inherited his father's fortune. Something I'm afraid his brother never came to terms with. For all of his flaws, Gerald was never dishonest. If you're looking for a miscreant in the family, it's Jim. Gerald was continually bailing his brother out of one misadventure or another. Any fool could have told him Jim would never change his ways.' She took a sip from her afternoon pick-me-up. 'It's curious, don't you think, how some of the most intelligent people see so little of what is going on right under their nose?' She paused. 'The end of the dig precipitated something of a crisis in the Hart household.'

Clare leant forward in her chair. 'What sort of crisis?'

'On the morning Gerald made his announcement, Estelle seemed to just fall apart. She was inconsolable. We were all shocked by the news, but her reaction was out of all proportion to the event. Of course, by the end of the week the whole village knew the real reason.'

'Which was?' Clare asked.

'Jim, with his inimitable sense of timing, had run off with Joyce Clifford.'

David was sitting beside Clare on the back seat of the bus back to Seacourt Park and Ride. He turned to face her. 'What did you make of Peggy?'

'I wouldn't like to get on the wrong side of her.'

'All part of her charm.'

'That and her penchant for Irish whiskey.' Clare smiled. 'At least now we know for sure there were two sun discs, we can rely on Gerald's excavation records.'

'But the bad news is somewhere along the line the sun disc from the excavation has been lost.'

'Lost! Didn't you listen to anything Margaret said in there? Jim Hart had access to the records and the archive. He spent half his life sponging off his brother and five minutes after the excavation ended he bunked off with the landlord's wife. It's as plain as day. Jim Hart stole the missing sun disc.'

'You can't go round accusing people of theft without a shred of proof.' And he knew British Heritage wouldn't take kindly to the idea of funding the project if it was at the centre of a police investigation. 'Besides,' he added gently, 'we've only got Margaret's word for what Jim was like.'

'I thought you liked her.'

'I do. But didn't you think she sounded the tiniest bit bitter about the Harts? You were the one who said you wouldn't like to get on the wrong side of her.'

Clare fell silent until the bus swung into the entrance to the Park and Ride. 'Estelle had access to the site records. She was married to one brother and working for the other. She might be able to give us an insight into what really happened.'

He'd had enough of this whole sorry saga for one day and he wasn't in the mood for a debate. 'We've got enough on our plates working out what we're going to tell British Heritage. The last thing we need is Peter on our backs, accusing us of harassing his mother.'

Margaret was as good as her word. Two days after the conversation in her office, an A5 Manila envelope arrived on David's desk containing the promised copy of the newspaper cutting. He was pleased with the way Clare had been progressing with the work on the archive, and more than a little relieved that she hadn't brought up the subject of speaking to Estelle again. After their journey back from Oxford, he'd wondered whether he'd been a little harsh on her. But from what Peter had told him, he knew he and Estelle had had quite enough to put up with from Jim without having to endure it all being raked up again.

David knew the chances of finding the missing disc were slim. He'd read somewhere that if the police didn't solve a crime in the first few weeks, they probably never would. So what hope did they have of tracking down a tiny gold disc that disappeared forty years ago? They didn't even have any proof that it had been stolen. Plenty of artefacts had gone missing over the years, mislabelled in museum stores or lost in garages and attics. After all, that was exactly how they'd found the Hungerbourne archive in the first place.

It wasn't until the afternoon, when Clare joined David in his office for tea, that he told her the newspaper cutting had arrived. He handed her the envelope. She opened it and sat quietly scanning the photocopied sheet in front of her.

He said, 'It doesn't help us very much, I'm afraid. Just confirms what we already knew. Richard Jevons gave his disc to the British Museum. You can see from the photo that it was Gerald he handed the disc over to. Only to be expected, as he was the BM's man on the spot.'

Clare was peering intently at the grainy image in front of her.

'Did you hear what I said, Clare? The disc we saw in the BM was handed over to Gerald by Richard Jevons.'

'No, it wasn't.'

'Are you getting enough sleep? Look at the photo. It's Gerald being given the Jevons disc.'

'Yes, but it's not the disc in the BM.'

'What?'

'You saw the one in the BM. It was perfect. This one has got a tear along its edge. Take a look.'

He all but ripped the photocopied sheet out of her hand. He spent a few seconds studying the image, checked the contacts listing on his PC, picked up his phone and dialled an outside line. 'Hi, Daniel, David Barbrook here. I'm trying to tie up a few loose ends. Would you happen to know whether any conservation work has been carried out on the Jevons sun disc?' A few moments elapsed before David continued. 'Hi . . . You're sure. OK. Thanks.' David replaced the telephone handset.

Clare shuffled forward in her seat. 'Well?'

'No conservation work has ever been carried out on their disc.'

'So the one they've got is the one from the dig.'

David nodded. 'It's the Jevons disc that's missing.'

CHAPTER SIX

'It seems to have disappeared sometime during 1973.'

David had been dreading this. Being at the centre of a criminal investigation wouldn't go down well with British Heritage, and without their funding there was no project. And without the project, Muir would have all the ammunition he needed to ensure his academic career was toast.

He'd finally grasped the nettle and agreed to report the theft of the sun disc to the police when Clare had pointed out that as soon as they published the excavation report it would be obvious to everybody, including British Heritage and the British Museum, that it was missing. So if they didn't report its disappearance, suspicion would inevitably fall on them. He could picture the smirk on the Runt's face now.

He was well aware that the police were likely to take a less than proactive approach to its recovery. He should be grateful he wasn't being met with outright derision.

As it was, the rotund, rapidly balding desk sergeant, who to judge by appearances was looking forward to his well-earned retirement, was already distinctly less affable than when David had introduced himself. 'I thought you said it had been stolen, sir.'

'Yes, Sergeant. Someone stole the sun disc that had been given to the British Museum by Richard Jevons in June 1973 and replaced it with the one found during Gerald Hart's excavations in August of the same year.'

The sergeant raised an eyebrow. 'Right, so the item definitely disappeared in 1973.'

'It could have been later.'

'How much later?'

'We can't be sure.'

'But you're sure it's missing?'

'Stolen – we think.'

'And you don't have any idea what happened to this disc between 1973 and the present.'

'No.'

'Right. Wait here, I need to have a word with one of my colleagues.'

David had to admit that, even to his own ears, the whole thing sounded far-fetched. He turned round, resting his elbows on the counter behind him and considered the two other inhabitants of the reception area. A doleful-looking teenager with a proudly displayed predilection for body art was slumped in the corner next to the vending machine. He was sitting next to a middle-aged woman wearing a billowing cotton skirt and drop earrings. On balance, David concluded she was more likely to be his social worker than his mother. The youth looked up at him, and David smiled. Adjusting the angle of his slump, the youngster raised a single digit in response. The woman continued to flick through the pile of papers she was holding without so much as a twitch.

'Right, sir.'

David spun round to discover the sergeant had been joined by a tall slim woman wearing a tailored trouser suit and open-necked blue blouse. Her long blonde hair was gathered together in a ponytail. It could have looked severe, but it didn't.

'I'm going to hand you over to one of our CID officers, Inspector Treen.'

He barely noticed the undisguised note of relief in the sergeant's voice. It wasn't just the policemen who were getting younger. Inspector Treen looked young enough to be one of his postgrads. He suddenly wished he'd taken the time to iron his shirt before he'd left the house this morning.

'Good morning. Dr Barbrook, isn't it? How can I help?'

Maybe this wasn't such a bad idea after all.

As far as Clare could see, everything Margaret had told them about the Hart family pointed to Jim's involvement in the disappearance of the Jevons disc. Gerald had clearly been used to clearing up his little brother's messes. And Gerald was the only person who would have had the opportunity to swap the sun disc from his excavations with the one Richard Jevons had given to the British Museum. But would he really have put his career on the line and risked his academic reputation to cover up his brother's indiscretions?

David had been insistent, to the point of obstinacy, that they couldn't be certain that Jim had stolen the sun disc. And while she understood his reasons for not wanting to speak to Estelle unless it was absolutely essential, she couldn't help wondering whether some of it was down to a reluctance to believe Peter's father might be a thief. In the end, they'd struck a deal. He would report the disappearance of the sun disc to the police and she would give up on the idea of speaking to Estelle.

Though she'd promised not to bother the wife, she hadn't said anything about not talking to the son. Which was why she found herself sitting in the lounge of Peter's first floor Marlborough flat. From the building's Georgian façade, she'd expected an interior of tastefully decorated eighteenth-century elegance. But the reality was light, bright and distinctly post-modern. Looking around the room, Clare found herself wondering if he ever read. There wasn't a book in sight. Maybe he wasn't the reading sort. It struck her that he was more likely to download his e-books to a reader than have a secret library hidden away somewhere.

Judging from the unblemished cream carpets, he had no children or pets. Function and style were all. Did he have a wife? David hadn't mentioned one.

Peter relaxed into the black leather sofa opposite the chair in which she was sitting. 'Sure you won't?' She shook her head and he filled his own glass from the bottle of Sancerre and replaced it on the coffee table that lay between them. 'So you want to know about the excavations.'

'I'm just trying to get a feel for the background to the dig – the set-up.' She'd decided on the drive over to Marlborough that she wouldn't share her suspicions about his father's involvement in the theft of the sun disc with Peter. After all, that was exactly what they were – suspicions. And she didn't want to get off on the wrong foot.

'I'm afraid my knowledge is probably a bit limited for what you're after. I was only a teenager at the time of the dig so I didn't know much about the technical side of things. And to be honest, fiddling around with bits of old pot was never really my thing.

I've always been more interested in the future than the past.'

'You didn't take part in the excavations?'

'No. Mother tried to press-gang me into helping out when they were short-handed. But I managed to avoid it. I think at one time she harboured hopes I'd follow in Uncle Gerald's footsteps.' He smiled. 'It didn't take her long to realise my interests lay elsewhere.'

'But your mother was involved in the excavations.'

He nodded. 'She loved it – spent all her free time helping Gerald. When he wasn't digging, she helped him with his preparation and his publications. She did quite a lot of his artefact drawings. That's where I get my creative gene from.' Clare looked at him quizzically. 'I'm an architect.'

He stood up and plucked a black-and-white photograph in a silver frame from the wall unit behind Clare's chair. 'Gerald was a good man. Good company, too. He had a wicked sense of humour. Right up until the last few months. He went downhill a bit then – especially after the fire.' He handed the photograph to Clare. 'That was taken a few years before the Hungerbourne dig.'

The photograph showed a gangly young Peter sitting cross-legged beside Gerald at the centre of a clearing in a small stand of hazel trees. A beaming Gerald was wearing a Davy Crockett hat several sizes too small for him while Peter was sporting a pair of fringed buckskin trousers and jacket, and sawing industriously at a small piece of wood with a knife. 'Mother took that on my fourteenth birthday. People who never met Gerald would have you believe he was a curmudgeonly old so-and-so. But they're wrong. He'd have done anything to make Mother and me happy. He bought me that whole outfit: the bowie knife, the buckskin jacket, the lot.' Peter's blue eyes lit up at the memory. 'I don't imagine you're old enough to remember *King of the Wild Frontier* or *The Alamo*?'

She shook her head. 'I was more of a *Bagpuss* girl.'

Smiling up at him, she handed back the photograph and he put it back in its appointed position. Relaxing here, she could see he'd inherited the Hart family charm.

'Your father was in the photo of the dig team. He worked on the excavation, too, didn't he?'

Peter's face froze.

Clare pressed on. 'Did he help with the recording side of things?'

'As I said, I didn't get involved with the dig.'

'But your father did.'

'If you want to know about my father, I suggest you find someone who gives a damn.'

She looked at the man in front of her. Despite his harsh words, his face seemed to betray the hurt of a young boy rather than hatred. As if aware of her ability to read his emotions, he looked down, unwilling or unable to reveal any more.

When she spoke, her reply was gentle. 'And that doesn't include you?'

His expression changed. 'I'm sorry. I shouldn't have taken it out on you. But I really don't see why I should have any reason to care about a man who abandoned his wife and child without a second thought.'

'You haven't had much contact with him since.'

'In forty years I haven't had so much as a birthday card. He never gave Mother a penny. Not a penny. If it hadn't been for Gerald, we would have been destitute. It's not everyone who would look after another man's wife and child without a murmur.'

It seemed Jim had been cut from the same mould as her own father. 'They're overrated, you know – fathers.'

'You sound like you're speaking from experience.'

'I have the advantage of not remembering mine. If he didn't want anything to do with us, I figured I was better off without him. Mum was enough for me.'

'How old were you when he left?'

'Just a baby.'

There was a long pause before Peter said, 'You know, sometimes I wish Father had left when I was a baby.'

'You think you would have missed him less.'

'Missed him! Jesus, I didn't miss him. I hated him – for what he did to our family.'

'You mean his philandering?'

'Sounds rather charming and old-fashioned when you put it like that. My father wasn't a philanderer, he was a wrecker – a wrecker of lives.' He replenished his glass. 'Do you have any idea what it's like to have a father whom you know everyone despises? Everyone from the village postman to the Lord Lieutenant knew my father was a shit. But no one was allowed to mention it. We couldn't have the family publicly embarrassed. The seventies weren't all about peace and love in the Hart household.'

'Didn't Gerald do anything about him?'

'He tried. He bailed him out more times than I can remember. But he didn't know about the worst of it.'

Clare looked at him quizzically.

Peter took a sip of his wine. 'He'd always been a drinker. Gerald knew that. But what he didn't know was that he'd started to threaten Mother.'

'Physically?'

Peter nodded. 'He was a bully and a coward.'

'Did you ever try to do anything about it?'

'I was just a kid. But I did screw up the courage to stand up to him once.' He fell silent.

'What happened?'

'Let's just say it wasn't only me that paid for it.'

She didn't want to push him any further. 'Do you ever wonder where he is now?'

'Truthfully, no.' He held her gaze. 'We've been better off without him.' He broke into an unexpected smile. 'You sound more interested in finding out where he is than I am.'

Clare chose her words with care. 'David and I are trying to sort out some confusion with the excavation records. Professor Bockford said your father had worked on them.'

'Professor Bockford?'

'Margaret Bockford. You would have known her as Peggy Grafton.'

'I remember Peggy. Ed Jevons had a bit of a thing for her.' A nostalgic smile spread across his face. 'She worked on the dig with Mother and Gerald. She was really keen. But Gerald more or less dragooned Father into working up there. Although I'm not sure exactly what he did. He was never one for manual labour, and I can't imagine Uncle trusting him with the record-keeping side of things.'

Clare hesitated. 'I don't quite know how to ask this.'

'Just ask.' When he smiled, he looked uncannily like the tall, handsome man in the Brew Crew photograph.

'Do you have any idea how we could get in touch with your father?'

'I haven't seen or heard from him in forty years. And I'm more than happy with that arrangement.' He paused for a moment. 'This really matters to you, doesn't it?'

Clare nodded. He got up and, without a word of explanation, left the room. She made her way over to the window. On the pavements below, shoppers bustled their way along the busy high street. For all she knew, Jim might be down there now. She probably wouldn't recognise him if he was. But if he had been responsible for the disappearance of the sun disc, he was likely to be a very long way from Wiltshire.

Peter returned, carrying a battered lever arch file which he placed on the coffee table. 'This might be of interest.'

She joined him on the sofa. He opened the file, revealing a collection of old bank statements. 'As well as leaving me the manor, Uncle named me as executor of his will. He made a number of minor bequests to charities and his favourite causes, but there was one rather more unusual stipulation. My inheritance of the manor and the residue of his estate was conditional on me continuing to make regular payments to a bank account. Uncle had set aside separate funds for the purpose.'

He pointed to a line on the uppermost of the fading bank statements that lay in front of them. Under the column headed 'Payment type and details' was printed: *Standing Order J. Clifford.*

Clare said, 'Joyce Clifford.'

'I see you're familiar with Mrs Clifford.'

'I came across her photograph in the excavation archives.' Peter looked straight at her. She tried to look him in the eye, but found she couldn't. She shifted uncomfortably in her seat. 'And Margaret Bockford mentioned her.'

'I imagine she also mentioned that Mrs Clifford was the cause of my father's exit from our lives. There's no reason for you to be embarrassed. It's my father who should be ashamed of himself.'

'She did mention it.'

Peter smiled, and Clare felt the tension between them dissipate.

'When the solicitor told me about the condition that Uncle had stipulated, I wanted to find out how long he'd been making the payments for. As David discovered when he sifted through Uncle's study, he was something of a fanatical record keeper. This file and a shelf full of others like it contain his bank statements going right back to the 1950s.'

'When did the payments start?'

'The first one I can find is September 1973.'

'He's been making payments to Joyce Clifford all that time.'

Peter nodded. 'Regular as clockwork.'

'That means the first one was made straight after the dig ended.'

'The only explanation that I can come up with that makes any sense is that Joyce was pregnant. Gerald would have wanted to make sure any child was provided for.'

'But why pay the money to Joyce?'

'He'd never have trusted my father with the money.'

'If you have to continue to make the payments, do you have any idea where they're being made to? If we're going to set the record straight and publish your uncle's work, we need to find your father.' And, though she wasn't going to say as much to Peter, finding Jim Hart was her best hope of tracking down the missing disc.

'You're welcome to all of the information I have, on two conditions.'

'Which are?'

'First, I don't want to be told anything about my father or his other family.'

'If you're sure that's what you want.'

'Quite sure.'

'And . . .'

'And you'll stay for dinner.'

Clare thought for a second of the chilled vegetable moussaka for one and the salad in a plastic bag sitting in the fridge of her flat in Salisbury.

'It's a deal.'

* * *

The drive up to North Yorkshire had been a long one, but a good night's sleep in a comfortable hotel in Malton and the journey through the purple and green mosaic of the North York Moors had gone a long way to reinvigorating Clare's spirits.

She parked near the marina in Whitby and set off on foot towards the harbour. The sky was overcast and the herring gulls and kittiwakes wheeling above her struggled to hold their course in the gusting wind. Crossing the bridge that connected the two halves of the town, she could taste the salt air tang on her lips. She still had no clear plan of action. But, on her approach from the car, she'd seen the great Gothic bulk of Whitby Abbey anchored to the cliffs above the spot where she now stood. Turning into Church Street, she began the climb uphill.

The building frontages on either side comprised a mixture of tearooms, guest houses and purveyors of seaside trinkets. A smattering of more upmarket shops was dotted among them. It was outside of one of these that she stopped to admire a display of antique jewellery. In the centre of the window was a large Victorian cameo brooch depicting the silhouetted head of a young woman carved from Whitby jet. The Victorians had a passion for jet, a passion matched by their desire to publicly mark the remembrance of their loved ones long after their death. It was a desire fuelled by the example set by their monarch. Strange that one woman's devastation at the loss of her husband should result in a mini industrial boom in a small Yorkshire town.

Until a few months ago, Clare would have thought Queen Victoria's reaction to Albert's demise self-indulgent. But in the weeks immediately after Stephen's death she'd tried to shut herself up and avoid the world. Her mother, on the other hand, had other ideas. She was an adherent of the bootstraps philosophy on life. And it had been her chivvying that had finally resulted in Clare deciding to return to the University of Salisbury to try to find some focus in her life. The brooch wasn't the sort of thing Clare would wear herself, but her mother would love it.

Her purchase pouched safely in a small package in her coat pocket, she resumed her climb, making her way up the steep steps signposted to the abbey. To her surprise, when she reached the top she found immediately in front of her not the Abbey but a low-slung, stout little church, with a sturdy tower and crenulations that seemed more fitted to a test of endurance than fulfilling heavenly aspirations. She turned and surveyed the full extent of her exertions and immediately regretted the impulse. Looking down the steps she'd just climbed made her feel a bit dizzy.

Turning back towards the church, she caught sight of a wooden bench on the seaward side of the building. Pulling her overcoat tight around her, she tucked herself onto one end of the bench. She watched, absorbed, as the little fishing boats in the harbour were buffeted by the increasing swell and enjoyed the sensation of feeling unencumbered by the need to behave as others might expect. She could choose to do exactly as she wished. So absorbed was she in her new-found freedom that she failed to notice the tank-grey clouds darkening overhead until she felt large cold spots of rain against her face. Her light overcoat was no match for the vigour of the elements and it was a long walk back to the car, so she decided to seek shelter in the church.

By the time she reached the little porch on the south side of the building, her hair was drenched. She removed her coat, gave it a good shake and hung it over her arm. A semblance of decorum restored, she pushed open the heavy wooden door and let out a gasp.

The interior of the church was crammed with a mishmash of

architectural forms and features entirely at odds with its plain exterior. The rounded chancel arch leading to the sturdy Norman tower she'd seen outside was only just visible. It was masked by a wooden gallery, in the centre of which was a pulpit. The gallery, supported on a confection of barley twist legs, ran right across the middle of the arch and around all four sides of the building. Between the pillars, the body of the church was crammed with row after row of high box-pews. But most remarkable of all was a series of huge metal pillars supporting what looked like ship's girders, forming a roof structure more at home on an ocean-going vessel than in a house of God. The windows set into the sides and roof of the nave picked up the nautical theme. Everything here reeked of the sea.

She dropped a couple of pound coins into the donations box by the door. The leaflet she took in recompense told her that a thousand years ago this place had been built by the monks of the abbey for the labourers that worked for them. But it was obvious to Clare that it had been the descendants of those labourers, shipwrights and fisherman, who'd made it their own. Here they'd found common cause and consolation. Every nook and cranny was stuffed with memorials and plaques to sailors and their families. Unlike the great abbey that had given birth to it, and whose jagged outline still dominated the clifftop skyline, the church had tenaciously clung to the spot where it had been planted.

Clare made her way up the nave. A sign on one of the pews read *For Strangers Only*. She sat down on the comfortable cushioned seat. This wasn't her place. She wasn't sure where was any more. She'd never understood how people found comfort in institutionalised religion. The whole concept was alien to her. After Stephen's death, she'd politely accepted the vicar's consoling words, grateful for his concern. If she was being honest she'd only agreed to a church funeral to make her mother and Stephen's parents feel better. The whole thing had left her cold. But this place was different. It was comforting in a practical way, right down to the wood-burning stove that stood slap-bang in the middle of it.

'Archaeology gets in your blood. Once it's running through your veins, you can't escape.' That was what Gerald had told Margaret Bockford.

Margaret had made no attempt to hide the fact that she felt personally betrayed by Gerald. But Clare knew that sometimes you had to make a choice between your career and the people you loved. Which was why she was certain that Gerald must have had a powerful reason for burying himself and the archive in the manor for the best part of half a century.

Peter had spoken of Gerald with such love and admiration. The Gerald he'd known was a good man; a man who fulfilled his obligations. But she seemed to be the only other person who believed that.

She unfolded her overcoat and reached into the pocket. Taking out her purse, she extracted a small scrap of paper. Several minutes passed while she remained looking down at the address and telephone number written on it. Finally, she reached into her overcoat once again, this time withdrawing her mobile phone. The battery icon showed low. It must have turned itself on, jangling around in the same pocket as her car keys. Keeping her fingers crossed, she dialled the number and waited. The palms of her hands felt clammy and she could feel her heartbeat quicken. She waited – maybe this wasn't such a good idea? She was about to flick the button to end the call when she heard a woman's voice. She hesitated.

'Yes. Hello. Do you have a room available for this evening? . . . I'm not sure . . . One night . . . Yes, that's fine . . . Mrs Clare Hills.'

She took a deep breath, folded the piece of paper and placed it carefully back in her purse.

Clare leant into the wind as she trundled her overnight bag towards the front door of the large Victorian villa. She narrowly managed to avoid being sideswiped by the sign reading *Captain Cook's B & B*, which swung violently from its metal bracket.

Before she'd even made it halfway up the rain-slicked brick path, she could see a figure hovering behind the frosted glass door. There had been no other cars in the small pull-in that served as a car park, which explained why her hostess seemed so eager to welcome her. The moment Clare reached the threshold of the porch, a woman in her early sixties opened the door. The fact of the woman's age hadn't deterred her from piling a mass of bottle-blonde hair high on her head and wearing a tight-fitting skirt that would have been a bold choice for someone half her age. With less make-up and a more classic taste in clothes, she might have been considered attractive. But the layers of foundation she'd applied with zeal gave her face a hardened, world-weary appearance.

'Mrs Hills?'

Clare nodded.

'Come on in out of the rain.' The woman relieved Clare of her bag as she divested herself of her dripping coat. 'You look all done in, dear.'

Clare looked down at her sodden shoes. A fog of exhaustion settled over her.

'Why don't you go on up and run yourself a nice hot bath and I'll make us a pot of tea for when you come down.'

The last thing she wanted was an evening making polite conversation. She'd been hoping to get a good night's sleep before she put her plan, such as it was, into action. But she didn't have the energy to argue and it might be the best opportunity she'd get.

Clare leant back in the bath and let the warm suds wash over her. Her expedition to Grimsby had, in part at least, been an attempt to run away from the increasingly unpalatable realities of life without Stephen. Up here, no one knew her and she'd relished the prospect of the anonymity. She needed time to think.

She breathed in the sweet delicate fragrance of the rose-scented water. But no amount of soothing bubble bath could expunge the knowledge of the letter that lay in its crumpled and still-unopened envelope at the bottom of her bag next door. At some point she was going to have to read it. She'd put it off for almost a week, wanting to be away from everything and everyone before she could face it. And now as she listened to each relentless drip from the leaking hand basin tap explode onto the cold porcelain below, she had her wish. She felt deeply and utterly alone.

She was well aware who the letter was from. She'd spoken to the steel-voiced young solicitor on the phone the week before it had arrived. He'd told her they would contact her again once they had 'clarified some of the detail' of her husband's 'financial arrangements'. Something in the way he'd emphasised that last word had made her begin to dread the promised letter. When it had finally arrived, she'd thrust it into the bottom of her handbag and tried to forget about it.

But she couldn't avoid it any longer. She got out of the bath, towelled herself dry and threw on her robe. Sitting on the edge of the bed, she unzipped her bag and took out the letter. It didn't actually say much. They wanted her to go down to London to discuss 'the situation' with her in person. For a moment, she considered ripping it into infinitesimally small pieces and depositing them in the bottom of the wastepaper basket. But she knew she wouldn't. She was going to have to steel herself. Things weren't going to be as straightforward as she'd assumed, and the worst thing about it was that she was going to have to face it on her own.

The residents' lounge was small but comfortably furnished. A large bay window gave a view over the tops of rows of slate-roofed houses to the sea beyond, an aspect that seemed to provide the only visible connection with the erstwhile seafarer whose name the establishment bore. Clare's hostess was sitting on a large well-worn sofa in front of a living flame gas fire that paid passing homage to art noveau sensibilities.

The older woman patted the vacant seat next to her, inviting Clare to join her. 'I thought you might like a slice of sponge to go with your tea. It's home-made.'

Clare shook her head. 'I'm fine, really.'

'Go on. A nice piece of Victoria sponge never did anyone any harm. And if you don't mind me saying so, you look as if you could do with some feeding up.'

Her hostess clearly wasn't going to take no for an answer. 'Alright, just a small piece.'

Up until now, her quest had proved a welcome distraction from her more mundane worries. But whatever her assumptions had been about the woman before she arrived, now that she was sitting here face-to-face with Jim Hart's mistress, Joyce Clifford appeared to be a thoroughly decent and kind human being.

Clare's head was throbbing and she was finding it difficult to concentrate on the task in hand. Deception didn't seem to agree with her. 'You really shouldn't have gone to all this trouble.'

'It's no trouble. It's a bit quiet here at the moment.'

'It must be difficult out of season.'

'To be honest, dear, it's a bit quiet any time these days. There's not much call for British seaside holidays when you can go to the Costas for half the price and ten times the sun. I've got my regulars, of course, but most of them are getting on a bit.' She leant towards Clare and smiled. 'It's nice to have some younger company.'

Clare accepted a huge slab of sponge cake, noting the wedding ring on the woman's hand. 'Does your husband run the B & B with you?'

'Husband!' She looked confused. 'I gave marriage up as a bad job years ago.'

'I didn't mean to pry. It was just that in the phone book it said Mrs Clifford.'

'I got divorced not long after I moved here. People weren't as broad-minded in those days. They liked their landladies respectable.'

'And that didn't include divorcees.'

Joyce Clifford shook her head. 'Keeping the Mrs and the ring helped smooth things over. People assumed I was widowed. They didn't like to talk about that sort of thing. It embarrassed them.' She took a sip of her tea. 'But what about you? I don't get many attractive young ladies driving expensive sports cars staying here. Not unless they're trying to get away from something – or someone.' She glanced down at Clare's wedding ring.

For a moment, Clare wasn't sure how to respond. This wasn't going at all as she'd planned. She was meant to be the one asking the questions. She plumped for keeping it simple. 'My husband died a few months ago.'

Joyce reached over and patted the top of Clare's hand. 'I'm sorry, dear. I sometimes forget not everybody's experience of men is the same as mine.'

Clare was touched by the unexpected display of warmth. 'You didn't consider remarrying?'

'I had a bit of fun in my younger days. There was somebody I thought I might have made a go of it with once. But I should've known better.'

Clare felt distinctly uneasy about the disarming candour with which Joyce Clifford was revealing her feelings. She couldn't go on with this pretence.

'Mrs Clifford . . .'

'Please. Call me Joyce.'

'Joyce. I need to be honest with you.' The older woman smiled nervously. 'I didn't choose your guest house at random.'

Joyce's shoulders drooped. 'I did wonder.' She hesitated. 'Has this got something to do with Gerald Hart?'

Clare nodded, trying to disguise her surprise. It hadn't occurred to her that Joyce Clifford might have been expecting her.

Joyce closed her eyes. When she opened them again, all colour had drained from her face. 'When I saw in the papers he'd died, I wondered how long it would be before I heard from his lawyers.'

'Oh no, you've got it wrong. I'm not a lawyer.' How could she explain why she was here? 'I'm sorry, Joyce. I should have been straight with you from the start, but I wasn't sure how to broach the subject.'

Joyce moved to the dresser that stood against the far wall and took out a bottle from the cupboard beneath. 'I think I could do with something a bit stronger than tea.' She poured two large schooners of sherry and returned to the sofa, carrying the two glasses and the remainder of the bottle perched on a tray. 'How did you find me?'

'Through Peter.'

'Young Peter. But he didn't . . .'

'He inherited Gerald's estate – and his obligations.'

There was a tiny but audible intake of breath from Joyce. 'He knows?'

Clare nodded. 'About the payments. Yes.'

Joyce's face was a mask of terror. 'Oh God! What am I going to do? If I lose this place I'm finished.' She put her sherry glass to her lips and drained it to the bottom.

This time it was Clare who extended a sympathetic hand to her companion. 'That's not going to happen.'

'You can't know that. He's not going to want to keep paying me, is he? Not now he knows about me and his dad.'

'I'd be lying if I said he was happy with the arrangement. But he doesn't have a choice. It's a condition of Gerald's will that Peter keeps paying you.' Joyce looked as if someone had commuted her death sentence. 'And he's not going to interfere if that's what you're worried about. He told me he wasn't interested in his father's other life.'

'So why did he send you?'

'He didn't. Coming here was my idea.'

'I don't understand.'

'Look, I'm an archaeologist.' It felt strangely satisfying to say that after all this time, even under these rather bizarre circumstances. 'I'm part of a university team working on the Hungerbourne dig.'

'But that was all done and dusted forty years ago.'

'When Gerald died we found the excavation archive in the manor.' Clare could see that Joyce was struggling to reposition her thoughts. Maybe it was time she tried a different approach. 'You were involved in the dig, weren't you?'

To Clare's surprise, Joyce blushed. 'Only because of Jim. So we could see one another without George – my husband – getting wind of it. Not that it did me any good in the end.'

'Why not?'

'George found out. He went mad. It wasn't the first time he'd given me a backhander, but this time it was bad.' She hesitated for a moment as if paralysed by the memory. 'I knew if I didn't get out then and there I might never do it.' The remembered fear in Joyce's eyes conveyed the truth of her words.

'Is that when you and Jim decided to leave?'

'He promised me he'd leave Estelle. So when George found out, I pleaded with Jim to go away with me. He laughed and told me to grow up. Said he'd got plans and they didn't include a "common little piece" like me.'

'So he didn't leave with you.'

Joyce replenished her glass and looked around her. 'Does this look like the sort of place Jim Hart would be caught dead in?'

Clare hesitated for a moment. 'Joyce, I'm not sure there's a polite way to say this so I'm just going to ask. Were you pregnant when you left Hungerbourne?'

'Pregnant!' Joyce snorted, her face reddened by a cocktail of anger and sherry. 'Now I see your game. Like father, like son. Peter wants to know if there are any other little Harts running around who might want a piece of Gerald's estate.'

'No, Joyce, I promise. It's not like that. Peter's a successful architect. He's a wealthy man in his own right. He really isn't interested.' How could she convince her? 'Do you remember the Jevons sun disc?'

'I should. I dug one up just like it.'

'Well, the Jevons one has disappeared and I'm trying to find it.'

Joyce's expression signalled her mistrust. 'Why the interest in me and Jim?'

'I thought Jim might have had something to do with it.'

Joyce said nothing, and for several minutes the two women sat in silence. Clare felt deflated. She'd really thought she was getting somewhere. But just as she was starting to think she'd misjudged things, Joyce drained her sherry, placed the schooner firmly on the tray in front of them and let out a long sigh. 'I've got no reason to protect the bastard now. Jim was in trouble.'

'What sort of trouble?'

'He was a gambler. It didn't matter what it was, Jim would bet on it. Money went through his hands like water. He liked the horses, but this time it was cards.' She hesitated, as if she were weighing something up. 'He'd got himself in deep and this time it seemed like his big brother wasn't going to bail him out.'

Clare shifted forward onto the edge of the sofa. This was more like it.

'It was one night after closing time during the dig. We'd had a lock-in. George used to tip one or two of the regulars the wink and they'd stay behind for a few hands of poker. At the end of the night he went out to see the last of them off and lock up, but he didn't come back. I thought he'd swanned off and left me to clear up on my own, as usual. But when I went out the back to empty the bins I heard him laying into someone.'

'Fighting?'

Joyce shook her head. 'Arguing. George saved his fists for people he thought wouldn't fight back. He never liked me around when he was doing business so I hung around by the back door where he couldn't see me.'

'Could you hear who he was arguing with?'

'That was the thing. It was Jim. It gave me a hell of a turn, I can tell you. The way George was going at it I thought he must've found out about us. But after a bit, when Jim was trying to calm George down, I started to get the sense of what they were saying. Jim told him everything was sorted, but that he'd have to pick his moment because Gerald was so obsessed with security. George wasn't having any of his old flannel, but when Jim told him he'd be able to pay back everything he owed and something on top, he started to quieten down a bit.'

'And you think he was talking about the gold.'

'Well, it makes sense, doesn't it?'

She nodded. It made a lot of sense. 'There is one thing I don't understand. Why was Gerald paying you?'

Joyce looked down at her hands, clutched tightly together in her lap. 'After George found out about me and Jim, and Jim refused to help me, I was in a right state. I couldn't go back to the pub – but I had nowhere to go.'

'What did you do?'

'There was never anyone around at the dig site at the weekend. So I thought if I could just rest up overnight in the site hut I'd be able to nip back into the pub in the morning when George was out walking the dog and get some of my bits together.'

Clare had a freeze-frame in her head of a young Joyce cowering in the corner of a cold, damp shed. 'It can't have been very comfortable.'

Joyce shook her head. 'It wasn't, but I was desperate. I was in too much of a state to get much sleep, but while I was lying on the hut floor trying to doze, I heard a car. I opened the door a crack to try to see who it was. It wasn't easy at first – it wasn't properly light. But once my eyes had adjusted I could see it was Gerald.'

'What was he doing up there at that time in the morning?'

'I couldn't work it out at first. But then I remembered what Jim had said to George about Gerald being obsessed with security. I figured he must be up there checking the site over. It gave him a right fright when he saw me, I can tell you. I must have been the last person he was expecting to see.' Joyce played with her earring. 'Gerald was no fool. He knew I'd been seeing Jim. So when I told him George had chucked me out it didn't take him long to work out why.'

'How did he react?'

'He was terrified. Thought I would cause some sort of scandal. He told me I had to leave Hungerbourne for good. Wouldn't even let me go back to collect my things from the pub. He scribbled his phone number at the British Museum on a finds card, shoved a wodge of notes into my hand and told me to contact him when I'd found somewhere to stay.'

'What did you do?'

Joyce shrugged. 'I did exactly what he told me to. I came up here, found somewhere to stay and phoned him. He said as long as I never went back or tried to contact anyone, he'd make sure I didn't go without.'

'And he kept his word.' Joyce nodded. 'And you kept yours?'

'It wasn't a difficult choice. There was nothing for me to go back for.'

CHAPTER SEVEN

Naked save for a rumpled cotton sheet, David lay motionless on his bed, enjoying the warmth of the spring sunshine and pondering the female gender. Clare had seemed restless and irritable since her weekend away. Exactly why that should be was a mystery to him, but then there was a lot about women, and Clare in particular, that had remained a mystery to him over the years.

But this weekend had taken a somewhat different trajectory to the usual and right now he was feeling rather pleased with himself. The smell of bacon cooking wafted up from the kitchen below. He reached for his robe and headed downstairs.

'This is too good to be true – a full English breakfast and a beautiful woman to share it with.'

'I can see we're going to have to work on your prioritisation skills.'

'I think I have them pretty well balanced.' He slipped one

arm around Sally Treen's waist and with the other reached over to pluck a slice of bacon from the grill pan that she was manoeuvring towards the two plates in front of her.

'Enough!'

'I don't seem to remember you saying that last night, Inspector.'

'I meant the bacon.' In one deft movement she deposited the grill pan on the worktop, turned and kissed him.

'Do you do this for all of your complainants?'

'Are you complaining?' She kissed him again, this time harder and more insistent.

'If you carry on like this we're going to see a good breakfast go to waste.'

She laughed. 'Breakfast on the patio?'

'Christ, woman, this is the Vale of Pewsey, not Tuscany. We'll freeze to death.'

'I thought you archaeological types were used to fresh air.'

He looked down at his robe. 'We normally wear rather more than this when we're digging.'

He busied himself preparing coffees from his lovingly reconditioned espresso machine and they settled down to breakfast at the large oak table in the middle of his kitchen.

'You're full of surprises. I wouldn't have had you pegged for the homely type, but this place is something else.'

He cast a disingenuously casual glance around the room. He had a particular sense of pride in the functionally rustic charm he'd breathed into this place. He'd bought it when he first moved back to Wiltshire. Not because of its idyllic location or its medieval origins, but because in its wrecked and – even the estate agent had been forced to confess – uninhabitable state, it was the only place he could afford on a junior lecturer's salary.

Sally looked down admiringly at the worn slate flags. He tilted his head to one side, studying her exquisitely cut hair as it brushed the shoulder of her blouse. He had the distinct impression that if he'd told her how many generations of decomposing animal dung he'd had to shovel out of the former byre to reveal that floor, she wouldn't be so keen on finishing her breakfast.

He settled instead for a satisfied smile. 'I thought the police had to proceed from a basis of evidence.'

'In my line of work you get an instinct for people.'

'And what did your instinct have to say about me?'

She leant back in her chair, eyeing him up and down. 'Political tendencies left wing. Not concerned with outward appearances.'

He adjusted the belt on his faded blue towelling robe. 'And what would you say now?'

'I wouldn't be able to make an objective assessment.'

'I thought you said it was instinct.'

'Instinct based on experience. What are you smiling at?'

'Exactly how many archaeologists have you met?'

'Including you?'

He nodded.

She looked sheepish. 'One.'

He raised an eyebrow.

'I was transferred into this job three weeks ago. The DCI before me took early retirement.'

'So if I'd reported the missing disc a month ago . . .'

'You'd be eating your eggs and bacon with a fifty-five-year-old bloke with a beard and halitosis.'

Clare had considered telling David about her trip to see Joyce Clifford. At first, she'd thought it might be awkward having to give him a carefully edited version of what she'd done on her weekend away. But as it turned out, the need for inventive retellings of her time in Whitby never arose. Aside from a polite enquiry about whether she'd enjoyed her weekend, he hadn't even mentioned it. She was unsettled to realise she felt more than a bit miffed by his total lack of interest. He was quite obviously preoccupied with something else.

She knew he'd been having a rough time with the Runt. But she'd assumed the funding he'd secured from British Heritage had solved that problem – at least for the time being. But apparently not. Since she'd returned from North Yorkshire, she'd hardly seen him. He'd spent most of his time tucked away in his office on the phone.

When she'd asked him how the police had responded to reporting the theft of the sun disc, he'd mumbled something about it being too early in the investigation to expect any progress. In fact, she thought he'd seemed slightly embarrassed. Even she had to admit she was surprised the police had shown any interest in a forty-year-old theft. But twice during the last week she'd overheard the departmental secretary putting a phone call through from Inspector Treen, the officer in charge of the case. Maybe it was the police involvement that had sparked the Runt's ire this time.

Well, she might not be able to share the information she'd gleaned from her trip to Whitby with David right now, but there was one person she owed an explanation to. After all these years, Peter deserved to know the truth.

When she'd phoned to invite him to dinner, he'd seemed pleased, but had insisted she let him make the arrangements. And she'd found herself looking forward to seeing him again.

Now, sitting in the comfortably plush surroundings of the gastropub he'd chosen, she was glad she hadn't let the few tattered shreds of her feminist principles that had survived her marriage to Stephen get in the way of her agreeing. The meal had been delicious and Peter had been charming company. He'd also insisted on picking her up from her flat, so by the time the waiter had deposited a coffee and a glass of port in front of her to top off the half bottle of Sancerre she'd polished off during the meal, she was feeling quite mellow.

Peter said, 'I wouldn't have taken you for a port drinker.'

She smiled a little guiltily. 'All of those dinner parties with Stephen's work colleagues gave me a taste for it.'

He took a sip of his coffee. 'You miss him a great deal, don't you?'

'We made a good team. We were comfortable with one another. I miss that.' She felt a twinge of conscience. What she'd said was largely true, at least until the last few months of their marriage. But she really couldn't face re-examining the minutiae of their relationship just yet.

He looked at her quizzically. 'I hope I don't make you feel uncomfortable.'

She shook her head. 'No, it's not that. It's just all a bit raw still.'

'I'd hate to think I was making things worse for you.'

She smiled. 'You know, in some ways I find it easier when I'm with you. We don't have a history. It makes things more straightforward. Everyone else seems to be treading on eggshells at the moment.'

'What about you and David? Do you have a history?'

Her attempt to conceal her surprise at the question was evidently unsuccessful.

'I don't mean to pry, but I've known David a long time. And over the years we've talked about things that matter to us.'

She felt as if the ground were shifting around beneath her. Her mouth felt dry. She took a sip of water and then another of port. Where was this heading?

'I thought it was women who were supposed to have heart-to-hearts.'

He didn't seem to have noticed her unease. 'More bar-room philosophy after one too many beers.' He smiled.

Clare edged her way forward cautiously. 'And my name cropped up in these philosophical discussions?'

He shook his head. 'Not exactly. David was never as gung-ho as the other chaps about discussing the women in his life. He had girlfriends, though none of them ever seemed to last very long. But he never turned up to matches bragging about his conquests. I suppose you could say we were kindred spirits in that respect. He told me that when he was younger he'd been convinced he'd know right away when he met the right woman. That whatever happened, things would work out if they were meant to.'

She'd never stopped to consider David's views on the philosophy of relationships before and she wasn't entirely sure she was comfortable thinking about them now. But she definitely wouldn't have thought of him as a fatalist.

Peter said, 'When I asked him why he'd changed his mind he said he'd met someone when he was a post-grad who he'd been certain he was meant to spend the rest of his life with. But things hadn't worked out as he'd hoped.'

She relaxed back into her chair. 'You thought that someone was me!' She laughed. 'Oh, Peter. Honestly. The only history David and I have is as friends. Our mutual passion was archaeology. We used to spend hours arguing about it. There was never anything more to it than that. He always knew that Stephen and I were an item.'

Peter's face relaxed. 'I probably shouldn't say this under the circumstances. But I'm rather relieved about that. David's a good bloke and I wouldn't want to put his nose out of joint by us becoming friends.'

She didn't want to ruin the evening. But she wasn't sure she was ready for the direction this seemed to be heading. Maybe it was time she shared with him what she'd discovered in Yorkshire. After all, he had a right to know the truth.

'There's something I need to tell you.' He looked at her quizzically. 'About your father.'

He stiffened in his chair, his face showing real anger for the first time since they'd met. 'That's a book I closed a long time ago, Clare. As far as I'm concerned, now that Gerald's gone, Mother is all the family I need.'

'Hear me out. It's not what you think.'

'This has been a lovely evening. Let's not spoil it by arguing. You won't change my mind.' He leant back from the table and folded his arms.

'Please, Peter.' She paused and took a deep breath. 'I wasn't entirely straight with you when I told you I wanted to contact Joyce Clifford about the confusion over the excavation records.'

Peter remained tight-lipped, but motioned his head forward in a curt nod.

'That was only part of the truth. Something is missing – some goldwork.'

'I thought all the gold was in the British Museum.'

'So did we. But one of the sun discs is missing – the Jevons disc.'

'The one found before the dig.'

She nodded. 'And it's possible your father was involved in its disappearance.' She looked across the table. What was going on behind those crystal-blue eyes? 'Do you trust me, Peter?'

'You know I do.' He held her gaze.

'Then let me tell you what happened in Whitby.'

He inclined his head in resignation, and Clare recounted what she'd learnt from Joyce Clifford.

‘So you see, there is no other family. Gerald was just trying to protect you and your mother.’

‘It sounds so like Gerald. And my father.’ He lapsed into silence before adding, ‘Odd, isn’t it. With everything my father did, you wouldn’t think I’d feel ashamed that he was a common thief.’

‘We don’t know that for sure.’ Even as she spoke the words she didn’t believe them. ‘Do you remember George Clifford?’

Peter nodded. ‘He used to run the Lamb and Flag.’

‘Do you remember your father being friendly with him?’

‘No. But I didn’t know all of Father’s friends. Mother wouldn’t have his drinking and gambling cronies anywhere near the house. Has Clifford got something to do with this?’

‘I’m not sure. It’s just something Joyce said. But I need to speak to him to find out.’

‘Will you let me come with you? If my father was responsible for the theft of the Jevons disc, I want to help find it. I owe it to Gerald.’

By the time Peter had dropped Clare back at her flat it was close to half past midnight. Despite the lateness of the hour, when she finally collapsed into bed she couldn’t sleep. A jumble of half-connected thoughts whirred around in her head. But it wasn’t her discussion with Peter that she couldn’t get out of her mind. It was a conversation she’d had fifteen years earlier, on her graduation day; when David had come bursting into the departmental common room to tell her about his fellowship at Newcastle.

She’d grabbed him by his broad shoulders and hugged him. ‘That’s wonderful, David. It’s perfect. Just perfect.’

As she drifted between slumber and wakefulness she could

still see the expression on David's face as she'd reached out a hand and pulled a beaming Stephen out of the crowd of students mingling behind her. 'You're going to be an academic, and Stephen and I are going to be married. Aren't we, darling?'

CHAPTER EIGHT

'Folk will do anything for money.' George Clifford seemed determined to prove the truth of his observation by insisting he would only talk to them for the price of a large whisky. He gestured impatiently for Clare to place the glass on the table in front of him. She complied, passing Peter his wine before setting down her orange juice and lemonade.

Clifford brought his bulk to rest against the back of his favoured corner chair and flipped a forefinger in the direction of Tony, who was pulling a pint behind the bar of the Lamb and Flag. 'Take the bloke who runs this place. Can't stand the sight of me – but he smiles and carries on like we were best mates. And why?'

Clare feigned an interested expression as he paused for dramatic effect.

'Because he wants my money – that's why.'

It hadn't proved difficult to track Clifford down. He was well known among the inhabitants of Hungerbourne. Well known, but not well liked. And Clare was beginning to understand why. George Clifford might once have been described as a bear of a man, but his ruddy features were the result of overindulgence and inactivity rather than jovial good health.

The few remaining strands of hair were secured in place with a generous slathering of Brylcreem. And before he'd uttered a word, Clare had decided that there was something deeply unpleasant oozing out of every pore of George Clifford.

'Most folks are like that.' He jabbed his finger towards Peter. 'Not your mother, though. She's got class.' Clifford took an appreciative swig of his whisky. 'As much as I'm enjoying our little chat, why don't you tell me why you and this lovely young lady want to speak to me?'

Before Peter had a chance to respond, Clare stepped in. 'I'm an archaeologist, Mr Clifford, working on the Hungerbourne barrow site.'

'And your coming 'ere is to do with his uncle turning up his toes.' Clifford nodded in Peter's direction.

Clare said, 'I've been looking at the finds from Gerald Hart's dig.'

Clifford crossed his arms. 'All very interesting, I'm sure. But what do you want with me?'

Before she could stop him, Peter blurted out, 'Some of the gold from the dig is missing – a sun disc.'

Clare shot Peter a sideways glance in an attempt to get him to keep his voice down, but she needn't have bothered. He was too intently focused on Clifford to notice.

Clifford, on the other hand, was a model of calm. 'Losing your uncle must have addled your brain, son. I'd not have gotten caught up with that shower on the dig if you'd paid me.'

Clare leant forward and lowered her voice. 'But that's exactly why you did get involved with them, wasn't it – for the money. From what I've heard, you had a hand in the disappearance of the sun disc.'

Clifford remained perfectly calm, unfolding his arms and throwing them wide in a gesture of dismissal. 'Not that old rubbish again. I thought Gerald had given up on all that claptrap years ago.'

So Gerald had known, or at least suspected, that Clifford had been involved. Maybe they were getting somewhere.

'You shouldn't believe everything your uncle told you. Cooped up on his own in that big old place day after day, no wonder he was away with the fairies.' Clifford tapped his head.

Peter leapt up, depositing his chair on the floor with a thud that turned every head in the bar. 'That's a lie!'

Clare placed a cajoling hand on his arm. At her touch, his anger seemed to dissipate. She mouthed a reassuring 'It's alright' in the direction of a concerned Tony as Peter righted his chair and sat down.

Clifford greeted the performance with amusement. Clare smiled as warmly as she could manage. 'Humour me, Mr Clifford. What did Gerald say about the missing disc?'

'He tried to say I stole it.'

Peter's voice was strained. 'And did you?'

Clare turned towards Peter, her hand resting once again on his arm, and whispered, 'This isn't helping.'

Clifford was still smiling. 'Well now, I can see you do take after your father. You want to mind that temper of yours – it'll get you into trouble one of these days.' He seemed to be feeding off the icy glare that Peter was directing towards him. He returned his attention to Clare. 'Don't worry, my love, I'm going to tell young Mr Hart here what I told his uncle. I never took nothing what didn't belong to me – unlike some. No, he needs to look closer to home.'

Peter struggled to keep himself in check. 'What exactly is that meant to mean?'

'You know the answer as well as I do – your father.'

'What makes you think Jim was responsible?' Clare asked.

'Because he told me so himself.' Clifford turned towards Peter. 'Even you couldn't deny your dear ol' dad liked a flutter. He was on his uppers more than once cos of it. And he came to me when the dig was on. Offered to pay off what he owed me in gambling debts – and more besides – if I'd ask around and find a buyer for the gold.'

'You were a fence.' Peter's eyes were fixed, blazing across the tabletop at Clifford. 'How could you do that to Gerald? It was his life's work.'

Clifford maintained a fixed smile. He took a sip of whisky before setting the glass down on the centre of the beer mat in front of him. 'I never said I agreed. I told him he could find the money to pay me how he liked, but I didn't want no trouble with the police. No, for once your father did something off his own bat.'

Peter said, 'Why should we believe you?'

'No matter to me what you believe. But you'd do well to talk to your pal Ed before you go accusin' folk.'

Peter looked as if someone had punched him in the stomach. For a moment, Clare thought he was going to be sick.

'What's Ed got to do with it?' Clare asked.

'Ed Jevons can speak for himself. But I'll tell you this – Estelle Hart wasn't the only person who had cause to be upset when Jim did a moonlight.'

* * *

'Are you alright?' Clare shot a sideways glance at Peter, who was sitting silently in the passenger seat beside her.

Barely a word had passed his lips since they'd left the pub.

He turned to face her, his expression blank. 'Fine.'

'Don't let him get to you.'

'He made me so bloody angry.'

'I gathered that from the flying furniture.'

'Sorry. It was all of that rubbish about Gerald being a nutty old man.'

'People like Clifford are emotional vampires. In a way, I feel sorry for him.'

Peter snorted his disagreement.

'No, really. The whole village obviously loathes him. I thought some of them were going to wade in with you when you flung that chair over.'

Peter managed a weak laugh and Clare fell silent, considering whether she should venture her next gambit.

Finally, she made up her mind. 'Interesting what he said about Ed.'

Peter turned away, staring out of the window. 'More rubbish from Clifford. The sins of the father and all that.'

Clare shot him a quizzical look.

'It's obvious, isn't it? He's trying to drag Ed into this to get at me. He's hated the Harts ever since my father ran off with his wife. Like you say, the man's an emotional vampire.'

'That was amazing, David.' The man in question was sitting beside Sally on her living room sofa with a self-satisfied grin on his face.

She'd spent the greater part of her day off cleaning and tidying her Devizes flat. Most of the plods she'd been out with had been too interested in beer and footy to pay any attention to her domestic arrangements. But, judging by what she'd seen of David's house, academics were a different kettle of fish. And that, as she had just learnt, apparently extended to their culinary skills.

'Where did you learn to cook like that?'

'I had four brothers.' He wiped his mouth with a serviette. 'And parents who were both hospital consultants. They were at work more often than they were at home. So it was a case of learn how to cook or starve.'

When she was a kid she'd lived on beyond-their-sell-by-date fish fingers and pizzas her mum had bought home from her twilight shifts at Tesco. But she had no desire to spoil the evening by dragging her family into it. 'I never really learnt to cook.'

'I could teach you.'

'I can think of things I'd rather be doing with you than learning how to cook.' She smiled and leant over to deliver a long, lingering kiss.

'You've persuaded me. But there's no point in letting good bubbly go to waste.' He reached over to the table, picked up what remained of the bottle of champagne he'd brought with him and topped up the two glasses. He passed her a glass and raised his own

'A toast. To the thing that brought us together.' She looked at him quizzically. 'The sun disc,' he said, chinking his glass against hers.

'Wherever it may be.'

'Not much further along then?' David took a sip of his champagne.

'To be honest, David, the chances of recovering it aren't great. We can't even establish when it went missing. And even if we do manage to find out who stole it, the likelihood of recovering it after all this time is a million to one.' She placed her glass down on the table. Taking his hand, she stood up. 'But I think I know something that will take both our minds off it.'

CHAPTER NINE

Clare straightened the pile of notes on her desk in the laying-out room and patted them contentedly. Everything was in place for the arrival of her eminent guest. David had managed to secure the services of a leading osteo-archaeologist with an enviable reputation in ancient cremation studies to examine the unexcavated urn. She'd had no time to dwell on her growing sense of unease about not telling him about her investigations as she'd busied herself preparing for Dr Granski's visit.

She glanced over at the large brown urn sitting on the Formica tabletop on the far side of the room, everything set out as the email had requested. She was congratulating herself on the efficiency with which she'd performed her task when the door clattered open, leaving the fire extinguisher shuddering in its wake.

'Is there anywhere to get a decent cup of coffee in this place?'

The accent was unmistakably west coast America. The owner was a petite woman in her mid-twenties with pale blue eyes and unruly shoulder-length beach-blonde hair that she'd attempted, not entirely successfully, to pull back from her face in a ponytail. She was dressed in old blue jeans, a Grateful Dead T-shirt and canvas basketball shoes that had seen better days.

Before Clare had time to respond, the woman swung her large camouflage rucksack onto the desk, causing the stack of papers Clare had placed there to cascade sideways into an untidy heap. Simultaneously, the newcomer jettisoned the crumpled Coke can she'd been carrying into the wastepaper basket by the desk.

The phone on Clare's desk rang, and she stood open-mouthed as the newcomer raised a hand in the air in a gesture demanding silence and picked up the receiver. Clare cast an anxious glance up at the wall clock. This couldn't be happening. Who the hell did she think she was? She had to get rid of this woman.

Clare said, 'Excuse me. What do you think you're . . . ?'

The young woman looked straight at Clare and raised a finger to her lips. Clare was speechless.

'Yup, yup. OK. I'll tell her.' She replaced the receiver and turned towards Clare. 'That was reception.' Clare nodded helplessly. 'They called to let you know' – she hung the words out one by one – 'that . . . I'm . . . here!' The younger woman watched in quiet amusement as Clare's expression flickered from incomprehension to confusion to embarrassment. Both women looked at one another for a moment before simultaneously breaking into uncontrollable laughter.

'Dr Granski?'

'Jo will do just fine. Not what you were expecting, huh?'

Jo was clearly determined to milk this for all it was worth.

Clare could feel her cheeks burning. 'I'm sorry. I didn't . . . I mean, David just said . . .'

'Don't worry. I get it all the time. How about we try to find some drinkable coffee before we get to work?'

Clare busied herself procuring two large mugs of filter coffee, thankful for a task to distract her from her embarrassment, while Jo set about her preparations for the examination of the cremation urn.

Clare could see why she'd developed such a formidable reputation. She was an intense worker, precise and focused in everything she did. It took her less than an hour to read through the large pile of papers Clare had prepared, making brief, one-line notes of her own in a small, neat hand in the spiral-bound notebook she'd extracted from her rucksack. When she'd completed her reading, she spent the next thirty minutes quizzing Clare about details from the notes and the site journals.

Clare breathed an internal sigh of relief when Jo finally said, 'I think that's about everything.' She smiled a warm, easy smile. 'Great job with the notes, by the way. This kind of thorough preparation makes a heck of a difference.'

Clare felt herself colour slightly – this time with pride.

Jo said, 'How about we get down to some real work?'

'We?'

'I need someone to assist. But if you'd rather not . . .'

'No, that would be great,' Clare said eagerly.

Jo delved into the bottom of her cavernous rucksack. 'Put these on.' She handed Clare a pair of thin, blue rubber gloves, then produced a roll of canvas which she untied to reveal a set of what looked like dental equipment. Jo laid them out side by side on the Formica tabletop next to the large mottled brown urn. Finally, she produced a small fine-meshed sieve which she placed on the other side of the urn.

Jo adjusted the position of the anglepoise lamp that was attached to the side of the table, focusing the pool of light onto the top of the pottery vessel. Picking up a small metal probe, she began scraping away at the surface of the soil in the top of the pot. She worked her way methodically across the mouth of the vessel, her hands moving deftly and precisely to loosen the earth within.

Clare watched as, one by one, tiny charred fragments of bone began to appear. Ensuring that each one had been completely loosened, Jo lifted them one at a time into a plastic box that Clare had provided for the purpose.

Jo asked, 'Ever done one of these?'

Clare shook her head.

'Like to join me?'

Clare nodded. 'Are you sure?'

'If I'm not sure, I don't ask.'

Jo passed her a metal probe identical to the one she was using. Clare's hand shook as she gripped the tool.

'No need to be nervous. The most important thing is to remember to keep going down in separate layers just like on a normal excavation. Stop if you see any changes in soil colour or texture.'

'Because you sometimes get more than one cremation in a vessel?'

'Right. You might get four or five separate individuals represented in one pot. Sometimes they've been deposited together and sometimes different cremations have been added at different times. So for each layer we'll put the soil through the sieve to capture any small fragments we might have missed, then we'll bag the soil matrix separately so we can analyse it later.'

After a few minutes, Clare began to relax.

Jo said, 'You're a natural.'

Working in companionable silence, it took the two women most of the morning to work their way through the upper half of the urn. The product of their labours comprised two large, carefully labelled plastic boxes containing fragments of burnt bone, and two clear plastic bags full of soil samples.

'Does it always take this long?' Clare asked.

'If you do it right. Sometimes it's slower. The soil in this urn is surprisingly loose. Normally it's more compacted.'

As she spoke, Jo began to work her way through the third layer of material. 'This is the easy stuff. The hard work starts when I get down to the analysis. That's the real cool part – when you get to know the people who were cremated.'

'So you can't tell much from looking at the material now?'

'Not everything. But sure, you begin forming an impression right away. See here.' Jo extracted a large singed piece of bone about two inches long from the layer they were working on and held it in the light of the lamp for Clare to see. 'The fragments in this layer seem larger and the bones themselves quite robust compared to the upper layers.'

'What does that mean?'

'Well, it looks like this one's been through a different cremation process. Probably the pyre wasn't as well made.'

'Is that usual?'

'It happens sometimes. Ceremonies change with time, or maybe the wood for the pyre wasn't properly seasoned. Hell, maybe it was just your English weather.'

Clare smiled. 'And the robustness of the bones?'

'Can't tell for sure yet. But if I had to take a punt I'd say the thickness and density of the bone means this was an adult male and the other two, in the upper layers, were women or children.'

'So does that mean . . .' Clare's voice trailed off as she began to pick away at a small amorphous blob just visible in the surface of the soil.

Jo looked up from her work. 'What have you got there?'

Clare shook her head. 'Not sure. You'd better take a look.' Clare moved aside and allowed Jo to take her place on the other side of the table.

Jo worked in silence, painstakingly loosening the soil from around the object. 'Get me another plastic box.'

Clare did as she was asked and, using a pair of tweezers, Jo carefully lifted the small grey object into the box.

Clare asked, 'What is it?'

Jo picked the clear box up and examined the shapeless little globule inside the container. 'Can't say for sure. It looks metallic. From the look of it, I'd guess it's been melted by the heat of the fire.'

Clare's eyes shone with excitement. 'That would mean it was placed on the pyre, wouldn't it? Part of the pyre cremation ceremony.' Clare looked at Jo. She could see she didn't share her excitement.

'Maybe . . . but it's the wrong colour for copper or bronze, and it's definitely not gold. I've never seen anything like this before. Not in a prehistoric context.' Jo set the box down on the tabletop and stared down at the urn, deep in thought.

Jo's reticence was beginning to worry Clare. 'But you've seen something like this somewhere else.'

'We're gonna have to run some tests. XRF, maybe.'

Now it was Clare's turn to look perplexed.

'X-ray fluorescence,' Jo explained.

'That would tell us the chemical composition?'

Jo nodded. 'And we'll need radio-carbon dates from all three cremation layers.'

'Not a problem. We've got the money for RC dates and I'm sure we can persuade British Heritage to fund the XRF.' The look on Jo's face was making Clare feel queasy. 'What exactly do you think it is?'

'If it's what I think it is, it's not British Heritage we're gonna have to speak to – it's the coroner.'

'The coroner! Oh, come on, Jo. What is it?'

'A filling.'

'A filling for what?'

Jo looked up, her pale blue eyes unflickering as they looked into Clare's. Her words were slow and deliberate. 'A dental filling.'

'That's impossible. This is a Bronze Age cremation.'

Jo shrugged her shoulders. 'I could be wrong. It might be something else entirely.'

But Clare knew Jo was right; the harmless-looking, dull, grey lump sitting in the clear plastic box in front of them was a dental filling. And she knew why Gerald Hart had gone to such lengths to ensure nobody got hold of the Hungerbourne archive while he was still alive.

CHAPTER TEN

Clare reached across the coffee table with the bottle and watched the Merlot glug into Jo's glass. Jo was lying outstretched on a pile of cushions on Clare's living room floor. Although she'd met the woman sitting in front of her less than twelve hours ago, it had seemed the right thing to do to offer her the use of her spare room while she was working at the university. She was glad she had.

Jo took an appreciative slurp of her wine. 'When are we going to tell David?'

'Not yet. We have to be certain. We'll need the results from the tests first.'

Jo gave a bemused shake of her head. 'Amalgam fillings weren't introduced until the eighteenth century. But it makes no sense – a modern cremation inside a Bronze Age urn.'

'What about the other two cremations we found above the one with the filling? Are they modern too?'

'Based on what I've seen so far, I don't think so, but we won't know for sure till we get the radio-carbon dates. If they're prehistoric, someone excavated them and deliberately placed them back on top of the more recent cremation.'

Clare swirled the inky red liquid round in the bottom of her glass. 'There's something you should know.'

Jo laughed. 'That's not a phrase I associate with good news.'

Clare hesitated, then looked up at Jo. 'I think I know who that filling belonged to.'

'You're kidding me.'

Clare shook her head.

Jo's eyes widened. She pushed herself into an upright position and sat cross-legged, staring at Clare across the top of the coffee table. 'You mean you know who the dead guy in the bottom of the urn was.'

Clare nodded. 'If I'm right, it's Gerald's younger brother – Jim.'

Jo slapped her wine glass down on the coffee table, her voice shifting up a tone. 'What the hell is going on? When David invited me down here, he didn't mention anything about modern cremations. Have you guys been holding out on me?'

Where to start? 'It's complicated. One of the gold sun discs from the site is missing.'

Jo's body was a study in concentration. 'Missing as in lost.'

'That's what David would like to believe. But I'm pretty sure it was stolen.'

'Who by?'

'Jim Hart.'

'OK. Back up. Gerald's brother stole the disc.' Clare nodded. 'What makes you think he's our cremation?'

'He disappeared at the same time the Hungerbourne dig ended. He was supposed to have run off with his girlfriend, leaving his wife and son behind.'

'Nice guy.'

'I tracked the girlfriend down – a woman called Joyce Clifford.'

Jo leant forward, elbows on the coffee table, entwined hands supporting her chin. 'Go on.'

'According to Joyce, Gerald paid her to leave Hungerbourne and stay away from the Hart family. What he didn't know was Jim had already dumped her.'

'Wow!'

'You haven't heard the best of it yet. I've seen Gerald's bank statements. He kept on paying her right up until he died.'

Clare got up, walked over to her bag in the corner of the room and withdrew a pile of photocopied sheets stapled together in one corner. Flipping over the first few pages, she found what she was looking for and handed the sheets to Jo. 'There's something else. I didn't think much of it when I first read it, but now . . . See what you make of it.'

Jo pulled herself upright, leaning with her back against the front of the sofa. While Jo read, Clare made coffee in the kitchen. The photocopied pages she'd given Jo were extracts from Gerald's site journal. Two entries had been ringed with yellow highlighter.

Friday 3rd August 1973

We have undertaken a great deal of work over the last several days. Our efforts have been directed towards the recreation of a Bronze Age cremation pyre. We are intending to use the methods and techniques that might have been employed during the period. We will record the details of the size and duration of the task and the traces left following the burning of the pyre.

I have selected a number of the male members of the team to assist me in the selection and acquisition of fuel. We chose a number of medium-sized trees from the grounds of the manor, sufficient so far as we could judge unto our needs. I had commissioned the local blacksmith in the manufacture of a number of bronze axes of the type sometimes referred to as palstaves and we set about felling the trees using these tools. Each tree was felled in a little less than half an hour.

This first task accomplished, I arranged for the felled timber to be transported to a site close to the top of the ridge overlooking the barrow cemetery. (I had chosen a site a short distance upslope from the barrows in order to ensure that no other as yet undiscovered archaeology was damaged in the pursuance of our task, but also, it must be confessed, to assuage the fears of some of my fellow residents, who feared that sparks from the blaze might take hold in some of the thatched buildings within the village itself.)

Much of today has been spent trimming the timber of its greenery. In hindsight, I realise we would have saved ourselves considerable effort had we done this at the time the trees were felled. We stacked the wood in a manner I have observed being used as part of Hindu funerary practice during my travels on the sub-continent.

There is considerable anticipation among the dig team about the outcome of our little experiment. A number of villagers have been quite open in voicing their opinion that we are 'quite mad' going to all this effort 'for no good reason'. All, that is, except the local butcher, who has had the good sense to stay quiet on the matter as he stands to benefit through the sale of an entire pig carcass, which I have ordered from him and which will take the place of the deceased on the pyre.

I am allowing a full month for the timber to dry out in situ and I'm hopeful that even the villagers may be won over by the project in the end. I have invited all of them to join us on the afternoon of Monday 3rd September (a bank holiday) to watch the culmination of our efforts.

Monday 3rd September 1973
Spoke to the dig team this morning. Commenced backfilling.

Clare set the coffee down on the table. Jo was hurriedly skimming the unmarked entries on the photocopied sheets.

Finally, Jo turned back to the 3rd September entry. 'Where's the rest?'

'That's it. That's the end of Gerald's entries in the diary.'

'But there's no mention of the results of the pyre experiment anywhere.' A look of awful comprehension spread across Jo's face. 'You found the urn in Gerald's attic.'

Clare nodded, half closing her eyes in a gesture of resignation.

Jo held up the dog-eared bundle of photocopies. 'Does David know about this?'

Clare shook her head.

'We've got to tell him. We're not just dealing with an antiquities theft any more.'

CHAPTER ELEVEN

'Jesus!' The clock on David's office wall read three minutes past nine. He hadn't even had his first coffee of the day and he'd just been told by one of the most respected bone specialists going that he had bits of Gerald Hart's baby brother sitting next door in the bottom of a Bronze Age pot.

He closed his eyes and cupped his head in his hands, slowly drumming his fingers against his forehead. No one spoke. He stood up and began to pace back and forth across the few square feet of clear carpet between his desk and the window. In the quadrangle below, students hurried to their first lectures of the day, unaware that the remains of a murder victim lay two storeys above them.

He turned to face Clare. 'Bloody perfect! We get our hands on the archaeological site of the century and you land us in the middle of a murder inquiry.'

Clare, perching uncomfortably on the edge of a swivel chair, stretched out her arms towards him, palms upturned. 'How exactly is this my fault?'

He didn't respond. Clare was right. She wasn't to blame for what was in the bottom of that damned urn. He picked up the polished stone axe that was lying on the corner of his desk. He turned the exquisitely crafted greenstone over in his hands, concentrating on the cooling feel of its glass-smooth surface. He took a deep breath and replaced the precious relic on top of the dishevelled heap of papers that it had come from.

He forced himself to smile. 'Look, I'm sorry I bit your head off. But we've got so much hanging on this project. We can't afford to do anything that might jeopardise our funding with BH. The archive being seized as evidence in a murder investigation is the last thing we need. It would give the Runt just the excuse he's looking for to close the project down.'

'All the more reason to find the missing sun disc. Can you imagine the publicity for the university? If we can find it, there's no way Muir could shut us down.'

David shook his head. 'It's a nice idea, Clare. But it was a long time ago and the police don't seem to be getting anywhere.'

'I don't mean the police. I mean us. We've already found Joyce Clifford and spoken to her.'

'We?' Confused, David looked from Clare to Jo.

'No. Not Jo, Peter and me. He came with me to speak to George Clifford and I'd never have tracked Joyce down to Whitby without him. He's been incredibly supportive.'

David's head was throbbing. 'Whitby! Un-bloody-believable. You tramp the length and breadth of the country with a man you barely know on some wild goose chase, and you don't even think to mention it to me. Why is that, Clare?' He ploughed on without giving her the chance to answer. 'How do you think Peter will feel when he discovers his uncle has concealed his father's cremated remains in the family home for the best part of four decades? Do you think he'll be supportive then? Who the hell do you think you are – Agatha fucking Christie? For once in your life, couldn't you consider the effect your actions have on other people?'

As soon as the words were out of his mouth, he regretted them.

Jo said, 'We don't know for sure the cremation is modern. Not until we get the XRF results and the radio-carbon dates back from the lab. I could be wrong.'

David said, 'Come off it, Jo. How often does that happen?' Jo opened her mouth to speak, but he held a hand aloft. 'I'm sorry you've been caught up in this. But we're not hacks working for some dodgy red top careering round the country on a treasure hunt; we're professional archaeologists.' He directed his gaze firmly at Clare. 'But clearly some of us don't have the faintest conception of what that means.'

For a moment, he thought Clare was going to say something, but she seemed to think better of it and instead slumped back into her chair, head lowered.

Good. What the bloody hell had possessed her? He sat down, flipped open the lid of his laptop and started fiddling with his mouse, determined to ignore the two women. Out of the corner of his eye, he watched Clare leave the room, pulling the door to with a click behind her. Jo, on the other hand, stayed put, sitting upright but relaxed in the ancient armchair, her hands palm-down on her thighs.

When she finally spoke, her voice was calm and measured. 'Do you want me to carry on with the analysis?'

He didn't answer. He wasn't angry with Jo. He was just angry, and now maybe a little regretful too. The old Clare would never have folded so easily.

'I asked you a question, David. Do you want me to carry on here?'

His eyes remained fixed on the computer screen. 'Of course I bloody do.'

'OK . . .' Jo strung out the word. 'What about Clare?'

'That's up to her.'

'I'm guessing that's not how she sees it right now. I'd say she pretty much thinks you don't want her within a million miles of this place.'

'Good. Maybe next time she'll come and talk to me before she embarks on some half-arsed quest.'

'That kind of implies there'll be a next time. Will there?'

He got up, avoiding Jo's gaze, and made his way over to the book-covered wall next to his desk. Plucking a journal from the shelves, he started to flick distractedly through it.

Jo remained sitting exactly where she was. David snapped the pages of the journal shut and returned to his desk, allowing the volume to drop onto the paper-strewn surface. He breathed in deeply, let out a slow sigh and lifted his eyes to look at Jo, who sat quite still, watching him.

'I think . . .' He hesitated, his voice softer this time. 'I think you know the answer to that.'

'Do you want me to speak to her?'

'Would you? I'd probably only make matters worse.'

Jo nodded and got up to leave.

'And Jo . . .'

She turned to face him in the doorway.

'Thank you.'

The door clicked shut and he sank back into his chair. For several minutes he stared straight at the faded poster of Avebury stone circles that was sellotaped to the back of the door.

How could this be happening to him? It was all such a bloody mess. If anyone had asked him, he'd have told them that when Clare turned up out of the blue he hadn't thought about her in years. It wouldn't have been true, of course. The truth was he'd never allowed himself to hope he would ever see her again.

At first, wary of reopening old wounds, he'd been unsure what to make of her sudden reappearance in his life. But the passing years had changed them both. They seemed to be able to rub along together happily enough now. He could enjoy her company without that sick-making combination of longing and hopeless frustration he'd suffered from before. That was all in the past now.

Looking back on the last couple of months, he realised that everything had gone so incredibly well since she'd reappeared that, despite the fact he didn't have a superstitious bone in his body, he'd come to regard her return as an auspicious sign. For once he was on top of things – in control of his life.

When she found the Hungerbourne archive, everything had just slotted into place. This was the first opportunity he'd had since he couldn't remember when to get on with some real archaeology, instead of clogging up the university intranet with meaningless pieces of paper and cramming reluctant students full of theory. Even the Runt didn't have anything to grumble about. The funding that the project had brought in would keep him off his back for months. And he couldn't think of anyone he'd rather share it with than Clare. She still shared his passion for the work, and – he'd thought – they trusted one another. It had been perfect.

True, he'd been concerned by her growing interest in Gerald Hart. But, at first, it had seemed understandable. She'd needed to throw herself into something, to try to get over Stephen's death.

Even when he'd finally reported the theft of the Jevons disc to the police, things had worked out better than he could have hoped. He'd known there was no realistic prospect of recovering the missing goldwork. But Clare had been right; they couldn't run the risk of being accused of stealing it themselves. And if he hadn't agreed to report the disc missing, he'd never have met Sally. That was one thing at least he did have Clare to thank for.

And that was what had made him so mad, though he couldn't have explained it to Jo or Clare – particularly Clare. He hadn't told her about Sally yet. He didn't want to turn it into a big deal and there was no reason he should feel guilty, but the timing could hardly have been worse, so soon after Clare had lost Stephen. Somehow he'd never managed to find quite the right moment to tell her. And now he couldn't avoid it. Clare and Sally were bound to meet. He was going to have to tell Clare about Sally, and having left it so long it would surely look as if he'd deliberately tried to hide it from her, or worse still that he was embarrassed.

To top it all, there was no way he could avoid having to explain this whole mess to Sally. He knew that whoever's remains were lying at the bottom of that urn, someone would have to tell her about it at some point and it was far better that the news came from him rather than someone else. Should he tell her now or wait until the test results and dates were through?

But that wasn't going to be the real problem. No. What he was really dreading was telling Sally about Clare's investigations. He knew she'd regard it as amateur interference.

He massaged his forehead with his fingertips. It was all such a bloody mess.

CHAPTER TWELVE

'Is that it, then?' Jo stood in the open office door.

Clare, bag slung over her shoulder, gazed steadfastly down at a copy of the Brew Crew photograph lying neatly sleeved in its polythene conservation wallet on top of her desk.

'Well!'

'You heard him. He doesn't want me around. And I can't say I blame him.'

Jo folded her arms, her head tilted thoughtfully to one side. 'Well, I do.'

'There's no reason for you to fall out with him. I was the one chasing around after the disc.'

'Yeah. Which came from the site you're employed to work on, right?'

'I don't . . .'

'Christ! You two really are a piece of work. Just answer the question. Is the sun disc from the site we're working on?'

'Yes, but I don't see . . .'

'Well, I do. So shut the hell up and start dealing with this like the rational human being you are.'

Clare fell silent. She didn't have the energy to argue.

Jo pointed at Clare's bag. 'And for Christ's sake, take that thing off your shoulder and sit down.'

Clare responded automatically, depositing her bag beside the desk and herself into the seat.

Jo drew up a chair beside her. 'Let's get this straight. David does not want you to leave this project.'

Clare opened her mouth to respond, but Jo's look was enough to dissuade her. 'Just now, he was angry. Though I can't for the life of me work out why.'

'He thinks I'm not up to the job.' Clare could feel her head thumping. She wanted not to have to think about this any more.

Jo sat perfectly still, looking directly at her. When she finally spoke, she said, 'I'll come clean with you, Clare. When David asked me to work on Hungerbourne, I was astonished he'd put you in charge of the day-to-day management. I couldn't understand how the hell he could put someone who hadn't even picked up a trowel in fifteen years in charge of something this important.'

Clare sat, shoulders drooping, hands lying limply in her lap. If Jo was trying to make her feel the full depth of her failings, it was working.

Jo continued, 'I thought he'd got shit for brains and told him so. But he insisted that if I wouldn't take the job with you managing the project, he'd find someone who would.'

Clare didn't know whether to feel flattered, embarrassed or angry.

She plumped for angry. 'Sounds like you two had quite a little chat.'

Jo's voice was matter-of-fact, unaffected by the sudden burst of hostility. 'I always insist on knowing exactly who I'm gonna be working with. This was no different. And from what I've seen since, I understand why David stuck by you. You're good, Clare – real good. If I hadn't been told otherwise, I'd have thought you'd been a pro all your working life.'

Jo looked as if she meant it. Clare felt her cheeks flush. She was beginning to regret her sarcasm.

Jo said, 'I get that he's frustrated. This gig is important to him – to his career. It's the biggest break he's had. Hell, it's probably the biggest break any of us will ever have.'

'I know, that's what makes it so awful. I've let him down.'

'You haven't let anyone down. I'm no shrink, but if you ask me, David's reasons for behaving like he did aren't just professional. It can't be easy knowing your buddy's pop is lying in the bottom of some urn that their uncle had stashed in the attic.'

Clare stared down at her hands, which were clasped together in her lap. 'No, I don't suppose it is.'

'But that doesn't make the way he behaved in there OK. He was way out of order.'

Clare looked up. 'I should have told him what I was doing. Without him, I wouldn't even be part of this project.' As much as she was enjoying her newly rekindled passion for archaeology, the reality was that she needed the money. But, given the circumstances, she could hardly tell David or Jo that. How the hell had she managed to end up in this position?

Jo raised her eyes to the ceiling in exasperation. 'Jesus Christ, Clare, have you listened to a word I've said? I know folks who'd kill to be in your position. You've got to decide whether you're prepared to throw that away.'

Clare looked around the room. Within these institutionally magnolia walls, the carefully ordered records and familiar buff boxes were crammed with the fragmented pieces of past lives – lives she was helping to rediscover.

When she'd come back to Wiltshire, she'd been searching for a retreat: a place of comfort and safety. She'd wanted to bury herself in potsherds and paperwork, to be completely absorbed by the minutiae of archaeological study. But archaeology wasn't about dusty artefacts and bits of paper. It was about real people, living and dead. And she'd forgotten how much that excited her.

Clare became suddenly aware that Jo was waving a hand in front of her face. 'Did you hear what I said? David wants you on this project. I want you on this project. End of. Are you in or not?'

Clare looked into Jo's steady blue eyes. 'I'm in.'

It took Clare several disorientating seconds to register the fact that the sound of reveille emanating from her spare room was coming from Jo's mobile. She'd been up until the early hours, rehearsing Jo for her appearance in the coroner's court, and had been hoping for a lie-in. Fat chance now.

She flung on her robe and padded into the kitchen in search of coffee. By the time Jo emerged, scrubbed and fluffed from the shower, Clare was making headway on her third cup of the day.

'Wow, look at you.'

Jo was dressed in a smartly cut dark blue suit and baby-blue blouse that had been carefully selected the previous night from Clare's wardrobe. Jo had managed to tame her unruly blonde hair sufficiently to ensure it was neatly constrained in a ponytail. She looked every inch the young professional. So why did she look so unspeakably glum? She hadn't seemed nervous when they'd been going over their notes the night before.

Jo pulled up a chair at the kitchen table. 'Any coffee left in that pot?'

Clare poured a mug of the hot liquid. 'Getting stage fright?'

Jo shook her head and took a slug of her coffee.

Clare remembered the ringtone. 'Bad news.'

Jo nodded. 'My boss at the institute. They're not going to renew my contract. No job means no visa. So it's goodbye, Blighty, hello, U. S. of A.'

It was early June, but it had been raining for weeks. The room was cold and a smell of damp hung in the air. Daylight filtered in through windows, which were smeared with grime and bird droppings, and the cheap veneer doors and chipped monotone paintwork made the room feel unremittingly brown. But the assembled mass of journalists and Hungerbourne residents in the coroner's court barely noticed the decor. They sat expectantly, their necks craned upwards, waiting for Jo's response. She was sitting on a raised plinth at the front of the room, her hands resting lightly on her knees in a state of prepared anticipation.

The coroner, a rotund man in his mid-fifties wearing an understated charcoal grey suit, was positioned on a podium to her left, a series of bundles of papers and folders laid out in front of him. His head was tilted attentively to one side, as if to emphasise the consideration he was giving Jo's reply.

'The remains are those of an adult male. He was probably in his forties when he died. The treatment the remains I examined had been subjected to was comparable to that of a prehistoric pyre cremation.'

'Can you be certain of that, Dr Granski?'

'Yes. The effects of pyre burnings on skeletal material are well attested in the literature.'

The coroner said, 'So the remains under consideration are of prehistoric date.'

'No. I said comparable to, not identical. The range of scorching was consistent with cremation on a pyre, but the size of bone fragmentation was unusually large and there was a larger mass of bone present than is usual in prehistoric cremations in this country.' The coroner looked at her encouragingly. 'Most Bronze Age cremations contain only a part of the remains of the deceased – what you might call a token of the whole.'

'Was that what alerted you to the possibility that the remains were not prehistoric?'

'That was unusual, but not conclusive.' She was beginning to warm to her theme. 'What clinched it was the presence of what appeared to be an amalgam dental filling.'

The coroner glanced down at his notes. 'And would I be correct in saying that you subsequently carried out tests that proved the item in question was a dental filling?'

'Yes, we ran an XRF test. X-ray fluorescence works by . . .'

He held his hand aloft and smiled. 'I think you've already established your level of expertise, Dr Granski. Are you satisfied that the test proved that the substance you identified was the remains of a modern dental filling?'

'Absolutely.'

'Are you able to estimate how old the remains are?'

'We took a sample from some of the cremated bone and ran a radio-carbon determination. The calibrated date came out at 1970 AD, plus or minus thirty years at two sigma.'

He gesticulated with his right hand in a gently encouraging motion.

'That means there's a ninety-five per cent probability that the person whose remains were in the urn died between 1940 and 2000.'

'Did your analysis reveal anything else?'

Jo drew in a deep breath. 'Yes. The individual concerned had been stabbed.'

There was an audible murmur from the back of the room.

'What led you to draw that conclusion?'

'There were peri-mortem cut marks on two separate rib fragments. Microscopic examination showed a combination of deep furrows and fine striations on the first fragment, consistent with the wound having been caused by a serrated implement.'

'Some kind of saw.'

Jo shook her head. 'Too thick for a regular saw – but it had teeth.'

'And what caused the marks on the second fragment?'

'They were from a knife blade.'

'Are you saying that two different weapons were used?'

'That would be a reasonable conclusion.'

'How serious would the wounds inflicted have been?'

'The angle of the cut marks indicates an upward thrusting motion. I'm not a physician, but in my opinion stab wounds in this area would most likely result in severe damage to internal organs, heavy blood loss and death.'

CHAPTER THIRTEEN

'Well done.' David, who'd been sitting, to his evident discomfort, sandwiched between Clare and Sally, sprang to his feet and clapped Jo on the back.

'It was nothing like I imagined. I thought it would be all wigs and gowns.'

'That's Crown Court, not coroner's court.' Sally's voice was dispassionately corrective.

Sally tugged at David's sleeve, drawing him a few paces to one side to speak with him. Heads together, voices low, they exchanged words. Clare watched as Sally nodded curtly in the direction of her and Jo, and then hurried through the double doors and out down the corridor.

Jo asked, 'What's her problem?'

Clare smiled. 'I think I am. I don't think Detective Inspector Treen approves of my methods.'

'Well, David sure as hell hasn't been seduced by her good-natured affability.'

'Seduced!' Clare felt a disquieting skein of recognition in the pit of her stomach.

Jo smiled conspiratorially at her. 'Come on. You must have noticed. The way he's been looking at her. All those phone calls. What did you think was going on?'

Clare hesitated. 'I thought they were discussing the case.' The truth was, she hadn't given a moment's consideration to the possibility that David might be seeing someone.

'Well, doh!' Jo's tone switched from flippant to concern in an instant. 'Are you OK?'

Clare shook herself. 'Fine.'

Jo looked unconvinced.

'Just tired.' Clare forced a half-smile. 'I can see I've got some catching up to do in the gossip stakes. Do you think I might respond to training?'

'Maybe an intensive course.' Jo laughed, raising an eyebrow in the direction of the double doors through which Sally had departed. 'One thing's for sure, you're more fun to be around than some people I could mention.'

Clare heard herself saying, 'Must go with the territory if you're in the police.' But her thoughts were elsewhere as she watched David striding back across the room towards them.

'Inspector Treen not joining us for lunch?' Jo asked.

He cleared his throat. 'No. She's got some phone calls to make.'

Jo leant back, avoiding his line of sight, and rolled her eyes into the top of her head. Clare suppressed the urge to laugh.

David snapped his head round and looked at Jo over his shoulder. 'Did I miss something?'

Jo stepped forward, slipping her arm casually through David's. 'Nah. You're just suffering from the innate guilt of a WASP in a liberal democracy.'

Sally Treen was undeniably attractive and brimming with the untrammelled confidence of youth. Clare found herself caught between wondering and wishing whether time would cast a pall over the younger woman's effervescent charms.

She glanced sideways at David. His strong, broad features were fixed firmly on Sally, who was sitting at the front of the room. He'd resisted the charms of enough undergrads when he was a doctoral student. Surely it couldn't be Sally's looks alone that had attracted him.

He placed a hand on her forearm. 'You OK?'

She nodded and he returned his focus to Sally. Who he slept with was none of her business. She tried to concentrate instead on what Sally was saying to the coroner.

'I became involved with the case when Dr Barbrook notified me of the results of the radio-carbon tests and the test on the material that turned out to be the filling.'

'Why did Dr Barbrook choose to notify you?'

David shifted slightly on the bench next to her. Was he blushing?

Sally replied without hesitation. 'I'd met Dr Barbrook some weeks previously when he'd reported the disappearance of a find from the Hungerbourne excavation archive.'

'And what exactly was missing?'

'A small gold and amber disc. But my understanding is that the purpose of the inquest is to look into matters directly related to the death of the deceased.' She flashed a smile at the coroner, who nodded. 'So I'm not sure the missing goldwork is relevant.'

'Have you established when this goldwork went missing?'

'No.'

'So in fact you have no way of establishing whether the artefact's disappearance was linked to the death of the deceased or not?'

'Well, no.' The words were dragged from her lips as if by some undesired but irresistible force.

The coroner glanced down at his papers. 'I'd like to pass on to the identification of the deceased. Has there been any further examination of the human remains subsequent to Dr Granski's investigations?'

'Yes. Preliminary enquiries . . .' She hesitated momentarily. Did anyone else notice the look Sally shot in her direction? Clare wondered. '. . . indicated that Mr James Hart – the brother of Dr Gerald Hart, who directed the excavations – went missing around the time the dig came to an end in September 1973. The forensic pathologist commissioned a DNA sample from the remains and further samples were taken from James Hart's son and his wife.'

'That is Mr Peter Hart and his mother, Mrs Estelle Hart.'

She nodded. 'Yes.'

'And this report' – he flourished a Manila folder in the air – 'states that the results of the DNA tests are consistent with the man whose remains were found by Dr Granski being the father of Mr Peter Hart.'

'Yes.' Sally nodded.

'Where was the urn from which the remains were recovered found?'

'In the attic of Hungerbourne Manor, the former home of Dr Gerald Hart.'

CHAPTER FOURTEEN

Unlawful killing. It was the verdict Peter had been dreading. The fact that it was the conclusion any reasonable person would have come to didn't make it any easier to take. Door cracked open, he'd listened to the verdict from the corridor. He had no intention of submitting himself to the press.

As he hurried down the stone steps at the front of the building, he heard quickening footsteps behind him. He glanced over his shoulder to see Ed had broken into a trot in pursuit of him. Peter turned away, but before he'd gone a few paces he felt Ed's hand on his shoulder.

'Hold up, old man.'

'Leave it, Ed. I need some time to think things through.'

'It doesn't change anything. You and Gerald and Estelle were more of a family to me than mine ever were. I'm not going to give up on you just because things have hit a sticky patch.' Ed gripped Peter's upper arms. 'We've always stuck together, haven't we?'

Peter nodded.

'I see no reason why things should change now.'

'We're not kids any more, Ed. This is different.'

Ed stepped back. His words were measured. 'I was there too – remember?'

Peter stood impassive, his gaze fixed firmly on the pavement.

Ed said, 'Your father was a difficult man.'

He couldn't deal with this now. He tried to turn away, but Ed blocked his path.

Ed said, 'I don't give a damn about other people's opinions. I do what's right. Come on, let's go and get a drink. Talk about this.'

'Peter!' Clare was breathless, her unfastened raincoat flapping in the wind behind her.

Startled by the unexpected interjection, Peter pivoted round to face her. But the reply came from Ed. 'Lovely to see you again, even if under somewhat unfortunate circumstances.'

Ed's attempt at preserving the social niceties dropped into silence. Peter and Clare stood motionless, hands by their sides, divided by more than just Ed's presence.

Ed ploughed on, 'I don't know about you, Peter, but I'm about ready for that G and T.'

'I'll catch you up in a minute.' Peter's voice was quiet but insistent.

Ed glanced from Peter to Clare and then, with an abrupt nod, turned and left them.

'Are you OK?'

Peter looked dreadful. There were bags under his eyes and his complexion was the colour of two-day-old porridge.

He raised his eyebrows in a non-committal gesture. She said nothing, but instead looked questioningly into his bloodshot eyes.

'Really, I'm fine. I've had worse things happen to me.' His words were ice-thin, devoid of belief.

Clare tried, unsuccessfully, to imagine what might be worse than this. The vigorous middle-aged man she'd met that first day at the manor now looked more as she'd come to imagine Gerald must have looked in later life: defeated.

'When you asked if you could help track down the sun disc, I never dreamt it would end like this.' She weighed her words. 'I suppose I'm trying to say I feel a sense of responsibility – towards you.'

There was the merest twitch of a smile at the corner of his mouth. 'You needn't, you know.'

Thin streaks of sunlight broke through the grey cloud, illuminating a tired-looking bench standing not far from the front of the red-brick monument to utility that comprised Swindon Civic Offices.

Peter gestured towards the bench's layers of peeling varnish and they sat down. 'There's only one person responsible for how I'm feeling right now.'

Clare waited, expecting him to enlarge on his comment. But instead he sat, hunched forward, silently staring out at the voyage of a wind-tossed crisp packet across the sea of municipal grass.

She shivered, pulling her raincoat up around her chin. 'Sally Treen is convinced Gerald was responsible.'

'It seems the obvious conclusion . . .' His voice trailed off before he added, as much to himself as to her, 'I thought we were free of him.'

'Your father.'

He responded with the echo of a nod. 'It's as if he's been sitting there all those years, just waiting for a chance to cause chaos for us all over again.' He pulled himself upright on the bench and turned to face her. 'You think that's callous.'

She said nothing. What was there to say?

'Anyone who knew Father will tell you he had it coming. He destroyed lives. Even from the grave, he's managed to wreck Gerald's career and ruin the chance any of us had of happiness.'

She asked, 'Do you think Sally's right about Gerald?'

His mouth twisted in an expression of pain. She prided herself on having a pretty vivid imagination, but she couldn't even begin to imagine how difficult it must be to contemplate the idea that a man you'd loved and respected all your life might be responsible for the death of your father.

'There's no evidence to suggest otherwise, is there? I loved Gerald, but he could be an irascible old bugger.'

'Do you honestly think he was capable of killing someone?'

He looked away from her. 'Do any of us really know what we're capable of?'

'You can't just give up on him. Gerald may have been a driven man, but just because he was passionate about his work doesn't mean he'd murder someone to protect it.'

'We don't know it was murder. My father had a hell of a temper, especially when he'd been drinking.'

'You think Gerald might have killed him in self-defence?' The thought that Jim's death might not be related to the missing gold had never crossed her mind.

Peter got to his feet. 'Look, Clare, I'm touched you care – about me and about Gerald. But right now I could do with some space.'

Clare stood up. 'I understand more than you think.' She raised herself onto her tiptoes and, somewhat to her own surprise, found herself planting a kiss lightly on his cheek. 'Now go and have that drink with Ed. I'm glad he's around to look after you.'

'No worries on that score. Ed's always been there for me.'

CHAPTER FIFTEEN

David rolled back the fraying canvas flap on the repair-pocked mess tent that would be the centre of their world for the next six weeks and drew in a deep breath of country air. The ground underfoot was sodden, his joints were already aching to the point of numbness and he was shortly going to be surrounded by sixty students of varying indifference to their task. But he still felt an overwhelming surge of relief at finally being out in the field preparing to dig.

The coroner's verdict hadn't come as much of a surprise. The peculiarities of the English legal system meant the culprit hadn't been named, but it was obvious to anyone with half a brain cell who was responsible. He knew that logically there was no way that British Heritage could lay the blame for any of it at his door. But the press attention hadn't been what they'd had in mind when they'd approved his funding application. They'd be watching his every move from now on, and they weren't the only ones. The Runt was on his case too. David had taken to letting his mobile go to voicemail whenever Muir called. The one good thing about the crap mobile reception around here was that it gave him a credible excuse for not getting back to the little Scots git.

Upslope, on the other side of the field, Clare was cocooned in something resembling a giant, ill-constructed kite. He smiled as he watched her wind herself further and further into the clutches of the clinging green nylon as it was whipped by the gusting south-westerly. The sky was grey and overcast. He rubbed his hands on the arms of his old army jacket in an attempt to dispel the soggy chill that made it feel more like autumn than early summer. They'd been lucky that the torrential rain of the last month had abated long enough for them to set up base camp.

He squished his way across the field towards Clare. 'You could have given Wilbur and Orville a run for their money with that thing.'

'Ha bloody ha. I thought these dome things were meant to be easier to put up than the old ridge tents.'

He stood back a few paces, the better to admire her courageous but ill-fated attempts to tame the flysheet. 'Depends who's putting them up. I think you're meant to start with the poles.'

'This isn't an anthropology field study. You are allowed to get involved with the participants.'

'And spoil the entertainment.'

Clare's expression told him he'd pushed his luck too far.

'Alright, mardy, let's see if we can't sort it out. We haven't got time to bugger about. The students are due to start arriving any minute and I want to have at least some of the more rudimentary elements of civilisation in place.'

'Worried some of the little darlings won't fancy it?'

'It's not them I'm worried about, it's their parents.'

Clare's eyes widened. She disentangled herself from the flysheet, snapped together one of the long metal poles and handed it to him. 'Parents. I wouldn't have been caught dead letting Mum drop me off at a dig.'

'It's all changed since our day. Mummy and Daddy want to know where all of their hard-earned cash is going now they have to fork out for little Johnnie's education. God only knows what some of them would do if they found out what life on a dig was really like.'

Holding two corners of the flysheet between her outstretched arms, Clare inclined her head backwards in the direction of the building that stood at the foot of the slope. 'So was it really the brightest move to pitch camp within spitting distance of the pub?'

David grinned. 'Some elements of fieldwork are a necessity; besides, Tony offered us a good rate on his field.'

'I bet you could see the pound signs light up in his eyes.'

'Never hurts to keep the locals on side.' He threaded a pole carefully into its nylon sleeve and gestured to Clare to pass him the mallet.

She tossed it to him and turned to pick up a metal tent peg from a pile behind her. Straightening up, she pointed her thumb in the direction of the Lamb and Flag.

'Looks like our first parent.'

He looked up from where he was crouching, trying to secure one of the pegs, to see a small, neat figure striding purposefully towards them. 'Oh, Christ!'

'Trouble?'

He lowered his voice almost to a whisper. 'Margaret Bockford.'

What was she doing here? As Margaret drew closer, he straightened up, mallet in hand, and waved.

Margaret pointed at the mallet. 'In some societies that would be construed as a threatening gesture.'

He hurriedly dropped the hand holding the offending implement to his side.

Margaret's face cracked an unexpected smile. 'I hope I haven't come at an inopportune moment.'

'We're just setting up. We don't really start until tomorrow,' he offered apologetically.

'And you're wondering how on earth you're going to get everything finished in time when this old duffer has turned up for the grand tour of the site before the excavation has even begun?'

He racked his brain for something politic to say, but to no avail. Clare and Margaret exchanged a knowing look. He had the uncomfortable feeling something was going on that he didn't quite understand. He looked from the older to the younger woman in search of an explanation.

It was Margaret who finally took pity on him. 'Will you explain, Clare, or shall I?'

He experienced a feeling of impending doom that he normally associated with preparing for exam boards.

Clare said, 'When Margaret heard about the inquest, she phoned me to find out how we were getting on with our search for the sun disc. I mentioned we were starting work out here this week and she offered to lend a hand.'

'All kitted out and ready for action.' Margaret swept her hands down from her chest to her knees, indicating her apparel: serviceable brown cords, a green polo neck sweater and a somewhat baggy but matching woollen cardigan. A pair of well-worn but still obviously purple Doc Martens added a dissonant note to the ensemble.

'I hope you don't mind me barging in like this, David. But when Clare said you were using volunteers as well as students, I couldn't resist.'

'You know you're always welcome, Margaret.' Had he sounded convincing? He'd been so looking forward to this. The last thing he needed was Margaret second-guessing his every decision.

'Right, young man, we women are perfectly capable of erecting a tent. Why don't you go and deal with that?' Margaret inclined her head in the direction of a large flatbed trailer that was just pulling in to the pub car park carrying a battered excuse for a Portakabin.

Resigned to the inevitability of the new regime, David started off across the field, the gusting wind dragging the words of the women's conversation towards him as he walked.

'He's not a good liar, is he?' Margaret said.

'No,' Clare said. 'He never has been.'

'A good sign in a man, I always think. Pass me that mallet.'

David was sitting, back pressed against the wooden slats of the tea hut, a lukewarm mug of almost undrinkable tea in his hand, surveying his team. They had more than a little in common with the Brew Crew of the original excavations. Jo had returned to London to see out the last few weeks of her contract at the institute. But in addition to Clare, Margaret and the students, their ranks had been swelled by Ed and his wife, Pat. Somewhat to David's surprise they had also been joined by Tony, the landlord of the Lamb and Flag, who, when he could escape the eye of the ever-vigilant Shirl, had proven to be more than proficient in wielding a trowel.

To his enormous relief, Margaret had settled into the role of humble digger without a murmur of dissent and hadn't once tried to gainsay him about his direction of the excavations. And when he'd drawn upon her expertise, her knowledge of the site and the earlier excavation had proven invaluable. She was apparently never happier than when trowelling alongside her somewhat younger companions. With few of the pretensions he'd observed among some of the other eminent professors of his acquaintance, her undisguised love of Irish whiskey had resulted in her quickly developing an almost mythic status amongst the student workforce.

David glanced across at Clare, who was sitting cross-legged in front of Margaret like some latter-day devotee at the feet of the be-cardiganed guru. Things hadn't been all plain sailing since Clare had joined the team. But he knew it had been his fault as much as hers. He should never have assumed they could just fall back into their old pattern of shared confidences and easy companionship.

He'd been a damned fool to have hoped, however fleetingly, that because Stephen was dead she might feel anything more than friendship for him. It was a chapter best left closed, and now with Sally maybe he had the chance to put it behind him once and for all. He took a last slug of the tepid brown liquid in his mug, upending the remainder of its contents onto the still-damp grass. He picked up his faithful old trowel, feeling the familiar bumps of the small wooden head that had been carved on its handle so many years ago, and stood up. 'Right, you lot, off your backsides!'

A chorus of groans and widespread muttering ensued as the ragtag workforce hauled themselves to their feet.

Taking a folded sheet of paper from his pocket, he turned

to Margaret, who remained seated in the carefully positioned wheelbarrow that she'd adopted as an impromptu armchair. 'How good's your surveying? Do you reckon you and Clare can spot the trench over the geophysics survey and bring us down here?' He pointed to a rectangle marked out over a fuzzy grey image of a round barrow lying just downhill from David's own trench.

'Despite appearances to the contrary, Dr Barbrook, this old bird is something of a dab hand with modern technology. Have total station, will survey.'

'Bet you a double you can't find the edge of the ditch and the grave cut first time.'

'You're on.'

Clare proffered her hand to assist Margaret in rising and cast a sideways glance to where the bright orange plastic case containing the twenty-first century version of a theodolite lay and grimaced. 'Maybe I should've mentioned I've never used one of these. Things were a bit more low-tech when I was last in the field.'

Margaret leant towards the younger woman and lowered her voice to a stage whisper. 'I never engage in a bet that isn't a racing certainty. I was walking these fields before David was born.'

Feigning ignorance of his role as stooge, David trudged upslope to inspect the trench he'd been labouring over for the last fortnight. In front of him, a rectangular area ten metres across had been stripped of its turf covering. In the centre, a ring of dark soil, the remnants of a narrow ditch, described a circle around a barely perceptible black-brown swell in the ground. Slightly to one side of the centre of this mound, and stretching out to the right, a second smaller trench had been cut as broad as David was tall. Within the trench, a small hole was visible. A lanky youth was crouching uncomfortably over the hole, about to resume trowelling.

David peered over his shoulder into the hole. 'Bottomed that thing out yet?'

The youth unbent from his tortured posture, looked at him nervously and shrugged his shoulders.

David motioned him aside. 'Let's have a look.' Kneeling down, he leant forward cutting his way expertly through the light sandy layer at the base of the hole with his trowel. There was a reassuring feeling of familiarity to the slight resistance of the soil as it encountered the worn steel of his trowel blade and transferred itself almost instantaneously to his fingers.

'Looks like that's it. A pit cut into the body of the mound. Organic silty fill. There was that large area of plough disturbance at the top, wasn't there?'

The youth nodded, looking down anxiously at the hole.

'What about the finds?' David asked.

The youth passed him a mud-splattered black plastic seed tray. Sitting back on his haunches, David picked his way through an assortment of burnt bone and coarsely made pottery. He rubbed his fingertips gently over the tiny fragments of burnt flint that some unknown potter had carefully kneaded into the clay almost thirty-five centuries before.

'The plough's pretty much mangled it, but it looks like a disturbed cremation deposit. I'd say you've found what's left of the pit the Jevons sun disc came from. The trench Gerald dug must have missed it by inches.' He stood up, wiped the soil from his trowel on his moleskins and took a step up onto the grass in front of them. 'If our GPS is right, the pit Gerald's sun disc was found in lies just here.'

'Are we going to open it up?'

David nodded. 'You bet. We need to tie the recorded position of Gerald's trenches in with ours.'

A broad grin animated the youth's previously inert features. This one might do alright, after all.

CHAPTER SIXTEEN

'Is that thing safe?' David headed downhill towards Ed, bracing himself against the familiar nagging pain in his knees.

Ed was standing on a small, flat plateau, halfway between the trench where David was digging at the top of the field and the cutting Margaret and Clare were laying out over the remnants of the second, as yet untouched, burial mound downslope. Around him the damp grass was littered with galvanised metal tubes as if some careless giant had been scattering toothpicks. To one side, a pile of wooden scaffolding boards had been neatly stacked.

Ed smiled. 'It's in better shape than you are by the look of it.'

David emitted a harrumph. 'Too much digging.'

'And too much rugby, from what Peter tells me.'

David nodded in the direction of the disarticulated skeleton of the photographic tower lying at Ed's feet. 'Have you checked this lot?'

Ed nodded. 'It looks pretty sound to me.'

'No offence, Ed, but I'd like to give it the once-over myself before it goes up.'

'None taken, old man. This thing looks like its seen some action in its time and that was a while back.'

'Where did it come from?'

'Peter found it in the manor outbuildings.'

He could take some comfort from that, at least. If Peter was willing to lend them this after everything they'd subjected him to over the last few months, he couldn't be feeling too badly disposed towards them.

'It was Gerald's. I tried to persuade him that he should sell off the old kit he had hanging around the place. But he wouldn't hear of it. Peter and I never could understand why.'

Maybe they couldn't, but David could. Getting rid of it would have meant admitting that he would never dig again. David couldn't even begin to imagine how he'd feel the day he had to hang up his trowel.

Picking a plank up from the pile, David flipped it over, running his hand across the rough grain of the pine. He looked up to see Ed trying to secure two pieces of steel together with an Allen key.

David said, 'You must have known Gerald pretty well.'

'As well as anyone round here.'

'Anyone except Peter.'

'He wasn't always around to keep an eye on the old boy.'

'Did he need keeping an eye on?'

'Oh, Gerald was all there with his cough drops, if that's what you mean. But he was pretty frail towards the end. I used to pop him round one of Pat's casseroles now and then.'

'That was good of you.'

'It wasn't much, really. Sometimes I'd stay for a chat. He liked to talk about the past – his work, I mean.'

'Did he ever talk about the excavation here?'

Ed shook his head forcefully. 'No.' He hesitated. 'Peter asked him about the dig once. It was the only time I can ever recall Gerald losing his temper. And now we know why.'

David returned the plank to the pile of timber beside Ed, thrust his hands into the pockets of his moleskins and turned to face him square on. 'How did Estelle take it when Jim disappeared?'

'Peter would know more about that than me.'

'I don't like to ask – under the circumstances.'

Ed hesitated. He seemed to be making up his mind about something. 'Peter's a pal, and I'm not one to tell tales.'

'But?'

Ed sighed. 'I don't suppose it makes much difference now. Estelle wasn't exactly the grieving widow.'

'Should she have been? According to Peter, Jim was a thorough going bastard.'

'That's only half the story.' Ed laid the two pieces of galvanised steel tubing he'd been holding on the ground. 'There's no way of putting this delicately. At the time, there was talk about Gerald and Estelle.'

David struggled to disguise his surprise. 'They were having an affair?'

'Let's just say they were very fond of one another. It was common knowledge that Gerald spent more time with Estelle than Jim ever did.'

'Are you suggesting Gerald killed Jim because he wanted Estelle for himself?'

'I'm not suggesting anything. Jim deserved everything he got.

Maybe Gerald had enough of the way Jim treated Estelle, maybe he didn't. Either way, I don't see what good it'll do dredging it all up now.'

The more David learnt about Hungerbourne, the more he began to get the uncomfortable feeling that there was something going on that he didn't understand.

Ed flipped his hands dismissively. 'Look, forget what I said. Nobody will ever know what really happened. And whatever Gerald did or didn't do, he's gone to meet his maker and Estelle is an old lady living in a nursing home. There's no sense in stirring up trouble.' Looking over David's shoulder, Ed nodded his head in the direction of the bottom of the field. 'If I'm not mistaken, there's someone else who thinks we're better off letting sleeping dogs lie.'

David turned to see Sally's car pull up in front of their makeshift office. Sally stepped gingerly out of the vehicle onto the rain-soaked turf. She waved, and he walked down to meet her. What with one thing and another, he'd hardly seen her since they'd started digging. Something he very much wanted to remedy, but this wasn't the sort of meeting he'd had in mind. She greeted him with a peck on the cheek.

'This is a surprise.'

'The chief insisted we take a stab at finding that missing disc of yours.'

'Refreshing to hear someone in the constabulary takes heritage crime seriously.'

Sally laughed. 'Not a chance. After the coroner's comments about the disc at the inquest, he's nervous the media will get hold of it. He wants us to make a show of it. So I thought I'd better at least see where the damn thing came from.'

David managed a weak smile. His social life had been colliding ever more frequently with his work in recent weeks and he wasn't altogether enjoying the experience.

'Well. Are you going to show me what you mudlarks get up to when you're not in your ivory towers?'

He swept his arm across the field in front of her in a gesture of welcome that belied his uneasiness. 'Step this way.'

She smiled and thrust her arm through his as he led her towards the open trench. He spent some minutes explaining the minutiae of their discoveries to date. 'So this is almost certainly where the plough cut through the pit that the Jevons sun disc came from.'

'That's the one that's missing.' She looked up at him.

He nodded.

'I've got a bit of a personal interest in this, then.' She shifted her gaze from the bottom of the pit to his face.

David looked down at her bemused. 'Why?'

She reached up and batted the back of his head playfully with the palm of her hand. 'Because, dopey, if it hadn't been for this hole and its contents . . .'

'Pit,' David corrected her. 'It's not a hole, it's a pit.'

'Hole, pit, whatever. If it hadn't been for this thing and its contents I wouldn't have met you.' She raised herself onto the tips of her toes and kissed him insistently on the lips. Despite David's embarrassment, he couldn't help his response as he drew her towards him and returned the kiss.

Out of the corner of his eye, David caught the amused expression of the lanky youth who was standing beside the pit, committing the details of its dimensions to paper. David scowled and the youth returned his attention to his clipboard. David held Sally at arm's length and looked down on her with a broad grin on his face.

She said, 'As I've used up my precious time to come and see this extravaganza, are you going to show me the rest of the place?'

'Sure.' His response was instantaneous. But he hoped this wasn't going to be a habit. He liked his life neat, ordered and separate. Play was play and work was his life. Things were getting confused and if there was one thing he hated, it was confusion.

Margaret poked at the glowing embers of the campfire with a broken length of hazel and watched the sparks dance against the star-speckled blackness of the night sky. Laying the improvised poker aside, she picked up the half-empty bottle of Jameson's from beside the log she was sitting on and poured another tot into her enamel mug.

The last of the students had retired to their beds in the campsite below almost an hour ago. She knew she'd regret it in the morning if she didn't do the same, but she found herself reluctant to follow suit. Lifting the mug into the chill night air, she silently mouthed the words, 'To you, Gerald.' Before she had a chance to place her lips on the metal rim, she heard a rustling behind her.

Craning her neck round, she strained her eyes into the darkness. 'Hello. Is someone there?'

There was no reply. *Must be the wind.* She took a long slug of whiskey. Being back here where it all started had made her realise how much she craved being out in the field again. Her chair at Oxford was the pinnacle of her career, but sometimes it felt more like a straitjacket than an accolade.

The embers of the fire glowed suddenly red as a gust deposited a blanket of sparks at her feet.

'Woe Waters.' The words drifted towards her on the wind.

She was imagining things. She rose unsteadily to her feet. Maybe it was time to find her bed.

'Woe Waters!' There it was again, louder this time.

She swung around, bottle in one hand, mug in the other. 'Who's there?' Silence. 'Speak up, do you hear me!'

The noise of muffled laughter drifted towards her from further down the hill. Probably kids from the village. She made her way downslope, swaying unsteadily. No bunch of yobs was going to make a fool of Professor Margaret Bockford.

'Clear off! Do you hear me? You've no business being here.' Her words fell into empty night.

She shuffled forward, unable to make out anything distinctly as she moved further away from the firelight. As her eyes adjusted she could make out the outline of a pile of planks near the foot of the photo tower.

More confident now, she strode forward. A sudden crack on her shins brought her crashing to the ground. The tin mug rolled away, but the Jameson's bottle shattered, depositing jagged shards of glass all about her. For several seconds she lay face down on the ground, listening to the rise and fall of her own breathing. Tentatively, she manoeuvred herself into a sitting position and put her hand to her face. No glasses.

What had she been thinking? Chasing apparitions in the middle of the night. Feeling around her, she retrieved her spectacles, but not without first cutting the palm of her hand on broken bottle glass. She reached into the pocket of her cardigan, pulled out her handkerchief and wrapped it round her bleeding hand. Rubbing her bruised shin with her good hand, she stood up.

What on earth would David and the others think if they could see her now? There was nothing for it – she would just have to set her alarm and come back to clear up the broken bottle before anyone found it. There was no way on God's earth she was going to let them know what a stupid, drunken old fool she'd been.

CHAPTER SEVENTEEN

From the moment she left Morgan's office, Sally had known the DCI was sending her on a wild goose chase. And nothing about the journey from Devizes to Whitby had changed her mind.

She also knew that the odds against solving a forty-year-old murder were astronomically high. The obvious suspect was Gerald Hart. The cremation had been found in his attic, and he seemed to have had sole control of the finds from the dig after it ended. But all of the evidence was circumstantial and Morgan, who had his eye firmly on the top slot, needed to keep the assistant chief constable off his back if he wanted to continue climbing the greasy pole.

They'd been lucky with the press so far. Thanks to an unlikely combination of royal baby fever, the cold-blooded murder of a serving British soldier and the Lords voting for gay marriage, the reporting on the coroner's inquiry had largely been confined to a few local papers. But she knew it couldn't last. Murder at the manor, ancient gold and a forty-year-old cold case – it was a tabloid editor's dream.

She'd already interviewed Jim Hart's widow and gotten precisely nowhere. Estelle had insisted the discovery of Jim's remains in the attic of the manor was as much of a shock to her as to everyone else. And, on balance, she was inclined to believe Estelle's claim that she'd thought Jim had done a runner with Joyce Clifford.

Sally had planned to spend this weekend with David. The wine she'd bought to go with the meal he'd promised to cook was still sitting in its carrier bag on her kitchen table. But Morgan was the boss; and in the force, when the boss ordered you to jump, you asked what over – a nugget of wisdom that seemed somehow to have escaped Tom West. Her sergeant had made his displeasure at having to drive the three hundred miles from Wiltshire to the North York Moors obvious in every conceivable way.

She'd encountered his type before. Every station had one: a tatty-suited, baggy-overcoated, fifty-something force lifer who knew everything and everyone. He'd been bloody-minded and difficult ever since she'd arrived in her new post. A word or two around the staff canteen confirmed what she'd suspected: he'd had an easy ride from her predecessor. But he was just going to have to learn to knuckle down and do things her way.

West reached the door of Captain Cook's B & B ahead of her. Three brisk raps with the lion-head knocker were eventually rewarded with the sound of heels clacking along a tile-clad floor.

The door opened and Sally thrust her warrant card forward, brushing past West. 'Mrs Joyce Clifford?'

The woman in front of them nodded warily.

'DI Treen and DS West, Wiltshire Constabulary. Can we have a word?'

Joyce glanced down at the card and looked the two strangers standing on her doorstep up and down. 'If you've come all this way, I don't suppose you'll be happy if I say no.'

West smiled. 'A cuppa wouldn't go amiss either.'

Sally shot him a warning glare.

'Come through. I don't want to disturb my guests.'

She followed Joyce down the Minton-tiled hallway. A half-glazed door to their right bearing the words *Residents' Lounge* in italic gold letters stood ajar. As far as Sally could make out, the guests Joyce had mentioned seemed to consist of one elderly gent warming himself by the gas fire.

At the end of the hallway, Joyce opened a solid Victorian door to reveal a light and airy kitchen. Sally could see, even at a distance, that the wooden units that lined the wall down the left-hand side of the room were handmade. To the right stood a scrubbed pine table and chairs, and a Welsh dresser bedecked with blue-and-white ware. Immediately in front of them, French windows gave onto a stone-flagged patio overlooking a good-sized garden. The room reeked of cash.

West pressed his nose against the French windows and looked out onto a neatly tended lawn and tastefully planted borders. 'Someone likes gardening.'

Joyce turned to face him from her position filling the kettle at the sink. 'I have someone in to give me a hand. But I like to potter during my quiet spells.'

Sally said, 'Like now, you mean?'

Joyce's face hardened. You could almost see the cracks in her pancake-thick make-up. 'You've caught us in a quiet patch – what with the bad weather.'

'Must be a worry. Financially, I mean.' She drew out a chair and, without waiting for an invitation, sat down at the opposite end of the table from where Joyce had seated herself.

Joyce had placed her chair at forty-five degrees to the table, as if to avoid facing her directly. West sat midway between them.

Arms folded, Joyce looked at Sally. 'I assume there's a point to all this. You're not here because you're concerned about the state of the tourist industry, and I haven't been to Wiltshire in nearly forty years.'

'When exactly did you leave, Mrs Clifford?' Sally asked.

'Summer 1973.'

'At the time of Gerald Hart's dig,' Sally said.

'Yes.'

'You worked on the excavation?' Sally asked.

'I helped out.'

'Didn't you find some of the goldwork? You made the national press. I thought some of the pictures were rather good,' West said.

Despite Sally's instinctive dislike of the man, she had to admit he knew what he was doing. Joyce sat upright in her chair, smoothed the flats of her hands down the front of her blouse and tucked a stray strand of her peroxide-blonde locks behind one ear. She smiled at West. 'I didn't take a bad picture in those days.'

'Jim Hart obviously didn't think so,' Sally said.

Joyce opened her mouth, but to her apparent relief the kettle boiled. She got up, filled a teapot and set it, mugs, spoons, sugar and a jug of milk on a green plastic tray. She waited until she'd finished placing the tray on the table and had retaken her seat before she spoke. 'Is that why you're here? Because of Jim.'

'You don't deny knowing Jim Hart?'

'Of course I knew him.'

West asked, 'In the biblical sense?'

Joyce twisted her head round to face him. 'What?'

Sally cast a warning look at him. 'What Sergeant West is trying to ask is whether you were involved in a relationship with Jim Hart.'

'What business is it of yours?'

West leant forward and picked up a mug from the tray. 'Since James Hart's cremated remains were found in the attic of Hungerbourne Manor, it's become very much our business.'

Joyce had the countenance of a woman whose world had just imploded. For a moment, Sally thought the older woman would faint.

'Would you like some water?' Sally nodded her head in the direction of the tap, and West duly obliged. She watched as Joyce took a couple of sips from the glass before resuming her questioning. 'Were you in a relationship with Jim Hart?'

'I was. He wasn't.' Her hands were shaking, but there could be no mistaking the anger in her voice. Sally and West exchanged bemused looks. Joyce said, 'Jim Hart only wanted me for what he could get.'

'And what was that, exactly?' Sally asked.

'What all men want – to get his leg over.'

West looked down at the table, apparently embarrassed by the universal guilt of his gender.

Joyce looked at Sally. 'I was young enough and stupid enough to think he wanted more. But I was just another one in a long line he'd used his flannel on.'

'And what did your husband make of all this, Mrs Clifford?' Sally placed the emphasis firmly on the 'Mrs'.

Joyce's eyes widened. 'You don't think George killed him?'

Sally said, 'We didn't say anyone had killed him.'

Joyce drained the rest of her water and placed the glass on the table. 'People don't cremate themselves, do they?'

She was beginning to think she might have misjudged Joyce Clifford. She obviously had her wits about her.

She said, 'I understand you spoke to a Mrs Clare Hills a few weeks ago?'

Joyce looked puzzled. Her reply came slowly. 'That's right.'

West said, 'Would you like to tell us what she came to see you about?'

'She was trying to track down some goldwork she said had gone missing from the dig.'

West looked at the small black notebook open in his hand. 'And you told Mrs Hills you didn't know the whereabouts of the missing artefact?'

Joyce nodded.

Sally said, 'But you told her something else as well, didn't you?'

Joyce looked from Sally to West and back again.

Sally said, 'You told her you were in one of the dig huts early one morning when Gerald Hart unexpectedly turned up on-site.'

She studied Joyce Clifford. Her face was devoid of colour, her body rigid against the chair back – as if braced against some impending disaster.

Joyce said, 'It was his site.'

West asked, 'You wouldn't happen to remember the date, would you, Mrs Clifford?'

Joyce snapped her head round to look at him. 'The date?'

Sally said, 'Oh, come on. You think you'd remember a day like that – one that was going to make you for the rest of your life.'

Joyce swung her head back to face Sally. 'I don't know what you're talking about. Like I told Mrs Hills, I was in that hut because I had nowhere to go. I needed to get away from George, while I figured out what to do.'

Sally said, 'We know that, Mrs Clifford. And I don't imagine you had any idea how lucky you were going to be when you bedded down for the night, did you?'

'Lucky! Are you mad? I was at my wits' end.'

Sally said, 'And then Gerald Hart turned up. Your knight in shining armour.'

'Pssh! None of the Harts were ever that.'

Sally looked at West. He read from his notebook, 'Saturday 30th August.'

Sally returned her attention to Joyce. 'The day your luck was in. The day you saw Gerald Hart doing something he didn't want anyone else to know about. The day you saw him burning his brother's corpse.'

The choice of the final word had been deliberate. It had the desired effect. Joyce slumped in her chair. Her shoulders heaved and she began to sob. She gulped in breath, struggling to keep herself under control. Eventually, after seconds that seemed to Sally like minutes, she regained her composure.

'How did you know?'

West said, 'Gerald kept a journal. He recorded all of the details of the pyre preparation in it.'

In Sally's opinion, it had been a lucky guess on West's part that what Joyce had told Clare about Gerald's visit to the site tied in with the date of the pyre burning.

West said, 'In your own time, Mrs Clifford. Just tell us exactly what happened that morning.'

Joyce got up and poured herself another glass of water. Standing at the sink, she drank it and poured herself a second before sitting back down. 'Like I said, I went up to the site to get away from George when he found out about me and Jim. I tried to sleep. It was perishing. But I must have dropped off eventually. Because next thing I knew, I heard a car. At first, I thought I was imagining it. But it got louder, and when I opened the door a crack to look out I could see Gerald's Volvo.'

She looked at Sally defiantly, almost as if she were daring her to contradict her. But Sally said nothing.

'Do you remember what happened next?' West asked.

Joyce turned to face him. 'It's not the sort of thing you forget. However hard you try . . .' She sat quietly, hands clasped together in her lap. Then, drawing in a deep breath, she straightened up in her chair. 'Gerald got out of the car, went over to the tool shed and got out a wheelbarrow. He pushed it over to the back of the Volvo. He had his back to me so I couldn't see what he was doing. But I could hear him huffing and puffing like he was shifting something heavy. Then he closed the boot and started wheeling the barrow up towards where all the wood was piled near the top of the ridge, above where we'd been digging.'

West asked, 'What did you do?'

'I followed him.'

Sally said, 'Wasn't that a bit foolhardy, Mrs Clifford?'

'If I'd known what he was up to I wouldn't have done it, would I.' She turned away from Sally to face West. 'I got as far as the tool shed. If I'd have gone any further, he'd have been able to see me out in the open.'

'How far away were you from Hart?' Sally asked.

'Thirty or forty yards, maybe.'

'What was he doing?' Sally asked.

'Once he'd got the barrow up to where the wood was, he tipped it out on the ground. It rolled down the slope a little way. It was wrapped up in a curtain. It was the same material as the ones from the drawing room in the manor.'

West looked at her as if unable to believe she should have concerned herself with drapery at such a moment.

Joyce turned to Sally to explain. 'I'd been up to the manor a time or two with Jim. I remembered them because I'd always thought they were such a pretty cream colour. But now there was a big rusty-coloured splodge all over the top half of them. I knew it was blood. Gerald had a terrible time trying to heave the thing onto the top of the wood. Eventually, he managed to get it over his shoulder and then sort of flopped it onto the top. It wasn't till then that I noticed he'd pitched a jerry can out of the wheelbarrow too. He tore a bit off the end of the curtain material that was flapping about. Then he doused the lot in petrol, lit the end of the material and chucked it on top. It went up with a hell of a whoosh.'

'When did you realise what he was burning?' Sally asked.

'Gerald had made a big thing of arranging a do for bank holiday Monday so everyone could watch. So what with the blood . . .' She closed her eyes as if replaying the image in her mind.

'Would you like a break, Mrs Clifford? This must be very upsetting for you.' Sally could still recall her own first encounter with violent death: a teenager, the same age as her sister's boy, Mikey. Unruly tufts of short brown hair poking out from beneath his baseball cap, she'd found him lying face down in a pool of his own blood on a concrete walkway. She had no doubt Joyce Clifford's distress was genuine.

Joyce shook her head. 'After all this time I'd rather just get it over with.' Nostrils wide, she drew in a long, deep breath. 'Once the fire took hold it didn't take long for the curtain material to burn off. Then it started to spit, and there was the smell.' For a second she raised her hand to her mouth, and then let it drop once more into her lap. 'That was when the cracking sounds started.'

West leant forward. 'Cracking sounds?'

Joyce nodded determinedly. 'That's when it happened. He looked at me.'

'Gerald looked at you?' West said.

'No. Jim did. Some of the fire collapsed and the head twisted round. It was shrivelled, black and sort of puffy, but I could see it was him. It was Jim.'

Sally felt distinctly queasy. When she'd attended her first autopsy, like two of the other first-timers she'd had to leave the room. But she had no intention of revealing her weak stomach to West. She leant back in feigned nonchalance.

She needn't have worried. He was too engrossed in what Joyce was saying to notice. 'Then what?'

'I think I must have screamed. I don't remember. Next thing I know Gerald was standing beside me down at the tool shed.'

'And that's when he offered you the money to stay quiet?' Sally said.

'At first he just kept shaking me.'

Sally asked, 'He tried to hurt you?'

Joyce shook her head. 'He just wanted to shut me up. I didn't know what I was saying. Eventually, I calmed down. He got his hip flask out and made me drink some brandy. Told me there'd been some sort of accident with Jim. I asked him why he hadn't called the police, or an ambulance or something. He said no one would have believed him.'

Sally said, 'You included?'

'I didn't know what to think. Jim had a temper on him. If they'd got into some sort of fight, anything could have happened.'

West spoke softly. 'But you didn't really believe him, did you?'

Her reply, when it eventually came, was even softer than his question. 'No, I don't suppose I did.'

'How much did he offer you?' Sally asked.

'It wasn't like that. He asked me why I was there. He knew about me and Jim. When I told him about the argument with

George, he took his wallet out of his pocket and stuffed some notes into my hand. Told me he'd help me get away and set up somewhere – see to it I was looked after. He even offered to drive me to the station.'

The amazement was evident on West's face. 'He left the body there while he drove you to the station?'

'No. He took me down to the tea hut, got a brew going and told me to stay there while he finished dealing with things.'

Sally said, 'Disposing of the body?'

'I didn't ask. He told me to stay put until he told me otherwise.'

'How long was he gone?'

'It was almost dark by the time he came back for me.'

'And you stayed in the tea hut the whole time.'

'Almost. I had to answer a call of nature.'

'But you didn't see anything more of what Hart was doing until he came back in the evening?'

'No.' She hesitated. 'But I think someone else might have.'

Sally was the first to pounce. 'Do you mean there was someone else up there?'

Joyce nodded.

'Who?'

'I don't know. A man – I think. He was moving about between the huts when I went out to have a tinkle.'

'What did you do?' Sally asked.

'Hopped it back inside the tea hut smartish. I thought it might be George.'

West leant forward in his seat. 'And was it?'

'I told you, I don't know.'

West chimed in, 'Surely you would have recognised your own husband.'

'I only got a glimpse. It could have been George.' She rubbed her forehead, staring down at the kitchen table. West went to speak, but Sally raised her hand and stopped him. Joyce looked up. 'It might have been George; it might have been someone else. I honestly don't know.'

'But it was definitely a man?' Sally asked.

'I think so – but it was so long ago. All I can tell you for sure is there was definitely someone up on-site that day besides me and Gerald.'

CHAPTER EIGHTEEN

The digging had been hard and the weather had closed in again. The wind and rain battered at the windows of the Lamb and Flag. The bar was, as it had been every night since the start of the excavations, thronging with students. A couple of weeks ago, Clare had thought life under canvas would be an adventure. Now the cosy bar felt like an oasis of comfort. Margaret had made the right choice, snugly accommodated in her room above where they were both now sitting.

But Clare was suffering from more than a case of the mid-dig blues. She felt pummelled – physically and mentally. Her hand dropped to the pocket of her jeans where she could feel the envelope pouched within. A handful of printed lines that had demolished the foundations of her new life before she'd even finished building them. It was taking all of her remaining energy to maintain the semblance of a conversation with Margaret.

Margaret said, 'I think there's something rather charming about using the original equipment – a certain nostalgic *je ne sais quoi.*'

She wrinkled her nose, unconvinced. 'You don't have to go up it.'

'If I was a few years younger, I'd offer to take the photographs myself. You get a marvellous view of the site from up there, you know. You're not of like mind?' Margaret lowered her head and peered over the top of her spectacles.

'I wouldn't mind using old kit if we were talking about wheelbarrows and spades, but that heap of junk is a different matter. I can't see why David won't just hire someone with a drone.'

'Drones cost money. And you know as well as I do that BH weren't overgenerous with the budget. If we can save some cash by using the old photo tower, we might be able to scrape enough together for some more radio-carbon dates.'

The two of them sat in companionable silence, Clare nursing her Shiraz while Margaret made inroads into her whiskey. Clare was an able and – if you caught her on one of her more immodest days, she'd admit – talented photographer, but her preference had always been to have two feet planted firmly on the ground. As a student, she'd managed to avoid going up the damn things. When she'd agreed to act as project photographer she'd presumed, erroneously as it turned out, that remote methods were always employed to take high-level shots these days. But with the old photographic tower to hand it seemed to make sense not to shell out money unnecessarily.

Margaret swirled her drink round in the bottom of her glass, then, draining its contents, set it down on the table. 'What are you planning to do?'

Unless she wanted to confirm all of David's suspicions

about her unprofessional attitude, she couldn't very well back out now. And in comparison to her other problems, it seemed laughable that she should be worried about it. 'As long as it's been properly checked out, I suppose I'll just have to get on with it and go up the thing.'

'No, I mean what are you going to do with your life? This dig won't last for ever.'

'I haven't really thought about it. I need to get Stephen's estate sorted before I can tackle anything else.'

'Hasn't that all been tied up yet?'

Clare shook her head. 'Stephen's business dealings were complicated.'

'How so?'

She didn't answer. She didn't know what to say. This wasn't a conversation she wanted to be having.

'Surely you must have some understanding of what he was doing with your money.' Margaret fixed her with a questioning look.

Clare rubbed the back of her neck. 'It was his money. He was the one with the career.'

'Forgive me, but isn't that a tad nineteenth-century? Marriage is meant to be a partnership.'

Clare struggled for a reply. Over the last few weeks she'd grown to like and respect Margaret, but she wasn't sure she was ready to talk about this with anyone. How could she explain it to someone else when she didn't understand it herself? She picked up a beer mat and began to shred small pieces of paper from its corners.

But Margaret was not to be dissuaded. 'Suddenly an abiding interest in real ale.' She reached over and plucked the beer mat from Clare's hand, placing it firmly down beneath her own glass. 'What's wrong, Clare? It will be shorter and less painful for both of us if you tell me now. I'll only keep asking until you do.'

Clare stared fixedly at the spot on the table that the beer mat had come from. 'Believe me, you don't want to know.' Margaret reached across the table and placed a hand on Clare's arm. Clare looked up into her soft brown eyes. Suddenly and quite against her will, she felt tears rolling down her cheeks. Her shoulders heaved and she let out a loud sob, attracting the attention of the students sitting at the next table. 'Oh, Margaret, it's all such a mess.'

Margaret reached into her pocket, withdrew a paper handkerchief and passed it to Clare. 'That's quite enough of that. This isn't the place.'

Clare looked at the older woman pathetically, seeking guidance. Margaret plunged her hand into her cardigan pocket once more and this time retrieved a key with a large plastic fob which she placed on the table in front of Clare. 'Go upstairs to my room, have a nice hot bath and try to regain some semblance of self-control. I'll join you in half an hour. By which time I expect to see you in a fit state to have a rational discussion.'

Clare was sitting, legs tucked beneath her, curled into an armchair and wearing Margaret's baby-blue towelling dressing gown. Margaret herself was perched on the edge of the bed facing her. Between them lay a small circular coffee table on which had been placed a box of paper tissues, a bottle of Jameson's and two glasses, each a quarter filled with the translucent umber liquid.

Margaret passed her a glass. 'Take a good slug.'

'I don't drink whiskey.'

'Nonsense.'

Lacking the energy to argue, she held the tumbler to her lips, sniffing its contents. She wrinkled her nose like a small child intent on refusing medicine. Margaret was watching her intently. She took a sip, the burning sensation descending from her mouth into her throat.

Margaret gave a satisfied nod. 'Now I want you to tell me about your current circumstances. I may stop you to ask questions. But you're not to leave anything out. Understood?'

Clare nodded.

'Right, when you're ready.'

She'd known when she'd acquiesced to Margaret's orders that this would be the outcome, and the reality of what that meant was only now beginning to sink in. But intermingled with her embarrassment at being forced to reveal the full awfulness of what had become clear to her over the last few months was relief at finally being able to tell someone. She sat quietly for a few moments trying to figure out how to put it into words.

'You know I lost my husband last year.'

Margaret leant forward from her perch on the edge of the bed and nodded.

'He was killed in a car crash. An accident. At least I thought . . .' Clare looked across at Margaret. 'I'm sorry, I'm not making much sense.'

The older woman's tone was firm but reassuring. 'Just tell me what you know. So far you haven't said anything beyond my comprehension.'

'No, of course not. I didn't mean . . .'

Margaret waved her apology aside. 'Go on!'

Clare raised her glass to her lips and took a second larger gulp of whiskey. She spluttered as it caught in her throat. Taking a tissue from the box in front of her, she dabbed at her mouth. 'No one else was hurt in the accident. What I mean is, Stephen was alone in his car and there was no other vehicle involved.'

'That at least was a blessing.'

She could feel herself in danger of bursting into tears again. She blew her nose on the tissue and took a deep breath. 'That was what I kept telling myself. I suppose at first I found it comforting that no one else was going through what I was.'

'And now you don't.'

She shook her head. 'Don't get me wrong. I wouldn't have wanted anyone else to have been hurt. But when the police investigated the crash scene they said they couldn't find any reason why Stephen's car had left the road.'

Margaret held her glass up in front of her, angling it slightly in Clare's direction. 'I presume they considered this?'

Clare nodded. 'Stephen was absolutely fastidious. He wouldn't touch a drop when he was driving. And the post-mortem showed he hadn't been drinking. He was on a straight piece of road. As far as the police could see . . .' She faltered again, but taking in a large gulp of air managed to suppress the urge to cry, '. . . there was nothing wrong with the car.'

She'd turned it over and over in her mind and she always came to the same conclusion. She was exhausted. She just couldn't go it alone any more.

Margaret said, 'There was something else.'

Clare nodded. 'The tyre tracks showed he'd been accelerating when he left the road. He just ploughed off the road through the hedge and into a tree.'

The two women sat without speaking for what seemed to Clare like several minutes.

Margaret was the first to break the silence. 'Did you have a happy marriage?'

'As good as most. Happier than some. At least I used to think so. But now' – she shrugged her shoulders – 'I can't help wondering.'

'If it was your fault he's dead?'

She nodded, staring down into the bottom of her glass.

'Look at me!'

She snapped her head up and found herself looking directly into Margaret's eyes.

'Don't you ever think that! We make our own choices in life.' The words were spoken with total conviction. 'Stephen was no exception, whatever happened that day.' Margaret replenished her glass. 'How long have you known all this? About the crash site evidence, I mean.'

'Since about a month after the crash.'

'So why are you so upset now? What's changed?'

Clare got up and made her way to a crumpled pile of clothes on the other side of the room and extricated a grubby white envelope from the pocket of her jeans. She handed it to Margaret.

Margaret took out a sheet of headed paper from the envelope and began to read. When she'd finished, she placed it back in the envelope and set it down on the table in front of Clare. 'That rather changes things, doesn't it?'

'The first few months were difficult. But once I got over the shock, I got to thinking there could have been any number of rational explanations. Maybe a bird spooked him. Maybe his foot slipped and he got it jammed on the accelerator. Maybe he fell asleep at the wheel. I suppose I began to accept I'd never know what really happened and I just had to get on with my life.'

'And now this.' Margaret gestured towards the letter and Clare nodded, sniffing into her tissue.

'Now it all makes sense. Why he'd want to kill himself.'

Clare nodded. 'There's no doubt. Stephen didn't have a penny when he died.'

'So what happened?'

'He specialised in property law. He had a lot of contacts in the property business, here and in the States; developers, agents, brokers. When the market took off a few years ago it seems he poured money into some financing scheme in the US.' Light dawned in Margaret's expression. 'I can't believe he was so stupid.'

'It must have seemed a seductive proposition if everyone around him was making easy money.'

'But to risk everything.' She shook her head in incomprehension. 'When things started going badly, he remortgaged the house.'

'You didn't know?'

Clare shook her head. 'The house was in his name. He'd even cashed in his life assurance policy. I thought we talked about everything. But he never even mentioned it. It's not just the money, Margaret. I could cope with that. I feel as if I never really knew him.'

Margaret put down her glass. 'I won't pretend I know how you're feeling. But I do know that wallowing in self-pity never helped anyone. You need to start thinking about practicalities. Have you got any funds of your own?'

She shook her head. 'There'll barely be enough left to clear my credit cards.'

'Have you got any assets?'

'My car, and I've got a small photographic gallery in Richmond. Stephen bought it for me as a present on our tenth anniversary, but it was always more of a hobby than a viable business. I couldn't bring myself to go back after he died – so I closed it.'

'Well, you're going to have to go back now. Commercial premises in Richmond must be worth something. You need to get yourself up there, find out how much it's worth and put it on the market. You can't sit in the middle of a Wiltshire field for ever. When I asked you what you were going to do, it was your intellectual life I was thinking about, not your finances. But you've got to sort out the money side of things before you can start thinking about the really big question.'

She looked at Margaret, nonplussed.

'What are you going to make of your life?'

Clare gritted her teeth and closed her eyes. She shook her head. 'I can't deal with this. Not now.'

'I know this is difficult, but you've got to start taking charge of your life.'

And the truth was the idea of running her own life terrified her. She'd never had to make a decision for herself. Her mum had been determined she would do everything in her power to give her daughter the opportunities she'd never had. She'd single-handedly taken command of Clare's life until the day she'd left for university.

She'd spent her first year in halls, lost, miserable and a little frightened until she'd met David. David seemed to take her on as his personal project. He encouraged and nurtured her talent, introduced her to all of his friends, and most importantly taught her how to navigate her way through university life. Then in her second year, at the May Ball, she'd met Stephen. Confident and self-assured, he seemed to have everything worked out. He knew exactly what he wanted and that most definitely included Clare. Her life's course seemed to be laid out before her.

Margaret's appraising look softened gradually into a smile. 'Why did you get involved with this project?'

'It just sort of happened.'

'Nothing just happens. There must have been a reason why you came back to Wiltshire. Why did you come back to the department? It's not the first thing most people would think of doing when they lose someone close – going back to their old university.'

She wasn't sure what Margaret was driving at, but she felt

distinctly uneasy about the direction the conversation was taking. She got up and walked over to the window. The rain clouds had been driven away by the whipping wind. And the moon outside was high and almost full, a single sliver of darkness shadowing its face. In the distance, towards the top of the ridge, she could just make out the white gash of the newly opened trench. As she turned away from the glass to face Margaret, she caught a movement out of the corner of her eye.

'There's somebody up there.'

'Where?' For a moment, Margaret looked worried. She rose to take a look for herself. 'I can't see anything. Probably just a trick of the light. Stop avoiding the subject!' Margaret sat back down on the edge of the bed. 'Why did you come back here?'

'I needed something to concentrate on; something to stop me thinking about Stephen.' Then, barely audibly, she added, 'I wanted to do something for myself.' She paused. 'I suppose I wanted to know, if things had worked out differently, if I could have made a go of it as an archaeologist.'

Margaret puffed out her cheeks and raised both hands in the air in a gesture of exasperation. 'Your inability to see what is in front of you is quite staggering. You *are* an archaeologist. Archaeology isn't about academic preferment or job titles. You either have it in you or you don't. You can teach the skills and cram people full of academic papers, but deep down, when you put it all together, there's something that boils down to instinct. God knows there were a lot of things I disagreed with Gerald about, but he always used to say, "Archaeology . . ."'

'". . . gets in your blood."' Clare smiled.

Margaret looked surprised.

'You mentioned it the first time we met.'

'Well, it was the one thing he was right about. You really

impressed me, you know, when you came to see me up in Oxford.'

Clare felt her cheeks flush. 'Really?'

'You were determined to find the missing sun disc, come hell or high water.'

'And look where that's got me. So far I've managed to implicate Gerald in his own brother's murder and Peter's hardly speaking to me.'

'You can't spend your whole life worrying about what other people think. If there's one thing I've learnt over the years it's that sometimes you just have to do what you feel is right.'

CHAPTER NINETEEN

Clare and David were standing alone by the tea hut, a bucket of soapy but rapidly cooling water at their feet. They were both bedecked in blue rubber gloves and clutching scrubbing brushes. On every other morning, the hut in front of them had resembled nothing so much as the cheap garden shed which in truth it was. But this morning it had been transformed by the application of a broad band of sunflower-yellow paint daubed across its wooden slats in letters a foot high.

THE WOE WATERS WILL NOT BE DENIED.

David stood back, arms crossed, surveying the scene. 'Pithy.'

Clare pushed the sleeves of her fleece up above her elbows, dipped her scrubbing brush into the bucket of suds and began to apply elbow grease to the task in hand. 'Can't you take anything seriously?'

David inclined his head in the direction of the trenches where the student workforce was beavering away with picks and trowels. 'If you had to read some of the garbage this lot churn out, you'd appreciate a nice concise turn of phrase.'

Clare shook her head. 'Doesn't it worry you that there's some weirdo creeping around here at night leaving us messages?'

'Don't be melodramatic. It's just kids.'

'It may have escaped your attention, but this neck of the woods isn't exactly stuffed with tower blocks and burnt-out cars.'

'Haven't you heard of the rural poor?'

'I haven't seen anything like this anywhere else in the village. Have you?'

David sniffed. 'Louts from Swindon on a joyride.'

She pointed her dripping brush at the water-streaked lettering and shook her head. 'It's the Woe Waters again. Just like the fire, and that letter I found in Gerald's site diary. There's obviously some sort of connection.'

'You said yourself Gerald thought that letter came from a local loony.'

'And that's exactly what worries me.'

'You know as well as I do there are more nutters per square foot hanging around archaeological sites than in any psychiatric ward. They're all full of piss and wind.'

It was obvious he wasn't going to change his mind. So there was no point pushing it.

She offered the bucket of soapy water up to him. 'I'm thinking of getting rid of the Mazda.'

Great dollops of yellow-tinged foam ran down his gloves and onto his bare arms as he turned to face her. His expression betrayed his horror. 'You can't. You love that car. And you're the only friend I've got with a car that's got any street cred.'

Clare laughed. 'I thought you'd be long past worrying about street cred by now. Besides, the Mazda isn't exactly practical for life in the sticks.'

'S'pose not.' David's expression had more in common with a sullen schoolboy than a respected academic. He dipped his scrubbing brush into the bucket of suds and added, almost casually, 'Does that mean you're intending to stick around?'

'I need the money.'

She held her breath, bracing herself for his reaction.

'Come off it. You're loaded. That bloody great house you two bought must be worth a mint.'

It had been difficult enough discussing it with Margaret, but David had never had any time for Stephen. And now she was beginning to understand why. She'd come back to Wiltshire to try to escape Stephen's ghost. But everywhere she turned there was something or someone reminding her of him. The last thing she wanted to do was stand over a bucket of lukewarm grime listening to David tell her how right he'd been about her choice of husband.

She slung her brush into the bucket, dousing David in filthy suds in the process. 'What the fuck would you know about it? You've never had a day's worry about money in your life.'

She regretted her uncharacteristic outburst as soon as it was over. David looked as if she'd slapped him in the face.

Without warning, Ed appeared from behind the site hut. Instinctively, Clare and David took a step apart. Clare could only marvel at the way in which David transformed his stunned expression into a model of calm professionalism. She, on the other hand, was only too aware of the tingling sensation in her cheeks that signalled her inability to disguise her embarrassment.

* * *

'Jo?' David pressed his mobile to his ear. From the Portakabin window he could see Clare pouring a bucket of murky water onto the grass. He hadn't wanted to give her anything else to worry about, but he couldn't let things go on like this.

'Hi, David. Found some Bronze Age bones for me to look at?'

'No. I'm after a favour.'

'Shoot.'

'I want you to look up a newspaper article from the time of Gerald's dig.'

'Let me get a pen.' He could hear a rustle of papers at the other end of the phone. 'OK.'

'From what I remember of the typeface, it'll be in *The Times* or maybe *The Telegraph*. You're looking for a headline that has the phrase "Woe Waters" in it.' He paused. 'And, Jo, I'd be grateful if you didn't mention any of this to Clare; she's got more than enough on her plate to worry about at the moment.'

'Sure. What's this about, David?'

'I don't know yet. But I intend to find out.'

From the first time she'd picked up a camera, Clare had found photography therapeutic. She'd been captivated by the almost alchemical transformation of a blank sheet of paper into a frozen moment in time. And though the detail of the process had changed with the advent of digital techniques, it still remained a magical business.

But now, as she stood at the bottom of the dull grey skeleton of the photographic tower, some of the magic was wearing decidedly thin. She checked the contents of her kit: camera bodies, lenses, filters, spare batteries – all in their proper place. She had no intention of climbing the thing more frequently than was absolutely necessary.

A few yards away, David was supervising a group of students who were clearing away the last few buckets and hand shovels from the muddied white surface of the rain-smeared trench she was about to photograph.

He pointed at her equipment bag. 'Do you want me to hand that up to you when you're at the top?'

She shook her head. 'I'll carry it over my shoulder. That way I don't run the risk of dropping it.'

And, more importantly, she didn't want anyone else up there making the tower wobble around. Closing the zip, she passed the strap over her head and positioned the bag snugly against her hip. She gripped the sides of the galvanised struts, the cold metal damp against her skin. Her palms prickled with perspiration. This was ridiculous. If she didn't start now, she'd lose her nerve.

She knew she'd be sunk if she looked down before she reached the top. Once she was up there she'd be fine. There was a solid wooden platform and a metal rail running right the way round the edge. She wouldn't let herself look down at David and the rest of the team assembled around the edge of the trench, but she was all too aware that they were watching her. Why didn't he tell them to go off and do something useful?

She began slowly, hoping it would be easier once she got going. But it wasn't. She felt just as nervous in the final two or three metres as she had at the bottom. Finally, she pushed her head above the last length of metal laddering and squeezed through the small purpose-made gap in the wooden platform. Steadying herself on the wooden boards, she took a deep breath. She couldn't say she was enjoying it, but she did feel a small glow of satisfaction. She'd made it. And providing she concentrated on the job in hand, everything would be OK.

Looking out across the site, she could see David standing in the middle of the trench holding a two-metre-long red-and-white-striped ranging rod.

He waved and shouted up at her, 'Where do you want me to put this?'

'Don't tempt me!' Even from up here she could hear stifled giggles from the students huddled together on the grass. 'Just to the left of where you are now. Pointed end up a bit. Perfect.'

David retreated to the edge of the trench. She unzipped her equipment bag and took out the camera. Removing the lens cap, she slid it into her pocket, then set about checking the camera settings. When she was satisfied, she hooked the strap round her neck and brought the camera up in front of her face to compose the shot. She widened her stance, craning her neck forward slightly as she peered through the viewfinder.

Lowering the camera, she called down to David, 'You're all in shot. Move everyone back behind the spoil heap.' She threw her hand out to her right, indicating where she wanted them to stand, and caught a gust of wind which momentarily unbalanced her. She grabbed the metal rail, thankful for its steadying presence.

'Are you alright?' It was Ed's voice from somewhere beneath the tower.

'Fine. Just not used to the pitch and the swell.'

She hoped he couldn't detect the false jollity in her voice. She did feel sick – sick to the pit of her stomach. But she was damned if she was going to throw in the towel now she'd got this far. She drew in a deep breath and brought the camera up in front of her face once more. If she could just get a slightly wider field of view, it would be perfect. She took half a step back.

It was then she felt it give. She had just enough time to process the fact that the wooden plank onto which she'd transferred her weight was sagging when she heard a cracking sound. As the plank gave way beneath her, she threw out both arms, instinctively seeking something solid. A tremendous jarring pain shot through her upper body as the muscles and ligaments in her shoulders strained against the force of gravity. The weight of the camera dangling beneath her dragged her neck forward, and there was a warm trickling sensation running down the inside of her thigh. *Oh Christ, this is no time to pee yourself.* It didn't occur to her that it might be blood.

CHAPTER TWENTY

George Clifford's house was a neatly kempt affair. A small area of regularly trimmed lawn at the front of the ex-council house was surrounded on two sides by regimental rows of French marigolds and begonias. Sally Treen couldn't tell a begonia from a hole in the ground, but she could see they'd suffered a beating with the rain and gales of the last few weeks. She allowed herself a satisfied smile when West fell dutifully in behind as she strode up the alternate pink and grey slabs of the garden path.

Her contentment was short lived. She rang the bell and glanced round and realised that his compliance was due only to his admiration for the ex-US-army jeep that took pride of place on Clifford's drive.

When Sally had asked around, the residents of Hungerbourne had been remarkably forthcoming. To a man and woman, it seemed they all detested him.

The uPVC door was opened by a small, grey-haired woman in her early sixties wearing the sort of housecoat that Sally's grandmother had favoured. Sally made her introductions and the woman scuttled away to a room somewhere at the rear of the house.

West leant over Sally's shoulder. 'Bit of a change from the first one.'

'Once bitten . . .'

The present Mrs Clifford returned with the news that her husband would see them in the living room. If it hadn't been for the lingering smell of fresh paint, Sally would have guessed the decor of the room into which they were led had last been updated in the eighties. George Clifford was enthroned in a necessarily voluminous armchair of which he filled almost every inch. His gaze was fixed firmly on a similarly ample wide-screen television perched on a Queen-Anne-style cabinet in the opposite corner of the room. He didn't speak when they entered, raising the remote to silence the sound on the television only when Sally and West disturbed his line of sight in order to seat themselves on the sofa opposite the fireplace.

His first words were addressed to his wife, who, apparently unsure of the social niceties relating to visits from the constabulary, had lingered by the door. Clifford flicked his head dismissively towards her and grunted, 'Close that on your way out.'

She complied without comment, any hint of defiance long since bridled. Sally had seen too many marriages like this one to waste time dwelling on the unfairness of it all. The mask she presented to Clifford betrayed only professional solicitousness. 'Thank you for contacting us, Mr Clifford.'

'Didn't have much choice given what's 'appened, did I?' He spoke with a gentle Wiltshire drawl that was at odds with the sentiment of his words.

'You said you had something you wanted to share with us that related to Jim Hart's death – something about the dig that took place here in the seventies.'

'It was a long time ago.'

It was all Sally could do to stop herself from screaming. She hoped Clifford wasn't going to turn out to be another attention-seeking time-waster. This investigation was turning out to be enough of a pain in the arse as it was. 'But you do remember it.'

'Course I do, woman. I'm not simple.'

Sally thought she caught the hint of a smirk on West's lips. She added it to a growing mental list of his misdemeanours and nodded at Clifford in recognition of the accuracy of his observation. 'Then you remember Jim Hart.'

He snorted. 'Not been allowed to forget him.'

Sally leant forward. 'Why's that, Mr Clifford?'

'All over the local papers.' He looked Sally straight in the eye. 'But you'll know that already.'

West said, 'The present Mrs Clifford isn't your first wife, is she?' Clifford made no reply. 'Do you see anything of your first wife, Mr Clifford?'

He tapped his nose with his forefinger, 'None of your beeswax.' He focused his attention on Sally. 'Just cos I phoned you don't mean you can come round here and start poking your nose in things what don't concern you.'

Sally said, 'I thought you wanted to help us with our enquiries into Jim Hart's death.'

'Still don't give you the right—'

Sally raised a hand to stem the flow of his indignation. 'The most helpful thing you can do right now, Mr Clifford, is answer Sergeant West's question. Trust us. It is relevant. Do you see anything of your first wife?'

'Why the bloody hell would I want to be doing that?'

Sally said, 'Why did your first wife leave you, Mr Clifford?'

'She didn't. I threw her out.'

'And that happened at the time of the first dig.'

'Dig! Bloody brothel, more like. They had all the young tarts in the village up there with 'em.'

West scribbled in his notebook.

'They?' Sally tilted her head towards Clifford expectantly.

'The Harts.'

'Surely Gerald Hart was a respectable academic.'

'Just because you've got money and work for some knobby museum don't make you respectable. Him and that brother of his were as bad as one another. Sniffing round any bit of skirt that came near 'em.'

This was better than she'd hoped. Had they finally unearthed another side to the older Hart brother? A motive for someone wanting to kill him? Or was it just sour grapes on Clifford's part?

West glanced down at his jottings. 'Who did you have in mind when you spoke of "young tarts", Mr Clifford?'

'The Grafton girl for one – decent parents, good home. Pretty young thing, she was. Wouldn't say boo to a goose till Gerald got his claws into her. Parents had her all lined up for a job in the bank in Marlborough. But once he got hold of her she didn't want nothing to do with it. Thought she were too good to stay round 'ere with the likes of us. Gerald was keen on her, alright. They were always up there alone on that dig of his getting up to God knows what. But one Hart wasn't enough for her. She had the pair of 'em dancing to her tune.' West raised an eyebrow. 'Word was Jim fancied his luck with Peggy, but Gerald put a stop to it.'

West said, 'But Jim had better luck with your wife.'

Clifford narrowed his eyes, but said nothing.

Sally said, 'How did you find out about Jim Hart and your wife, Mr Clifford?'

Clifford snapped his head round to face Sally. 'That's none of your business neither!'

She straightened up in her seat and looked Clifford straight in the eye. 'One of the people we're talking about was murdered, Mr Clifford. So it's very much our business.'

Clifford snorted and levered his considerable bulk into a more comfortable position. 'I knew she were up to something – spending all that time up there.'

West said, 'Your wife hadn't previously shown an interest in archaeology, then.'

Sally could see he hadn't taken to Clifford.

Clifford said, 'No more than Jim Hart had – did it to keep in with his brother. Make sure he stayed close to the money.'

West asked, 'And why did your wife do it, Mr Clifford?'

'Because she was a tart!' The final word was spat out with all the venom Clifford could muster; Sally suspected it was more the result of a long-festering wound to his pride than the memory of true love betrayed.

'How did you find out about the affair?' Sally asked.

'He told me.'

'Jim Hart told you he was having a fling with your wife?'

Clifford nodded brusquely. 'I slung him out of the pub one night when he was slewed.'

Sally cast a questioning look in West's direction.

'Drunk, ma'am.'

Clifford continued, 'He was shouting the odds and didn't have the money to pay his bill. I told him he'd had enough and he wasn't getting any more till he could pay for it. When I chucked him out, he turned round and told me I ought to 'ave a word with my wife cos she gave him whatever he fancied for free.'

'And what did you do?' Sally asked.

'Told him to bugger off and not bother coming back.'

'And that was all? Weren't you even a tiny bit angry?' she asked.

'Of course I was bloody angry. But I wasn't going to fetch him a clout and lose my licence.'

'What about Joyce?' Sally asked.

'I told her to pack her bags and get out.'

'That's not how she tells it.'

Clifford looked shocked. He clearly hadn't expected them to have spoken to Joyce. He grunted. 'Can't believe a word she says.'

'Joyce was under the impression that when you parted company you might seek to do her some sort of harm.'

'I can't account for what she might've thought.'

'Did you go after her when she left?'

'Why would I do that when I'd slung her out?'

West said, 'You were angry. What man wouldn't have wanted to make Jim and Joyce pay for publicly humiliating you?'

Clifford was silent.

West persisted. 'You followed her up to the dig site.'

'No.' Clifford's voice was calm and steady.

'Do you deny going up there on the morning after you found out about the affair?' Sally asked.

'Of course I bloody do. Jim Hart was welcome to the little trollop. I wouldn't 'ave had her back under my roof if you'd paid me.'

'And you're absolutely sure you didn't go anywhere near the excavations that morning?'

'The nearest I got was the lane that runs up past the bottom of Old Barrows Field, when I was walking the dog.'

More in desperation than expectation, Sally asked, 'Did you see anyone else when you were there?'

'No.'

She'd been hoping he might have caught a glimpse of Gerald Hart. But his response was firm, his tone matter-of-fact and, unfortunately, all too believable. West closed his notebook and stowed his pen in his jacket pocket. She'd been right all along. Their trip to North Yorkshire had been a complete waste of time.

Then Clifford leant forward in his chair, wheezing as he did so. The corners of his mouth were turned up in the suggestion of a smile. 'Come to think of it, I did see someone.'

It was obvious to Sally that Clifford was enjoying jerking their chain. And, despite herself, she couldn't help some of her frustration seeping into her tone. 'And who was that exactly, Mr Clifford?'

He paused, then said, 'Young Ed Jevons.'

Sally glanced at West. She hoped Clifford couldn't read the surprise on his face as easily as she could. She needn't have worried. Clifford was too caught up in his denouncement of the residents of Hungerbourne to notice. 'Ed had been sniffing round the Harts for years. Gerald's little lapdog. He's the same with the son.'

'Where was Ed Jevons when you saw him?' Sally asked.

'On the lane leading up to the site. I remember cos he was running hell for leather – nearly knocked me clean over. There was smoke coming from the top of the field. It looked like someone had lit Gerald's bonfire up on the ridge and the clip he was going it crossed my mind he might 'ave had a hand in it. I tried to catch hold of him to ask him what he'd been up to but he just belted past me back towards the village.'

'Did you mention this to anyone else at the time?'

Clifford shook his head and smirked. 'No skin off my nose if some youngster having a bit of fun pissed on high-and-mighty Gerald Hart's plans.'

Sally could see he wasn't going to make this easy for them. 'What plans were they?'

'The bonfire was meant to be part of some big shindig Gerald had got up on the Monday. Bloody waste of good timber if you ask me. Never 'appened in the end.'

'Did you ever ask Gerald why?'

He shook his head. 'No need. It was as plain as the nose on my face. Soon as Jim hopped it with Joyce, Gerald shut up shop.'

'Only Jim didn't leave with your wife, did he, Mr Clifford?'

'I didn't know that then, did I.'

CHAPTER TWENTY-ONE

'Clare! Are you OK?' David bellowed from behind the spoil heap.

'What do you fucking think?'

He fumbled frantically through the jumble of clothes and equipment deposited behind the spoil heap. He ripped open the inside pocket of his jacket so forcefully he almost jammed the zip. *Breathe, make yourself breathe. She'll be alright.* He dialled 999. It seemed to take an age of disparate and unnecessary questions before they finally told him emergency services were on their way.

'I'm coming up.' It was Ed, somewhere directly below her. The tower was swaying from side to side with the motion of his movement.

'Jesus, Ed! I don't know what I'm hanging by.' Her world suddenly lurched to the left. And somewhere below something large hit the chalk with a metallic thud. 'Shit! What are you doing?'

'Take it easy. You look pretty well wedged in. I'm going to climb past underneath you to take a look.'

David could see what Ed was trying to do, but he could also see the danger of it. All four legs of the tower were lashed down, but the ropes were only intended to brace it against the wind. Ed was going to have to swing round the outside of the tower to get past Clare. And that meant he could bring the whole thing crashing down.

'Hold up, Ed!' David sprinted to the base of the photographic tower, hauling five of his burliest male students with him.

'You three get round the other side and hang on to that bottom rail. We'll do the same here. Any of you let go and you can forget any chance of passing your finals. Got it?' He craned his neck backwards to see Ed positioned just to one side of Clare's dangling legs.

Ed's words drifted up to Clare. 'Looks like you've got a few cuts and bruises, but you don't seem to be in too bad a shape, all things considered.'

'What was the thud?'

She was aware her breathing was shallow. But she couldn't be sure whether her difficulties were physical or whether it was the result of the rising panic that threatened to overwhelm her.

'Top length of laddering hitting the deck. You must have dislodged it when the boarding broke. I'm going to have to climb round the outside of the tower to get to you.'

'I don't care how you do it. Just get on with it. I'm not sure how long I can hold on like this.'

Ed squeezed his torso out through the steel cross-braces.

Hooking one arm over what remained of the wooden planking, he levered himself far enough up to reach out and grab the safety rail above his head. Once his grip was secure, he pushed off with his left foot against the crossing point of the metal brace below and hauled himself, stomach first, onto what remained of the wooden staging. He pivoted his legs round onto the wooden boards and Clare found herself face-to-face with him.

'How are you holding up?'

'With great bloody difficulty. My left shoulder's beginning to cramp.'

'We'll soon have you out.'

Ed slithered across the wooden staging, arching his body upwards to avoid putting weight on the splintered plank which was pointing downwards at an angle and had come to rest on Clare's chest. He shuffled into a kneeling position in front of her. Leaning forward, he looked down through the hole from above.

'We'll have to get rid of the camera and the equipment bag.'

'Can you lift them off?'

'The camera strap's snagged around part of the splintered plank and the bag's wedged beneath the plank on this side.' He patted the plank across the top of which Clare's right forearm was braced. His hand cupped to his mouth, he shouted down to the ground below. 'David, move everyone away from the bottom of the tower.'

David's reply was muffled by the wind. 'Don't try anything daft, Ed. The emergency services are on their way.'

A cold stab of fear shot through Clare when she heard Ed's reply. 'Can't wait.'

For several seconds, nothing seemed to be happening. Then David's voice drifted upwards, barely audible this time. 'All clear down here.'

Ed shuffled forward on his knees and leant over her. She could feel the heat of his body next to her face, suddenly aware she could smell perspiration; the scent of her fear and his exertion.

'It'll all be over in a moment.' He dropped his right hand to his side and with his left gathered up both halves of the camera strap. Suddenly and without warning he withdrew a knife from the leather sheath on his belt, slashing downwards with one hand whilst pulling the strap taut around her neck with the other.

She felt a ringing shudder vibrate through the tower as the camera smashed into the metal framework on its earthward journey. 'What the fuck are you playing at?'

'We needed to get rid of it to get you out of there.'

She opened her mouth, then shut it again. She was in no position to argue. She stretched her aching neck muscles as far backwards and forwards as her stiffened shoulders would allow, enjoying the relief from the additional weight.

Ed leant forward again. He inserted the knife blade beneath the strap on her right shoulder, drawing the blade away from her neck in a sawing motion. With no way of tensioning the material, it took longer this time. The back edge of the knife chafed against the skin beneath her T-shirt. Then all at once the upper half of her body felt lighter. This time there was only a muffled thud as the padded equipment bag hit the ground.

'What now?' she asked.

'I'm going to remove the two parts of the splintered plank in front of and behind you.'

It wasn't a plan that appealed to her. Once the plank was gone she'd be able to see what was underneath her – precisely nothing. But she didn't have a choice. 'Can you start with the one behind me?'

Obligingly, Ed manoeuvred around her. Sliding the small portion of broken plank behind her outwards, he pushed it gradually over the edge of the tower until it finally reached tipping point and joined the camera and equipment bag below. Resuming his position in front of her, he gripped the remaining section of plank in both hands, pulling it gently away from her chest. He gave a heave and she heard the sound of splintering wood. Heard but not saw. Her eyes were clamped tightly shut.

She strained every muscle in her upper body in an attempt to lever herself upwards. But it was useless. She smiled grimly at Ed, the muscles in her face contorting now with the effort of merely sustaining her precarious position. 'I should've kept up those gym subs.'

The sound of a mobile phone ringing below was followed by David's voice. 'That was the fire service. They'll be here any minute with one of those cherry-picker jobs.'

Was she imagining it or did his voice sound strained, unconvinced by the message he was conveying? She had a sudden urge to yell down to reassure him. To tell him everything would be alright. But every muscle in her shoulders and arms was screaming at her to give up the effort.

She looked into Ed's face. 'I can't wait.'

He nodded. 'This may hurt.'

Her teeth were gritted with effort. Ed stood up and spread his legs to distribute his weight across what remained of the platform. Knees bent, he dipped down in front of her.

'I'm going to pull you up. Ready?'

She blinked her assent. The whole of her body was cold with sweat. A freezing spasm of cramp shot through her upper arms. What the hell was he waiting for?

She screamed, 'Do it!'

She felt Ed's muscles tense as he inserted his arms beneath her armpits and heaved. For just a moment she thought she felt him release his grip. With every scrap of strength she had left, she swung her weight onto her left side. A burning sensation in her shoulder, as if someone had inserted a red-hot knitting needle, was followed almost instantaneously by the reassuring feel of solid wood beneath her. And for the second time in twenty-four hours she found herself blubbing uncontrollably.

From somewhere, Ed produced a pressed cotton handkerchief. After all he'd just done, he seemed suddenly awkward and uncertain.

'No need for that. It's just shock.'

'I don't mean to sound heroic or anything, but it's not shock. It's my shoulder. It's bloody killing me.' And suddenly she began to laugh.

CHAPTER TWENTY-TWO

'Any news from the hospital?' Ed set a pint of 6X down in front of David.

'Margaret phoned to say they were keeping Clare in overnight. But aside from a dislocated shoulder and a nasty gash on her leg, it looks like she got away with a few bumps and the odd splinter. With a bit of luck, she should be up and about in a few days.'

Ed's face twitched into a smile. 'Do you think the insurance will pay out on the camera?'

'I doubt it. But under the circumstances, the least I can do is make sure Clare isn't out of pocket.'

'Won't be cheap. It looked like expensive kit.'

David picked up his pint and stared down into the bottom of the clear, dark liquid. 'I still don't understand how it happened. I checked the whole thing over myself. There was nothing wrong with it.'

'The hours you've been working, I'm surprised you can still see straight. And you've got to admit that tower wasn't exactly in the first flush of youth. Anyone in your position might have missed a weak bit of timber.'

David looked up at Ed. He wanted to punch him square on the jaw for even suggesting he might have been responsible for what had happened to Clare. But, if truth be told, Ed was only voicing what he'd been thinking himself.

'When everyone else is down here having a jar in the evenings, you're tucked up in the Portakabin with your plans and record sheets. You need to cut yourself some slack.'

It was true. He had been working long hours. Maybe it was a sign that he was getting older – he wasn't able to keep on top of things like he used to. The thought that his actions had come so close to causing anyone's death was appalling. But knowing that someone was Clare? It was almost unbearable.

'I'm the site director, Ed. I'm responsible for this lot.' He swept his arm around the student-crammed bar. 'That means there is no slack. First thing tomorrow I'm going to check over what's left of those boards.'

Ed took a long, slow sip of his gin and tonic. 'You'd be better off sticking the bloody lot on the campfire and forgetting about it. You don't want to risk the health-and-safety Gestapo sniffing round and closing the place down.'

David spluttered, almost choking on his pint. He slapped his glass down on the table in front of him. 'Jesus Christ, Ed! We can't afford to do anything that will compromise us with the HSE.'

Ed leant forward and whispered, 'But that's why you should get rid of it. I had them snooping round my place a while back when we had a bit of an upset with a baler. They made my life a bloody misery.'

David glanced around him, uncomfortably aware that the rest of the room had fallen silent. Tony stood behind the bar, arms crossed, giving them a reproving stare. Ed sat quietly, sipping his gin and tonic.

David lowered his voice. 'I know you mean well, Ed. But we can't just go round destroying evidence.'

'Your choice, old boy. But I know what I'd do if I were in your shoes.' Ed stood up. 'Want another?'

David's head was throbbing. He wasn't in the mood for a jovial pint. He shook his head. 'No thanks. I'm shattered. I think I'll call it a night. I'd have thought you'd be knackered too after your heroics today.'

'I suspect I've had more practice at heaving heifers about than you have.'

David stood up to leave and, despite himself, had to struggle to suppress a laugh. 'I wouldn't let Clare catch you making that comparison if I were you.'

Jo attached the JPEG of the newspaper article to the email, pasted David's email into the address line and hit send. He'd been right; she'd found it in *The Times*. She picked up the photocopy of the original from her desk.

ANCIENT CURSE THREATENS DIG

An ancient legend has returned to haunt the spectacular dig site at Hungerbourne, Wiltshire. Sources close to the excavation have revealed that a mysterious curse has struck, leaving the future of the excavation hanging in the balance.

The discovery of a priceless gold and amber artefact known to archaeologists as a sun disc sparked the most important dig for a generation. Experts say the find is more than three thousand years old.

But villagers believe the discovery of the gold at the very moment when an intermittent stream, known locally as the Woe Waters, was rising is the cause of an astonishing run of bad luck that has befallen the endeavour. Before the project even began, one of the dig huts was burnt to the ground. And now the dig director has had the tyres on his car slashed and a brick thrown through a window of his nearby manor house.

Excavator Dr Gerald Hart of the British Museum has dismissed the curse as 'superstitious nonsense'. The dig continues . . .

Reading it again didn't make her feel any better. She'd done some dumb things in her time, but this was beginning to look like one of the dumbest. David had asked her not to tell Clare and she'd agreed. At the time it had seemed like the right thing to do. Clare had enough to deal with. But she was beginning to wonder whether she'd made the right decision.

Clare struggled to lever herself into a sitting position, her dislocated shoulder twinging painfully in its sling. Beneath her, she was uncomfortably aware of ruched plastic sheets beneath starched cotton. She turned to face Margaret, who was sitting on a vinyl-covered armchair beside the hospital bed.

'If you don't do as the doctor told you and lie flat you'll be in here for a good deal longer than one night.'

'I don't have time for this, Margaret. I need to get out of here.'

Throwing back the sheet that covered her with her good arm, Clare swung round until her legs dangled over the cold metal bed frame. She shivered as she felt the rush of cold air on her back where her gown gaped open.

'Will you pass me my clothes? They're in a plastic bag in there.' She pointed her good arm in the direction of the standard-issue cabinet beside the bed.

'Certainly not.'

'Fine. I'll get them myself.'

She tried to disguise a grimace as she stood up and attempted to move towards the cabinet. With surprising agility for a woman of her years, Margaret sprang to her feet, interposing herself between Clare and the cabinet.

'Oh, for heaven's sake!' Margaret reached inside and retrieved a clear plastic bag containing Clare's clothes. 'You'll do yourself a mischief carrying on like this.'

She thrust the bag at Clare, who flopped back onto the edge of the bed.

'Would you pull the curtains round, please?'

Margaret complied, then sat down again and pointed to Clare's sling. 'How exactly do you intend to dress yourself with that?'

Clare had no intention of asking for help, but without it she was going nowhere. Perched on the edge of the bed, bare feet dangling above the vinyl floor and plastic bag clutched defiantly in her hand, she stared at Margaret.

Finally exasperated, the older woman held out her hand. 'Bag!'

Even with Margaret's assistance she took several minutes to achieve a full state of dress. And her trouser leg remained flapping from hip to ankle like an unruly sail where the nurse in A & E had cut it in order to dress her leg wound.

'Sit still, will you!' Margaret reached into her handbag and retrieved two safety pins from an inside pocket, as if she'd been keeping them there for just such an occasion. It took a few moments more to achieve her end. 'It might be a bit draughty, but at least you won't offend public decency. Now before I take you anywhere, I want to know why you're so determined to get out of here.'

'I have to get back to site.'

'You're not serious. If you think for a moment David is going to let you go back to work before you've had time to recuperate properly then you've taken leave of your senses.' Margaret drew back the curtains surrounding the bed and lifted the corner of the blind in front of the window. 'And even if he would, it's dark out there now.'

'I know, but I've got to get back there tonight.'

'What on earth for?'

'I need to check out the tower.'

'The tower!'

An elderly lady in a crocheted blue bed jacket in the next bed turned and glowered at Margaret. Margaret lowered her voice, instead leaning forward so that Clare had no doubt about the full force of her disapproval. 'Now I know you're crazy. If you think I'm going to let you go anywhere near that death trap you're mad. I know I said it was a good idea to use it. But I was wrong.'

Clare knew the last word had been dredged from her lips at considerable cost.

'I don't think you were.'

Margaret looked at her in consternation.

'I've been lying here flat on my back thinking about what happened. David went over that tower with a fine-tooth comb. There's no way he would have let anyone go up it if he thought there was anything wrong with it.'

'Least of all you.' Margaret smiled knowingly.

She felt herself flush. 'Not anyone. I've been over and over it in my head. I'd barely put my foot on that plank when it gave way. It wouldn't have done that if it was sound.'

'So you do think David missed something.'

Clare shook her head. 'Someone tampered with the wooden staging after he checked it.'

'But why would anyone do that? You could have been killed.'

'I did notice.'

Margaret seemed to be deliberating over her choice of words. 'I know you've had a terrible time of it lately. And shocks like this can be very unsettling even when one's feeling quite robust.'

'Why does everyone keep saying that? I'm not in shock. I'm perfectly *compos mentis*. You weren't up there. That boarding had been got at and if you'll just take me up to site, I'll prove it.'

'You're not going anywhere near the dig until you've had a chance to rest.' Margaret halted her protests with an imperious wave of the hand. 'No argument or you're going nowhere. Is there anyone to keep an eye on you if I take you back to your flat in Salisbury?'

'No. But I feel fine.'

'You are patently not fine. But I'm willing to make a deal with you. First, though, I need to make a phone call. You stay right where you are.'

Clare collapsed back onto the pile of pillows, frustrated and furious with her own physical weakness. She was lying on her side, considering her options, when Margaret returned a few minutes later wearing an expression of triumph.

'Right, here's what we're going to do. Clearly you're in no fit state to stay under canvas. So I'm going to drive you back to the pub and you're going to stay in one of Tony's rooms, where, with a little help from Shirl, I'll be able to keep an eye on you.'

There was no point in prevaricating; Margaret already knew

about her financial situation. 'I appreciate what you're trying to do, Margaret, but I really can't afford it.'

'The financial arrangements are none of your concern. Your responsibility is to concentrate on getting better.'

Clare considered the proposal for a moment. 'What about the tower?'

'First thing tomorrow morning I will personally check out every inch of that planking.'

CHAPTER TWENTY-THREE

Clare leant back into the pillows piled high behind her and took a sip from her steaming mug of coffee. For the last few days, Shirl had clucked and fussed around her as if she were her own daughter. Clare's first instinct had been to protest, but she'd quickly given in and allowed herself to enjoy being cosseted. Cocooned in her comfortable little bedroom, she was thankful for the respite from the realities of the outside world.

The cream walls, cheerfully unpretentious floral-print curtains and bed linen reflected her hostess's personality perfectly. And now, glory be, sunlight was streaming in through the window overlooking the hillside where the team was digging. The improvement in the weather was matched by an upturn in her spirits when Margaret had finally acquiesced to her request to bring her the pile of papers and journal articles that now lay scattered about her.

She set her mug down on the bedside table and picked up the photocopied pages that lay in her lap. The subject of her attention was a paper about barrows, written almost a century before Gerald had begun his Hungerbourne excavations, by a Dr John Thurnam. He'd been just one in a long line of antiquaries including John Aubrey, William Stukeley, Sir Richard Colt Hoare, and latterly Gerald Hart, who'd been at the forefront of the study of prehistory in these parts over the last few hundred years.

She craned her neck forward to watch the students digging on the hillside opposite. Did they have any idea what a venerable tradition they were part of? Salisbury was a top-notch university. Most of them would end up with sensible, well-paid jobs – accountants, marketing execs or city bankers. If they wanted any sort of security they would decide, as she had, that their futures lay outside of archaeology. But in the last few months she'd come to realise security was an illusion.

It felt like a lifetime since she'd decided to forsake a career in archaeology. It hadn't been an easy decision. But the joy on her mum's face when she'd told her that Stephen – a solicitor-in-waiting – had asked her to marry him had told her everything she'd needed to know about her choice.

When she'd first given up archaeology, she'd had no idea how much she would miss it. She'd been too busy building her new life with Stephen. There was the wedding to plan; setting up home together; making new friends and hosting dinner parties for his clients. But as time passed their life together had fallen into a rhythm. And that was when the unexpected pangs of loss had threatened to overwhelm her. She couldn't bring herself to watch a TV documentary about archaeology – much less pick up a book on the subject. They reminded her of the life she might have had.

Stephen hadn't questioned it. He'd always thought her degree subject was an indulgence – whereas his own was a stepping stone to his career. She'd told herself she was being daft. The chances that she would have made it as an archaeologist were infinitesimally small. And even if she had, an archaeologist's pay, unlike Stephen's chosen profession, could never have ensured her mum was properly provided for. Stephen's relationship with his mother-in-law was the stuff of Les Dawson's nightmares. In so many ways he'd been the model husband.

But since his death she'd begun to learn that nothing was quite as it seemed. At first, she'd thought she'd end up hating Stephen for what he'd done. Gradually, almost without realising it, he'd become not just the centre of her world but the whole of it. And then one day without warning he and it were gone. Her first reaction when she discovered the unholy mess Stephen had left behind was anger. But try as she might, she couldn't sustain it.

Her resentment had turned inwards. He hadn't forced her to marry him – she'd jumped at the chance. She begun to realise that – to begin with at least – she'd used him as her security blanket, luxuriating in the shelter he'd provided from the harsher realities of life. She'd chosen her own path in life. She couldn't blame him for that.

Had the seeds of her dissatisfaction been obvious to Stephen before the crash? Maybe even before they were obvious to her. She'd never been entirely comfortable with the way he lavished her with gifts. But it was his way of showing how much he loved her, so she'd let it pass. Were his money-making schemes his way of trying to put things right between them?

Now he was gone and, if she was honest, she knew it might not be too many years before her mum was gone too. 'We make our own choices in life,' Margaret had said. And at the moment she had the square root of nothing to show for hers.

She looked down at the article she was holding. Since returning to Wiltshire, she'd become acutely aware that they were part of an older tradition. Almost without realising it she'd found herself hoping that in a few hundred years' time someone would look back at the work she was doing and think of her as being part of this place and its fabulous past. She'd rediscovered her ability to lose herself completely in her work. Being able to step into that long-disappeared world was all that had sustained her in her darker moments. It might not pay much, but it provided her with an entirely different sort of security.

Her musings were brought to an abrupt end by a rap on the bedroom door, and Shirl's head appeared from behind the woodwork. 'You up to visitors, love?'

She wasn't at all sure she was, but she couldn't bring herself to say no to the woman who'd been the source of so much comfort over the last few days. So she smiled and nodded.

'I'll send him up.' With no explanation of whom 'he' might be, Shirl turned on her heels, her muffled clip-clopping receding down the stairs.

She barely had time to set her coffee down on the bedside table and run her fingers through her hair before there was a second knock on the door and Peter Hart's tall, slim frame stood in the doorway. His concerned expression transformed into a smile the instant he saw her sitting up. He thrust a bunch of brilliantly coloured dahlias at her. 'Not shop-bought, I'm afraid. They're from the manor garden.'

'And all the more lovely for it. They're beautiful, thank you.' She tilted her head upwards and, as he leant down, she planted a gentle kiss on his cheek. 'I'll ask Shirl if she's got a vase I can borrow.'

She laid the flowers on the bedside table. Peter looked about him for a suitable space in which to sit, but every spare inch was occupied by books and papers.

She waved her good arm. 'Just throw that lot on the floor.'

He scooped up a pile of journals and placed them on the carpet, then settled down in the armchair. Pushing aside a sea of paper, he pulled the chair closer to her bed and pointed to the sling from which her arm was suspended. 'Does it hurt?'

'A bit, if I try to move it. I feel a bit of a fraud. But the doctor told me I've got to keep it on for at least another week – come what may.'

'I came as soon as I heard. I bumped into Pat this morning in the post office. She told me what happened.' He paused, his voice softer. 'I wish someone had let me know sooner.'

'David wanted to tell you, but I wouldn't let him.' She hesitated.

'Why on earth not?'

'I wasn't sure you'd want to see me.'

'I'd hoped you might think better of me than that by now.'

She looked away, unwilling to meet his gaze. Peter's charm was undeniable. He was attractive, thoughtful and intelligent. Any woman would be flattered. But she wasn't at all sure she could cope with his attention right now.

He rushed to fill in the silence. 'How are you really?'

Grateful for the change in subject, she looked up. 'Pretty much as you see. Dislocated shoulder, a few cuts and bruises – I'll live.'

'Only just, by the sound of what Pat told me.'

'Did she tell you that it's only thanks to Ed that I'm still here to tell the tale?'

He smiled broadly. 'She did mention it.' He leant forward conspiratorially. 'To tell you the truth, I put her version of events down to the over-exaggeration of a proud wife. As soon as you're feeling up to it, she's invited us round to dinner at their place.' He shifted slightly in his chair, his face flushing crimson. 'If you'd like to, that is.'

Her eyes sparkled with quiet amusement. Her every instinct told her it was a bad idea, but she found herself saying, 'That would be lovely. Holed up in here, I haven't had a chance to thank Ed for what he did. Without him they'd still be scraping bits of me off the Downs.'

Peter's pallor drained to match the grey of his sweatshirt. 'What exactly happened?'

'Someone tried to kill me.' The words were matter-of-fact.

'You're joking.' Her expression told him she wasn't. 'But surely if that were the case, the police would be investigating?'

'You'd think so, wouldn't you? But Sally Treen thinks I'm hysterical.'

'But there were witnesses. Pat said the whole dig team was there.'

'Yes, but all they saw was me crashing through the planking. They didn't see what caused it.'

'I don't understand.'

'It's quite simple, someone was trying to kill me – or at least kill one of us.'

'What on earth makes you think that?' Peter's expression was a mixture of concern and disbelief. Despite his best efforts, it was clear Sally wasn't the only one who didn't believe a word she was saying.

'David insisted that he check over the whole tower personally before he'd let anyone go up it. It was perfectly safe. But when he went back to look at the thing afterwards he found the planking I went through was totally rotten.'

'Couldn't he have missed it the first time round?'

She shook her head. 'That's what David says – he's blaming himself for what happened. But I know him. There's no way he'd have missed it. He'd never put anyone's life at risk.' What she really meant was that David would never put *her* life at risk, but Peter was the last person she was going to share that with.

'Not deliberately, maybe, but mistakes happen. And I'm as much to blame as David. That tower had been knocking about at the manor for years. I should never have lent it to the dig. It was obviously well past its sell-by-date. If you want to blame anyone, blame me. I'm the one that nearly got you killed.'

That was all she needed: David and Peter competing over who was to blame. She wanted to scream. 'You're missing the point. The person at fault is whoever tampered with the planking.' Peter just stared at her. 'Great! Now you think I'm nuts too. Sally's convinced David I'm overreacting. One less off the crime figures, I suppose.'

'I'm sure if Sally thought there was the slightest chance that this was anything other than an accident, she'd have pursued it.'

What the hell did men think with? David clearly wasn't the only one who'd been swayed by Sally's all-too-obvious charms. But she really wasn't up to arguing about the way in which DI Treen was going about her duties.

Peter said, 'I know you've had a difficult time of it lately . . .'

'Let's get one thing straight, Peter – whatever you, or David or Sally Treen think, I'm not deranged. Someone saw to it that whoever used that thing was going to get hurt. And they didn't give a damn if someone was killed in the process.'

'But why would anyone do such a thing?'

'You of all people should know we disturbed more than a few layers of dust when we found that archive. Someone wants to make sure we aren't around to disturb anything else.'

'But it doesn't make any sense – not now it's all out in the open about Gerald and my father.'

The duvet was tucked securely around her, but despite the pretty room and the sunny day, Clare felt suddenly cold and glum. The more people who told her Gerald was a murderer, the less she seemed able to believe it. 'We don't know for sure that Gerald killed your father.'

'The police seem pretty certain.'

'Don't you find it strange that nothing happens in Hungerbourne for four decades and as soon as that urn turns up, people start plunging from towers?'

'Are you suggesting my father's killer is still alive?'

She elevated her sling-bound arm with a wince. 'From where I'm sitting, it seems like a reasonable conclusion.' She slumped back onto the pile of pillows behind her, suddenly aware of how tired she felt.

Peter paused. 'Even supposing it wasn't an accident, what makes you think whoever killed Father was responsible?'

She angled her head back against the crisp cotton, closing her eyes as if to intensify the glass-refracted heat of the sun as it touched her skin. 'It's a pretty strong motive for wanting us as far away as possible from Hungerbourne, wouldn't you say?'

'There is an alternative.'

'Like what?'

'Maybe someone has a vested interest in preventing you from finding the Jevons disc.'

'But that doesn't get us very far, does it? Even George Clifford doesn't know where the disc is.'

'You believed him!' Peter sounded incredulous.

'I don't like the man any more than you do. But if he'd been involved in the theft, he would have been better off denying all knowledge.' She shook her head. 'No. I think he was pretty frank with us about his part in the affair. The most likely culprit is whoever killed your father.'

'I think I've found something that will interest you.'

He withdrew a folded A4 sheet from his wallet and handed it to her. It was a photocopy of another of his uncle's bank statements. She cast her eyes down the list of names and numbers. 'I don't see what this tells us. We already knew Gerald was paying Joyce.'

Peter gesticulated at the sheet. 'Look at the entry above that.'

'Royals Removals £2,500.' Clare laid the paper down on the duvet in front of her. 'Why would Gerald need a removals company? He wasn't planning to move, was he?'

Peter shook his head. 'Look at the date of the payment.'

She read it out. '10th February 2012. So?'

He nodded. 'A fortnight before the fire.'

Her eyes widened. 'You think this is Gerald paying for the archive to be moved into the manor attic.'

'Don't think – know. I looked Royals Removals up in the phone book. They're based in Reading. The chap I spoke to remembered the job because it had been such easy money he couldn't believe there wasn't some sort of catch.'

'And was there?'

He shook his head. 'Apparently, Gerald asked them if they could come and move some boxes. They told him they'd need to come round and give him an estimate and, because of the distance, they'd have to charge him for the fuel costs. As Gerald was an old boy the chap suggested he'd be better off getting someone from his own area to do the work. But Gerald was absolutely adamant he wanted them to do the job – whatever it cost.'

'Two and a half grand for moving a few crates across the yard. I bet they bit his hand off.'

'It was only payable on condition they did it at night and told no one about it.'

'So why did they tell you?'

'When I told them Gerald had passed away and I was his executor they seemed to think it didn't much matter any more.'

'But why would Gerald want the archive moved?' She was beginning to form her own ideas on the subject, though she could hardly bring herself to believe it.

'I'd been trying to persuade Gerald for years he should hand the archive over to a museum. But he wouldn't hear of it. And then there was all of the hoo-ha over the visitor centre proposal. Things got really nasty for him in the village. Half the village blamed him for it because he dug the site in the first place and the other half wouldn't talk to him because he wouldn't let them have the archive to display there. So as the British Museum already had the goldwork, I made a few enquiries of my own with them. When I mentioned it to David, he offered to write up the site. I didn't realise he was going to write to Gerald about it.'

'He'd have to, Gerald was the excavator. You arranged all this without Gerald knowing?'

'I was worried sick about him. If I'd told him before I'd spoken to the British Museum, he'd have told me it was none of my business.'

'Which it wasn't.' She knew Peter had acted out of concern,

but she couldn't shake the idea that Gerald must have seen it as a betrayal.

'Worrying about the security in the coach house was driving him to distraction. It seemed to consume his every waking minute.'

'What happened when he got David's letter?'

'He refused outright to countenance the idea. I tried to persuade him it was for the best, but he wouldn't have it. In the end, he asked for a bit more time to think it over and I thought he was coming round. Then the coach house went up in flames and it was too late.'

'You thought the archive had gone with it.'

He nodded. 'Which was exactly what Gerald wanted me to think. A few days before the fire, he told me he'd seen someone hanging around the outbuildings. Said he was so worried he'd phoned the police.' Peter shook his head slowly from side to side. 'I could never understand how someone managed to break into the coach house so easily. He was out in that yard night and day in all weathers, checking it was securely locked up.'

'You think Gerald set the fire himself.'

Peter nodded. 'It must have scared the old boy rigid when I told him I'd spoken to the museum. The only thing I can't work out is why he went to the bother of having the stuff moved. If he'd let it burn, the evidence of what happened to my father would have gone up in smoke for good.'

'It's almost impossible to entirely destroy human remains in a normal fire – modern crematoria have to get up to nigh on a thousand degrees centigrade and then pulverise what's left to turn it into ashes.' Peter grimaced. 'Gerald would have known that. Maybe he didn't want to take the risk.' She looked into the face that reminded her so much of Gerald's and smiled. 'Besides, your uncle was an archaeologist to the core. He could never have destroyed the rest of that archive.'

And, Clare thought, *Gerald Hart was a man who had long ago decided he would put his personal ethics ahead of his reputation.*

CHAPTER TWENTY-FOUR

Clare shifted in the cast-iron chair, trying to get comfortable. From her seat on the terrace of Ed's farmhouse, she could see a purple-streaked sky above the darkening Downs. The elevation of the great chalk land mass of the Marlborough Downs ensured that even on the warmest summer's day the air grew cold more quickly here than those unfamiliar with the area expected. And she found herself shivering at the damp chill in the air.

Ed raised his brandy glass. 'Your good health!'

She reciprocated the gesture. 'The continuation of which is largely due to you.'

Ed looked down at the table. Was he embarrassed? He didn't strike her as the sort of man who would be reticent about his achievements. But then her track record in sizing up people – and men in particular – didn't seem to be up to much lately. Casting her mind back to her first impressions of the man, she felt a twinge of guilt. She was the one who should be embarrassed. Without him she wouldn't be sitting here.

From somewhere deep inside the house, the sound of Pat and Peter's laughter drifted towards them, accompanied by the clatter and chink of plates and cutlery. Her injury had excused her from offering to help clear away the remnants of Pat's cassoulet. Clare's neck was sore from the weight of the foam sling that still hung from it. But with every sip, the suffusing warmth of her cognac worked its magic, easing the tension in her muscles.

They sat in companionable silence, enjoying the last embers of the day and the diminishing birdsong. It was several minutes before either of them spoke.

She said, 'It must be strange for you having us descend on you like this, especially when you were part of what happened here the first time.'

For a second, he looked perplexed, but his confusion was fleeting. 'You mean the excavation.'

She nodded.

'Digging up at Old Barrows Field again has certainly brought back memories.'

'A lot must have changed in Hungerbourne since the first dig.'

He tilted his head to one side and smiled. 'I'd just like to emphasise that I was astonishingly young when the first excavation took place.'

She had to confess, he could be very charming when he put his mind to it. But his expression morphed from easy charm to earnest reflection in the time it took for her to process the observation. She realised for the first time that things must have been almost as difficult for him as they had for Peter over the last few months.

She set her glass down on the table. 'I was so excited when

I found the archive. I couldn't quite believe our luck. But Gerald's death seems to have been a catalyst for a lot more than just our project.'

'I gather you've had a bit of a rough time of it lately.'

A few weeks ago, she'd have been less than thrilled with the idea of discussing her private life with Ed, but now she found herself willingly confiding in him.

She nodded. 'When David asked me to work on the archive with him, I was relieved to have something positive to get my teeth into. But now it feels like I lifted the lid on Pandora's box when I opened that first crate.'

'You sound as if you might be regretting it.'

She didn't reply.

He gestured towards the rapidly dissolving silhouette of the hills. 'When you've lived here all your life and spent every waking minute out on the Downs, they're as much a part of you as breathing. You come to realise it's all very simple.'

She smiled. 'I wish I had your certainty. Whoever left that message on the tea hut doesn't want us around.'

'You're not going to let a bit of nonsense like that put you off, are you?'

Clare stayed silent. It wasn't just the tea hut incident; there was also her 'accident' on the photographic tower. But she knew that, like David, Ed believed that was exactly what it had been – an accident.

'People don't understand what this place is about. They take it all for granted.'

'Incomers, you mean?'

Ed shrugged. His tone was considered, deliberate. 'They're all the same, incomers or not. They don't give a damn about what it is or what it means. They don't feel it. They live on the landscape like . . .' He faltered, his voice straining with emotion. 'Like parasites.' A trickle of clear brown liquid slopped over the edge of his glass as he brought it down onto the tabletop, creating a sticky pool on the cold, metal surface.

The force of his words made Clare start in her seat, but Ed didn't seem to notice. She'd had no idea how intensely he felt about this place. He was obviously every bit as passionate as she and David were about its importance. For a few moments, she considered not pursuing the questions she'd already determined to ask him. They seemed faintly ridiculous now, disrespectful even. But he was her best chance of finding the sun disc – not to mention who wanted her dead. The velvet blackness of the night had all but enveloped them by the time she steeled herself sufficiently.

'David said you spent a lot of time with Gerald in his later years.'

Ed turned towards her, his tone warm and responsive. 'Working in town, Peter couldn't always be around as much as he'd have liked. So I used to help out. I'd drop in on the old boy. Make sure he was alright.'

'Did you know he kept the Hungerbourne archive at the manor?'

'He never talked much about the dig.'

'Why was that?'

Clare sensed more than saw Ed stiffen in his seat. 'I would have thought that was obvious now.'

'Do you think Gerald killed Jim?'

He hesitated for a moment before replying. 'I was very fond of Gerald. I don't want to believe he was responsible. But what other reason could he possibly have had for keeping Jim's ashes under lock and key for all those years? What I can't understand is how he managed to keep something like that a secret.'

'Do you really believe he was capable of killing someone?'

'You didn't know Jim. He would have tried the patience of

a saint. He was a first-class shit. Fancied himself as lord of the manor, but never showed any sign of acting like a gentleman.'

'He was in money trouble, wasn't he?'

'Peter told you, I suppose.' He peered into the semi-darkness as if straining to make out her expression. She made no comment, choosing neither to confirm nor deny his assumption. 'Estelle and Gerald did everything they could to keep Jim's gambling debts quiet, but they were on a hiding to nothing. Jim tapped up half the county for money at one time or another.'

'How much did he owe?'

'I don't know, but it must have been a fair whack. He was desperate to get his hands on cash. I heard him arguing with Gerald about it more than once. At the time I had the impression that Peter didn't know what was going on. But looking back now, I think he was just too embarrassed to let on.

'Peter and I had something in common. We both had lousy fathers. A friendship forged in adversity, you might say. My own father was never physically aggressive, not in the way Jim was. But he was a detestable penny-pinching bully. As soon as I finished school, I started work on the farm. I'd never wanted anything else, but the old man was as tight as . . .' He seemed to be on the verge of using an expletive, but thought better of it. 'Well, let's just say he was the meanest man I've ever met. He paid me a pittance. I was no different from any other young man. I wanted to be able to do what my friends were doing; have a few drinks and be able to treat one or two of the girls to a night out.'

With his curly, light brown hair tingeing into grey and his strong, muscular face, Clare was reminded again of the Brew Crew photograph. He must have been popular with the ladies when he was younger.

Ed seemed almost to have forgotten she was there. 'He sat in his armchair like some crumbling dictator issuing his decrees. Do you know what he said when I complained? He told me I should be grateful.' He snorted. 'I was nothing more than cheap labour to him.'

Through the flickering red cast of the tea-light, she could see that his eyes still blazed with the injustice of it all. He fell silent, staring out into the night. The ill will he bore his father was evident. But she still couldn't bring herself to feel the same compassion for Ed that she did for Peter. They'd both had a choice about what they'd do with their lives. Peter had gone out into the world and forged a life of his own. Ed, on the other hand, had chosen to stay. And, looking round at the farmhouse, he didn't seem to have done too badly for himself.

A breeze rustled through the hedgerow that divided the garden from the fields beyond. She sipped her brandy and pulled the cream cable-knit jumper that was draped around her shoulders closer to her. Ed looked up and shook his head as if trying to dislodge an unbidden memory.

'Ed, can I ask you a question?'

He smiled. 'I find it difficult to refuse requests from attractive young ladies.'

She tried to smile, but couldn't quite manage it. 'It's about something someone told me about Jim's disappearance.'

'Who, exactly?'

She leant forward in her seat, trying to make out his expression in the flickering candlelight. 'George Clifford.' She let the name settle on the rapidly chilling night air. 'He suggested you had a reason to be upset when Jim left Hungerbourne.'

'As did Clifford, but that was true of half the village.'

'Look, I'm going to level with you: Clifford suggested you were involved in a plan to steal the Hungerbourne gold.'

Ed hesitated, then after a moment looked her straight in the eye. 'I'm not going to lie to you, Clare – I was. But not in the way you might think.'

He paused, turning his glass round thoughtfully in his hand. He looked up at her, his expression one of regret. 'You have to understand I'm not proud of my part in all this. I overheard Jim and George arguing outside the pub one night.'

'About the gold.'

Ed nodded. It seemed half of Hungerbourne had known about Jim's plan.

Ed said, 'Jim was pleading for time, telling George that once he got hold of the stuff from the dig he'd be able to pay him off. Jim didn't see me sitting in the shadows nursing my pint until he went to go back inside. I thought he was going to have a heart attack when he caught sight of me. He shoved me up against the wall and told me that if I didn't keep my mouth closed he'd make sure it was shut permanently.'

'What did you do?'

'I told him I'd tell Gerald about his sordid little plan.'

Something about the righteous indignation of Ed's reply brought a smile to her face. 'I don't imagine he took that very well.'

He shook his head. 'When he realised threats of physical violence weren't going to work, he offered me money. He said I could help him out. He told me he needed someone who was on the inside at the dig to pull it off – someone Gerald trusted.'

Ed fell silent.

'And?'

'I said yes.'

He stared down at the table, seemingly bereft of an explanation. When he finally looked up, there was desperation in his voice. 'I had no intention of going through with it. I just wanted to teach him a lesson. Jim treated everyone like dirt and I was sick of it. I thought that if I could find out what he was planning, I could stop him – and maybe make a few bob on the side in the meantime.'

Her expression, even in the half-light, must have betrayed her thoughts.

She took a deep breath. 'So what happened?'

'Jim popped me a few quid and I played along. I had to have solid proof if I was going to take it to Gerald. Without it, no one would have believed me. Even if Gerald was sympathetic, he wasn't likely to believe the word of a kid over his own brother. So I began to follow Jim, tried to work out exactly what he was planning to do.'

'And did you find out?'

Ed shook his head. 'Before I got a chance, Jim disappeared.'

'And you said nothing to Gerald about any of this.'

'When Gerald shut the dig down, there was no mention of missing goldwork. Jim did a runner and Gerald never spoke about him or the dig after that. I had no idea whether Jim had taken the gold or not. Gerald would never have been able to live with the shame if it had become public that some of the artefacts from the site had been stolen by his own brother. And I could hardly ask him about it, could I? If Jim had nicked off with the gold, there was no way I could tell Gerald I'd known what Jim was planning and taken money to keep quiet.'

'But now we know that Jim didn't go anywhere, with or without the gold.'

'So it would seem.'

'So what do you think happened to the missing sun disc?'

'Your guess is as good as mine. I assume Jim did the deed and got rid of it. Gerald wasn't easily roused to anger, but he took his archaeology very seriously. When he found out – well, the evidence of what you found in that urn speaks for itself.'

Could Ed be right? Had Clifford lied? If Jim had given Clifford the disc before he met his maker, it might have provided Clifford with a very comfortable little pension scheme. And if Clifford was involved in the disappearance of the sun disc, who was to say he wasn't responsible for the Woe Waters threats and what had happened on the photo tower?

CHAPTER TWENTY-FIVE

Clare was only too well aware that she had no way of proving Gerald was not a murderer. And neither was she any closer to finding out what had happened to the missing sun disc. But she had more pressing concerns at the moment – like how she was going to keep her financial head above water.

She'd followed Margaret's advice and put the Richmond shop on the market. She'd never really had any reason to wonder what it might be worth before, and to her amazement the estate agent had valued it at considerably more than she'd thought possible. And, given what she'd learnt about the full horror of Stephen's financial arrangements, she was going to need every penny she could lay her hands on.

Which was why, now that her shoulder had finally healed enough for her to drive, she found herself sitting behind the wheel of an economical but thoroughly unglamorous Fiesta with 50,000 miles on the clock. She'd imagined she would find the moment she handed over the keys of her beloved coupé difficult to bear; but in the event, the acquisition of a sizeable cheque had softened the blow considerably.

She pulled out of the garage forecourt and headed for the Salisbury ring road, wearing a self-congratulatory smile. By the time she'd reached the dig site, her enthusiasm for her new mode of transport was undimmed. In fact, she experienced an altogether unexpected sense of freedom as she bumped the little blue box over the rutted grass. She pulled up beside David's Land Rover and gave the bonnet of her new acquisition an affectionate pat.

'Isn't that a bit of a retrograde step?'

She looked up to see a familiar figure framed in the Portakabin doorway.

'Jo! What are you doing here?'

'That's nice. I hike all the way down from the big city to be here and . . .'

Before Jo could say another word, Clare enveloped her in a hug. Clare could feel her cheeks burning as she stepped away from Jo. Public displays of emotion weren't normally her thing. Jo rested her hands on Clare's shoulders, surveying her friend's face, her expression betraying her concern. 'Are you OK?'

'Fine.'

'Really?'

Clare nodded, maybe just a little too enthusiastically. 'Really – I'm absolutely fine. Just pleased to see you. I thought you'd be off to the States by now. Have they extended your contract?'

Jo shook her head and smiled. 'David's offered me a project-funded post down here at the university. So here I am.'

Clare made no attempt to hide her delight. 'That's amazing news. I can't believe he didn't say anything. And neither did you!'

'He made me swear not to tell anyone.' Jo tilted her head to one side. 'I kind of got the impression he was worried about you. It crossed my mind that that was why he offered me the post.'

'He offered you the job because you're the best at what you do.'

Jo's face broke into a broad smile. 'I'd like to be all British and argue about it, but it just so happens it's true. Besides, scratch the surface and we high achievers need cold, hard cash just as much as the rest of humanity. And I got to like this neck of the woods last time I was down here.' She slapped Clare on the back. Clare winced as the pain shot through her shoulder. 'Crap. Sorry. I didn't think.'

She brushed aside the apology. 'You don't really think David appointed you to babysit me, do you?'

Jo shrugged and laughed. 'If he did, I'd say he's backed the wrong horse, wouldn't you? But he is worried about you, and so am I.'

'I'm old enough to look after myself. I don't need a nursemaid.'

Jo raised her hands in a defensive gesture. 'Hey, what's so wrong with having people care about you?'

Clare let out a long sigh and smiled. 'I'm sorry. After everything that's happened around here lately I guess I'm just a bit on edge.'

Jo raised an eyebrow. 'How about we rustle up one of your vile English cups of tea and you tell me about it.'

'Give that fucking thing here!'

Clare had ignored the ruckus coming from the other side of the tea hut for as long as she could. But there was no mistaking the strain in Jenny's voice. The young post-grad site assistant was clearly finding the students from her trench too boisterous to handle. Clare abandoned the pretence of enjoying the mug of tepid brown sludge masquerading as tea and went to investigate.

Drawing herself up to her full five feet six, she bellowed, 'Enough!'

Two male students whipped their heads round to see where the command had come from. Jenny had interposed herself between these two and a third student, who must have been at least six feet four and was wearing a T-shirt with the word 'Wolfmother' emblazoned across his chest. She seemed to be trying to persuade him to hand something to her.

'They must be able to hear you lot down in the village.'

Wolfmother dropped his hands to his sides in a clumsy attempt to distract attention from the object at the centre of the dispute.

'I'm sorry, Clare. I was trying to get them to give it to me.' Jenny pointed to where the object had been a second ago.

Why did this sort of thing only happen when David was off-site?

'Hand it over to Jenny now!' Clare ordered.

Wolfmother grinned. 'Chill! We were just having a bit of fun.'

Clare motioned for him to hand over the offending article. 'Give!'

Wolfmother held the knife out towards her, his head drooping. Out of the corner of her eye, Clare could see the other two students smirking. At moments like this, she wished she had Margaret's glasses so that she could peer disdainfully over them. She settled instead for a withering sidelong glare. Satisfyingly, the smirks disappeared instantaneously.

She looked down at the object in front of her. It was a knife almost a foot long. The long metal blade was in-turned towards the tip and serrated down one edge. A metal cross-piece divided the blade from the remnants of a tattered leather-bound handle. It was a bowie knife.

She raised her eyes to Wolfmother's. 'What the hell do you think you're doing bringing that thing onto site?'

'I didn't.'

Clare looked at the other two students. 'Which of you clowns was it?'

They both shook their heads.

'Well?'

'We found it,' Wolfmother said.

'Where?'

'In the old dude's trench.'

She looked at Jenny questioningly. The younger woman said, 'It was in the backfill in Hart's trench.'

Clare turned to Wolfmother. 'Well, it's Jenny's trench now, so hand it over to her.'

He waved the knife in Jenny's direction. 'But she said we could keep it.'

Jenny's face reddened. 'That was before I knew where you got it from.'

Clare said, 'Give it to her!'

Wolfmother passed the knife to Jenny, who was looking decidedly uncomfortable.

'In case you're in any doubt, one more step out of line and my recommendation to David will be referrals on your fieldwork reports for the lot of you. Got it?' Reluctantly, one after the other they all nodded. 'Now clear off and get some work done.'

Clare watched as the undergrads trudged uphill towards the trench. Once she was sure they were out of earshot, she turned her attention to Jenny. She knew that the younger woman had been having a rough time of it lately. According to the dig rumour-mill, her long-term boyfriend had dumped her in favour of someone who spent more time at home with the living than in the middle of nowhere with the long-dead. Along with knackered knees and an unhealthy relationship with alcohol, it was one of the occupational hazards of life as an archaeologist. And it looked to Clare as if she was having a tough time dealing with it. The last thing she wanted to do was to add to the poor girl's misery by giving her a public dressing-down.

Clare turned to Jenny, who was staring down at the grass. She lowered her voice, gesturing over her shoulder with her thumb towards the trio as they disappeared up the hill. 'That lot can be a pain in the backside when they put their minds to it. If they get too much to handle just come and let me know.' There was no outward sign that the younger woman had registered a word Clare had said. 'Jenny!'

This time she looked up, but said nothing.

'David needn't know if that's what's worrying you.' Clare waited, but there was still no response. 'OK, have it your way. But that thing is from an archaeological context. So I want it bagged, tagged and on my desk before you leave site today.'

Clare pulled up outside George Clifford's house, slotting into the space vacated by a battered Suzuki four by four. She turned towards Jo, who was in the passenger seat. 'Are you sure about this? I'd hate you to lose your job before the ink's even dry on your contract.'

Jo unclipped her seat belt and grinned. 'My trips to Wiltshire are the most excitement I've had since I came over here. Don't get cold feet on me just when things are getting interesting. Besides, it's got to be better than spending our day off bussing the students to and from the laundromat.'

Clare laughed, though she couldn't help feeling a tinge of guilt about leaving that particular pleasure to Margaret and Jenny. But Margaret seemed to be enjoying her time with the students and Jenny hadn't seemed bothered one way or the other.

The doorbell was answered by Clifford's wife, who ushered

them into a small, gloomy front room and seated them on the Dralon-covered sofa before departing.

Clifford was ensconced in his armchair – curtains drawn, television on – watching an episode of *Ice Road Truckers*.

He nodded at Clare. 'Now then, who's your friend 'ere? Bit of an improvement on the last time we met. Don't think I've had the pleasure.'

He stuck out a clammy paw in Jo's direction.

'Doctor Josephine Granski,' Clare said, emphasising the 'doctor'.

'Doctor, is it?'

Jo eased her hand out of his grip as he clung on for just fractionally too long. 'Jo will do just fine.'

He turned to face Clare. 'I don't suppose this is a social visit.'

Clifford seemed to be able to get under her skin with astonishing ease. It was an ability she resented, but she was determined not to let him wind her up. 'No, it's not, Mr Clifford. We just had one or two more questions we were hoping you might be able to help us with.'

Clifford's smile set like pre-cast concrete.

Peter's aggressive approach hadn't helped much last time. Maybe she'd have more success if she tried to butter him up a bit. 'I'm afraid we haven't had much luck in our search for the missing sun disc since the last time we met. And, at the moment, you're our best chance of finding it. When we spoke before, you mentioned that Ed Jevons had cause to be upset when Jim left Hungerbourne. Did it have something to do with the missing gold?'

Clare watched as the ends of Clifford's lips turned upwards, entirely in contradiction to the rest of his face, which betrayed no semblance of a smile. He said nothing.

Jo stepped in. 'I'm sure even on this side of the pond it wouldn't look good if the cops found out someone was concealing information about a homicide.'

'I thought you were here to find out about the missing gold.' He paused. 'And anyway, that lovely young inspector seemed to think the man who killed Jim Hart had gone to meet his maker.'

'You've spoken to Inspector Treen?' Clare couldn't conceal her surprise.

As far as she'd been able to make out from what David had said, Sally lacked all enthusiasm for pursuing both the missing goldwork and Jim's murderer. So why the interest in George Clifford?

'When I heard that Jim Hart was dead, I thought it was only right I should make sure the police 'ad all the facts. So I told the inspector what I know. And that's the last word I'm going to say to anyone about that bloody dig.'

Jo said, 'To give them your side of things, you mean, before you became a suspect.'

Clifford leant forward. 'I'd go careful if I were you. Folk round 'ere don't take kindly to being accused of murder.'

Reaching into her bag, Clare pulled out a sheet of paper and waved it in Clifford's face. 'Whatever happened to Jim, we know he never left Hungerbourne. So what happened to this?'

Clifford took hold of the photocopied newspaper article. It showed Richard Jevons presenting his sun disc to Gerald. He glanced at it before letting the sheet of paper fall to the floor. 'You're joking. That's not what you're looking for, is it?'

Clare and Jo exchanged bemused glances.

He pointed at the image now lying upturned beside his armchair. 'If you think I 'ad anything to do with that piece of junk going missing, you need your head read. You're all the same. You think cos a man don't speak like a toff he ain't got two penneth o' brains.' He started to laugh, a peculiar, high-pitched, child-like chuckle. When he finally stopped, he broke into a broad grin, and jabbed his finger emphatically at the sheet of paper. 'Look at it!'

Jo picked up the paper and examined the picture. But Clare had no need. She had a terrible feeling she knew what he was about to tell them.

'If I'd have wanted to nick something from that dig I wouldn't have wasted my time with that. Who'd have given decent money for damaged goods when they could have the real thing?'

Jo looked perplexed. 'The real thing?'

'That's right. The one Joycey found.'

Jo turned to Clare. 'I don't understand. It was this disc – the one found before the dig – that was stolen.'

Clare nodded. Out of the corner of her eye, she could see Clifford smiling. She detested the man, but the cold sinking feeling in the pit of her stomach told her he was telling the truth.

Jo puffed out her cheeks and clenched her fists. 'That guy is a total slimeball.'

'He gives me the creeps too. But that doesn't necessarily mean he's lying.'

Jo clipped her seat belt into place and turned to face Clare. 'You believe him!'

Clare slipped the Fiesta into reverse and manoeuvred it out onto the road. 'Unfortunately, I do. Just about the only thing everyone I've spoken to agrees about is that the robbery was planned well in advance.'

'So?'

'Like Clifford says, no one in their right minds would deliberately steal a damaged sun disc when they could take their pick from any number of other pristine pieces of goldwork from the dig.'

'Unless things didn't go to plan. Maybe they were interrupted.'

'That would certainly suit Sally's version of events. Gerald discovers Jim stealing the disc and ends up killing him.'

'I know you and Sally don't get along, but you've got to admit that as a theory it's got a lot going for it.'

Clare's grip on the steering wheel tightened. 'How I feel about Sally Treen is neither here nor there. But as a theory it leaks like a sieve.'

'Why?'

'If Gerald found Jim stealing the gold and killed him, where is the sun disc? We would still have it, along with the one from the excavated assemblage.'

It was a few minutes before Jo replied. 'So what's the alternative? Jim gets interrupted when he's stealing the gold and only manages to take the damaged disc. Then someone else kills Jim and makes off with it. Do you think he had an accomplice?'

Clare shrugged. 'I suppose it's possible.'

'But that doesn't explain how Jim's remains ended up as a heap of burned bones in Gerald's attic.'

'No. But it would mean there might still be someone out there with a damned good reason for not wanting us poking around in the past.'

CHAPTER TWENTY-SIX

A light sprinkling of rain earlier in the evening had ensured Jenny had the canal-side pub garden to herself. She was exhausted. She and Margaret had spent the day herding the undergrads around Swindon and then, when they'd finally got back to camp, she'd had to supervise the chores duties too because Clare still wasn't back from wherever the hell she'd buggered off to. She listened to the gentle lap of water as the barges bumped gently against their moorings. It all seemed so perfect. Really it was anything but.

Nothing seemed to be going her way. She'd known things weren't right between her and Karl for a while. She was always the one to phone him. A couple of weeks ago, she'd finally plucked up the courage to ask him what was wrong and he'd denied there was a problem – but she knew he was lying.

She had to see him to sort things out. She couldn't face talking about it with David, so instead last week she'd gone to see Clare and begged a couple of extra days off. She'd spent the whole train journey from Pewsey to Exeter determined to have it out with him. When she'd arrived at his place unannounced, he'd made it clear he was far from pleased to see her. When she'd demanded to know what was wrong, he'd put it down to being uptight about finishing his master's dissertation. He'd been in a strop the whole time she was with him.

By the time she got back to Wiltshire, she'd managed to convince herself he was stressing because his folks had forked out a fortune for him to be there and now the shit was about to hit the fan. But when she'd texted him to tell him she'd got safely back to the dig site, he'd texted back to say he'd decided they should take a break, maybe see other people. By which she took it that he was already shagging whoever owned the blouse she'd found chucked behind his sofa that he'd lightly dismissed as belonging to his sister, Kerry, who – he'd claimed – had been down from London to see him the week before.

Bastard! He'd known she wouldn't speak to Kerry – they hated one another's guts. She'd wanted to tell him to go fuck himself. But instead she'd found herself telling him it was probably for the best, and maybe they could stay in touch, and then proceeded to drink the best part of the half bottle of vodka she'd been saving for the end-of-dig party.

She'd woken with a screaming headache she'd been unable to shake all day, despite drinking enough water to drown a fish. The last thing she'd needed was a row with Clare about that bloody knife. It wasn't her fault the lads were a roaring pain in the arse. Anyway, what was the big deal about a rusty piece of junk?

By the time she'd got back to camp, she'd just wanted to collapse in her tent for a couple of hours before dinner. She couldn't believe her eyes when she'd found her tent flap thrown back and most of its contents – including her bras and knickers – strewn across the grass outside. The lads in her trench had been winding her up for days, but they'd gone too far this time. When she confronted them, they seemed to think it was funny. They denied all knowledge. Which was when she'd lost it – started yelling and screaming at them. Then Clare had rocked up and had another go at her. It wasn't fair; she was the victim, but she was being treated like she was the one in the wrong.

She'd spent the past couple of days worrying herself sick that Clare would tell David. She was sure to, if she hadn't already, and she could say goodbye to any hope of a reference. This was meant to be her golden ticket – everyone had heard of Hungerbourne. But everyone knew everyone in archaeology. And once word got out, she could kiss any hope she'd had of a career in archaeology goodbye too. She wished she'd never signed up for the bloody dig in the first place.

A train clattered by on its way to the little red-brick station just up the road. Maybe it was time to cut her losses.

A shadow fell across the table in front of her, and she glanced up from what remained of her vodka and orange juice to be greeted by a familiar smile. 'Hello. Hope I didn't spook you.'

She shook her head. 'Just thinking.'

'Not always good for you, that. Want another?'

She nodded. Maybe her luck was changing.

CHAPTER TWENTY-SEVEN

'Hello, you. What a lovely surprise.' David stood up and moved towards the doorway to greet Sally.

She stood stock-still on the threshold of the Portakabin. The surprise she had in store for him was anything but lovely. She prided herself that she'd learnt how to deal with these situations professionally and sympathetically. But she had no idea yet how she was going to break it to him. She'd had far too much experience of doing this sort of thing since she'd joined the force. Whatever people might assume, it never got any easier. And standing here now, with David looking at her expectantly, she wondered where the professional young DI had gone.

'What on earth's wrong? You look dreadful.'

'Do you have a student called Jenny Shelton on the dig?' She knew the answer already. She'd seen her on her last visit to the site a couple of days before. Jenny had been sitting cross-legged beside a trench, poring over a ring binder full of paperwork. But she couldn't take any shortcuts. Everything had to be done by the book with this one.

David nodded, clearly confused. 'She's a site assistant – one of my MA students. Is there a problem? Has she got herself into some sort of bother? Honestly, Sally, she won't say boo to a goose most of the time, but when she's had a few it's a different story. At the end-of-dig party on our last excavation she drank herself under the table – literally. I found her sleeping like a baby on the floor of the bar. She was so drunk it took two of us to carry her back to her tent.' He smiled at the memory.

'Sit down, David.'

He complied, depositing himself into his mud-stained chair.

'Jenny is dead.'

'Dead.' He repeated the word without intonation.

'A dog-walker found her early this morning – in the Kennet and Avon canal in Pewsey.'

'I don't understand.'

'Yesterday was the dig day off, wasn't it?'

He nodded. 'Yes, you know it was. Are you sure about this, Sal? There must be some sort of mistake. Jenny can't be dead.'

She wanted to be able to reassure him. She'd thought she was used to breaking bad news, but she'd never had to deliver it to the man she'd just spent the night with before. 'I'm sorry, David. There's no mistake. There'll have to be a formal identification, but I saw her myself.' The image of Jenny's bloated face swam into her memory.

The realisation that she had seen the young woman's lifeless body lying cold and sodden on the towpath seemed to jolt him into action. He stood up. 'Oh, Sal, I didn't think. Do you want to sit down? Can I get you something? Tea, or would you prefer coffee?'

She'd seen this reaction in people before; the need to block out the unbearable news they'd just received with some form of activity. But this wasn't just another bereaved relative; this was David, her David. The sudden realisation that she thought of him that way felled her as soundly as any crowbar-wielding thug. She had an overwhelming urge to wrap her arms around him. But she had to treat this like any other unexplained death she encountered. The canteen grapevine had already sussed she was seeing one of the archaeologists from the dig. It wouldn't take long for word to reach DCI Morgan that the dead woman worked for the man that Sally was sleeping with. And he would be less than happy if David received that news from anyone but her. Even then, he wasn't going to be a ray of sunshine when she told him.

There was no guarantee that he'd let her stay on the case. And in the meantime, she couldn't afford to put a foot wrong. If Jenny's death turned out to be anything other than an accident she might be forced to make a tough choice.

'I'm used to it, David. It's my job.' It was partly true, though she'd never entirely come to terms with the sight of sudden death. At times like this, she envied the detachment some of her colleagues appeared to have when they dealt with the discovery of the newly dead and its aftermath.

He looked hurt. Had she been too short with him? Maybe, but she couldn't afford to let that distract her. 'When did you last see Jenny?'

'It must have been yesterday morning – she and Margaret were about to head off into town with the students.'

'And do you know what she was planning to do when they got back?'

'No. Margaret might know, but Jenny had been keeping herself to herself lately.'

'Any idea why?'

'I got the impression she was a bit down. I think she'd been having a rough time of it.'

'How do you mean?'

'Some sort of trouble with her love life, I think. I don't know the details. You'd be better off speaking to Clare about that.'

She moved on without acknowledging the suggestion. 'Would you have said she was depressed?'

'You think she killed herself!' He seemed to take her silence as affirmation. 'Look, Sally, I was her lecturer, not her best friend. If at all possible, I avoid getting tangled up in my students' personal lives.'

'I'm just trying to get an idea of her state of mind.'

'Then you'd be better off talking to a psychiatrist.'

'Look, David, I'm just trying to get to the bottom of what happened to Jenny and I could really use your help.'

He closed his eyes for a second and let out a deep breath before opening them again. 'OK, point taken. Jenny is – was – a quietly optimistic soul usually. She rolled with life's punches and got on with whatever she was asked to do without making a song and dance about it.'

'You sound as if you liked her.'

'I did.' He paused as if weighing something up. 'She was an intelligent young woman. Not a rocket scientist, but bright and hard-working too. I used to think she had enough about her to ensure she'd make a go of it in archaeology when she finished her master's.'

'You sound like you might have changed your mind about that.'

He nodded. 'I don't feel good about saying this, but to tell you the truth her work hadn't really been up to scratch lately. She seemed distracted – stressed. The undergrads in her trench had noticed. They started playing her up on-site. I even thought about getting rid of her.'

'She was that bad?'

David nodded. 'This site's so important we can't carry a site assistant who's not up to it. But, in the end, I couldn't bring myself to do it.'

If things were that rough for the girl, maybe that explained why he'd immediately assumed that whatever had happened to her had been linked to booze. The smell of alcohol on Jenny had been strong enough that Sally could still smell it even after her body had spent the night floating in the canal.

'Can you think of anything at all that might have caused her to want to harm herself?'

'Like I say, she seemed very down.' He paused before saying, 'There was one thing. But I don't suppose it was important. I think there was some sort of to-do about her tent.'

'What sort of "to-do"?'

'Apparently, a couple of nights ago she got a bit hysterical when she came back from site. Started accusing some of the undergrads in her trench of ransacking her tent.'

'Ransacking?'

'Jenny's words, not mine. She said someone had been into her tent, been through all her stuff, then deposited the contents of the bag containing her personal laundry outside on the grass.'

'Was anything missing?'

He smiled for the first time since the start of their conversation. 'Not everything's a crime.'

It was true that she did view life through glasses with a darker tint than most of the inhabitants of rural Wiltshire. It was the job; there was no escape from it. It consumed your every waking moment and taught you to look for the worst in everyone and everything you came across. But there was more to it than that. Her early memories weren't as warm and cosy as David's comfortable middle-class upbringing. She knew he was only teasing, but it didn't stop her feeling that sometimes she needed the Clifton Suspension Bridge to cross the gap between his world and hers.

CHAPTER TWENTY-EIGHT

'It was pretty grim, to tell you the truth.' A sudden gust caught the French windows overlooking the patio and Ed got up to close them. The freshening wind was accompanied by rain and before he'd regained his seat, heavy drops of water were running in rivulets down the glass.

Sally Treen, West and Ed were sitting around the coffee table in the latter's well-appointed drawing room. Sally had spent a good deal of the last few days trying to tie up the loose ends with Jenny's death. Dealing with the aftermath of the totally pointless waste of a young woman's life made investigating a forty-year-old murder with a long-dead perp seem like an even more pointless waste of police time and her energy. But what Morgan wanted, Morgan got.

At least, to her surprise, Ed had admitted that he was on-site when Gerald had cremated the body. In fact, everything he'd told them so far backed up Joyce Clifford's version of events. According to Ed, he'd arrived on-site only after the body had been burned and was unrecognisable. He claimed Gerald hadn't seen him and he appeared to have no idea that he and Gerald were not the only two people on-site that day.

It was a mystery to Sally why so many people seemed determined to believe Gerald hadn't killed his brother simply because he came from a nice respectable home with all of the advantages in life. But she couldn't help feeling a certain satisfaction that the evidence seemed to be backing up her instincts.

'Why didn't you report what you saw to the police? You let a murderer walk free.'

'I was seventeen, for Christ's sake, and I'd just seen my best friend's uncle roasting someone on a bonfire.'

She raised an eyebrow. 'Are you saying you were in some sort of shock?'

'No, Sally, I'm saying I was bloody petrified. The moment I realised what Gerald was doing, my world turned upside down.'

She bristled at the intimation of familiarity in the use of her first name. 'The truth is you were a witness to a murder and you failed to come forward.'

'But I didn't see anyone being killed.'

'So you're saying that when you saw Gerald cremating his own brother alone, on a hilltop in the middle of nowhere, you thought he'd died of natural causes.'

She sat impassive, apparently unmoved by the image she had conjured up. But inside she shivered. What sort of a man could do that to his own brother and then calmly stash his crushed-up remains in the attic of his own house? In her experience, murder knew no boundaries. Even the most apparently respectable people proved to be completely lacking in morals.

'You must have realised it was Jim – once you found out he'd disappeared. But you still chose not to say anything.'

'Of course I had my suspicions. But I wasn't certain until the inquest.'

'You don't seriously expect us to believe that, do you, Mr Jevons?'

Ed slumped back into his seat, his head on his chest. Then, pulling himself upright by the arms of his chair, he leant forward. 'Put yourself in my shoes. Peter was my best friend and Gerald was more of a father to me than mine had ever been.'

Ed stood up and placed both hands on the mantelpiece. He let the solid block of hewn limestone take his weight and then, drawing in a deep breath, turned to face them. 'Jim was a bastard. He treated Estelle and Peter like shit, and Gerald was constantly bailing him out of one mess or another.'

West looked up from his notebook. 'What sort of mess?'

'Money, mostly. Money and women. Jim's two favourite pastimes were gambling and other people's wives.'

'Did Jim's wife know about the other women?'

Ed nodded. 'Estelle was an intelligent woman and Jim never went out of his way to hide his indiscretions.'

Sally said, 'And Estelle didn't object?'

'What do you think?'

'How exactly did Gerald bail Jim out?' she asked.

'Most of the women Jim hung around with were old slappers.'

West raised an eyebrow. His glance towards Sally didn't go unnoticed by her.

Ed managed a diffident shrug by way of apology. 'A few quid from Gerald normally sent them packing. Gerald must have known every bookie in Wiltshire by the time he'd finished paying off Jim's debts. Even then the smug little shit wasn't satisfied.'

'He wanted more?' Sally thought back to their conversation with George Clifford. 'Was Jim blackmailing Gerald about his affair with Peggy Grafton?'

Ed snorted. 'That frigid little—' He stopped short, seeming to think better of whatever he was going to say. 'Peggy Grafton wasn't having an affair with Gerald, or with anyone else for that matter.'

'But Jim was intending to squeeze his brother for more money.'

'Not so much squeeze as take. Jim was planning to steal the gold from the excavations.'

West asked, 'How did you find out?'

Ed returned to his seat. He placed his elbows on the arms of the chair, resting his chin on his steepled hands. He seemed to be trying to make his mind up about something. West looked at Sally questioningly. She lifted her hand slightly in response and gave the merest suggestion of a shake of her head. West blinked his understanding.

After what seemed like an age, Ed clasped his hands together and dropped them into his lap. 'Jim offered to cut me in on the deal – to shut me up.'

'To shut you up?' Sally's tone brightened. Now they were getting somewhere.

'I overheard him talking about it.'

'Who to?' Sally asked.

Ed shrugged. 'They were outside the pub – it was dark.'

'Did you accept?' Sally asked.

'I played along. I wanted to get proof of what Jim was planning to take to Gerald. So I needed to convince Jim I was serious. Gerald didn't trust him as far as he could throw him. But Jim knew Gerald trusted me. So he asked me to find out what Gerald's security arrangements were.'

She allowed herself a smile. She couldn't condone Ed's behaviour, but she was beginning to see how his mind worked. 'Is that why you followed Gerald up to the dig site?'

Ed nodded. 'I knew I might never get another chance to do something about Jim. But, if I played along with him, I could make sure I had enough on the bastard that he couldn't wheedle his way out of it.'

CHAPTER TWENTY-NINE

The party of Americans who passed through Hungerbourne that morning on their B-road tour to Avebury and Stonehenge could have been forgiven for thinking they'd arrived in November rather than August. It had started to rain mid-morning and hadn't stopped. By lunchtime, most of the roads that ran along the valley bottoms on the Downs were impassable by anything other than a four-wheel drive. The Hungerbourne, which had been trickling for weeks, had turned into a torrent. Bubbling down the narrow coomb that ran past the barrow cemetery, it disappeared into a culvert beneath the village high street only to reappear on the far side of the manor.

They'd tried sitting it out in the huts up on-site to see if the weather would improve. But by lunchtime it was obvious, even to David, that trying to carry on digging would wreck more archaeology than it revealed. So he'd called them all off-site to let everyone try to dry out.

David, Clare, Margaret and Jo were sitting around a trestle table in the mess tent, taking solace from four mugs of steaming coffee. Margaret produced a small hip flask from the pocket of her cardigan and proffered it to the assembled company.

Only David accepted, pouring a generous slurp into his chipped Bath Rugby mug. 'What are we going to do for the rest of the day? There must be something productive we can get this lot to do.' He nodded in the direction of the bedraggled collection of students behind him. They were hanging an assortment of sodden clothing and sleeping bags over wooden benches that were ranged around an old Calor gas heater that Tony had unearthed from his garage.

Clare warmed her hands around her mug. 'They've had enough, David. Trying to work in this is no joke and they're not used to it. They're whacked.'

Margaret said, 'Why not give them the afternoon off? Let them get the bus into Marlborough. It might cheer them up to have some free time.'

David grimaced. 'If this weather keeps up, we won't be finished when the machines come in to start backfilling. We should at least get them to wash some of the finds.'

Margaret said, 'Go easy on them, David – losing Jenny like that has been really rough on them.'

'It's been rough on all of us, but we can't afford to lose any more time. I've already got British Heritage on my back over the newspaper articles. They've hauled me in for a meeting in Swindon this afternoon.'

Jenny's death had made the nationals. When the press had come sniffing, some of the locals had been only too willing to spout rubbish about the legend of the Woe Waters. And things had only got worse when someone – he suspected one of the students – had told them about the graffiti on the site hut. So before he or anyone else could do anything to stop it, one unfortunate young woman's suicide had morphed into the ancient burial ground with the killer curse. King Tut's tomb, it seemed, had nothing on the Hungerbourne dig site.

David knew there was every chance that British Heritage had called the meeting to tell him they were pulling the plug on his funding. Clare and Jo would lose their jobs and the Runt would take great pleasure in ensuring his name was top of the list when the next round of departmental redundancies hit. But worst of all was what this must be doing to Jenny's parents. God only knows what they must be going through. It was bad enough losing your only daughter like that without being hounded by a pack of muck-raking journos.

Clare said, 'The finds will never dry out in this weather. The pottery will turn to mush.'

Margaret peered over the top of her spectacles. 'She's right. And you're not going to help matters by making this lot even more miserable than they already are.'

He knew he should be the one trying to keep their spirits up – to keep the team positive. But despite his best efforts, he couldn't find anything about the current situation to be positive about.

'I know,' he conceded.

'Why don't you give them the rest of the day off and ask for a few volunteers to help sort out the plans?' suggested Jo.

Margaret pushed her spectacles back towards her brow from the end of her nose and smiled. 'Wise words from the colonies – a rare thing.'

Jo grinned.

For an instant, David felt the briefest flicker of relief. 'Everyone agreed?' They all nodded and he slapped the flat of his hand down on the rough wooden surface of the table. 'Settled.'

Clare said, 'There's a flaw in the scheme.' The others turned and looked at her. 'Most of the plans are in the office up on-site.'

'No problem,' Jo said. 'David and I can go collect them in the Land Rover.'

David glanced down at his watch. 'If we get a shift on we should just be able to get up there and back before I have to head off for my meeting with BH.'

David and Jo splashed their way up to site in the Land Rover, fording pools of water more like small lakes than puddles. He pulled on the handbrake and patted the top of the steering wheel. 'The old rust bucket has her uses.'

Jo opened the passenger door, swinging her body round to enable her to push off against the footrest. A moment of resistance was followed by a loud ripping sound as her jacket caught on a metal rivet on the door surround.

'Shit!'

David made his way round to examine the damage.

She raised an arm aloft and looked at him accusingly. The two sheets of Gore-Tex previously forming the front and back of her waterproof now flapped freely in the whipping wind and rain. 'Lovable old rust bucket, huh?'

David looked crestfallen. 'Nothing's perfect.'

He made his way round to the rear door of the Land Rover and began rummaging beneath a midden of buckets and plastic bags. Jo was fiddling with a large bunch of keys, trying to find the right one to open the office.

David tapped her on the shoulder. 'Here, Clare, left this in the back.' He thrust a bundle of muddied red fabric towards her. 'Put it on then, before you get drenched!'

She hurriedly pulled on Clare's bright red waterproof, flinging her own into the back of the Land Rover in exchange. Suitably attired, she turned to David. 'Why don't you back up to the office steps so we don't get the plans soaked?'

It took the two of them less than ten minutes to select the sheets of drafting film they needed and roll the plans up into neat cylinders for their journey back to base camp. They stacked them all into two plastic carry boxes, and David hefted them into the back of the Land Rover.

He glanced down at his watch. 'If we get a move on, I should just be able to get over to Swindon in time for the meeting.'

She was checking distractedly through the pockets of her unaccustomed waterproof. Finally, she looked up at him. 'I can't find the keys.'

David raised his hand in the air and dangled the Land Rover keys in front of her.

'No, the site hut keys. I had them to open the office and now I can't find them.'

David let out a long, low sigh.

'You get the plans back to the others at camp and get off to your meeting,' she suggested. 'I know they're here somewhere. I'll have to go through the office.'

'How are you going to get back?'

'I've got legs.'

'I'm really not sure about leaving you up here on your own, Jo.'

She knew what he meant. They hadn't talked about the newspaper article since she'd joined the dig. But she could see he'd been more than usually cautious about security around site. And Jenny's untimely death had made them all the more aware of how precarious and precious life was.

'I'll be fine. I'm not going to be up here long.'

She could sense his anxiety as he touched her lightly on the arm. 'Promise me once you've locked up you'll go straight back down to camp.' She nodded. He hesitated for a moment, then said, 'If you're sure?'

She nodded again, gesturing towards the Land Rover. 'Get going.'

It took her longer than she'd anticipated to solve the problem with the keys. Unable to find them, she'd had to root through the tool box to find a spare padlock before she could secure the office. By which time the torrential rain had transmuted itself into an all-enveloping cloud which seemed to permeate every inch of her skin.

She cursed under her breath, pulled the hood of Clare's waterproof up tight around her face and began the trudge down the lane back towards camp. Approaching halfway on her journey, the width of the lane diminished, its grass verge narrowing. Water gushed downhill over the potholed tarmac surface like a river filling a dry stream bed. She struggled to gain her footing as she climbed onto the narrow verge to avoid the cascade, grateful for the reassuring squelch of her gum boots in the saturated turf.

Behind her she could hear the low thrum of a diesel engine. She turned aside. Her back against the straggly remnants of the ill-kempt hedge, she leant against the prickles of the blackthorn to give the driver room to pass. It sounded like a four by four. But the impenetrable shroud of moisture that swathed the whole of the Downs prevented her from seeing either driver or vehicle.

It seemed to have pulled up behind her. Maybe it was David, having come back for her. She was about to step down into the road to check when the pitch of the engine shifted up a notch and the lights reared up towards her. Raising her hand in front of her face, she tried to shield herself from the dazzling glare of halogen. She pressed herself backwards, forcing herself to endure the hypodermic intrusion of sloe thorns through skin. Her boots dug into the grass verge, sending a scree of mud sliding onto the road surface below, unbalancing her into the hedge in the process.

For a second, the noise of the engine quietened and the beams of light wheeled away from her line of sight. She rolled sideways and tried to manoeuvre herself onto all fours to push up against what remained of the hedge and regain her footing. She was aware of the palms of her hands being punctured by the thorns ripping into the soft skin. But, with one hand clutched to her side in an attempt to dull the sharp pain in her ribs, somehow she managed to scramble upright.

She could hear the diesel engine idling. *They could have killed me. They could have damn well killed me!* They just seemed to be sitting there. Well, she wasn't going to let the bastards get away with it. She stepped towards the vehicle, rehearsing the stream of invective she would deliver. Then suddenly the engine roared. Two beams of light angled up over her head and she felt the sickening impact of metal on bone.

'Sounds like David's back.' Tony was standing behind the bar, drying up glasses. He inclined his head in the direction of the car park from where the sound of a low chugging engine was coming.

Margaret looked up from behind the plan she'd been studying and laid it on the table in front of her. Tony had allowed them to commandeer a corner of the bar as a temporary office and she was surrounded by ring binders full of mud-smeared context sheets.

When the door opened, it was Ed, not David, who appeared. She watched as he divested himself of his tweed cap and Barbour, shaking silver pearls of water first from its waxed surface and then from himself in a manner that reminded her of an old Labrador she'd once had. She smiled. 'You look like a man who could do with a drink.'

'Astute as ever, Peggy.' Her displeasure at his use of the diminutive was muted when he added, 'Care to join me?'

'You could twist my arm.'

'G and T for me, a whiskey for Peggy and whatever you're having.' Tony dutifully obliged. Ed raised his glass to hers. 'To old times.'

'I'd rather drink to the future.'

He nodded, chinked his glass against hers and took a long slug of G and T.

The strained expression on his features was all too apparent. 'Rough morning?'

'I've had the police round at my place asking questions about Gerald and the first dig.'

'Only to be expected in the circumstances.'

'I could have done without it.'

'I suspect that's a common reaction to finding the police on one's doorstep.'

Over Ed's shoulder, Margaret saw the door to the ladies' swing open.

'Where's mine?' Clare grinned across the bar.

Ed jerked his head round, causing the glass in his hand to lurch sideways and slop a trail of colourless liquid onto the sleeve of his jacket. Margaret watched the colour return to his complexion as he placed his glass carefully on the bar and mopped up the damage with a tissue.

He smiled at Clare and cleared his throat. 'What would you like?'

She joined them at the bar, placing a hand briefly on his arm by way of an apology. 'Glass of Shiraz, please. Hope you haven't got a dicky ticker, Ed?'

'I think it's the police that have given him a bit of a fright,' Margaret said.

Clare looked quizzical.

'I've had Sally Treen round at my place asking questions.'

Clare offered a sympathetic smile.

'I imagine they'll get round to us all eventually,' Margaret said.

Ed looked around the bar. 'No David or Jo?'

'David's at a meeting and Jo's still up on-site.' Margaret walked over to the window, wiped away the condensation and peered out. The blanket of low-hanging cloud was getting thicker. 'Someone ought to go and look for her. It's been nearly two hours.'

Clare said, 'I tried her mobile. There was no reply. She always turns it off when she's working. You know what she's like. She's probably got caught up in something at the office.'

CHAPTER THIRTY

'I can't stand it; we've been here hours and we still have no idea how she is. Even that paramedic wouldn't tell us anything.'

It was Clare's second trip to Great Western A & E in a month and she was enjoying this one even less than the first. She was sitting next to Margaret on the hard plastic chairs in the waiting area. David was pacing the floor in front of them.

Margaret wrapped an arm around Clare's shoulder, enveloping her in the fuzzy green wool of her cardigan, and looked over towards David.

He dropped onto his haunches, pressing Clare's hands between his. 'If it's anybody's fault it's mine. I could see the weather was foul; I should have insisted on driving her back to camp. But all I could think about was that bloody meeting with British Heritage.'

Clare sniffed. 'No, I should have gone to look for her when Margaret suggested it. God knows how long she'd been lying there when they found her.'

David shook his head. 'If I hadn't given her your jacket, her mobile wouldn't have been in the back of the Land Rover when you tried to phone her.'

Margaret said, 'Oh for pity's sake, listen to the pair of you! Carrying on like this isn't going to help anyone. None of us are to blame for what happened to Jo. And what she needs right now is our love and support. It's our job to make sure she gets through this.'

Clare looked up into David's steady grey-green eyes. He squeezed her hands and nodded.

The double doors at the end of the corridor swung open and a female doctor wearing green overalls entered the waiting room. She looked exhausted. Clare wiped her eyes and blew her nose with a paper hanky that Margaret produced from her cardigan pocket.

The doctor glanced down at her clipboard. 'Is there anyone here with Josephine Granski?'

They all nodded.

'Are you relatives?'

David stepped forward. 'We're the nearest thing she's got on this side of the Atlantic.'

She offered a practised smile. 'You'll have to do, then.'

Was the smile a good sign or a consummate professional trying to soften the blow? Clare couldn't bear it any longer; she had to know.

She stood up. 'Is she . . . ?'

'She's just come out of surgery. She's sustained multiple fractures to her ribs and her left femur, as well as a depressed cranial fracture.'

Clare couldn't help thinking that Jo would have known what that meant. 'Is she going to be OK?'

'It's too early to say for sure. Her ribs will heal in time and we've cleaned and pinned the fractured femoral shaft. The depressed cranial fracture is the biggest risk. The good news is that we've managed to remove all of the bone fragments cleanly. So now it's just a question of waiting to see.'

Clare asked, 'Can we see her?'

'We're going to need to keep her sedated for a while, I'm afraid, and then we'll need to run some tests. I'm very sorry; that's really all I can tell you at the moment.'

As soon as the doctor departed, Clare blew her nose loudly on the tissue, trying to clear her head. Margaret reached forward and touched David on the leg. He bent down to listen to her. 'Why don't you take Clare outside to get some fresh air? I'll stay here.'

He looked at her, uncertainty written across his face.

Margaret offered a reassuring smile. 'If anything happens, I'll come and find you.'

David guided Clare towards the front doors of the hospital. But outside, darkness had already fallen, and the wind and rain were battering against the windows. So they settled for a hot drink in the RVS shop.

He stirred his tea with a plastic swizzle stick. 'I phoned Sally earlier to see if she'd heard anything.'

Sally Treen was the last person Clare wanted to talk about, but it seemed churlish to dwell on her own feelings given what Jo was going through. She stared down into her cup, unable to muster any enthusiasm for the subject. 'Oh?'

He went to take a sip of his tea, but set it down again as soon as his lips touched the steaming brown liquid. 'Their take on it is that it was probably an uninsured driver or someone who's been disqualified. It happens a lot, apparently – and we get more than our fair share with Swindon on our doorstep.'

She fiddled with the wrapper of the Kit Kat David had insisted on buying her, but she felt no inclination either to eat it or to respond to him.

'When Margaret phoned and told me about Jo, I shot up to site to take a look for myself before coming over here.' She looked up, attentive now. 'The visibility was crap, but the police signs were still up so it was easy enough to find where it happened. There's a damn great hole in the hedge where Jo was rammed through it.'

She felt sick just thinking about it. It must have shown.

'Come on, have a sip of your tea.'

She shook her head.

'The verge was pretty churned up, but I could make out the tyre marks clearly enough.' He pulled his phone from his jacket pocket and tapped the screen a couple of times before handing it to her. 'Take a look.'

She sat motionless, staring at the image on the tiny screen. 'Does this mean what I think it means?'

David nodded. 'There were four sets of tyre marks. They all seem to be from the same vehicle. Whoever was driving must have hit Jo, reversed and then had another go just to make sure.'

She felt suddenly light-headed. 'What are the police doing about it?'

'Nothing. Sal's spoken to traffic. Zero visibility, no witnesses, and nothing but a few muddy tyre tracks. Unless Jo can give them a description when she comes round, Sal doesn't think they'll be able to do anything.'

They sat in silence for several minutes. They both knew what they were thinking, but neither of them dared say it: *If she comes round.*

'There's someone out there trying to kill people, David. They killed Jim Hart. And they've tried to kill me and Jo. And then there was poor Jenny.'

'What happened to Jenny has shaken all of us, but everything points to her taking her own life.'

'I know that's what the police think, but after everything that's happened how can you be so sure?'

He said nothing.

'Oh, come on, David. We've had threats about the Woe Waters daubed all over our site huts, one person's dead – two if you include Jim – and Jo is in there fighting for her life. We're way past a bit of bad luck here.'

'Please don't tell me you think there's something in this "curse of the Woe Waters" nonsense.'

'No, of course I don't. At least not in the way you mean. But there's obviously someone out there who does believe in it or at least wants everyone else to. And they're prepared to do whatever it takes to stop us finding out what really happened in Hungerbourne the first time round.'

'The police believe Jim's killer is dead. Sal told me she'd interviewed a witness who saw Gerald burn Jim's body on the pyre.'

'Jesus, David, Sally Treen isn't the fount of all bloody wisdom.'

He looked shocked, hurt even, but he said nothing.

She lowered her voice. 'I'm sorry. But don't you see? That doesn't prove Gerald killed Jim, just that he helped get rid of the body.' She jabbed a finger towards his phone. 'Besides which, Gerald didn't put Jo in a hospital bed.'

'That doesn't change the fact that unless Jo can give them something to go on, the police won't be able to take it any further.'

'But they have to!'

David shook his head. 'It's not going to happen, Clare.'

'We can't just leave it like this.'

He looked straight at her. 'And we won't.'

CHAPTER THIRTY-ONE

The Pines was a name singularly unsuited to a sprawling Victorian villa on the outskirts of Marlborough where the last stretch of coniferous forest had disappeared centuries before.

David could see that someone had gone to considerable expense to disguise the true nature of the place. The entrance hall looked more like a well-appointed country club than a care home. And the besuited manager guided David and Clare into a tastefully decorated lounge with the effortless grace of a well-polished maître d'.

The entire establishment seemed to be in denial. But David had spent too long watching his own father's decline in an identical institution to be blind to the realities of its daily business. And he couldn't help wondering what it must be like to come through those outsized doors knowing that the only way you would be leaving was feet first.

It must have been worse for his father – a medical man who would have been only too well aware of what lay ahead. Until recently, he'd never actually voiced his opinions to David on his son's very different career choice. But whether it was no longer having his wife around to temper his natural inclinations or as a consequence of his worsening dementia, any inhibitions he had on that front had vanished. David had become used to being greeted by a barrage of verbal abuse on his visits to the care home, as his father detailed his manifold deficiencies. He recalled with particular clarity the afternoon when his father had informed him that he'd wasted his life 'scrabbling around in dead men's shit'.

But he would happily have borne any number of such tirades rather than suffer the alternative. More often than not of late when he'd visited, he'd had to introduce himself to his own father and witness the confusion and fear that followed. As a consequence, his trips back to Derbyshire had become less and less frequent, until he'd reached the point when he'd considered stopping them altogether.

And now as he shuffled about on the leather Chesterfield, he felt decidedly uncomfortable. If he could have walked away there and then he would have. But that wasn't an option. It was time for him to start facing up to his responsibilities. He was the one who'd invited Jo down here and involved her in all this. After the incident on the photo tower and reading that article Jo had dug out for him on the Woe Waters, he'd known there was more to it than a few rotten planks and a bunch of kids with a spray can. He should have been more careful.

If he hadn't abandoned Jo up on-site, she wouldn't be lying in a hospital bed right now. He had no idea what they'd managed to get themselves tangled up in, but he was determined to put a stop to it.

His self-recrimination was summarily halted as the manager returned, pushing a wheelchair. Its occupant was instantly recognisable as the tall, slim woman from the Brew Crew photograph. Estelle Hart was immaculately dressed in a three-quarter-length taupe skirt and cream blouse with a single string of pearls hanging from her neck.

Peter had given him the impression that his mother was at death's door. And as a consequence, David had done everything in his power to postpone this moment for as long as possible. But Estelle Hart looked remarkably hale and hearty for a wheelchair-bound eighty-something. If he hadn't known, he'd have thought she was ten years younger.

Could he have misinterpreted what Peter had said? He dredged his memory banks, trying to recall exactly what Peter had said. After their conversation, David had made it abundantly clear to Clare that neither she nor anyone else from the project should go anywhere near Estelle. And despite everything that had happened since, to his surprise she'd done exactly what he'd asked.

Clare looked just as perplexed as he was. Had his insistence that they mustn't involve Estelle put Jo in hospital or, worse still, cost Jenny her life? He pushed the thought from his mind. There was no point dwelling on it. Margaret was right: self-recrimination wasn't going to help anyone. They were here now and Estelle was their best chance of sifting fact from fiction when it came to the events surrounding the first Hungerbourne excavations.

'I'll get someone to bring you some tea.' The manager straightened the green and brown scarf draped elegantly over Estelle's shoulders. 'Now make sure you don't overdo it, Estelle.'

She dismissed him with a flick of her wrist. 'Honestly, Charles, don't fuss! You're as bad as Peter.'

David waited until Charles had closed the door behind him,

leaving the three of them alone, before he spoke. 'Thank you for agreeing to see us, Mrs Hart.'

She smiled. 'When you rang, you told Charles you were friends of Peter. But I didn't quite understand why you wanted to see me.'

He hesitated and Clare gestured for him to get on with it. He'd rehearsed umpteen different opening gambits in the car on the way over here. He'd finally settled for a preamble about continuing Gerald's work at the barrow cemetery.

But as he looked into Estelle Hart's sharp blue eyes he could see that flannelling her was never going to work. 'A friend of ours – Dr Josephine Granski – is lying in a hospital bed because somebody tried to kill her.'

'I'm sorry to hear about your friend, Dr Barbrook, I really am, but I don't see what it has to do with me.'

David said, 'We think the attempt on Jo's life is connected in some way to your husband's death and the disappearance of a Bronze Age sun disc that came from the Hungerbourne barrow cemetery.'

Clare cut in. 'And possibly to the death of another young woman on our dig team too.'

He cast an admonishing glance at Clare. 'We can't be certain about Jenny – the police think it was suicide. But the fact is, Mrs Hart, Jo is in hospital and if it hadn't been for Ed Jevons' quick thinking, Clare here might have been killed too. So we're hoping you might be able to shed some light on what this is all about before anyone else gets hurt.'

Estelle said, 'Of course I'll help in any way I can, but I'm really not sure what I can tell you that would be of any use.'

He said, 'To be honest, we don't know either, Mrs Hart. But somebody seems prepared to go to any lengths to prevent us from digging into Hungerbourne's past and you're our best hope of finding out why. Anything you can tell us about what happened at the time of Gerald's excavation may help.'

Estelle turned to Clare and smiled. 'Peter told me about your accident, my dear. I know he was worried about you, but he didn't mention the unfortunate young woman who took her own life or your friend Dr Gretski.'

'Granski,' David corrected gently.

Estelle ignored him, her attention focused firmly on Clare. 'Tell me what happened to your friend.'

'She was the victim of a hit and run.'

'And you think it was deliberate?'

David cut in before Clare could reply. 'We know it was. The driver ploughed into her, reversed and then had another go to make sure they finished the job.'

Estelle put her hand to her mouth. 'But why would anyone want to kill her?'

Clare fixed David with a glare. 'They didn't.'

Estelle said, 'I don't understand.'

'They were trying to kill me.'

David turned to Clare. 'What?'

'There's no way anyone could have known it was Jo on that road. The only people who had any idea she was up on-site were you, me and Margaret. When they found her, Jo was wearing my waterproof with the hood pulled right up. Whoever was behind the wheel thought it was me.'

His heart was pounding. Was it possible? Had there really been two attempts on Clare's life? He nodded. 'It makes sense.'

Estelle looked from David to Clare. 'It doesn't to me, I'm afraid.'

Clare said, 'Peter told you about the missing goldwork.' Estelle nodded, but didn't say a word. 'I've been trying to find out what happened to it. So far I've managed to establish that it was the

Jevons sun disc that was stolen and then replaced with the one from Gerald's excavation. Whoever did it must have had access to both the excavation archives and the British Museum collections. And there's only one person who fits the bill.'

'You're not seriously suggesting Gerald stole it, are you? Archaeology was his life; he would never have done such a thing.'

'I know, and I didn't understand that either until I realised he must have been covering for someone.'

'That someone being your husband, Mrs Hart,' David said.

He searched Estelle's face for a reaction, but none was discernible.

Clare said, 'As far as the police were concerned, when your husband's remains were found in the attic of the manor that meant Gerald was a murderer. But it didn't explain what had happened to the sun disc, or why Gerald paid to have the archive moved into the manor and then set fire to the building it had come from.'

Estelle said, 'Now that really is absurd. Gerald would never have done that.'

Clare said, 'He paid over the odds for a removals company from outside of the area to move it from the coach house to the attic in the manor, no questions asked.'

'That's insane. Why on earth would he set fire to his own property?'

Clare said, 'That's something we were hoping you might be able to tell us.'

Estelle said nothing, instead staring determinedly down at her hands, clasped tightly together in her lap.

Clare said, 'If you don't believe me, you can ask Peter. He was the one who found the copies of Gerald's bank statements that proved it.'

Estelle looked up, the colour drained from her face. 'Leave Peter out of this! He has nothing to do with it.'

'Then tell us who has, Mrs Hart.' David leant forward in his seat and lowered his voice. 'The police think they've got everything worked out. They're convinced that Gerald killed Jim. But Clare has been telling me right from the start that there's something not quite right about it. I didn't believe her at first, but after what's happened in the last few weeks, I'm beginning to think she's right – that somebody else was involved.'

Estelle remained tight-lipped.

Clare said, 'We know Gerald cremated Jim's body. We even know where, when and how. But what we don't know, and what I can't understand, is why Jim's own wife didn't realise something was wrong at the time.'

For the first time since they'd arrived, Estelle looked flustered. 'I thought he'd run off with another woman.'

Clare said, 'Joyce Clifford.'

Estelle nodded.

David hadn't wanted to make this more difficult than it had to be but, despite her advancing years, Estelle Hart was clearly a woman who knew her own mind. 'That was very convenient, wasn't it?'

'Being abandoned by one's husband for another man's wife is not my idea of convenience, Dr Barbrook.'

'You weren't on the best of terms with Jim before his death, were you? Peter has told me more than once how much he detested his father and why.'

Estelle maintained her silence, refusing to be goaded.

He could feel the colour rising in his cheeks as he spoke. He cleared his throat. 'There's something about the Joyce Clifford affair that doesn't ring true to me. When a man leaves a woman, he doesn't just walk out and leave all of his possessions behind. He takes them with him. And from everything I've learnt of your husband, he was a man who liked his luxuries: good suits, expensive cologne, fast cars. It seems to me he would have taken anything he could lay his hands on.'

Estelle was visibly rattled. 'I don't know what good you think picking over old sores like this is doing your friend, Dr Barbrook.'

'You were Jim's wife. You must have noticed that he took nothing with him.' David glanced at Clare. She looked impressed. 'Gerald was no fool. He would have known that after he died someone was bound to examine the archive and work out who was in that cremation urn and very probably how they died. And yet he seems to have been perfectly content for everyone to know he killed his own brother.

'Everyone tells me how much he cared for you and Peter. But if that were true, why was he willing to let you endure all of the innuendo and stories in the press about the family that he must have known would follow the discovery of Jim's remains? Why would anyone subject their own flesh and blood to that? I keep asking myself: what could possibly be worse? I can't work it out, not after he'd gone to so much trouble. Even paying off Joyce Clifford to make sure she stayed away – to ensure that you and Peter remained secure and untroubled.'

Estelle gestured towards a jug of water and a glass sitting on a small side table. David filled the glass and handed it to her. She took two small sips before passing it back to him. 'Gerald was a gentle man – so unlike Jim. But he believed in loyalty. He would have gone to any lengths to protect the people he cared for.'

'Are you trying to tell us that Gerald did kill Jim?' Clare asked.

Estelle raised her right hand. 'I've been unable to share this with anyone for four decades. It would be easier if you would allow me to tell it in my own way.

'The last few months have been more difficult than any of us would have wished. Losing Gerald, then having his name dragged through the mud. What has sustained me is the knowledge that it was what he wanted. But he would have detested the idea that anyone else might get hurt because of it. Least of all someone Peter is fond of.'

David felt decidedly uncomfortable as he watched the smile that Estelle lavished on Clare.

'It's time to end it.' Estelle turned to David. 'You're very astute, Dr Barbrook. I was fully aware that my husband had not left with Joyce Clifford. He would never have left me.' David couldn't mask his surprise. 'I know what you must be thinking. But believe me, I had no illusions about Jim. I knew he felt nothing for me, but if he'd ever tried to leave me and Peter, Gerald would have cut him off without a penny. And life without easy money was inconceivable for Jim.'

'But you knew about the affair?' Clare asked.

'Oh heavens, yes. It wasn't the first and I very much doubt it would have been the last. I had passed the point of caring about Jim's dalliances. His philandering and gambling were minor irritations I'd learnt to live with. It was his drinking that made life unbearable. I'm not sure whether you will understand this' – she looked from David to Clare – 'but I think you might, my dear. You're an attractive young woman' – Clare blushed – 'and attractive young women attract men like Jim – wastrels.'

David shifted in his seat.

'I knew what he was like from the start. But he was utterly charming and such fun to be with. In the beginning, I would have forgiven him anything. But then he started to drink; really drink. And he changed. He became abusive – at first just verbally, but then physically too. I'm sure I don't have to paint you a picture. For a while, I thought I might be able to stop him drinking.

Persuade him that we should try to make a go of it for Peter's sake. But nothing changed. And then he started to threaten Peter.'

He leant forward in his chair. 'Did Gerald know?'

She shook her head. 'Not at first. He knew Jim drank too much and he knew about the arguments, but he had no idea that Jim hit me. I didn't want anyone to know how bad it was – least of all Gerald. I made all of the usual excuses: slipping on wet floors, walking into furniture.'

'But why hide it? If Gerald had known, surely he could have helped,' Clare said.

'If I had my time again, maybe I would. Lord knows I've thought about it often enough.' Estelle shook her head, staring down at the carpet. She seemed caught halfway between the present and a darker place. She lifted her head, looking first at Clare and then David. 'I didn't tell Gerald because I was afraid of what he might do. You see, I'd known for a long time that Gerald was in love with me.'

David lowered his eyes to the floor, unable to meet Estelle's gaze. Ed had been right; there had been more than the affection of a brother and sister-in-law between Gerald and Estelle, at least on Gerald's part.

'What happened when he found out?' Clare asked.

'He didn't find out how bad it was until it was too late.'

'Too late?' Clare said.

'Until I'd killed Jim.'

The words rattled around inside David's brain, jumbled, making no sense. '*You* killed Jim.'

Estelle nodded. 'Everything Gerald did was to protect me.'

Clare said, 'He must have loved you very much.'

Estelle turned to face her, eyes glistening. 'He gave up his career, his friends and his reputation.'

'How did it happen?' David almost whispered.

Estelle took a cotton handkerchief from her sleeve and dabbed at her eyes, then sat with it in her lap, twisting it first one way and then the other. 'This is the first time I've spoken about what happened that evening with anyone other than Gerald.' She closed her eyes and took a deep breath before opening them again. 'I came home one evening to find Jim in Gerald's office with the safe door open. I didn't even know he had the combination. He'd been drinking. When I asked him what he thought he was doing, he started yelling and shouting. I tried to shut myself in the kitchen to get away from him. But I couldn't get the door locked in time. And it just made him worse. He was raving. He grabbed hold of me and started shaking me. I kept screaming at him to stop. But he wouldn't. He kept banging me against the table. I thought he was going to break my back. I tried to use my hands to brace myself against the tabletop. Then I felt something – a bread knife. I just took hold of it and rammed it towards him as hard as I could. It was all over very quickly. There was blood everywhere. I didn't know what to do. Then I heard Gerald's car.'

'Where was Peter when all this was going on?' Clare asked.

Estelle was emphatic. 'Out. He'd been with Ed Jevons all day – drinking, we later discovered.'

'What did you do?' Clare said.

'I didn't do anything. I was useless. When I saw all of that blood I nearly passed out. I was shaking like a leaf. Gerald ordered me to go upstairs, run a bath and go to bed. He told me he would deal with it. I was like an automaton. I just did exactly what he said.'

For a few moments they all three sat in silence. As if no one knew exactly what the correct etiquette was during a confession to a killing.

Clare said, 'If we're going to stop anyone else getting hurt, we need to know what happened to the sun disc.' Estelle nodded. 'You said the safe door was open.'

She nodded again.

'What was in it?' Clare said.

'Gerald kept the goldwork in there. At the time I was in too much of a state to ask Gerald what had happened with the safe. It wasn't until later that he told me the disc was missing. Gerald thought Jim must have stashed it somewhere. He almost tore the house apart looking for it. But he couldn't find it. Eventually, he came to the conclusion that Jim must have given it to someone before I'd found him. Gerald had heard whispers around the village that something was being planned, but he could never get to the bottom of it. That's why he was so obsessive about security.'

'But why was the Jevons disc in the safe in the first place?' Clare asked.

'Gerald had taken it out of the British Museum to compare it with the one he'd found during the excavations. They were identical in every way, apart from the damage. He was convinced they were made as a pair.'

David rubbed his hand across his chin and nodded thoughtfully. 'They almost certainly came from different barrows. It'll be interesting to see what the radio-carbon dates from the associated remains are. We'll need DNA analysis to see if there's any kin relationship between them.'

For a moment, Estelle's face softened, the spark that had been so evident in her eyes at the beginning of the interview returning. 'You sound so like Gerald. Everyone says Peter takes after his uncle. I suspect the village gossips thought he was his father. But I never really saw it. Peter has always been a much more restrained sort of a man than Gerald. Gerald had such a passion for what he did. It was his whole life.' All at once the energy seemed to drain from her. 'Sometimes I wonder whether Peter ever really got over not having a father around.'

David placed a hand gently on Estelle's. 'From what Peter's told me, you and Gerald were all he ever wanted or needed.'

She smiled at him, squeezing his fingers with hers. Then, easing both of her hands away from his, she placed them resolutely on the arms of her wheelchair. 'Where's that tea we were promised?' She manoeuvred herself over to a small brass buzzer mounted just above the dado rail in the corner of the room. Within seconds an assistant had arrived and was duly despatched in search of the missing beverages.

Clare said, 'Why did Gerald decide to move the archive and set fire to the outbuildings? What had changed after all these years? Was he scared of something?'

Estelle shook her head. 'Not scared – worried. About eighteen months ago he came to see me. I could see he was preoccupied with something. At first he wouldn't tell me what was wrong. Peter had been trying to persuade him to give the archive to a museum for some time. Gerald just ignored him. But then he got a letter from a researcher at a university offering to help him publish it.'

David looked at the floor.

'Naturally, he refused. Gerald knew he could fob Peter off, but once other people started showing an interest in the archive again, wanting access . . . Well, he just couldn't let that happen. When he told me he was going to destroy the archive, I couldn't believe it. But he insisted it was the only way. When I heard about the fire, I knew he must have been responsible.'

David felt a knot of recognition twist in his stomach. He could barely believe it. This was his fault. His letter had been the catalyst for all of this. He looked at Clare. The thought that he had been responsible for putting her life at risk, however indirectly, made him feel sick.

Estelle was right; he had more in common with Gerald than he'd thought. In the end, Gerald would rather have seen his own reputation in tatters and be remembered as a murderer than have the woman he loved implicated or destroy the archaeology that had been his life.

They sat in the lay-by on the A4 looking west towards the Overton Hill round barrow cemetery, HGVs and vans dousing Clare's Fiesta with spray. The one thing they were agreed on was that whatever decision they reached, they both had to be able to live with the consequences.

Clare made her views quite clear. The right and proper thing to do was to go to the police and repeat what Estelle had told them. David was equally forthright in letting her know that they shouldn't withhold that sort of information from Sally.

What disquieted David most was not that Estelle had killed Jim, but that Peter had tried to dissuade him from talking to her. Did Peter know that his mother had been responsible for his father's death? Had he been trying to protect her? But neither David nor Clare could believe that was true. If Peter had known he would never have risked inviting David to Hungerbourne or asking him to publish Gerald's journals.

But whatever Peter's motive, the fact was that Gerald and Jim were both dead while Estelle and Peter lived on. What purpose would be served by incarcerating an elderly woman already suffering from a debilitating illness? Besides, after everything he'd already gone through, the psychological effects of Peter discovering his mother had killed his father were unfathomable.

It was patently obvious that Estelle couldn't have been

responsible for what had happened on the photographic tower, the attack on Jo or, come to that, Jenny's death. Whoever had been responsible wasn't interested in covering up Jim's killing. They were trying to stop anyone discovering the truth about what happened to the sun disc.

And so they decided. They would not be the people to reveal Estelle Hart's secret.

CHAPTER THIRTY-TWO

David returned from his trip to Marlborough to purchase supplies to find Clare sitting at his desk in the Portakabin, studying the contents of a large plastic bag.

He had thought it would prove difficult to continue with normal life knowing a secret of such enormous proportions. But in the event, he felt neither guilty nor anxious that they might be discovered. Sharing the decision with Clare had made it easier; not so much because the burden of knowing the truth had been halved, but rather because he was comforted by the knowledge that it bound them together in the same way that Estelle had been bound to Gerald.

But despite everything Estelle had told them, they were still no closer to retrieving the missing sun disc or discovering who had put Jo in hospital. What worried him most was that it was common knowledge that Clare had been asking questions about the sun disc. Ergo, someone thought she was too close to discovering the truth about its disappearance. And that meant she was still in danger. There was no way he could ask Sally for help. Not least because he couldn't risk what Estelle had told them coming out. So keeping Clare safe was entirely down to him.

He scraped the mud from his boots on the metal door surround and nodded in the direction of the bag she held in her hands. 'What've you got there?'

'Take a look for yourself.'

He slipped the knife out of the plastic finds bag and smiled. 'It's an old bowie knife. I had one just like it when I was a kid – all the lads round our way did.' But there was no hint of a smile on Clare's face. She obviously wasn't in the mood for exchanging childhood reminiscences. 'What's up?'

She shrugged.

'Where's it from?'

'The backfill in Gerald's trench.'

He reinserted the knife into the bag and slid it back towards her across the tattered desktop. 'In my highly trained professional opinion, that thing is most definitely not Bronze Age.' But when he saw her reaction his failed attempt at humour morphed into concern. 'What's wrong, Clare?'

She glanced across at the open door. He got up and closed it, before seating himself at the desk opposite her.

She looked at him. 'You don't get it, do you?'

He didn't.

She sighed. 'Estelle told us Gerald dealt with everything after she killed Jim. And we know Gerald closed the dig down straight away. And that thing' – she pointed at the knife – 'was found in the backfill in Gerald's trench.'

David stared down at the contents of the bag. 'You think this is the knife that killed Jim?'

Clare nodded.

He got up and walked over to where she was sitting. Feet tucked up underneath her, she looked like a depressed pixie. He laid a gentle hand on her shoulder and spun her round through ninety degrees to face him.

Crouching down, he pressed her hands between his and looked into her soft hazel eyes, the tiny golden flecks tarnished with worry. 'This has really put the wind up you, hasn't it?' He paused, choosing his words carefully. 'That is absolutely not the knife that killed Jim. Estelle told us she stabbed Jim with a bread knife. Remember? This is just some of the normal end-of-dig crap that gets chucked into the backfill.' He squeezed her hands between his. 'What Estelle told us, it's not easy stuff to deal with. But we've made our decision and we've got to stick to it. We've just got to keep our heads down and finish the job we came here to do.'

Clare raised her eyes to his, smiled and nodded. It brought him no comfort. He recognised that smile. It said, 'For external consumption only'.

CHAPTER THIRTY-THREE

'How are you feeling?' Clare set the copy of the report down on the bedside cabinet and looked up to see Jo lying, hair pulled back from her face, looking towards her.

On the far side of the hospital bed, a long snake of plastic tubing led from Jo's forearm to an intravenous drip hanging from a metal stand. The top of her head was swathed in bandages and her face was a terrifying palette of autumnal shades, streaked through with ruddy cuts. A criss-cross of jagged stitches ran down one side of her face and beneath her chin.

Jo touched two fingers to her mouth and croaked, 'Dry.'

The sign hanging above Jo's head said *Nil by Mouth*. A direction Jo made it very obvious she was less than happy about when Clare pointed it out. After a brief discussion with the nurse, she returned with a small cup of water to moisten Jo's mouth, though she had to endure the indignity of being made to spit its contents into what looked like a cardboard bedpan afterwards.

'Thanks for coming.'

'You didn't expect me to abandon you in here, did you? You had us really worried for a while.'

'It takes more than a crap bit of Brit driving to keep me down.' Jo's mouth ceased the attempted smile at the point where the corner of her mouth met one set of stitches.

Clare nodded in the direction of the nurses' office. 'They tell me you don't remember what happened.'

Jo went to shake her head, but winced at the attempt. 'I remember locking the office, and setting off back to camp. Then the next thing I remember is coming round with the nurse standing over me.'

Clare looked at Jo. She was always so confident and competent in everything she did that she'd never stopped to consider how young she was. But lying there swathed in protective wrappings, with the ephemera of life stripped away, she looked so fragile – almost childlike. It was a Jo entirely at odds with the force of nature who had breezed her way into the department on that first morning. She glanced down at the floor, blinking away tears.

If there was any other way, she wouldn't do this. She would leave Jo to recuperate in peace. But she had no choice. There was a killer out there somewhere and Jo was the only person who could tell her what she needed to know.

'What did David have to say for himself when he came to see you?'

'I haven't seen him. The only people I've seen besides you are Margaret and Peter. Peter brought me those.' Jo directed her gaze towards an exotic and very obviously expensive bouquet of flowers in a vase on the bedside cabinet. 'One of the nurses told me David had been in. But I was out for the count and they didn't want to wake me.'

Clare wasn't sure she should have started this conversation. But she knew it was too late to stop now. She dragged her chair closer to the bed.

She leant forward, her face close to Jo's. 'There's something I think you should know.'

Jo's eyes widened. 'What's happened? Is everyone OK?'

Clare rested her fingers lightly on Jo's hand and smiled. 'We're all fine. It's about your accident.' The emphasis on the last word was unmistakable. She had Jo's full attention. 'David went back to have a look at the spot where it happened. You'd been rammed clean through the hedge.'

Jo pointed to her bandaged head. 'I didn't think I'd got this at one of your English tea parties.'

'You really can't remember anything at all about what happened?'

'Like I said, I remember heading down the lane. The weather was just awful – I could hardly see a thing. David had given me your waterproof from out the back of the Land Rover. And I pulled the hood up real tight to keep the rain out. So I guess I wouldn't have heard or seen much before I got hit anyhow.'

'Jo, I know this is difficult. But you need to think. This is really important. Can you recall anything at all about the vehicle that hit you?'

Jo looked exhausted. 'I've told you I don't remember anything. Some asshole hit me and drove off. End of.' Jo paused. 'What's this about, Clare? Have they caught the driver? Do they know who it was?'

Clare shook her head. 'It's not that.' She took a deep breath. 'David found multiple sets of tyre tracks.'

'There was more than one of them?'

Clare shook her head. 'No, they were all the same vehicle. A four by four by the look of the tread marks. But the thing is, it didn't just hit you once. They had a second go. What happened to you wasn't any sort of accident. They were trying to kill you.'

'Back up a little. I know I'm pretty bust up, but my brain is functioning just fine. The waterproof I had on was yours. There's no way anyone could have known it was me under that thing. If they were trying to kill someone, it wasn't me – it was you. And the way I see it, it wasn't the first time.'

Clare nodded. 'I know – that thought had crossed my mind too. I'm so sorry, Jo; I think I'm the reason you're in here.'

'Screw that. I'm here because of the son of a bitch driving that four by four.' Jo signalled towards her mouth for another sip of water and Clare duly obliged. 'This has to be connected to Jim Hart's death somehow. Have you been rattling skeletons in too many closets?'

Clare laughed. 'That's rich, given what you do for a living.'

But Jo's expression was entirely devoid of humour. 'If I'm lying in a hospital bed because some mad bastard wants you dead, I think the least I deserve is to be taken seriously. We need to figure out who wants you dead.'

'It's not just me, Jo, not any more. Whoever ran you down doesn't know you can't identify them. And that makes you a target now too.' Clare held Jo's hand and gave it a squeeze. 'Do you trust me?'

Jo smiled. 'I guess having the same person trying to kill us must count for something.'

Clare picked up the report from the bedside cabinet. 'I've been going over your report on Jim's cremation. And I need your professional opinion about something.'

'My memory might not be so hot right now. But bones I can do.'

Clare wedged another pillow behind Jo's head as she winced, struggling to lever herself into a semi-upright position.

'You said in your report that the marks on one of the ribs were caused by a weapon with a serrated edge.'

Jo nodded. 'That's right.'

'Could it have been a bread knife?'

Jo raised an eyebrow. 'A bread knife.'

Clare nodded, but didn't elaborate.

Jo thought for a moment before shaking her head. 'Well, no. No way.'

'Are you absolutely sure?'

'Sure as anyone can be. A bread knife would have been all wrong. Whatever the weapon was, it had substantial serrations – teeth.'

Clare said, 'And the marks on the second rib fragment. They were caused by a blade with a more conventional cutting edge.'

Jo nodded. 'That's right. They're entirely different.'

Clare looked around, glancing over her shoulder towards the office at the end of the ward before picking up her bag from the floor and withdrawing the plastic bag containing the bowie knife. For a moment she had a vision of alarm bells ringing and orderlies running towards her. But as she slipped it onto the edge of Jo's bed, the only sounds were the rising and falling notes of the elderly lady's snoring in the neighbouring bed.

Jo picked up the bag, looking first at its contents and then the numbers written across the plastic in bold black marker pen. 'This came from site.'

She nodded. 'From Gerald's backfill.' She paused. 'Could it have caused both sets of cut marks?'

Clare watched as Jo examined the knife again, turning it over again and again until finally she was satisfied. 'Yes. I think it could. This could be the knife that killed Jim.'

Looking down at the great sweep of land that lay at her feet, Clare could see why Barbury Castle's Iron Age builders had chosen this spot to create the ancient earthworks on which she stood. Below her, a series of sinuous green lines threaded their way across the landscape, marking the boundaries of ancient fields. Some had been tilled and harvested by the same hands that built the hillfort over two thousand years ago.

At the base of the hill, the fields flattened out into an expansive plain, set in the middle of which was the sprawling mass of concrete and tarmac that was now Swindon. Somewhere within the network of ring roads and thrumming railway tracks lay a young American woman who'd given her the news that she'd expected but dreaded hearing.

She leant into the gusting wind, pushing through the drizzle as she navigated her slippery course along the chalk-incised crest of the bank. The air was chill and damp. She jammed her hands down into the pockets of her new waterproof. Her fingers clasped the plastic bag containing the knife, the handle of which poked a little too conspicuously out from beneath the pocket's Gore-Tex flap. She hadn't been able to bring herself to leave it in the car. It felt like the one thing connecting her to the truth about what was really going on at Hungerbourne.

She slithered her way down the bank, her thoughts a kaleidoscope of competing versions of reality. At one moment forming a discernible pattern, the next dissolving into unrecognisable fragments. Estelle had lied to them – that much was obvious. But why? It seemed unlikely she was trying to protect Gerald's reputation. After all, Estelle had implicated him in covering up the aftermath of Jim's death.

She trudged the muddy footpath back to the Fiesta, deep in thought, barely noticing her surroundings as the drizzle thinned and the cloud began to lift. Her concentration was broken by the metallic jingle of an ice cream van coming from the car park. She smiled. That sort of optimism should be rewarded. She ordered an ice cream with a Flake and sat down at a picnic table situated close by a life-sized reconstruction of an Iron Age round house. She began her methodical dissection of the sugar-laden treat with the Flake, hoping the energy intake might boost her powers of reasoning.

For a Saturday during the school holidays, the country park was quiet. No surprise given the weather. But a handful of hardy parents were resolutely ignoring the elements, determined to make their offspring enjoy their day out. A few metres away from where Clare was sitting, a family group were trying to have a picnic in the lee of the round house. Mum was fighting a losing battle with plastic plates and paper serviettes as the wind whipped at the corners of the blanket on which she'd staked out their territory.

In the doorway of the Iron Age hut, dad and son, a youngster of no more than eight or nine, were engaged in mock battle. The boy, face set in earnest concentration, was dressed in a horned helmet and wielding a small plastic sword. Dad, meanwhile, was forced to make do with decidedly inferior equipment and had selected a short length of hazel from among the wind-blown debris in the nearby shrubs as his weapon of choice.

The little boy parried and thrust, but, lacking his father's reach, was finally outmanoeuvred as dad sent the plastic helmet tumbling to the floor with a deft blow. He plucked the helmet from the ground and perched it precariously on his own head as the youngster proceeded to give him a good striping with the flat of his plastic blade in recompense for the theft.

Clare licked her ice cream and watched the mother looking on proudly at her two boys. For the briefest moment, more out of curiosity than envy, she wondered what it would have been like to have been part of that sort of family. But having a dad around was no guarantee of happiness – look at Peter.

Clare shuddered. For several moments she sat quite still until the sensation of cold, sticky ice cream trickling down between her fingers jolted her into activity. She rammed the remains of the cornet into a nearby rubbish bin and wiped her hands with a paper tissue. Fumbling in her pocket for the car keys, she made her way to the Fiesta and climbed in.

She took her mobile out of her bag and dialled David's number, trying to calm her breathing. 'It's me. I need you to meet me at the manor.'

'When?'

'Now.'

'But I—'

She cut him off short. 'Estelle lied.'

'What?'

'She's been lying to protect Peter. I'll explain when I see you.'

'You can't be serious? You think Peter killed Jim?'

'I'm not arguing, David. I've got proof. I'll see you there in twenty minutes.'

'Wait! Don't be a bloody idiot, Clare.'

She pressed the disconnect button.

Clare barely registered the presence of the speed camera signs on the long, undulating road that switchbacked its way through acre upon acre of open wheat fields between Barbury Castle and Hungerbourne. She prided herself on being a good judge of people. But she'd been wrong about Stephen and now it seemed she'd misjudged Peter too.

Her heart was pumping double-time as she slewed the Fiesta round onto the manor's gravel drive. Pulling up in front of the house beside Peter's black BMW four by four, she hurtled out of the car and up the steps, jamming her finger into the decrepit bell seated beside the flaking front door. No response. She wiped the grime from the hall window with the flat of her hand and peered in. There were no evident signs of life.

She returned to the front door, hammering on it with her fist. 'Peter!'

Finally, she heard Peter's muffled voice coming from somewhere beyond the hallway. 'Steady down. You'll have the door off.'

When he opened it, the same engaging smile played on his face that she remembered from the day she'd first met him. He looked her up and down, surveying her breathless state, his expression one of anxious concern. 'My God, Clare, what on earth's the matter?'

He was a cool character. She had to give him that. But then he'd had years of practice.

She made a conscious effort to control the tremor in her voice. 'I need to talk to you, Peter – now.'

He looked perplexed, but said nothing; instead, he held the door open and ushered her inside. The shabby elegance of the drawing room was a stark contrast to the clean, functional lines of his Marlborough flat. An open laptop and mobile on the side table next to the wing-back chair by the fireplace were the only visible concessions to modernity. Expecting him to sit in the chair, she perched on one end of the sofa opposite the fireplace.

But, instead, he sat down beside her. 'You're lucky to catch me. I'm only here because I'm still waiting for the electrician to turn up to give me a quote for rewiring this place.' He looked at her, apparently trying to take stock of her unaccustomedly serious expression. 'What's this about?'

Now that she was here, faced with confronting him on her own, she realised she had no idea what to do. Peter seemed to mistake her hesitation for distress and slid his hand forward to rest on hers. She snatched her hands away, depositing them firmly in her lap.

He craned his neck forward, peering into her face. But she looked away, unwilling to meet his penetrating blue eyes. 'What is it, Clare? You're frightening me.'

She glanced down at her watch. Where was David?

She drew in a breath and looked at Peter. 'I need to talk to you about something. Something I swore to David I'd never discuss with anyone else.'

Peter stiffened. 'What's between you and David is none of my business.'

'It's not just between me and David. It involves someone else.'

He looked at her questioningly.

Clare said, 'Your mother.'

'My mother!'

Whatever he'd been expecting, this obviously wasn't it.

'A few days ago David and I paid her a visit.'

Peter shifted slightly on the sofa. 'What on earth for?'

'Can't you guess?'

Peter leant back and looked at her. She had the impression he was examining her – reappraising what this new Clare signified.

'I haven't the faintest idea what you're talking about. If you've got something to say, why don't you just come out and say it.'

Clare glanced down at her watch again. She'd been certain David would be here by now. Surely he wasn't going to let her down when it really counted.

'For pity's sake, Clare, what is this about?'

She couldn't stall him any longer. She'd said too much to stop now. 'Your mother told us she'd known about your father's death.'

Peter's eyes left hers. He mumbled, half to himself, 'She knew?'

Clare nodded, her eyes fixed firmly on his face. 'She told us Gerald had been protecting someone.'

Peter's eyes returned to hers. He looked bemused. Could she have got this wrong? She told herself not to be such a fool. He'd kept this act up for almost three quarters of his life. It must come as easily as breathing to him now.

Well, she wasn't going to allow herself to be manipulated again, not by Peter or anyone else. 'She told us she'd killed your father.'

She held her breath, waiting for his response. He looked genuinely shocked. He stood up and made his way over to the window, staring out down the long sweep of the drive. For a few moments neither of them spoke.

He turned to face her. 'You're lying.'

His tone was cold and distant. She was surprised to find she felt hurt by it. But then she hadn't had much practice at this sort of thing. And as he remained motionless in front of her, her hurt began to change to fear.

'Why would I lie? Estelle told us she stabbed your father. If you don't believe me, you can ask David. He'll be here any moment.'

She fervently hoped that was true. Where the hell was he?

Peter's expression was one of complete incomprehension. 'I don't know what sort of game you're playing, Clare, but I don't believe you. My mother isn't a murderer. Why would she say she killed my father when she didn't?'

'She told us Gerald helped her cover it up. He disposed of your father's body.'

He shook his head, waving his hands in the air in a frantic gesture of denial. 'This is nonsense.'

What had she expected? That he would admit everything and meekly offer to turn himself in? She'd been a naïve idiot. He'd allowed everyone he supposedly loved and cared for to take the blame for his actions for the last four decades. Why on earth had she expected him to behave any differently with her?

She stood up. Her cheeks scorched red with anger. 'You've used me, Peter, and you've hurt the people I care about. There was a time when I couldn't have believed this of you. It was bad enough that you were prepared to let everyone believe Gerald was responsible for your father's death. But then somewhere along the line you got the idea you could silence anyone getting close to the truth. But surely even you aren't prepared to let your own mother take the blame?'

He shook his head. 'I've told you. My mother is not a murderer.'

'I know.' She spoke the words slowly, deliberately. 'We found something buried in Gerald's backfill. A bowie knife. Sound familiar?'

She could feel the weight of the knife jostling in her jacket pocket. What the hell had she imagined she was going to do – confront him with it? Face him down and demand an answer? That didn't seem such a good idea right now. In fact, as she sat here, murder weapon in pocket, with Peter just a few feet away on the other side of the room, there was quite a lot about her decision-making skills that she was beginning to question.

He said, 'I don't know what you're talking about.'

Her mouth felt dry. But she'd gone too far to back down now. 'No.' She almost spat the single syllable at him. 'You wouldn't, would you. You'd rather allow your uncle and your own mother to clean up your dirty work. I've seen the knife before, Peter. You showed me a photo of it when I came to your flat that first time. Remember? The photo of you and Gerald.'

She struggled to control her anger. Tears pricked her eyes. Her shoulders heaved. The rest of her words came in huge gulping sobs. 'How could you? How could you stand there in cold blood and show me that photograph, knowing you'd killed him with it?'

All at once his expression changed from blank denial to limp exhaustion. His shoulders sagged and he seemed to shrink in front of her. He shuffled the few feet from the window to the chair as if in a catatonic state and folded into it. And there he sat, bent forward, head in hands.

His words when they eventually came were directed towards the floor. 'I didn't know. Not when I showed you that photograph.'

Clare stood up, just a few feet in front of him. 'Oh, please. What do you take me for? Are you seriously trying to tell me you didn't know you'd killed him?'

He repeated the words. 'I didn't know. Not until that day in the coroner's court. You can't begin to imagine what it's been like since I found out.' He looked up at her, his blue eyes unblinking.

Her voice was flat, drained of all emotion. 'What happened?'

He held his arms outstretched, palms upturned, in front of him. 'I don't remember all of it. Ed and I had been drinking. There was a place we used to go to up in the copse. I was in a bit of a state by the time I got back here and I wasn't feeling too good.

'I went into Gerald's study to help myself from his whiskey decanter. And that's when I found my father with the safe door open. I screamed at him and asked him what the hell he thought he was doing. But he just looked at me and sneered. If I'd been sober, I'd never have spoken to him like that. But after everything Uncle Gerald had done for him, I was furious. I knew he was a bastard, but I never dreamt he'd stoop to stealing from him. I remember shoving him and then him taking a swing at me. After that I don't remember a thing. I must have blacked out. When I came to I was in my bedroom with the most almighty hangover, a lump the size of an egg on the back of my head and a black eye.'

'You seriously expect me to believe you can't remember stabbing your own father.' The disbelief on Clare's face was obvious.

'If you think it's unbelievable, just imagine how I feel.'

'And if you think I have any sympathy for you then you really don't understand me at all, Peter. I don't care how you try to justify this to yourself. But you damn near killed me with that stunt of yours on the photographic tower and what you did to Jo was unspeakable.'

Peter's face was filled with horror. 'What? You think that was me? No, no.' He shook his head violently from side to side. 'You've got to believe me, I would never . . . I could never . . .' He stopped mid-sentence, and plunged his head into his hands. For a few moments he sat in total silence. Then, taking a deep breath, he said, 'I'm not trying to deny killing my father. I'm just saying I don't remember it. And I could never hurt you, or Jo.'

'How can you expect me to believe that? You killed your own father, for Christ's sake.' She couldn't bring herself to look at him. She'd thought they had so much in common. She'd allowed herself to be comforted and flattered by his attentive charm.

'Whatever you think of me, I'm not going to let my mother take the blame for something I did. Ever since that day in the coroner's court when I found out Father was dead, I've been going over and over it in my head – trying to make sense of what happened. Please, Clare, I need you to understand.'

She stood, arms folded, lips clamped shut, unable to reply for fear of what she might say.

'When I came to the next day, Mother didn't say a word to me. But Uncle Gerald gave me a hell of a rollicking. He told me Mother had found me spark out, covered in my own vomit, lying in the hallway. The whole house reeked of bleach for weeks afterwards. I thought it was where the maid had cleaned up my vomit. But they must have cleaned it, mustn't they – the two of them.' His head sank back into his hands, his fingers digging deep into his forehead. 'Oh God. Mother and Uncle Gerald out there on their hands and knees scrubbing away my father's blood.'

It was all Clare could do to stop her gaze being drawn through the open door towards the Minton tiles beyond. But there was one thing she still needed to know.

Her voice was calm and steady. 'Think, Peter. You said the safe door was open. Did you see what was in it?'

He shook his head.

'You don't remember anything else?'

He took his head out of his hands, and closed his eyes for a moment before opening them again. 'When I woke up, someone had cleaned me up and put me to bed.'

He held his hands out in front of him, turning them over palms upwards and curling his fingers towards him. He seemed to be examining them. 'There was dried blood under my fingernails. What with the black eye and the lump on the head I thought it must have been where I'd been fighting with Father. I tried to explain, to tell Gerald about finding Father with the open safe, about fighting with him. I was terrified of what Father would do to me. But Gerald wasn't having any of it. He told me I wasn't to speak of him. Said we wouldn't be seeing him again. When I asked why, Gerald went mad. Said Father was a disgrace.

That he'd brought nothing but shame on the family. I'd never seen him like that before. I thought he was mad at me because I'd been drunk – acting like a lush just like my father. Of course, it wasn't long before the entire village knew Father had done a bunk with Joyce Clifford.'

Clare's voice was softer now. 'Or thought they knew.'

Peter looked up at her and nodded. 'You do believe me, Clare, don't you?'

'What I believe really doesn't matter.' She struggled to keep her tone even and dispassionate. But the truth was, despite everything, she did believe him, and that meant she was still no nearer to finding out who was trying to kill her.

'It does to me,' he said quietly.

She looked down at the faded woollen kilim on the floor in front of her and said matter-of-factly, 'You've got to tell the police, Peter. Tell them exactly what happened, before they figure it out for themselves.'

He nodded.

'Was there anyone else, anyone at all, who might have known what happened?'

He didn't get to answer. Outside, she could hear the sound of a car pulling onto the gravel drive. David. Finally! She walked over to the window and looked out to see two uniformed constables in a marked police car, and Sally and West climbing out of a silver Lexus. And trundling down the drive behind them was David's Land Rover.

'What is it?'

Peter got up and walked over to where she was standing. He looked out of the window, then without a word walked over to the sofa and sat down. Someone was banging on the back door. He stayed staring blankly at the unlit fireplace. He was still gazing inertly into the empty grate when there was a crash accompanied by the sound of splintering wood, and Sally and West, followed by an out-of-breath David, entered the drawing room.

Peter ignored Clare and David, turning instead to face Sally.

He spoke quietly and without fuss. 'I killed him. I killed my father.'

Sally nodded at West. He read Peter his rights, cuffed him and led him outside.

Clare turned to face David. 'Friendship means nothing to you, does it? Couldn't you even allow him the dignity of turning himself in?'

David opened his mouth but, seeming to think better of it, closed it again.

It was Sally who replied. 'Some people have the sense to realise these things are best dealt with by the professionals.'

Clare thrust her hand into her jacket pocket and handed the bag containing the knife to Sally.

'What's this?'

'I'd have thought a professional would recognise a murder weapon when they saw one.'

Clare marched out of the room without another word. Standing on the front steps, she watched as an utterly compliant Peter was led through the driving rain into the waiting squad car. Glancing over her shoulder, Clare caught sight of David staring out of the drawing room window. His eyes were fixed so intently on the back of Peter's head, he didn't notice her watching him.

When she turned her attention back to the drive, Clare thought she saw the hint of a smile flick across Sally's face as she climbed into the passenger seat beside West. It was all in a day's work to them. And her mind drifted back to another rain-sodden afternoon and another young female police officer standing on her front doorstep. When she'd delivered the news of Stephen's death, she'd wanted to stay, but Clare had refused. When she'd finally left, Clare had closed the door behind her, pressing her back against the wooden glazing bars and sliding down to sit crumpled on the cold, hard Minton tiles. And there she'd stayed for she couldn't remember how long, the veneer of normality ripped away, her life shattered beyond repair.

CHAPTER THIRTY-FOUR

'I'm not sure drinking in here was such a good idea.' Clare had positioned herself so that she could see the door from the table where they were sitting in the corner of the Lamb and Flag. Not for the first time this evening, she was looking towards it anxiously.

'You can't keep avoiding him.' Clare ignored Margaret. 'He's off out somewhere with Sally this evening. Besides, you can't blame him for what happened.'

'It wasn't what happened, it was how it happened.'

'Meaning?'

'He shouldn't have contacted the police.'

'Oh, don't be ridiculous. What did you think he would do? He was in the department in Salisbury when you phoned him – miles away. He'd have to have been out of his mind not to have called the police after what you told him.'

Margaret was right – Clare knew it. She'd known the police would have to be involved eventually. But she'd phoned David because she trusted him. He was Peter's friend as well as hers. She hadn't really thought it through, but she'd assumed that somehow together they could talk Peter into handing himself in. After everything he and Estelle had gone through, she'd figured that he deserved at least that.

She blamed herself every bit as much as David. She had every right to be angry with Peter – he'd killed his father. But, in truth, she felt sorry for the teenage Peter. Her anger had been directed firmly at Peter the man. She'd trusted him and he'd deceived her. She'd believed every word of his lies and he'd made her look like a fool.

Margaret's expression was reproving. 'Aren't your sympathies somewhat misplaced? He admitted killing his father. And after what happened to Jo and poor Jenny, you must see he had to be stopped.'

Clare lowered her voice. 'Peter had nothing to do with what happened to Jo. And we can't be sure that Jenny didn't take her own life.'

'That's not what you were saying a few days ago. And what about what happened to you? It was Peter who lent us the photo tower.' Margaret hesitated for a second as if she was considering something, but seemed to think better of it.

'I seem to remember everyone else had that down as an accident at the time.'

The two women sat in silence.

It was Margaret who spoke first. 'Don't you think you're being just a tiny bit naïve, Clare? I've known Peter all his life and I would never have dreamt he was capable of killing his father. But none of us can be sure what we might be capable of in extreme circumstances.' Margaret peered over the top of her spectacles.

'We can't change reality, however much we might wish to. We just have to find a way to live with it.'

Whatever Margaret might believe, she hadn't seen the look of horror on Peter's face when Clare had confronted him. She'd been convinced he was telling the truth: that he wasn't responsible for what had happened to her or Jo. And she still wanted to believe that, but where a few short months ago she would have trusted her instincts, now she wasn't so sure.

'How could I have been so wrong about him, Margaret?'

'Don't be too hard on yourself. You didn't know Jim. There are a good many people in this village who would have cheered Peter to the rafters if they'd known he'd killed him.' Margaret paused. 'And it seems to me that everything Peter has done since has been born out of desperation.'

Clare swirled the dregs of her Shiraz around in the bottom of her glass. 'Gerald must have cared a great deal about Peter to do what he did for him. Were they alike?'

Margaret shook her head. 'In looks, maybe, but not in any of the important things.' Clare raised a quizzical eyebrow. 'It's not what you think. They both took after Peter's grandfather in appearance. But Peter lacked the Hart self-confidence as a boy, whereas Gerald and Jim both had it in spades. Peter was much more self-effacing. Temperamentally he was more like his mother. He was a quiet child. Ed was his only real friend.'

Clare said, 'They seem to have stayed pretty close. Not all childhood friendships survive. I can't remember the last time I saw any of the kids I went to school with.'

Margaret said, 'You've got to remember that seventies Hungerbourne wasn't the well-heeled commuter village it is today. It was a tiny isolated village stuck out in the middle of the Downs. There weren't many boys of their age around, and Peter hero-worshipped Ed. A classic case of opposites attracting, I suppose.'

'But they had one thing in common, didn't they. They both hated their fathers.'

Margaret pursed her lips. 'I suppose that's true. I can't imagine either the Jevons or the Hart households were easy places to grow up in. But I was thinking more of their interests. Ed was always going to take over the farm. It was more than simply a family inheritance. He had a real affinity with the land – a sense of connection to its past.' Margaret took a sip of her whiskey and smiled. 'Ed and I spent a lot of time together when we were young.'

Clare laughed. 'I wouldn't have had Ed down as your type.'

'And you would be right – though not for want of trying on his part in his teenage years. But we shared a common interest.'

Margaret halted her explanation. The sound of raised voices was coming from the car park. Clare turned her head round towards the window in an effort to make out what was happening outside.

Clare couldn't see anything, but she could hear Tony's booming baritone. 'Look at the state of you. You should never have driven down here.' A door crashed against a wall. 'I'll call you a taxi.'

'No bloody blow-in is going to tell me what I can and can't do. Issheinthere?' Ed's words staggered into one another. There was another crash as woodwork hit brick and Ed himself staggered through the doorway.

Tony rushed in behind him and tried to interpose himself between Ed and the table where Clare and Margaret were sitting. But Ed shoved him to one side, sending him crashing over a bar stool and landing him with a resounding smack onto the flat of his back.

Ed gripped the edge of the table and leant forward towards Clare. She swayed backwards, trying to avoid the reek of brandy on his breath.

'Couldn't leave it alone, could you? We were fine before you stuck your nose in. Didn't anyone ever tell you that people get hurt when they mess with things they don't understand?'

Tony rolled onto his side and, gingerly touching one hand to the back of his head, tried to get to his feet. Transfixed by the scene unfolding in front of them, the students and villagers sitting around the bar watched in stunned silence.

Ed moved backwards, releasing then re-grasping the edge of the table in an oscillating motion that made Clare feel queasy.

He screamed at her, 'You called the police!'

Clare stood up. 'You should get your facts straight.' She glanced down at Margaret, who shook her head. 'And who phoned the police is irrelevant. You can't bury the past. You have to deal with it.'

It was Margaret who spoke next. 'How do you think carrying on like this is going to help Peter? God knows he could do with some real friends right now.'

Ed straightened up. 'Why you . . .' He didn't finish the sentence. He snatched Clare's wine from the table, swung back his arm and lashed it into the wall, spraying the two women with shards of glass and leaving a trail of sticky red liquid dribbling down the black-and-white print of the barrow cemetery that hung behind them.

Ed unbalanced forward.

Tony got to his feet. 'Enough!' Catching Ed by the arm, he twisted it up behind his back and shoved him against the bar. Tony's breathing was heavy. 'Call the police, Shirl.'

Shirl glanced over towards the door. 'No need.'

'What the . . .' It was Sally.

Tony gave Ed's arm another tweak. 'He's rat-arsed. Took a pop at me and tried to attack Clare and Margaret.'

'Right, Mr Jevons, you're going to spend tonight making friends with our custody sergeant.'

* * *

Sally was sitting at a small Formica-topped table in the middle of the interview room. Opposite her, someone had positioned a grey plastic chair. The narrow slit of frosted glass let into the wall high above to her left offered little in the way of illumination even in the hours of daylight. She could have been anywhere on planet Earth. She wondered if the public realised the average copper spent more time incarcerated than most cons.

She rubbed the back of her neck. The low-level buzz of the strip light wasn't helping her headache. Arching her spine backwards, she placed her hand to her mouth, trying to suppress a yawn. The scrawny young PC standing on the other side of the room offered an embarrassed smile. She glanced down at her watch. What was taking them so long? There was no chance she'd get to see David this evening.

The door swung open and a jowly-faced middle-aged sergeant entered with a gaunt-looking Peter. In the time since she'd last interviewed him, he clearly hadn't shaved. He sank down into the seat opposite her. She nodded and the constable started the tape machine. She spoke the time and date, and listed those present. Peter sat with his hands in his lap, his gaze fixed firmly on the tabletop that divided them.

Sally looked down at the papers in front of her. 'Thank you for being so forthcoming, Mr Hart, about the circumstances of your father's death.'

He raised his head and shrugged his shoulders.

'During your last interview, you told me you had nothing to do with the hit-and-run accident in Hungerbourne.'

'I don't know what else I can say to convince you.'

Sally looked into his brilliant blue eyes. Most people wouldn't be able to bring themselves to believe he was lying. But she'd had too much experience of people's capacity for deception to be so easily persuaded. She leant across the table and lowered her voice. 'If I were to believe you, Mr Hart, that would mean there's someone else out there with a reason for wanting Mrs Hills dead. Don't you think that would be a bit too much of a coincidence?'

'You mean Jo?' he corrected her.

Sally shook her head. 'Dr Granski was wearing Mrs Hills' jacket. The person responsible' – she looked directly at him – 'was trying to kill Mrs Hills.'

'If you think I want Clare dead, you're insane.'

'You supplied the photographic tower from which Mrs Hills nearly plunged to her death a few weeks ago. Mr Hart, isn't it true that you've perpetrated a sustained campaign of intimidation and violence against Mrs Hills and her colleagues?'

'No, no. I had nothing to do with any of it.'

Sally leant back in her chair, arms folded, and tilted her head slightly to one side. 'One of your friends seems to have taken exception to Mrs Hills' behaviour on your behalf.'

'What?' He looked confused.

She allowed herself a self-congratulatory smile – it was an old ploy, but an effective one. 'Ed Jevons attacked Mrs Hills in the bar of the Lamb and Flag.'

He pulled himself upright, his eyes wide with alarm. 'Is she alright?'

She ignored the question and consulted her notes. 'He told her that "People get hurt when they mess with things they don't understand." What do you think he meant by that, Mr Hart?'

'Shouldn't you be asking him that?' He paused. 'Is Clare alright?'

'No major injuries. But Ed Jevons was drunk. And very angry.'

'What about?'

'Your arrest.'

She watched as he sat, head in hands, so that she could no longer see his eyes. He ran his fingers through his hair and breathed in deeply before lifting his head again. 'You have to understand, Ed and I are like brothers. He's been a better friend to me than I've had any right to expect.'

'Well, he certainly demonstrated whose side he was on tonight.'

'Ed's always been very protective towards me. After the inquest, I was in a bit of a state. He knew something was wrong.'

She gave him an encouraging nod.

'He took me for a drink. Once I knew for sure it was Father in that urn, I had to tell someone. I told him everything. Do you know what he said?'

Sally just looked at him.

'He told me he already knew. Do you understand what I'm saying? He knew I'd killed my father. All these years and he's said nothing. He said it didn't matter.'

'To him, maybe.' Sally let the implication of her words linger. 'How did he know?'

'When he brought me home drunk that day, he was worried how my parents would react. So he hung around to check that I was OK. He saw the whole thing through the hall window.'

She hoped she was managing to disguise her surprise. Did he really have no idea of the implications of what he was saying? He'd just provided her with the name of a witness – if she could get Ed Jevons to talk, that would stand up far better in court than a confession to something the accused claimed not to remember.

'He saw my father attacking me. The fight. Everything.'

So that was his angle. He was going for self-defence. The most convincing lies were always a version of the truth. If he'd persuaded his childhood chum to go along with this one in their cosy little chat after the inquest, it would explain why Ed was beginning to get so nervous about his role in the cover-up.

Her tone hinted at her incredulity. 'So he watched you kill your father and stood by and did nothing?'

'When he heard Gerald's car he legged it. What Ed did in the pub – I don't condone it. But he was trying to protect me. If you're going to blame anyone for all this, it should be me.'

She cursed inwardly. She could have done without this. She'd only released Ed Jevons a few hours ago. But if she was going to prove Peter Hart's guilt, she'd have to bring Jevons back in for questioning.

CHAPTER THIRTY-FIVE

Clare stared down at the faded ink on the single sheet of foolscap in her hands and shivered, shocked by the startling ring of familiarity.

She was sitting at the end of a long wooden table in an upstairs room of Wiltshire Heritage Museum in Devizes. A large Gothic window set into the wall behind her flooded the room with natural light. The window, in combination with the functional plastic chairs stacked against the wall to her left, reminded her of a church vestry.

When David had asked her to do some research on the flint collected from the area surrounding the barrows, she'd jumped at the chance, grateful for an excuse to take her away from the oppressive atmosphere that hung over the excavations. Three long, low cardboard boxes lay on the table in front of her. Beside them, the curator had deposited a small, blue cardboard wallet containing a sheaf of notes and letters written by Reverend Hemmings, the erstwhile vicar of Hungerbourne. The letters spanned a forty-year period from 1935 to 1974. Their subject matter centred on prehistoric stone tools collected from the fields in his parish.

But these were no dusty museum accounts. Interspersed with the recording of the artefacts were tales that revealed the reverend's interest in local folklore. Skimming through the pages, she'd discovered stories of unsuspecting travellers lured to their doom by ethereal nocturnal music emanating from the barrows, an otherworldly horseman and the dreadful consequences of the running of the Hungerbourne excavation.

More slowly this time, she read the passage she was holding again.

The tales foretell that when the bourne rises, suffering inevitably follows. The Woe Waters will not be denied.

In her mind's eye, she could see the sunflower-yellow letters daubed across the tea hut.

'Got everything you need?' She gave a start. In front of her stood the curator, a wizened little man in his early sixties who was standing beside her, absent-mindedly cleaning his spectacles on his green woollen tie.

'What?' She looked at him, momentarily disorientated, then nodded automatically. He smiled and, apparently satisfied, turned to leave. As he reached the door, she called out after him, 'There is one thing.' He turned to face her, expectant, his hands clasped together in front of him.

'Has anyone else looked at these records recently?' she asked.

He shook his head. 'The only person to have touched them in my time here is me, when I re-bagged the flint.'

He departed, seemingly satisfied that his duties had been discharged.

Coincidence, then. Maybe she was starting to get paranoid.

She fanned the letters out on the tabletop in front of her. The reverend, it seemed, had possessed more staying power than the curators with whom he'd conversed, because the names of the addressees changed on a regular basis.

The letters were accompanied by lists of objects found, together with sketch maps of their locations, all penned on whisper-thin and now-yellowing paper. She smiled. Hemmings displayed all of the traits of a fellow enthusiast.

Knowing from her experience as an undergrad that once she had her hands on the artefacts themselves she would find it difficult to drag herself back to examine the documents, she decided to complete her study of the letters and lists before examining the flint.

The early letters were dominated by questions to the curator of the day, but as time passed Hemmings seemed to have developed more confidence in his own abilities. His epistles after the Second World War contained more assertions than questions, with Hemmings expounding on a series of his pet theories. By the late sixties, the cleric's handwriting had become shaky, with an increasing frequency of ink blots and smears in evidence. For the first time too in these letters, he intimated he was no longer collecting all of the material himself, but had commissioned others to carry out the task. His mind had obviously remained willing and, judging by his letters, able, but his flesh, it seemed, had weakened.

Next she turned to the accompanying pages of notes, lists and pencil sketches. With the exception of the increasing frailty of the handwriting in the later pages, they appeared at first reading to retain pretty much the same format throughout; locating all of the finds to their nearest field, with annotations detailing the month and year of discovery.

But as she devoted more time to individual pages, she noticed minor differences. Some of the sketch maps had pairs of capital letters written in their top left-hand corner. Was it some sort of site code? She spread the pages containing the maps out in front of her. The letters didn't correspond to field names. But individual pairs of letters did appear again and again with the same fields. She examined the dates on the maps and on the letters. The pairs of letters only appeared on the maps showing material collected during the late sixties and early seventies; the same period during which Hemmings had been forced to resort to using others to do his collecting for him. No great mystery, then. They must be the initials of the people who'd collected on his behalf.

Clare withdrew her laptop from her bag and made notes about the documents in front of her, then turned her attention to the boxes containing the stone tools. The material inside the boxes was in clear plastic bags. The brown paper bags that had originally contained the flints had been retained but consigned to the status of artefacts themselves, having been placed in large plastic bags at the rear of each box. The reason for their replacement became obvious when she examined them. They were in a poor state of repair, their pencil-written labels now barely legible. But someone had carefully transcribed the words from the paper bags onto their modern plastic equivalents.

Going through each box in turn, Clare cross-checked the details on the bags with the details of the letters she'd recorded on the laptop. They were identical in every way except in the case of the later discoveries. For these, the names of the finders had been recorded in full on the bags. She'd known already from what Margaret had told her that she would find her name among the list of young collectors and, sure enough, there was Peggy Grafton, her name appearing against a whole series of different locations.

But there were others too whose names were less familiar: Patrick Sweeney – Hungerbourne Bottom; David Clifford (a younger sibling of the irascible George, perhaps) – Small Penning.

And there was one other, familiar but unexpected: Edward Jevons – Old Barrows Field.

The unstarched cotton of the curtains hung limply down, framing Clare's view of the bustling marketplace from the open window of the Bear Hotel in Devizes. She nursed her orange juice in the near-empty bar. The attempt at ventilation had failed to dissipate the stifling heat. Not the heat of a classic English summer, but a sticky oppressive heat. Neither the temperature nor the half-eaten mozzarella and tomato baguette that lay abandoned on her plate had done anything to help her make her mind up about what she should do.

She leant back in her chair and checked her watch. Six-thirty. They'd be off-site by now. She plucked her mobile out of the bottom of her bag and punched in Margaret's number.

'Professor Bockford speaking.'

Clare could hear the sound of chattering voices, and the clatter of plates and cutlery in the background. 'Margaret, I'm still down in Devizes. I need to check something with you.'

'Can't it wait? I'm in the middle of sorting the chores team out.' Margaret sounded as if the heat of the day was getting to her.

'No, I don't think it can.'

There was an unmistakable exhalation of breath at the other end of the line. 'Very well. Fire away.'

'The common interest you and Ed shared. Was it fieldwalking for Reverend Hemmings?'

'Yes. He roped in several local youngsters to help.'

'Was Peter one of them?'

'Once or twice, maybe, but Ed and I were the only two who stuck at it. Peter didn't have the slightest interest in archaeology. I always thought it was a bit of a disappointment to Gerald. But Ed and I were out in all weathers collecting.' The memory seemed to lighten Margaret's mood. She chuckled. 'These days I suppose you'd say Hemmings operated on a productivity basis. When we found something really good he would tell us one of his tales.'

'About the local folklore.'

'That's right. How do you know that?'

'I've been reading Hemmings' letters. But that's not important. Margaret, who actually found the first sun disc?'

'Ed, of course. Why do you think it was called the Jevons disc?'

Clare finished the call and set her phone down next to her tepid orange juice. The prickle of perspiration on the palms of her hands wasn't due to the warmth of the evening. How could she have been so stupid? The disc was named after the son, not the father. She wiped her hands on her black jeans and picked up her mobile.

'David Barbrook.' His voice was faint, the signal poor.

'Where are you?'

'Up on-site.'

'Still?'

'I've found something.'

She didn't have time for a debate on archaeology now. 'Does that mean you'll be on-site for a while?'

'Looks like it. Why?'

'I need to talk to you.' The line crackled. 'I'm going to come over.'

David slipped his mobile into the pocket of his moleskins, picked up his trowel and knelt down in the middle of the trench. A dark brown spread of soil in front of him marked the site of a pit. There was no indication it had ever held a wooden post. That tallied with Gerald's records of it containing a cremation. Like others he'd dug in the past, except in this one Joyce Clifford had unearthed a sun disc.

He began again, scraping away at a small concavity within the large dark splodge of earth. It shouldn't take long to bottom it. The dip was filled with a mixture of chalk rubble and a lighter gingery-coloured soil and, as his team's records suggested, it had been formed by someone digging into the fill of the earlier pit. Not unusual in itself. But why was there was no mention of this second feature in Gerald's records?

David sat back on his haunches, trying to make sense of the conundrum. What was the sequence? A large pit had been dug into the chalk bedrock in the Bronze Age. The contents of that pit had been excavated and removed by Gerald's team during the 1973 dig. At the end of the season, the pit had been backfilled; he could tell that from the remains of the decaying Woodbine fag packet poking out of the top of the fill of the larger, darker splodge. And then the spoil from the excavations had been used to recreate the profile of the barrow mound. All perfectly normal at the end of an excavation. But why had someone dug another much smaller hole into the top of Gerald's backfill and then filled it in again, before the mound had been reconstructed?

He sighed. It probably wasn't very important in the grand scheme of things. But it was a puzzle. And he didn't like puzzles – he preferred solutions. He ran his fingers through his hair and wiped the perspiration on the sleeve of his shirt. The warm and humid weather of the last couple of days was beginning to take its toll. He'd almost had enough. He was looking forward to a cool shower, a pint and an evening with Sally. But he needed to finish this before he could call it a day.

He leant forward again, pushing the metal blade of his trowel into the loose chalky soil. As he dragged it backwards it hit something solid. Probably a stone. But he'd better check. He hunched forward over the hole to get a closer look. His arms and back felt suddenly cold. He looked up to see a tall figure silhouetted by a penumbra of sunlight.

David put his hand up to shield his eyes. 'Shit, Ed! You nearly gave me a heart attack.'

Ed made no attempt to move out of the glare of the sun. 'Been busy while I've been away?'

'Just tying up a few loose ends. You know how it gets at the end of a dig.'

Ed nodded slowly. 'Oh yes. I know how it gets.'

David had the uncomfortable feeling he was missing something. Did Ed consider him guilty by dint of his association with Sally? 'Look, mate. I'm sorry about what happened with Peter. I know you two go back a long way.' Ed stood perfectly still, his head cocked to one side. 'I can understand you were angry, but Sal was just doing her job.'

Ed raised a hand, pointing towards the hole in front of David. 'Don't let me stop you finishing what you're doing.'

David leant over again. Using his fingertips, he began to feel around the soil he'd loosened. He could feel something metallic against his skin. He was aware of Ed shifting slightly to one side as if to get a better view. The sun's rays poured into the void left where Ed's body had been and caught the edge of the object David had begun to reveal, directing a deep golden beam of light onto his chest. For a second, he knelt entranced as the pattern of light played on his shirt.

'Beautiful, isn't it?' Ed said.

David gazed at the object in front of him. He recognised it immediately. 'Yes.'

'Well, pick it up! You only find something that exquisite once in a lifetime.'

David picked the small golden object up. The pitted disc at its centre was the colour of caramelised blood orange. He ran his fingers around the edges of the encircling gold, removing the soil that stuck to the concentric circular indentations that ran around its circumference. He stopped and looked up, his fingers encountering a rip in the surface of the tinfoil-thin metal. Ed's expression was calm, almost serene.

With a moment of dreadful clarity, David realised that here standing in front of him was his solution. 'That's not true, is it, Ed? You've found it twice.'

Ed smiled. 'Not exactly. It was never lost.'

Ed reached out a hand, palm upturned, and motioned to David to pass him the disc. David didn't move. Now that Ed was no longer silhouetted by the sun, he could see Ed's other hand was far from empty. He was holding a shotgun. David's arms felt like jelly. He was pretty sure if he hadn't been kneeling, his legs would have too. He looked down at the glittering object in his hand, struggling to process the full implications of what was happening.

'I didn't have you down as a stupid man, David. Hand it over!'

The sweat poured off him. Every instinct he possessed was screaming at him to do what Ed was telling him. But he couldn't. He wouldn't make it easy.

He clasped his fingers tightly around the disc. 'So you can make it disappear again?'

Ed pulled the stock of the gun closer to his body, his finger caressing the trigger. 'It's going back where it belongs.'

'You won't get away with this.'

Ed whipped the shotgun through one hundred and eighty degrees, gripping the barrel with both hands halfway down its length. For a split second, David thought he was going to give him the gun. Then Ed drew the weapon back in an arc above his shoulders and David felt the wooden stock crash down against the side of his skull.

CHAPTER THIRTY-SIX

Clare bumped the wheels of the Fiesta over the rutted pasture. With all the rain, the site had begun to turn into a swamp. But the warmer weather of the last few days had hardened the tyre tracks, which now resembled the scars of giant talons that clawed their way down the lush green hillside. She parked up behind the site huts and climbed out. The mud-streaked cream rectangle of the most recently opened trench was visible from where she stood. No sign of anyone there. David must be in the office or in one of the trenches higher up the slope.

The secured padlocks on most of the ad hoc collection of temporary structures told her they'd been locked when the team had knocked off for the day. The door of the tea hut stood open but as she approached she could see it was empty. David's Land Rover was parked outside of the Portakabin. She climbed the breeze-block steps that were caked in drying mud and pushed at the door. Rows of black plastic seed trays crammed with pottery and flint were drying neatly in their racks against the back wall, but there was no sign of anyone in the front of the office. He must be in the back.

'David. Are you there?'

No response.

She made her way into the tiny room behind the partition wall. It was empty. She was aware of an uneasy tightness in her chest. It just wasn't like him. Going off and leaving all of the finds and records unsecured.

A green plastic ring binder lay open on his desk. It contained completed context sheets. One sheet for each posthole, pit or layer they'd found, numbered and filed sequentially. The snap-to clasp on the binder was open. She flicked through the sheets. One was missing, from the trench they'd reopened on the barrow that Gerald had dug.

Next to the binder lay a photocopied sheet she recognised immediately as a page from Gerald's site diary. She picked it up. skimming through its contents: a description of the pit that had contained the cremation urn and the second sun disc. Maybe David had spotted a discrepancy between Gerald's records and the newly completed sheets. He was probably up there now, checking the record against the pit. But what could possibly be so important that he'd forget to lock up? She peered through the dirt-streaked window. He'd better get a move on. If he left it much longer, the light would be gone.

Pulling the Portakabin door closed behind her, she spun the combination on the new lock. The muscles in the backs of her legs strained as she hiked up towards the top trench. She could hear the wind blowing through the trees in the plantation at the edge of the field and her skin prickled cold with goosebumps.

The smell of rain was in the air. The oppressive hot weather of the last couple of days was drawing to a close. Stopping to catch her breath, she looked uphill. She could make out the white chalk outline of the bottom of the trench, but she couldn't see anyone. Then she glimpsed movement. Someone behind the spoil heap. She waved. The figure stopped for a moment, returned her wave, and then once more disappeared behind the mass of earth.

She let out a deep sigh of relief and trudged on upwards. When she reached the edge of the trench, the figure rounded the front of the spoil heap. She gave a jolt of startled recognition as she realised it was Ed.

He said, 'A little late to be up here on your own, isn't it?'

'I'm looking for David. I was supposed to meet him here.' She'd assumed Ed was still securely locked up. She hoped her face didn't betray her disquiet.

'You've missed him, I'm afraid.' His tone was affable; as if the events of the last couple of days had never happened. He smiled. 'Don't worry, I'm not about to put in a repeat performance of yesterday.'

Clare scanned the trench in front of her. In the middle, she could see the large, dark brown splodge signifying the pit recorded on the page of Gerald's journal that she'd found on David's desk. Just off centre of the pit was a much smaller hole. Beside it lay a small pile of soil, a half-filled plastic bucket, a metal hand shovel and a trowel.

She said, 'David left the context records out down in the Portakabin. I thought he'd come up to check something.'

Ed climbed into the trench. 'That was me, I'm afraid.' He made his way over to the pit and, picking up the trowel, scraped up the pile of soil and deposited it into the plastic bucket with the hand shovel.

'But his Land Rover's still here.'

Ed straightened up, pursing his lips and, looking her straight in the eye, unblinking, shrugged. 'He got a phone call. Said Sally was going to pick him up.' He paused, raising an eyebrow. It was as if he was daring her to argue with him. 'I offered to finish up here and take his Land Rover back to camp afterwards.' He produced a set of keys from his trouser pocket and dangled them in front of her. 'You'll have to excuse me if I work while we talk.' He pointed skyward with the trowel. 'I want to get finished before the light goes.'

Clare watched as he knelt down in front of her, the bottom of the trowel visible in his hand. A skein of fear twisted deep in the pit of her stomach. Poking out beneath Ed's little finger she could see a small carved wooden head worn smooth with years of use. It was David's trowel.

Clare steered the Fiesta gently up onto the grass verge at the side of the lane and switched off the engine and headlights. Ed had lied to her; she was certain of that. But she couldn't afford to dwell on the implications of what that might mean. She needed to find out where David was.

Reaching over onto the back seat, she rummaged around in the bottom of her bag. Where the hell was her mobile? Her fumbling fingers finally found what she was looking for. The number she wanted was definitely not in her favourites list. But she was glad now that she'd listened to David and kept it in case of an emergency – though she was pretty sure this wasn't what he'd had in mind.

The backlight on the phone seemed dim. When she checked the battery icon on the top of the screen, there were no little blue bars showing. Damn. It must have joggled itself on in her bag again. Finding the number she wanted, she punched the dial button and prayed there was enough juice left to make the call. It was ringing. Sally's voice was calm and efficient. Voicemail.

'Sally. It's Clare Hills.' She checked the clock on the dashboard. 'It's half-eight. I've just been up to the dig site and Ed's up there. He says David's with you. But I think he's lying. I don't know what's happened, but David's in danger. I'm going back up there. If you get this message, please hurry. And Sally: don't come on your own.'

It had been a long day and Sally could have done without the meeting with DCI Morgan. She'd hoped he'd be pleased she'd got a confession for the Hart murder from the son. But he'd been more concerned that she'd released a witness from custody without questioning him about the killing. And she'd had to admit she was no nearer to finding out what had happened to that bloody gold disc. She sighed. It could have been worse. At least he hadn't chewed her out in front of West.

West was still there when she got back to their office. He looked up from his desk on the far side of the room. 'Kettle's not long boiled.'

Sally nodded, but said nothing. He'd only hung around to gloat. She made her way over to the kettle on top of the filing cabinet and, spooning two large teaspoons of instant coffee into a cracked Swindon Town mug, she poured the tepid water on top. Reaching into the top drawer of her desk, she withdrew a small, pale blue plastic container, dispensed a single white granule into the solution and stirred.

She sat at her desk, flipping through the pile of papers in front of her. Nothing that couldn't wait. Pushing the pile to one side of the crowded surface, she took a swig of coffee. It was lukewarm and tasted like floor sweepings, but the caffeine did the trick.

West looked up, and pointed towards the suit jacket hanging from the back of her chair. 'Your mobile rang a couple of times while you were with the chief.'

She reached behind her into her jacket pocket and fished out her phone, scrolling through the missed calls.

The first was a voicemail from David, telling her he had to work late. 'How about meeting up for a drink in the Lamb and Flag when I get through – about nine-thirty? Would you be a sweetie and ask Shirl to rustle me up one of her specials?'

She smiled. When she'd joined the force, she'd worried that she'd never find anyone who could cope with the hours. She'd seen enough of her colleagues' relationships destroyed by the job in the years since. But David seemed to be trying to give her a run for her money on that score. She listened to the next voicemail. 'Sally. It's Clare Hills.'

Sally hit the delete button. The last thing she needed was another one of Clare's half-baked theories. Why did David put up with her? She wasn't sure she really wanted to know the answer to that question. But she was damned sure she wished Clare would get on with her job and leave the police work to the professionals.

She'd had enough of Hungerbourne for one day. She walked outside into the corridor. Through the frosted glass pane that divided them, she could see West watching her. She turned her back to him and scrolled through her contacts to find David's mobile number. When she rang, it went straight to voicemail. She left a brief message telling him she couldn't make it and that she'd ring him later, then searched for another number.

'Tony? It's Sally. David left a message for me to meet him at your place, but I can't make it and I can't reach him on his mobile. Could you ask Shirl to put one of her specials by for him? Thanks. About nine-thirty.'

Clare looked down at the phone in her hand. She hit 999 and waited. The light flickered and dimmed and then disappeared entirely. She put the mobile to her ear. For a moment there was a faint buzzing and then nothing. Disgusted, she threw it into the footwell of the passenger seat.

She stretched her neck backwards, pressing her head into the velour headrest and exhaled. There was no choice. She slipped the keys out of the ignition and climbed out of the car. Easing the door shut behind her, she stuffed the keys into her jeans pocket.

This far away from the village, the silence was broken only by a single blackbird protesting against the fading light. In the valley below, the windows of the Lamb and Flag, phosphorescing like flares in the last remnants of twilight, only intensified the enveloping darkness. She hesitated. Should she try driving down there to get help? She dismissed the idea. There wasn't time. She had to find David – if it wasn't too late already.

She turned away from the pub's familiar outline. This time thankful for the fading light, she crouched low, tracking the hedgerow and edging her way up the lane as quickly as she dared without risking detection. At the entrance to the field, she stopped. She couldn't take the chance that Ed might see her.

Dropping to her knees, she crawled towards the cover of the nearest site hut. She poked her head around the corner of the wooden tool shed far enough to get a view up towards the trench where she'd last seen Ed. But there was no sign of him.

She pushed the palms of her hands down against the damp grass, levering herself upwards until she was squatting on her haunches. There was a noise. She pressed her back flat against the thin wooden slats of the shed and listened. There it was again – a muffled scraping. She spun round in her crouched position and, straining her eyes, peered around the side of the shed into the deepening gloom.

In the last wash of daylight above the barrows, she could just make out the outline of a hunched figure silhouetted against the skyline. She narrowed her eyes, forcing them to focus on the distant image. As the figure drew closer, she could see that the hunched appearance was because they were bent forward, arms outstretched towards the ground, dragging something heavy.

Even before she could see it she knew. It wasn't something, it was some*one*. A wave of panic engulfed her. This was madness. She should have gone for help. Coming back to find him on her own was just the sort of lunatic scheme David would have warned her against. Trying to control her rapid breathing, she closed her eyes and inhaled deeply, drawing the cooling night air down deep into her lungs. For several moments she remained motionless in her crouched position, attempting to still her thoughts.

Opening her eyes, she forced herself to look again. The scene in front of her had changed. The light that now illuminated the ramshackle collection of structures belonged to the moon. The figure appeared to be heading for the small cluster of huts only about thirty metres from where she was crouching. As he turned downslope she could see Ed's face bathed by the gunmetal-cold moonlight. His arms were hooked beneath David's shoulders, his features taut with the strain of manoeuvring the inert body.

She was surprised by his strength. David was no lightweight, but Ed had managed to drag him over two hundred metres. She watched in appalled fascination as he bumped David's backside and ankles over the doorsill of the tea hut and deposited him with a thud on its wooden floor. She could just make out the bottom of David's legs through the open doorway. For a moment, she thought she saw one of his boots twitch. She couldn't be sure, but there was still a chance. She had to do something.

Ed had disappeared from view. She could hear him doing something in the back of the hut. But there was no time to worry. She edged around to the door of the tool shed and withdrew her keys from her pocket. She felt for the metal padlock, inserted the smallest key on the fob and turned. To Clare, the dull click as the lock opened resounded across the hilltop like Big Ben striking the hour. But, thankfully, neither this nor the creaking of the rusty hasp as she eased open the door seemed to be audible from the tea hut.

She slipped inside. The interior of the hut was almost pitch-black. She stood still for a few moments, trying to let her eyes adjust to the reduced light levels. There was a strong smell of earth and damp metal. A sliver of moonlight pierced a gap where one corner of the structure met the roof. The thread of silver illuminated the top of an upright wooden handle belonging to one of the pickaxes stacked along the back wall of the shed.

As she stood in the dark and the silence, she became aware of the sound of someone rummaging around in the other hut. Then the noise stopped. What was he doing? There it was again. This time the rummaging was followed by the clang of metal on metal. The gas burners!

In desperation, she reached out for one of the pickaxes in front of her. She shuffled forward, feeling for the long wooden handle. There was a deafening clatter of wood and metal, and she gasped for air as something struck her in the ribs, knocking her backwards and forcing her onto the floor in the corner by the door.

'What the fuck!' The raw expletive came from the tea hut.

Thudding footsteps crashed across a wooden floor. Then closer, on the grass outside. Almost on top of her now. She struggled to right herself, but she was pinned down by something heavy skewed across her chest. She felt the reverberation of the hut walls against her back as the door was flung open. Framed against the moonlight in the doorway, Ed's looming figure seemed huge. He raised his hand. She turned her head to one side and shut her eyes, raising her forearm across her face to shield herself from the inevitable blow.

It didn't come. Ed reached across her and, with a single movement, flung back the metal object that had pinned her to the floor. She opened her eyes, unbelieving. In the light streaming in through the doorway, she could see now that her captor had been a wheelbarrow. He was leaning forward now, his face right over hers. She could feel his heavy breath and smell stale garlic. His shoulders and neck were taut with anger.

His words seared like erupting magma. 'I should have known I couldn't get rid of you that easily. You never do what you're fucking told!'

He leant his head back, angling it to one side as if examining the exhibit in front of him. All at once the anger and irritation seemed to dissipate from his body. The cold night air rushed into the space between his face and hers, and she gulped down clean air.

He stood up, offering her his hand. For a split second she considered refusing. But some innate instinct made her reconsider. She mustn't antagonise him. She knew what he was capable of. If she was going to have any chance of getting herself and David out of here alive, she had to delay for as long as possible. She held out a trembling hand.

He wrapped his hand firmly round hers, his long, delicate

fingers contrasting with the roughness of his farmer's hands. His palm was clammy with sweat and he adjusted his grip to gain more purchase. He took the strain of her weight. Then, giving a sharp tug that wrenched at her shoulder socket, he pulled her viciously towards him and landed a punch in the middle of her stomach.

Doubled up in agony, she heaved, unable to take in air. She dropped forward onto her knees, moonlight spotlighting the floor in front of her as he shifted sideways. There was a sharp pain at the back of her head. The force of the blow thrust her sideways, her head clattering off the side of the upturned wheelbarrow and coming to rest on the floor. The rough wooden planking felt surprisingly warm against her cheek and she was dimly aware of wondering whether the splatters of blood on the two well-polished Oxford brogues in front of her were hers or David's before she slipped into blackness.

'He could have rung himself.' Shirl was standing, hands on hips, behind her husband.

'I don't know why you're so upset.' Tony bent down and slotted a box of cheese and onion crisps beneath the bar.

'You weren't the one who cooked it.'

'You can always slip it in the microwave for him later.' Tony stood up.

Shirl emitted an audible harrumph. 'Why did he have to get her to do his dirty work for him?'

Tony turned round and placed a hand on Shirl's shoulder, lowering his voice. 'Give it a rest, love. I'm sure he had a good reason for asking Sally to phone. It's not like he hasn't worked late before.'

Margaret deposited an empty tumbler onto the bar. With

the practised skill of a landlady of long standing, Shirl's frown transformed from a scowl to a welcoming smile in an instant. 'What can I get you, Margaret?'

'Another of the same, please, Shirley.'

Shirl slipped the tumbler under the optic. 'Tight for time on the dig?'

Margaret's expression was quizzical. 'Things are going rather well. We should finish the last two trenches before the machines come in on Tuesday.'

This time Shirl found it impossible to retain the professional façade. Her disgruntlement was clear for all to see.

Tony laughed. 'Don't mind Shirl. She's got the hump because she's cooked David one of her steak and kidney puds and he hasn't turned up to eat it.'

Shirl looked abashed. 'It's just not like him. He's usually such a gent.'

Tony leant towards Margaret and winked. 'Between you and me, I think Shirl's a bit sweet on our Dr Barbrook.'

Shirl cast Tony an admonishing glance and handed Margaret her replenished glass.

Margaret handed Tony a five-pound note and frowned. 'Shirley's right. It's not like him to miss one of her specials.'

Shirl leant forward across the bar. 'Sally told Tony he'd be here by half nine.'

Margaret glanced down at her watch and peered out into the night. 'It's too dark to be working up there now.'

'You don't think there's been another accident, do you?' Shirl asked, glancing over to where Jo was sitting working her way through a pile of site records.

Margaret handed her untouched whiskey back to Shirl. 'I'm going to go up and take a look.'

'I'll come with you,' Jo volunteered, raising herself gingerly from her corner seat and reaching towards where her crutches were leaning.

Tony folded back the hinged lid of the bar. 'You're not going anywhere, young lady. You can hold the fort here for a few minutes, can't you, Shirl?'

Shirl nodded.

'Get your coat, Margaret. Looks like the weather's closing in.'

CHAPTER THIRTY-SEVEN

Clare opened her eyes to the sight of David's size thirteen boots inches away from her face. Her head was thumping and her ribs hurt like hell. Beyond the scuffed black leather and mud-caked rubber she could make out a cardboard box beneath the legs of a wooden trestle table, out of the top of which spilt a pile of empty glass bottles, drinks cans and plastic milk containers. She was lying on the floor of the tea hut.

The memory of Ed's face inches from her own obliterated the scene in front of her. Where was he now? She listened, but could hear only the sound of the quickening wind catching beneath the flapping felt of the hut roof. Pools of light flashed and vanished like the pulsing beam of a lighthouse through the scratched Perspex windows as the scudding clouds covered and then revealed the silvered surface of the moon.

She hauled herself into a sitting position. Moving onto her knees, she felt a sharp pain in her ribs where she'd been hit by the wheelbarrow. She turned to face the closed door and gently tried the handle. It was locked.

She turned her attention to David. His head was lolling to one side. She ran her fingers down the trickle of sticky dark brown liquid visible beneath his short sandy hair. Holding her arm to her ribs to dull the pain, she placed her ear close to his mouth, but she could hear nothing above the sound of the gusting wind. She placed two fingers on the side of his neck just below the angle of his jaw and prayed. There it was, steady and warm against her fingertips – a pulse. Thank God.

Outside, a door slammed, followed by footsteps. She hurriedly manoeuvred herself back into her former position on the floor and closed her eyes. The metallic click of a key turning in the padlock was followed by the whining rasp of an unoiled hinge as the door swung open. She felt a sharp impact in her side and, despite her best efforts, couldn't prevent the yelp of pain that followed the brogue contacting her injured ribs.

'I thought I heard you.' Ed stood over her, a shotgun in his right hand. He jabbed the barrel in the direction of the far corner of the hut. 'Up the other end!'

She pulled herself upright, half crawling, half sliding across the wooden planks until she sat wedged upright against the back wall, beside David's head. Keeping the gun trained on her in one hand, with his other he dragged the cardboard box out from beneath the trestle table where the gas burners stood, swinging it round in front of her. Plucking a glass cordial bottle out of the box, he set it down on the floor between them.

He stepped back outside of the hut and, reaching down, produced a battered jerry can and thrust it towards her.

He poked it towards the bottle with his foot. 'Fill it.'

She didn't move.

He screamed the words. 'Fill it!'

Her head was pounding. She reached forward, grimacing at the pain in her ribs as she pulled the bottle towards her and started to manoeuvre herself towards the door.

'No you don't!'

'I can't see. I need the light from the door.' She stared up into his eyes, refusing to look away.

He nodded brusquely and waved the end of the shotgun barrel at the corner by the door.

She placed the bottle on the floor in front of her and with a tilt of her head indicated that he was blocking her light. He stepped sideways, positioning himself to ensure he could keep the gun trained on her. With his other hand he reached inside his wax jacket and produced a hip flask and flipped the lid.

She looked up at him. 'The Woe Waters. It was you, wasn't it?'

He took a swig from his hip flask and cracked a self-congratulatory smile. 'A message even a blow-in could understand. You know, this could all have been avoided if you'd just listened and left everything as it should have been.'

'As it should have been. With Peter believing he killed his father. Was keeping Peter out of the way while Jim stole the gold Jim's idea, or had you planned to get rid of Jim and set up Peter from the start?'

He grinned at her, but said nothing.

'All you had to do was get Peter drunk and deposit him back at the manor, where you knew he'd find his father stealing the goldwork. Using Peter's knife, was that planned too? Or did you just grab the first thing that came to hand?

'You told me you only got involved with Jim's plan so that you could shop him to Gerald. But the truth is that you wanted more than Jim was offering. You wanted it all yourself. When it came down to it, you were nothing but a murdering little sneak thief.'

The corner of his lip lifted in a sneer. 'You understand nothing. It was never about the money.'

She unscrewed the lid of the jerry can. A gust of wind blew the first spots of rain through the open doorway and the smooth, deep smell of Ed's brandy mingled with the sharp metallic tang of petrol. 'So where is it?' She looked down at the open fuel container in front of her. 'You've nothing to lose by telling me now.'

'You think you know it all, don't you? But there are some things you'll never know. It's back where it belongs and this time it's going to stay there.'

She managed to raise a hollow smile. 'I bet it put the fear of God up you when you heard Gerald's car. What did you do – grab the first thing that came to hand? One pitiful little disc. Damaged goods – not a very heroic haul.'

Ed's face contorted into a snarl. 'That sun disc is mine. I found it and no one has the right to take it from me. Not my father. Not Gerald. Not Jim. And not some upstart bitch like you.'

He swung the barrel of the shotgun down towards the top of the bottle. 'Get on with it!'

With the bottle gripped between her knees and trying to hold the metal canister steady in her shaking hands, she tipped it up and began to pour. The oily odour intensified her headache, the jab of pain to her side making her wince as she dropped the metal can back onto the floor with a dull thud. 'You know all about taking things from people, don't you. You took any hope of a normal life from Gerald and Estelle, and now you're doing the same to Peter. You've destroyed their entire family.'

'The Harts wanted something for nothing. Jim wanted money,

Gerald wanted glory. I watched them all, living in that house – my grandfather's house – playing at lords of the manor. They bought their way into this village. They don't understand any more than my father did. Any more than you do.'

Looking up at Ed, she thought she caught a glimpse of movement on the wooden floor behind him. 'All of these years, your friendship with Peter, was it all a lie?'

'He was the worst of the lot. I felt sorry for him at first. Our fathers were both bastards.' He snorted derisively. 'He followed me round like a puppy. It was pathetic. I tried talking to him – explaining about this place. Do you know what he did?'

She looked up at him. In the dim light she could just make out his eyes. But from here on the floor where she was kneeling, they had no definition. Pupil and iris merged into a soulless black void.

'He laughed. He wanted out. He wanted nothing to do with Hungerbourne. He had everything and understood nothing. Just like you. You think you're so fucking smart, don't you? But if you hadn't come snooping round here, none of this would have happened. Everything would have stayed as it was meant to be.'

Now she was quite certain. Just behind Ed's foot, David raised an index finger from the floor. She had to keep Ed occupied.

'Is that why you tried to kill me, and nearly killed Jo in the process, to stop me snooping around?'

'I tried to warn you off, but you were too stupid to listen. You left me no choice.'

'But you had a choice with Jenny, didn't you? She'd done nothing. Did you just have a taste for it by then?'

Ed hesitated. For the first time, he looked uncomfortable. He shook his head. 'You can't pin that on me. Jenny was down to you. I heard you arguing with her about the knife – I couldn't run the risk of the police getting hold of it.'

Clare struggled to process what he was saying. He'd thought Jenny still had the knife. Her decision to spare Jenny the humiliation of a public dressing-down had cost Jenny her life. She replaced the cap on the jerry can, struggling to control her accelerating heartbeat. She held up the container for Ed to take.

'Down there!' He pointed behind her and she complied. 'Now take one of the tea towels out of there.' He slid the cardboard box across the floor with his foot until it was within her reach. 'Tear a strip off. Long enough so that it will fit in the bottle with some of it sticking out of the top.'

Clare caught her breath. Her eyes bulged with sudden understanding.

He laughed. 'I thought archaeologists were used to working out cause of death. I see you've finally managed it.'

Behind Ed's leg, she could see David reaching across his body with his right arm.

She raised herself up into a kneeling position and, taking one of the dirty tea towels in both hands, ripped at the material as hard as she could, praying her efforts would mask the noise of David's movements.

She stuffed one of the ripped strips of cotton down into the neck of the bottle and held it up in front of Ed. 'Not original.'

Ed smirked, reaching forward toward the incendiary device. 'But very effective.'

Behind Ed, David drew back his arm. In his right hand she could see the glint of something metallic. She held her breath and swayed backward, moving the bottle out of Ed's grasp.

Something circular flew through the air and clattered against the hut wall behind Ed's right shoulder. He spun round to see a teapot lid spinning on the floor in front of him. David heaved himself sideways, rolling against the back of Ed's legs and bringing him crashing to the ground. They were scrabbling around on the hut floor, Ed face down and David trying to keep him pinned there.

David yelled, 'The gun. Get the gun!'

Ed's arms were thrashing around wildly in the darkness at the back of the hut. She flung herself forward. Ignoring the pain in her side, she groped around on the floor beside the two men. Finally, her fingers found the stock of the shotgun. She tried to pull it towards her, but Ed must have had hold of the other end. He was too strong for her. She grabbed at it, but her palms were heavy with sweat and the shiny wood slipped from her grasp. She clung onto the stock with one hand, the searching fingers of her other finding the metal loop further up the gun. Suddenly, Ed yanked backwards. There was a shuddering bang, an agonised scream and the two men on the floor lay still.

Margaret and Tony heard the shot as they turned into the gateway. The paramedics said it had been Margaret's quick thinking in improvising a tourniquet that had saved Ed's life. Though whether he'd thank her for it was doubtful. The shot had shattered the whole of the lower half of his arm and done considerable damage to the side of his face.

Ed was being bundled into an ambulance under West's watchful eye. It seemed that half of Wiltshire constabulary had turned out to the scene of the shooting – including Sally. David and Clare were standing wrapped in foil blankets, leaning on the bonnet of a squad car. Despite Sally's attempts to persuade him, David was refusing to go to hospital to be checked over.

'If you think I'm getting in the same ambulance as that lunatic, you've got another thing coming.'

Sally turned to Margaret. 'Can't you make him see sense?'

'I make it my policy never to get involved in domestics.'

Sally flung her hands in the air and let out an impatient sigh. 'I've got things to do. We'll talk later.' She turned and made her way towards the site huts.

As soon as Sally had gone, Margaret withdrew a small hip flask from the pocket of her blood-stained cardigan. 'A drop of this'll do you more good than a trip to A & E.'

Clare raised her hand. 'Oh no you don't – I've seen quite enough of those things for one night. Besides, there's something I want to ask our all-action hero before he hits the juice.'

'Don't say I didn't offer.' Margaret headed off towards Tony in search of a more grateful recipient.

Clare turned to face David. 'When I phoned earlier, you said you'd found something.'

He smiled knowingly and nodded. Then, making his way over to the back of his Land Rover, he rummaged around inside until he found a torch. He walked a short distance uphill and gestured towards Clare. 'Coming?'

Together they rustled their way up to the edge of the top trench. He scanned the torch beam across the exposed surface. The air about them was still now, but the mud-smeared chalk was dotted with large damp splodges where the promised storm had threatened then dissolved away to nothing. The shaft of light came to rest on a dark area in the middle of the bedrock, which contained a small, empty depression lying just off centre.

She looked at him, seeking answers. By way of explanation, he stepped into the trench and offered her his hand. She declined it, instead leaning on his shoulder to lessen the pain in her ribs as she descended. Together they made their way to the spot where a bucket, hand shovel and David's trowel still lay. Clare shivered.

He looked at her. 'You alright?'

It seemed a strange question coming from a man who had the upper part of his cranium encased in layers of gauze bandage. She smiled and nodded, drawing the foil cape closer round her shoulders.

He picked up the trowel and handed it to her, then tracked the torch beam to a spot several metres away where a few days previously a lanky youth had found an empty cremation pit. But now the pit was full of loose chalky soil.

David held the torchlight over the mottled earth. She tried to kneel down, but the pain in her ribs was so sharp that she was forced to straighten up again. Swapping the torch for his trowel, David knelt down and began to dig. Within seconds, he stopped. She watched intently as he put down the trowel and began to brush away the remaining soil with his fingertips.

'Back where it belongs,' Ed had said. And sure enough, there in the torch light was the Jevons sun disc. Perfect except for one irreparable flaw. Ed had been as good as his word. He'd put it back where he'd found it: in the pit his plough had ripped it from all those years ago.

CHAPTER THIRTY-EIGHT

David inclined his head towards Clare. 'Not a natural orator.'

'Ssh!' She turned towards him, her expression enough to silence further commentary.

It was no wonder Peter looked nervous; there must have been over a hundred people jammed between the glittering display cabinets of the Prehistory Gallery of the British Museum. There were academics, newspaper journalists, several TV news crews, a clutch of second-rank politicians that Clare recognised but couldn't name and a coachload of Hungerbourne residents who had been bussed in by British Heritage for the occasion. All hanging on Peter's every word.

A set of glass cabinets to either side of the low platform on which Peter stood displayed the goldwork from the Hungerbourne excavations, the case to his right containing in its centre the two reunited sun discs. Peter was impeccably dressed in a dark grey suit, white shirt and baby blue tie that complemented the colour of his eyes. Behind him, a copy of the Brew Crew photograph had been blown up to cover the rear wall of the gallery. David had made it very clear that as one of those depicted was presently incarcerated for the alleged murder of another, he considered it an inappropriate choice. Daniel Phelps had agreed, but there had been no swaying British Heritage, and they were footing the bill. But when Peter had seen the image it hadn't bothered him – which seemed to Clare to be the important thing. If the events of the last few months had taught her anything, it was that you couldn't change the past – however much you might want to.

Peter clasped the sides of the lectern and leant towards the microphone, his gaze flicking between the paper in front of him and his audience. His hands were shaking and there was an audible tremor in his voice. 'So now the results of my uncle's work can finally assume the place they deserve at the heart of this great museum.'

Applause rippled through the room. A flurry of camera flashes went off and Peter stepped down from the plinth. The crowd began to disperse towards the tables of finger food and champagne that were ranged around the room.

David clapped Peter on the back. 'Well done, mate.'

'Was it alright?'

Margaret, who had dispensed with her battered cardigan in favour of a Harris tweed twinset, said, 'Gerald would have been proud of you.'

He beamed a relieved smile.

Margaret peered over her glasses and widened her eyes at Peter. 'Haven't you got something else to tell us?'

Standing beside Margaret, he turned to survey the small group.

David, sporting the M & S blazer that had served him through all of the formal occasions he had so far encountered in his academic career, was sandwiched uncomfortably between Sally and Clare. Jo stood on Clare's other side, the impact of her ordeal now barely visible except for a small white scar on her forehead.

Peter said, 'I've been offered a partnership in the States.' Clare was aware that he was looking directly at her. 'And I've decided to accept. So I'm going to sell the manor.'

Clare was surprised at the relief she felt, but she managed to return Peter's smile.

'And I've given some thought to what Gerald would have wanted to come out of all this.' He turned to David. 'Margaret tells me you've been trying to get the finance together to set up a research institute at the university.' David nodded. 'If you'd let me, I'd like to donate the funds from Gerald's estate. Once the Inland Revenue has taken its whack, it won't be as much as I would have liked. But Margaret says if you could take on some commercial work as well it should be enough to get you started.'

David opened and closed his mouth like a goldfish. Sally gave him a prod. 'Say thank you.' Then she added in a whisper, 'That'll keep Muir off your back.'

'Bugger that little runt! It means we can get stuck into some real research for a change.' For just a second, Clare thought he was going to hug Peter, but at the last moment he extended his arm, shaking Peter vigorously by the hand. 'It's incredibly generous of you, mate.' Then David spun round on his heels to face Clare and Jo. 'Well, how about it? Do you fancy being the Hart Research Institute's first employees?'

Jo nodded enthusiastically, but Clare stood stock-still. She felt Jo's elbow in her side. 'Say something, dope. Before he changes his mind.'

Clare looked into David's steady grey-green eyes, his expectant expression reminding her of Gerald's words. *Archaeology gets in your blood. Once it's running through your veins, you can't escape.*

It would be a struggle. She'd barely earn enough to scrape by on an archaeologist's salary. She hesitated, acutely aware that everyone's attention was focused on her.

A broad smile erupted across her face. 'Yes.'

Margaret stepped forward, swallowing her up in a voluminous hug. Over Margaret's shoulder, Clare could see David looking directly at her, a satisfied grin stretching across his broad features.

She returned the smile and David opened his arms, herding the little group towards the tables between the glass cases. 'Now can we please get stuck into some of that free bubbly?'

ACKNOWLEDGEMENTS

ACKNOWLEDGEMENTS

This is a work of fiction and the characters, events and organisations within it are imaginary. The places are a blend of the real and the imagined, and Hungerbourne, though fictitious, is inspired by a hamlet in the Marlborough Downs. The ancient goldwork is based on discoveries unearthed from one of the burial mounds in the Stonehenge landscape. Today, they form part of the collections of the Wiltshire Museum, Devizes; at the time of writing, they are on display in the Stonehenge visitor centre exhibition.

Many people have helped make this book happen, but any faults or errors that remain are my own. I would particularly like to thank my publishing director Susie Dunlop and publishing manager Lesley Crooks and all the staff at Allison & Busby. And I owe an enormous debt of gratitude to Diane Banks, for having faith in both me and this book, and to Kate Burke and the team at Diane Banks Associates Literary & Talent Agency.

Few writers' journeys are straightforward and mine was no exception. My writing would never have seen the light of day without the friendship and encouragement of Mari, Mo and Carole.

NICOLA FORD is the pen-name for archaeologist Dr Nick Snashall, National Trust Archaeologist for the Stonehenge and Avebury World Heritage Site. Through her day job and now her writing, she's spent more time than most people thinking about the dead.

nicolaford.com
@nic_ford